THE
ROAD
TO
DELANO

To my Huckleberry friend.
With much love.

JOHN DeSIMONE

THE ROAD TO DELANO

RARE BIRD BOOKS
LOS ANGELES, CALIF.

THIS IS A GENUINE RARE BIRD BOOK

Rare Bird
453 South Spring Street, Suite 302
Los Angeles, CA 90013
rarebirdbooks.com

Set in Minion
Printed in the United States

10 9 8 7 6 5 4 3 2 1

Library of Congress Cataloging-in-Publication Data

Names: DeSimone, John, author.
Title: Road to Delano / John DeSimone.
Description: Los Angeles, CA : Rare Bird Books, [2020] |
"A Genuine Rare Bird Book"—Title page verso.
Identifiers: LCCN 2019051699 | ISBN 9781644280317 (hardback)
Classification: LCC PS3604.E758 R63 2020 | DDC 813/.6—dc23
LC record available at https://lccn.loc.gov/2019051699

FOREWORD
By Marc Grossman

THIS NOVEL, *THE ROAD to Delano*, embraces the moral courage it takes to make the difficult decisions life often imposes on us and to make them count for something good. The most dramatic choices, the ones with life-changing consequences, often are required of us "against our will," in the words of the ancient Greek philosopher Aeschylus.

Such an event is at the heart of this story when Latino and Filipino strikers were confronted with intractable violence on vineyard picket lines around Delano, California in 1968. They had to decide how to respond to abuse, humiliation, and violence from growers and their agents.

In Cesar Chavez's mind, there was only one response that would break the back of the grower's resistance to a peaceful redress of their grievances—it was nonviolent action. For him, a moral issue that required the deepest courage and self-discipline to practice. As a devout Catholic and student of Eastern religion, including Zen Buddhism, he saw all human life as a gift from God, and no one, grower or farm worker, had the right to take it for any cause.

Cesar was convinced of the power of nonviolence. He believed that when you practiced nonviolence—instead of just reacting to attacks from opponents—you controlled the fight.

Cesar did not believe in taking shortcuts. He saw violence as a shortcut people turned to out of anger and frustration.

He understood that although nonviolence appeared weak at first glance, it was powerful in practice. As he said many times, "There is no defeat in nonviolence."

He was convinced that if the strikers controlled their impulse to fight back, and through determined persistence used their creativity—change would come.

When some mostly young male strikers talked about resorting to violence, Cesar felt he had failed as a leader to teach them to show patience and faith in nonviolence. In an ultimate act of moral courage, he demonstrated what it meant to be willing to continue the hard work and sacrifice winning demanded. That is why he fasted in February and March of 1968.

Strikers and supporters—and people from all walks of life—saw Cesar lose thirty-five pounds in twenty-five days. Some strikers and union staff left the United Farm Workers, but most hearts were moved by the fast. Dr. Martin Luther King Jr. and Senator Robert F. Kennedy were also deeply moved. All of this was because one man was prepared to die for his beliefs.

Talk of violence stopped. The strikers continued their arduous struggle over two more long years until the grape boycott convinced growers to sign their first union contracts in 1970, establishing the UFW as the first enduring farm worker union in American history. Cesar never lost faith in the poorest and least educated, believing they could challenge one of California's mightiest industries and prevail. That faith is still at the heart of the movement.

In the twenty-four years, I worked with Cesar Chavez, first as a volunteer in the 1960s and then as his speechwriter and personal aide, I witnessed many of those life-shaping moments where an act of moral courage defined a person and paved the road to their futures.

I first learned of the cost of moral courage through his eldest son, Fernando, when we were both college students. We have remained close friends. I still call him Polly, his nickname around family.

Cesar was so dedicated to the movement, that he spent little time with Fernando. They never played catch. They never went to a baseball game together. In a way, they were distant, but he was still Cesar's son. Fernando's experiences in Delano during the grape strike paralleled those of Adrian Sanchez's character in the novel, but they were worse because he was Cesar's son. Fernando responded to merciless harassment in high school by mixing it up with grower and Anglo town kids. He left Delano to live in East San Jose with his grandparents, Cesar's parents, Librado and Juana Chavez, with whom he was close.

At the height of the Vietnam War, Fernando filed as a conscientious objector with the Bakersfield draft board, which considered his application for all of a few minutes before rejecting it. Fernando told his dad he would refuse the draft. Cesar said, "That will take a lot of moral courage. You could go to prison. Are you prepared to do that?"

"I don't know, but I think it's the right thing to do," Fernando replied. He was drafted and refused induction.

This was the era of Nixon and his enemies' lists. Later we learned hundreds of FBI agents were spying on Cesar and his union, in Delano and across the country during the grape boycott. Cesar's FBI file was 1,434 pages long, although "no evidence of Communist or subversive influence was ever developed," according to a 1995 story in the *Los Angeles Times*.

FBI agents took Fernando away in handcuffs. His trial for draft evasion was at the federal courthouse in Fresno in 1971. Cesar stood by his son and testified in his defense. Early one morning, I joined Cesar, his wife, Helen, and some of their children leaving for court from their little house on Kensington Street in Delano. The youngest, twelve-year old Anthony started crying, "I don't want my brother to go to jail." They had to leave him behind.

Michael Tiger, a prominent Selective Service criminal defense attorney, represented Fernando pro bono. Tiger exposed government misconduct in singling out Fernando for special treatment because of his dad. The conservative federal judge dismissed the jury and ordered a directed verdict of acquittal. Cesar did not easily express personal sentiments, but Fernando knew his father was proud of him, and in later years, they worked to patch things up. The trial inspired Fernando to become a successful personal injury lawyer.

Moral courage comes in many shapes and forms, but its ability to shape and form our lives is immutable because it forces its practitioners to use the gifts and talents for a higher good.

Cesar's influence rippled beyond the farm worker movement. He believed that everyone should develop their abilities and talents. When at the union office, he spotted young people with talent, especially if they came from a farm worker or working-class family, he convinced them they could become accountants, administrators, attorneys, or negotiators. Sure, he wanted results at the office, but he saw the greater good of helping individuals fulfill their dreams— dreams some didn't even know they had.

Today, Chavez's family members, movement colleagues and I meet hundreds of women and men he personally influenced. There was a young woman who wanted to escape the fields by becoming a teacher's aide. Cesar convinced her to be a teacher. Now she is a school district superintendent. There was the young UFW paralegal, a striker's son, who became a lawyer at Cesar's urging. Now he is a Superior Court judge in Kern County, where Delano is located. The list goes on and on.

Wasn't that what he also wanted for farm workers? To sit across the bargaining table from their employers as equals and not just take orders all their lives.

By instilling hope and confidence in people who never had them, Cesar inspired an entire people to create their own future. These elements also shine through in this book.

Today, too few people seem willing to risk their livelihoods, much less their lives, for principle. Our times cry out for heroes to inspire us, and the example of Cesar Chavez becomes all the more relevant and instructive.

In this novel, Jack Duncan and Adrian Sanchez, the story's protagonists, come from different worlds. One is the Anglo son of a grape grower; the other the Latino son of a grape striker and picket captain. But during stormy and heroic times, they both grapple to make their own decisions about moral courage and in doing so discover common ground through shared values and experiences.

That is a valuable lesson for their times and in our own. It is why *The Road to Delano* is an important contribution to telling the full story of what happened more than fifty years ago.

MARK GROSSMAN
Spokesperson
Cesar Chavez Foundation
Keene, California

Sugar

1933

SUGAR DUNCAN WAS KNOWN around Lamoille County as a gambler who could farm, but Sugar called himself a farmer who understood a sure bet. He grew up a plowboy on a hardscrabble patch of Vermont hill country and had calluses before he knew he had brains. It was in the seventh grade, in Pete Colburn's barn, waiting out a driving rain that he found his power. While playing seven-card stud he could see the patterns, he understood the odds. He lived by the bluff, and he lived well as far as a child of the Depression could. Before he reached high school, they were calling him Sugar because he was sweet about taking their money.

While his college buddies baled hay and slopped pigs to pay their way through Ag school at Vermont U, Sugar found it more profitable to relieve the hooligans and rumrunners of their easy fortunes at the card table above Markham's Grill over in Providence. After four years of playing cards and a new degree, he left town to farm where the land hadn't been wiped clean of its strength.

Sugar rode west to California's Central Valley in a Pullman with a new pair of tan and white brogues stuffed with cash packed in the bottom of his steamer. FDR had just signed the Cullen-Harrison Act ending Prohibition, and a fifth of whiskey was now as cheap as an acre of California farmland. He hadn't any choice. Returning to Vermont would mean he'd starve. With gasoline a luxury, his father had resorted to using mules to plow his hundred acres. Milk and corn prices had fallen so sharply, a farmer could live better by killing his cows than by selling their milk. California was the place he could make a living. And he intended to make that living as a farmer—eventually.

A couple of weeks after arriving in Frisco, Sugar stood on the running board of a dusty Model T on the road leading into Delano and surveyed the flatlands of the valley planted in golden September wheat. He removed his hat, wiped his brow with the sleeve of his seersucker suit, and his instinct told him *there* was a sure bet.

He ensconced himself in the Fairmont Hotel on Nob Hill. Each night around six, he made his way downstairs to a back room where he took up residence with a fresh deck of cards and a new bottle of Jim Beam, thankfully back in production, and waited. It didn't take long for his table to fill. About a year later, he bought his first section of land.

➤

ON A MISSION TO see an angel, Sugar debarked the Nob Hill trolley at Taylor and California on a foggy Sunday morning, after a long night of wagers and bluffs. Grace Cathedral's carillon was in full melodic stride, pounding out a hymn he hadn't heard in years. He paused midway up the ascending concrete steps, the tip of its campanile obscured in thick fog, trying to recollect its name. He'd not heard that song since he'd left the Methodist church as a teen. The Methodists didn't have bells that could sing like this stone and stained glass beauty now emerging from the mist of the rising morning. Neither did Methodists take kindly to boys who gambled.

The crowd swelled up and carried him along in a cavalcade of San Francisco's best citizens in their finest clothes. The building itself was a monument to European Gothic, with soaring stained glass windows, buttresses, candelabras of beaten silver, and hard oak pews. Striding down the wide center aisle, he nodded at several men he'd become acquainted with in the back room of the Fairmont. The altar was a majestic slab of marble, adorned with satin cloth and golden candlesticks. Three stained glass Palladian windows rose four stories behind it.

In the warm umbra of the early light, he waited to see for himself what Mr. Dalton, a colleague in cards, had meant by angels appearing during the service. Not that he disbelieved in the possibility of divine intervention, he just wanted to witness it for himself. The choir assembled in a rustle of white robes trimmed with red satin stoles.

According to the Order of Service, they began with "*Jesu, meine Freude*" and while it wasn't ordinary, it wasn't angelic to Sugar's tastes. At least not in the way Dalton had described a divine manifestation. At the refrain, a raven-haired singer stepped forward, a few light steps and she settled in a sliver of light from above. The choir hushed. The congregation quit their fidgeting. She lifted her voice, and something inside him ascended along with her, sweeping him up, so even the German lyrics took on a secret meaning. The importance of the lyrics magnified by her conviction, a message from God, undecipherable, but absolutely true. Her music expanded to fill every cubit of the vault. When she finished the quietness of the miraculous settled over the congregation, a hushed moment of wonder. She melded back into the white-clad choir. A part of Sugar refused to return, still soaring high, shiny and lit by the sun. He perused the Order of Service again: Soloist Miss Shirley Gray. Now here was a dark-haired angel he had to meet.

Shortly after purchasing his fourth section, Sugar drove his shiny black Model A back along the road to Delano, with a lovely and satisfied Miss Shirley Gray bundled in the seat next to him. She wore a white cotton dress in the new style almost to her knees and a silk scarf to tamp her beautiful black hair down against the sweep of dry valley air rushing across the flatlands. And she had the long slender fingers of a pianist, the daintiest of hands that Sugar wanted desperately to hold in his.

Sugar parked along the shoulder of the dusty county road. He helped her out, then led her through the scrub and mesquite. Not a tall man, but neither was he short, he had the build and stride of a man who had worked the land, though his hands had gone soft from playing cards. His black hair was swept back under a new fedora, and he was dressed in a new Brooks Brothers suit, with a pleat cut to the pants and two-tone white and tan oxfords. Shirley picked her way, slipping her slender legs through gaps in the brush; with dainty steps she skirted the holes and dips.

Not far off the road, they stopped on a gentle rise to survey the sparse landscape in silent awe. His suit jacket flapped in the breeze. Water in Spring Gulch that cut across the southwest corner glistened blue in the brightness. The sky appeared so translucent he considered the possibility of seeing straight through to heaven. She pushed her hair under her scarf and had to work to keep her skirt from flying up. Her hand shielding her dazzled eyes, she turned full around taking in the flat expanse and let out a low sigh.

"This would be a nice place to build a house," Sugar said.

"A farmhouse?"

He turned to her. "Why a farmhouse?"

She couldn't conceal her smile. "I always wanted to marry a farmer and live on a farm." Her cheeks now blushed. He took up her hand in his, fresh and light, the skin of her palm as smooth as a baby's face.

"What about marrying a gambler?"

"Never." She stepped away, letting his hand go before he could read her eyes. For all of his acumen in divining the facial expressions of card players, he was at a loss to understand the game she was playing. Driving home, he thought of explaining his view of gambling and farming, how they both entailed managing risks, calculating odds, and the subtle art of placing a bet. But she'd already revealed her hand. She would marry a farmer. He realized then that if she had said she dreamed of marrying a gambler, he would have no use for her. He had every intention of playing his last game—soon. He just needed a better stake.

A few days later Sugar visited the offices of Collette and Sons and signed a contract to build an impressive Victorian home on the site that had made Miss Shirley Gray sigh with undeniable pleasure. Something like the grand mansions that stood on Nob Hill, he told old man Collette, who listened while stroking his heroic mustache.

Mr. Collette built the three-story Victorian with two turrets, gabled roof with dormers, and a wide veranda on the rise Shirley had enjoyed, in the southeast corner where Spring Gulch swept by. A natural spring ran in a culvert fronting his acreage, bequeathing the riparian land rights.

In March of '39, he escorted the new Mrs. Shirley Duncan down the aisle of Grace Episcopal Cathedral. Descending through the gauntlet of rice to their waiting Cadillac, he now owned four thousand acres of the most fecund soil west of the Mississippi. When he proposed to her, she had reminded him that she wouldn't tolerate any more gambling. He sealed the deal with a promise that he had played his last card game and would plant his land that spring.

So the year before their wedding, he had planted all his land in durum wheat. When Sugar wasn't watching his supervisor, Isidro Sanchez, work a crew of men plowing in John Deere tractors from an hour before dawn until an hour after sunset, he spent time in his farm office on the second floor planning and figuring. Across from his office, Shirley set up her sewing room with the new Singer machine her mother gave her as a wedding gift. When she wasn't sewing dresses and shirts or a new buckskin jacket for Sugar, she played her Steinway grand in the parlor, running through Chopin and Schubert. In the late afternoon, Sugar would lean against the doorway in the hall, one foot across the other, his planter's hat askew on his head like a man on the hunt. She'd break into a high fevered Benny Goodman or his favorite jazz piece, and he'd sit close by, tapping his foot to the time and smiling like a man who'd eaten ice cream his whole life and was better for it.

In the evening, when the heat had dried out every ounce of a man's efforts, Sugar took Shirley's hand and led her into the parlor and stacked their favorite albums on the phonograph. The sound of jazz and swing filled the house. They fox-trotted across the floor, their bodies swinging and pulsing to the beat. Her scent a promise of her treasure. Sugar held her close as a certainty against all the uncertainties. And they kissed in the vanilla moonlight that streamed in through the tall windows, her slimness against his, warm and powerful and urgent.

➤

ONE DAY SHIRLEY BROUGHT coffee on a silver serving tray up to his office. She wore a new spring dress, white with purple violets splashed across it from the hem to the collar, one she made herself. Sugar introduced her to a well-dressed man with slicked-back hair black as coal. He rose when she entered, a tan planters' hat in his hand. She set the coffee service down on a Queen Anne side table and poured two cups, and took one to her guest.

Both of the men stood. "Shirley, this is Herm Gordon."

Herm held out his hand. "Nice to meet you, Mrs. Duncan. Sugar's told me a lot about you."

"And what do you do?"

"I'm with Lacy's Farm Equipment," he said while fingering the brim of his hat.

"Herm says they're coming out with a new combine that'll harvest fifty acres an hour," Sugar said.

"You say so," she said.

"Three times faster than what we have now," Sugar said.

"You say so." She handed him the cup and saucer.

He took the coffee. "I do," Herm said a broad smile on his face.

"Do you take sugar, Mr. Gordon, or cream?" She motioned toward the tray.

"No, thank you. I always drink mine black." He stirred the coffee with the silver teaspoon, tapped the rim once, and set it on the saucer.

"Herm's been selling farm equipment in the valley for years. He's seen it all. He thinks our place will be one of the most productive around."

She handed Sugar his cup and saucer and looked over the salesman one more time.

"Yes, Ma'am," Herm nodded. "Usually farmers aren't too friendly to new ways, but not Sugar."

"You look way too young to have seen that many harvests, Mr. Gordon."

Herm smiled, and two dimples formed in the center of his cheeks, both fired with a flash of blush. "Good food and fresh air. It keeps me young."

"Herm also said we might look into planting grapes. There's a trade group over in Delano that's made up mostly of grape growers. He thinks I should join."

"You think so, Mr. Gordon," she said.

"Grapes are the biggest cash crop. It's the future of Delano as long as labor's so cheap and we get the water."

Sugar set his cup down and looked at her inquisitively as if wondering what she would say.

"Well," Shirley said, touching her throat. "Then maybe we should plant some grapes."

"A couple of hundred acres in the east sector to start." Sugar pointed toward the large plat map on the wall.

Herm nodded, and Sugar smiled, and he asked her to sit with them as they talked of hardiness and climate and varieties. Sugar favored wine grapes, Herm table grapes.

"I love Thompson Seedless," Shirley said. "I could eat those forever."

The men gave each other knowing looks. "Well, then, let's start with Thompsons," Sugar said.

Sugar prospered during the war years because everything that could be eaten was in high demand. The US military coveted his high-protein durum. And his land had the highest yields an acre of any in the valley. Shirley took advantage of the good years and had a half-acre set aside behind the house. She reminded Sugar she didn't want any planting up to the porches just to maximize the yields. He had a wooden fence built around her parcel where she planted a garden. Shirley in her woven sun hat and pedal pushers, she laid out neat rows of vegetables and flowers and she purchased seedlings for apricot, peach, and orange trees. And in the heart of the garden, she built a grape arbor, cool and shady, where she often rested from the afternoon heat.

Around the oak in the front yard, she sowed Bermuda grass that would take the heat and wear of the large family she and Sugar were working on, but that hadn't taken root yet. Soon the tree would spread its thick limbs, and she'd hang a swing from it and rock her boys in the silent rhythms of the Central Valley breezes.

The year the Sears and Roebuck opened in town, Shirley bought a brand-new Singer sewing machine, one that could do thirty different stitches, and had a foot pedal. She enlarged her sewing room on the second floor by taking over a second bedroom and turned out dresses and shirts for farmers' wives who came to the house to be measured and choose patterns.

It seemed every few days she had a new dress—winter dresses with heavy fabrics; spring dresses white with flowers; bright summer dresses, light and swishy; and autumn always brought out the burnt oranges and browns. She sewed dresses to dine in, to dance in, and to listen to music in, and practical dresses to work in, which had all the elegance of the city, but with large pockets for gloves and scissors and trimmers and small spades.

Shirley didn't like the cars being covered in dust from the wind that often blasted down from the foothills. So Sugar built a car barn on the east side of the house, in the same style of the three-story Victorian. They painted it tan with dark brown trim to match the house whose two turrets, dormer windows, slender brick chimneys, and peaked roofs with gingerbread trim rose three stories above the parched brown fields, a castle on an isolated plain.

In the years after the war life settled in for them and Sugar sold every bushel he grew. By 1950, Sugar's first table grape harvest had grown to two hundred acres, and he knew the future was in grapes. Prior years he'd sold them to winemakers because thir appearance didn't matter. But table grapes were different. Appearance and sweetness were as important as price, and table grapes cost three times what vineyards paid.

Some of what he knew about grapes he learned at the dinner table. Shirley would only set her table with grapes that were the sweetest tasting, had a consistent golden hue, and had the fewest marks of rot and pests. If he could please her, he could satisfy any woman in America. His Thompsons pleased her immensely.

"It's like eating raindrops coated with sugar," she said one night at dinner, after plucking a few damp golden grapes from a bowl. There was a sweet satisfaction that ran across her smile that traveled right up into a happy squint in her eyes. If he could grow the best grapes in the Central Valley with his own brand, he could ship them all over the world. But he'd need a completely new way of farming. The work and cost to convert his land would stretch every financial resource. He'd have to do it soon because wheat just didn't bring the profit it once had.

Though anything a man planted around Delano seemed to grow taller and thicker than in other parts, Shirley didn't get pregnant until early 1950. One evening, both of them sat in the parlor, after she'd learned she was expecting their first child, listening to Benny Goodman on their Victrola when the announcer broke in. Shirley crocheted. Sugar read a book. They both set down their work at the sound of President Truman's voice. The president spoke in a grave tone, one that matched his declaration of a national emergency because of the North Korean Communist's attack on peaceful South Korea. He had considered using an atomic bomb to stop them.

Shirley stifled a gasp. "An atom bomb," she said, shaking her head, "again?"

Sugar shushed her with a hand, and he bent to the radio. She pursed her lips and listened.

"He's sending MacArthur to kick them damn communists' butts," Sugar said when the radio address finished.

"But a nuclear bomb, honey? If he used it the whole world would be in flames again."

Sugar smirked at the sly grin that crept across her face. "See, already you understand the difficulty communist subversives would have in our own community," he said. "We got MacArthur on our flank ready to reap havoc, Truman in DC ready to drop the A-bomb, and the mothers of America protecting our farms. Those dirty Reds can't win for nothing."

She laughed and held out her hand, and he took it. She drew him toward her, and placed his warm palm on her stomach, and went back to crocheting. "We'll soon have more to think about ourselves."

Comfortable beside her, Sugar felt warm with that consideration.

Later that year she delivered a 7lb. 4oz. boy on the third of December around midnight, as the silvery moon rose full over the land. She wanted to name him Jack, after her grandfather, but Sugar wanted Paul.

"Paul? You don't have any relative named Paul."

"I like Paul. It's from the Bible."

She looked at him, her head askance. "I know that."

"I spent a lot of time reading the Bible when I was younger. It's a good book."

The baby made one of those sucking noises that distracted both of them. Shirley pulled him away and gently held him while Sugar placed a cloth diaper on her shoulder. She settled the boy on the white square and lightly tapped his back. After he burped, she held his tiny body in front of her.

"I think he looks like Jack? But then I can see Paul too."

Sugar brushed at a tiny wisp of hair on his head. "You're right about that. He's going to be a man among men, well-trained in the ways of the land."

After all the baby's noises ended, she held him under his arms and lifted him high in the air, letting his little feet dangle. "Well then, how do you do, Mr. Paul Jack Duncan? Welcome to Duncan Farms."

Sugar smiled and touched her cheek with the back of his hand

Sugar and Shirley soon began calling their son Jack. Like his father, he took to the details of farming. One cold morning, after the final wheat harvest, Jack rode the tractor with Isidro as he prepared the land for planting grapes. Year-old vines were stored in their canisters on the north side of the ranch. When spring warmed the air, they would begin planting. Jack rose early during that spring planting to watch the men loading the young plants on flat trailers before leaving for the fields. Rising early became second nature to him, like every good farmer. Before school, he fed the chickens in the small coop his mother built behind the car barn and brought in fresh eggs before catching the bus on the county road.

Summer evenings, with the land resting in the heat, the family would sit out on the large porch that wrapped around the front and side of the house. They watched the fireflies light up the night air and listened to the croaking of tree frogs under the starlight while they drank sweet lemonade squeezed from the fruit grown in Shirley's own garden. Sugar told jokes and stories as the three of them rocked back and forth on the porch swing, Jack squished between them like a ripe watermelon aching to break open, while they swirled away the still evenings.

➤

THE YEAR JACK TURNED eight, just after the grape harvest, Shirley sat at the kitchen table, one hand on her stomach the other over her mouth, a glass bowl on the table in front of her. Jack brought her a glass of water and set it on the table. Jack was hoping for a baby brother. She'd told him they wanted so many more brothers and sisters, but it had been hard for her to get pregnant. The doctor had advised extra caution, afraid she would miscarry as she had before. So she had decided to stay home when Dad went to the annual Association meeting in San Francisco where he'd been invited to speak.

On that Friday in November, after Dad turned out of the driveway on his way to Frisco, the phone calls started up again.

They'd changed their number three times over the past year and a half. Each time the calls would stop for a while, then a month or so later start up again. Every time the phone jangled in the hall or the kitchen, Shirley would sit up real straight and get this far-off look in her eyes as if she already heard what was being said on the line. She never told him who called or what they wanted, but Jack knew they disturbed her. Dad never said much about them either. But one night after Jack went to bed, when they thought he was asleep, he could hear the two of them up late talking about something. There was a sternness in their voices, so he knew it was something important. At times they argued. Then it would be quiet till the deep darkness of the morning, the phone would ring again, and between each metal jangle the house took on a vacant silence. He imagined his parents lying awake down the hall, staring into the darkness, holding their breaths, hoping it would stop. But it kept on. Then they would stop for a time. And they all breathed a sigh that maybe whatever had caused them to ring in the first place had passed by them.

Friday evening, Jack ran to answer it in the kitchen, but she called to him. He pulled up short, wishing he could lift the receiver to hear that voice. Maybe he might recognize him. He'd shoot his eyes out next chance he had, just for causing all this fear.

"Leave it alone." She called to him in her don't-mess-with-me voice.

Jack held up, waiting for it to stop. Dad planned on returning after the banquet on Saturday night. He didn't want to be away too long with Shirley needing him as she did. So in a day or so this ringing would pass.

When the kitchen phone rang later that afternoon, they both stared at it.

"That could be Sugar." She stared at the black rattling instrument. "He's probably in Frisco by now." She rose and answered it. She listened for a while, her eyes turning frightened then angry. "Stop calling here." Her voice was controlled, but Jack knew she was afraid. She dropped it on the cradle. From the slump of her shoulders, he could see her fear. She had one hand to her forehead, another on her mouth.

"Who is it, Mom? I'll kick his butt."

"You'll do no such thing."

He thought she dabbed at her eyes before she turned to sit back down. Jack ran upstairs to his room, loaded his BB gun, pumped it up, and leaned it against the wall by his bedroom door. He knew where Dad kept his hunting rifle and shotgun in the bedroom closet if he needed them. At the bottom of the stairs, he stood where he could see into the kitchen one way and another way to the front door.

When she didn't hear from Sugar on Saturday morning when he promised to call, she paced the kitchen, a worried look on her face. She kept saying as much to herself as to him that everything was okay. After the Association meeting, Dad would probably make the rounds at the jazz clubs in Frisco, probably listened until the sun came up. Jack kept thinking to himself that Dad was just fine, having fun somewhere, telling jokes, laughing and smoking cigars. He would call soon.

She kept up a constant patter of reasons why he hadn't called. When the phone rang Saturday at midmorning, she hustled to the hall extension on the second floor. She gave a cheery "Hello." Jack could tell by the sudden tightening of her face, the voice on the other end wasn't Dad's. She held the phone in the air for a moment, then dropped it to the cradle as if it was contaminated, wiping her sweating palm on her dress.

"Who was that, Mom?" Jack stood a few feet down the darkened hall. When she didn't answer, he asked again.

"Just a wrong number."

After church on Sunday, she paced the hall by the telephone, forgetting the time until Jack called to her that he'd made a dinner of tuna fish sandwiches and lemonade. There were more calls, and out of her anxiety, she answered them all, but after listening for a few moments, she'd slam the receiver down hard on the cradle.

Late Sunday she called his hotel. He always stayed at the Fairmont, but they had no record of him checking out. They called back later to tell her his belongings were still in his room, but none of the hotel staff had seen him since Saturday. Was he home and forgot to pack and check out? Did she want his clothes shipped?

Monday she spent hours calling the hospitals. He hadn't been admitted to any of the local ones, but one woman asked if she'd called the police. She did and was switched to a detective who handled missing persons. The man kept her on the phone, which made her wonder if they'd found his body and this cop was trying to figure out a pleasant way to deliver the news.

Tuesday she sat on the rose-patterned sofa in the parlor with her face in her hands when Jack left for school. When he got home, she still had not risen from her place by the phone. She asked him to make some lemonade and maybe sandwiches for them. When he brought in a tray full of food and drink, she took the glass he offered in one hand and ran the other through his longish brown hair, but she didn't take a sip.

Wednesday he didn't go to school. She sent him to the door when neighbors stopped by. Later that day, she heard men talking to Jack at the door, voices she didn't recognize. Men in police uniforms—one tall and thin, the other short and stocky—stopped asking questions when they saw her. When she noticed the brown Plymouth parked behind them in the drive, something came untethered, and she moved around as if she was trying to float away. She squeezed Jack's shoulder, and he held her hand tightly.

"Can I help you?" she said, talking to them through the screen.

"Mrs. Duncan," the first man said in uniform, touching the brim of his white Stetson.

"I'm Sheriff Gates. Can we talk?"

"I'm listening," she said.

"We're here about Sugar."

She folded her arms and turned from the door. The two men stood on the polished wood of the cool hallway, hats in hand. The short one built like a whiskey barrel nodded toward Jack. She stood in the hall considering for a long moment. She invited them into the parlor and turned to Jack.

"Honey, come over here." The two stood together in front of the sofa. "He's a part of this." She fixed her eyes on the two.

"If you say so," the sheriff said. He introduced Detective Sergeant Kipps of the San Francisco PD.

"All the way from San Francisco, Detective Kipps?"

"Yes, Ma'am. I was asked by Sheriff Gates to report on your husband's stay at the Fairmont Hotel."

"What did you find?"

Kipps hesitated. Sheriff Gates nodded at him. Kipps cleared his throat.

"We have his belongings from the Fairmont in the car, Ma'am."

She bit her lip. "Where's Sugar?"

"That's what we've come about," the sheriff said. "We found his car on Highway 7, heading east, right over the Kern County line."

Mom's eyes turned suddenly hard as if she was tightening up expecting a big blow. "Yes."

"As close as we can tell, he ran off the road and crashed into a deep gulley."

"Where's Dad now?" Jack nearly shouted.

Neither of the men said anything; their eyes turned furtive.

"We found him in the vehicle," Sheriff Gates said in a consoling whisper. "There was nothing we could do for him." From his low tone, almost like a voice you'd use when telling someone good night, Jack wasn't at all certain what he was saying.

Mom closed her eyes and stood motionless. All the air of expectation seeped out of her as if she could sigh right through her pores. Her whole spine went slack, and she slid right onto the sofa. Jack sat beside her, and she clutched his hand. The two men took a step forward, but she held up her hand. Her eyes were downcast for a long while as if she were gathering her thoughts.

Dad in a car wreck? People got in wrecks and were fine. But these men were acting strange, and Jack wanted to know where he was now. If they found him then why wasn't everyone happy about it? There was a light tapping at the screen door.

"That's Sugar's luggage," Sherriff Grant said. "You want him to bring it in now?"

"Why didn't he check out himself?"

Kipps cleared his throat. "Witnesses report he spent the evening at the tables in the backroom of the Fairmont all night after his speech. He never went back to his room. Rumor is he ran into some trouble at the tables."

"Sugar gave up gambling twenty-five years ago, Mr. Kipps," Shirley said, getting her matter of fact tone back under her. She squeezed Jack's hand tighter till the little bones in his knuckles hurt, but he didn't say anything. Jack tried to figure where Dad might be, and why they couldn't help him, and why the sheriff would have to bring Dad's luggage all the way out here.

"I doubt if those rumors are true." She put a finger to the corner of her eye and wiped something away.

"All five men who played with him had the same story," Kipps said.

"He's not a gambler, Mr. Kipps."

There was another tapping at the screen.

Shirley glanced up. "Let the boy in."

The sheriff went into the hall and returned with a young fellow carrying three pieces of luggage and a leather briefcase. He settled them on the floor right in the doorway between the hall and the parlor then straightened up. The nameplate on his breast pocket read Cadet Earl Kauffman.

While the sheriff whispered to Shirley, Jack fixated on his father's suitcase. If that was Dad's stuff, then he wasn't coming back. And the house around him that'd been so full of everything he could ever want was suddenly empty; a vast place opened inside, dark and vacant. His world slowed, and snippets of the talk reached him—"car crushed…gambling and drinking…morgue…must identify the body…sorry for your loss…."

He shot up from his seat and turned to his mother's Steinway behind him, where Dad used to stand and listen to her play, and smile while he tapped his foot. And Jack thought he saw him there, holding his hat, brimming with satisfaction after a day of work, nodding at him to come over and join the fun, the room emptied, and he knew.

Scalding streams flowed down his cheeks, and he ran, banging through the kitchen. Mom's plaintive voice, calling for him, faded as he slammed out the back door into the yard, trounced across her garden, and bolted flat out into the vines, screaming as he tore into Dad's fields, green and freshly brushed by the afternoon breeze.

Chapter 1
The Combine

1968

THE VOICES FROM THE fields woke Jack early on Saturday. The musky odor of grapes sifted into his bedroom even though his closed window was shut to the morning cold. He pulled back the drape and row upon row of trellised vines emerged from the gauzy twilight. They stretched to the horizon on three sides of his house. He thrust the window up and leaned out, and a biting wind chilled his face. Thick dark clouds filled the sky, and the voices of workers trimming and bundling echoed in the morning stillness. In these quiet moments, he imagined the land calling to him. Did it matter anymore that all of it was gone?

"Jack, you up?" his mother called from downstairs.

Off to the east, a red bruise ran across the rugged spine of the Sierra peaks. The air heavy with moisture, it was time to get on the road before a storm rolled in.

Jack slipped into his jeans and plaid shirt, tall and sinewy, hardened from work and sports. Ella, his girlfriend, always told him he never fought his clothes like some guys; they moved with him. He didn't know what to say when she said things like that. He brushed back his blond crew cut and stooped to tie his boots, then he snatched his sheepskin coat off the hook by the door. His mother called again. The day was already half gone from the tone of her voice.

In the kitchen, he grabbed a piece of toast, slurped some coffee, and bolted outside.

He mounted the cab of his father's dirt-splattered combine parked by the rickety porch of the Victorian, now tired and sagging. Jack fired it up and the engine idled under his throttle foot. The strong pulses surprised him after all those years of sitting idle. He revved it up, ready to make its last run into Delano.

The cab of the boxy, once-bright yellow combine, now the peeling paint, was pocked with rust, perched over the rotary thresher blade in front, raised for road travel. The square separation box that stripped the stalks of their grain pods hunched behind him. Most of the gauges worked—fuel, oil, temp, volts. He flicked on the headlights in the gray morning, two above on the cab's roof and two below, illuminating the rusting threshing blade.

"Mr. Lacy's waiting for you." His mother stood on the porch, her arms crossed over her chest. Her back erect, and her gray hair pulled back in a ponytail, still marked with the leanness of one who worked the land.

Despite his sheepskin coat with the collar up and a knit cap over his crew cut, the damp chill sunk through. He tugged on the rim of his cap, snugging it tight, ready to go. The importance of the moment weighed on him. She was counting on him. He eyed the road at the end of the drive.

"I'm expecting you back by ten." Tall and pensive, she studied him with her steely gaze. Fatigue, worry, or both, Jack wasn't certain, had settled around her eyes, etching thin branches that fanned out to her temples. "Don't stop for anybody. If any of those strikers get in your way, just plow through them, you hear?"

He nodded, but he wouldn't be plowing through anyone. With this beast on the road, folks naturally gave way.

Standing on the porch with an expectant look in her eyes, she suddenly appeared younger, fresh-faced and fearless, the way she must have looked to his father before he went off to work his fields. Before their life had become unraveled and they had to sell everything, down to the last working piece of the old ranch to keep a roof over their heads.

He ran his hand over the control panel. This is where his father used to sit. He gripped the wheel. Somehow, it had become a measuring device for what his father had missed all these years. The baseball games he had never seen Jack play, the fun they never had together. He pushed down hard on the brake pedal and fiddled with the front rotor switch. If he spun these blades, would they speak to him? Maybe there was some lever here he could pull that would fill in all the blanks in his life, that would tell him why his father had left them to their own fates. He shook his head. He was just fooling himself—there was no way of knowing what his life would have been like with his father around. Now was an excellent time to be rid of this memory-laden contraption.

A shaft of brightness broke through. Shielding his eyes, he squinted into the sun peeking from behind an ominous bank of black-bottomed clouds. He had to get moving before the sky broke open.

Ella waited in her black-and-gold trimmed El Camino under the spreading oak tree at the front of the yard. She had agreed to follow him. If the machine broke down, she could drive him into town for help. Ella waved, and her long brown hair caught in the rising wind, covering her face. They had met their sophomore year, and now they both were graduating in June. He signaled back, released the brake, and eased out the clutch, which gave off a whiny clank as he shifted into first. The boxy contraption rolled forward, rattling and jiggling, out of the yard.

He turned into County Road 33, a hard-packed dirt road. A chill damp wind kicked harder against his face. He passed the Dakota family's fields that already sprouted a spring crop in some of the straightest rows he had ever seen. The air smelled of dark earth, freshly upturned and dark with moisture. The sun ducked in and out from behind a bank of black-bottomed clouds blowing right at him.

He had driven in this weather. It wasn't pleasant, but the land had never swallowed him whole. It was eight miles to Delano and Lacy's Tractor dealership. About an hour and a half drive if he trotted this beast.

The wind whipped his face. At one time, the cab had side windows, but they had long ago disappeared. The windshield had one working wiper. The rubber blade had rotted away, but it might help some. He pressed the accelerator, taking it up to six miles per hour, but the motor cowling behind him vibrated violently, so he eased off.

His mother's angst over driving these roads in a rickety combine wasn't hard to understand. These weren't the easiest of times around Delano. She wouldn't stop reminding him of what had happened just last week down the road. Thugs had waylaid a carload of strikers and busted out their windshield, their headlights, and threatened their lives unless they left the county. But no one would bother a guy in a combine going about his business.

A muddy road was the biggest threat. If the combine got stuck in the mud, it would take a couple of tow trucks to yank it out. Something his mother couldn't afford. She needed every penny to open her shop.

After crossing over Highway 99, County Road 33 turned into Cecil Road. The road was a straight shot into town, but the combine was too wide to take directly into town, so he would need to hang a right on D Street, and then turn left onto Kelly Avenue. Lacy's Tractor Dealership was right on the corner of Kelly Street and F Street. It would be an easy drive.

Ella drove close behind with her lights on. He made the turn on D Street, and it was a straight run down a freshly graveled dirt road that gently undulated with the land. It sliced through pastureland. Drainage gullies ran along each side.

The rain began in sporadic windswept sheets. He buttoned up his jacket, pulling the sheepskin collar tighter against him. Heavy rain beat in slanting waves on the thin roof. The wind whipped water into his face, soaking his jacket, running down his jeans. He gritted his teeth and leaned forward peering into the gray. Already runoff gathered in shallow pools in the road.

He switched on the wiper. It smeared the water around in a blurry mess, so he shut it off. The road softened, and the big machine wobbled on the uneven road, threatening to bog down. He gunned the motor and squinted to see through the deluge. Once, then again, the tall slick tires slipped in the soggy earth, and the cab rocked in the wind. He willed the machine to keep moving, hunched forward over the wheel, face to the stinging wind.

The clouds lowered and heaved toward him. He held the machine steady on the center crown. If the motor didn't die on him, he could make Delano before he froze or drowned. He plowed slowly through a puddle halfway up the tires, feathering the clutch and gas to keep moving. Not too fast so the tires wouldn't dig in.

At a deeper depression, he trotted the combine down the muddy slope, slow and steady, keeping his progress firm, until the left rear tire lost traction. A swift current pushed him to the right. Downshifting to first, he throttled it up, easing the clutch out until the front wheels of the boxy machine plowed on. The motor strained as he gassed it. The rear wheels grabbed, and he slushed forward up and out of the mud onto the graveled road.

The El Camino stopped at the opposite edge. He halted and leaned out of the cab. She would never make it through. Ella yelled at him from the half-open door. The rain swiftly plastered her hair to her face. She would backtrack to the 99. Get off the dirt road, and wait for him where Kelly Street crossed under the 99. That's where the pavement began. He waved her off and moved on. If he stayed in one place too long, the combine would sink. He had to push on.

Rain pelted him in windswept sheets, obscuring his sight to just feet. Creeping along he saw two red eyes staring at him off to his right through the watery veil. He cupped his hand over his eyes, blinking away the water. Could be a driver standing on his brake pedal, run off the side of the road. He rolled closer. Sure enough, it was a white Cadillac, late fifties, with a black landau top. Its rear taillights were two bullets of red in the gloom, and the front wheels were off the road in the water-filled gully. The tail fins stuck out into the road like an artifact from space half buried in the mud. He crept up beside it. Was someone hurt?

The driver door opened and a man in a three-piece suit stepped into the downpour. He wore a black fedora that shed water off in sheets. Obscured by the brim of cascading water, the man stood tall in the rain as if it were a sunny day, grasping a silver metallic attaché case like Mr. Franks his math teacher at school used.

A fool city boy for sure. He would drown out here behaving like that. Jack inched the machine closer to the tall, lean man, dressed like a slicker among the pastures. The rain slacked a bit, and the man lifted his chin and gave Jack a steady gaze. He did not seem at all distressed.

Jack leaned toward him. "You look familiar, Mister. Do I know you?"

The man touched the brim of his hat, "Herm Gordon. I've known you since you were a child, but you probably don't remember me. I was a friend of your father."

Sure, the man in the photos with Dad in the farm office. The guy with his arm around Dad in the plowed field. Jack set the brake. The combine idled. A bright beam broke through a patch of dark sky.

He clambered down into the muddy road. Herm extended his open palm ignoring the fact he was being soaked by a downpour. They shook. "Pleased to finally meet you, Jack."

"If you need a lift, hop on the running board, Mr. Gordon. I can take you into Delano."

"I don't need a ride, Jack. I have something for you." He held out the silver briefcase. "Could you step into my car for a few moments?

I want to show you some important documents that pertain to your father. Then you can be on your way."

He patted the case. Water dripped off his flat brim down his shoulders. "We don't have a lot of time, Jack."

Jack shook his head at the craziness. The rain slowed, and he sighed thinking about stopping for some fool in an ill-fitting suit. But this wasn't just any old guy. Herm Gordon was a longtime friend of the family. He looked the same from the photos, only with creases down his cheeks.

"I've got to get this machine into Delano before it floods. Do we have to do this now?"

"I need to show you this before you sell the combine."

Jack stepped back a pace. "How'd you know about that?"

"Heavens, Jack, Chuck Lacy over at Lacy's Tractor is one of my best friends. I worked for him for more than forty years. He mentioned your predicament to me. I knew you'd come right down this way since this is the most direct route into Delano for big farm equipment. Besides—," his voice broke off for a moment as if lost in a memory, taking in the creaky machine that idled just a few feet from him. A note of sadness flickered across the man's eyes.

"Besides what, Mister?

"I sold this thing to your dad. What, thirty years ago, now." The man turned to the road. "We drove it right along here to get it to your place."

"And you know why we have to sell this?" He jerked a thumb over his shoulder.

"Everyone knows, Jack. The county published the tax sale notice in the papers. But that's not the point. Lacy told me you'd be bringing it in today, so I figured this is where'd I'd get a chance to talk. I know why you shouldn't have to sell it."

Jack edged forward. "What?"

"Time's slipping away, Jack. If you don't show up soon in Delano, your mother will be on the phone with the sheriff. But before you sell that machine, I have some information for you. You need to know the truth about your father. Besides, it looks like the suns coming out and the road will be drier soon if you wait it out a bit."

Jack lifted his cap and wiped the water from his face. What good would it do to bring that up now? He had to get to Delano. Jack stared at the man. He couldn't completely stifle his curiosity about his father.

"What do you know about my dad?"

Herm Gordon patted the case and turned to the Cadillac DeVille. The big car angled off the road with its right front wheel in the ditch and the left on the lip of the slope. To reach the drivers' door, you had to step into the muddy ditch, but the back door was an easy step right off the road. Herm opened the DeVille's back door, the interior dark and inviting. He motioned for Jack to enter.

"How long's this going to take?"

"Not more than five."

Jack studied the road ahead. The rain had lifted, and the car and combine lay in a patch of warming yellow light. Ahead, clouds of fog gathered on the road. If he waited five minutes, the way would firm up, and the mist could blow off. But he'd need to get going before the Tule fog set in.

The combine's motor sounded strong and would idle just fine for five minutes. Jack slid into the back seat and sank into the plush upholstery. The air smelled sweet like cherry tobacco.

"I'm sorry about the water and the mud, Mr. Gordon." The car was warm and dry and felt comfortable after that jittering ride.

"Don't worry about that, Jack." He settled in and slammed the heavy door. The dark brown upholstery with brocade ropes across the back of the seats made him feel like he was in a rich man's limousine. He had seen cars like this in town but never been in one. He glimpsed the combine out the back window, but he couldn't hear it. The quiet was eerie but pleasant.

Herm took off his fedora and tossed it in the front seat. He wiped back his gray hair, wringing out the water. He retrieved two hand towels from the front seat, handed one to Jack.

"Take off your coat and dry yourself off," Herm Gordon said. "You'll be more comfortable."

Jack didn't want to, but it had become soggy. He shrugged out of it and laid it on the front seat, then dried his face and hands. Herm flopped down the hand rest between the seats and put the case flat between them. He snapped the two latches, lifting the lid toward Jack. Gordon rifled through papers inside the case, looking for something, his eyes crinkling with concentration.

"Here it is." Herm pulled out a thick manila envelope.

Jack fidgeted. Had he made a mistake getting in the car? He should go right now, get on with his trip.

"What's so urgent I've got to see it right now?"

"Patience, my boy." Gordon opened the flap. With one eye on Jack, Herm slid out a document, stamped with official seals and signatures.

"This is a copy of San Francisco PD's police report."

"Why don't you come by the house and show this stuff to my mom? She's the one who would want to see it."

Herm spoke low and deliberate. "Your mother's seen it." He slid the police report back in the envelope and set it on top of the silver case. "I think you ought to know the truth about your father."

"What truth?" Jack ground his teeth as he studied Herm's face. This man knew his father well. There were photos of the two all over the farm office wall. It was likely the man knew something his mother would never tell him. His mother probably had already told him everything she planned to say about his father. She had a reluctance to give him too many details about how they lost the land. That had always bothered him. Here in the oddest of place, at this crucial moment, the truth just happened to meet him on the road.

He tried to figure if Herms showing up here was a coincidence or an answer to what he'd always craved.

He turned and eyed the combine through the back window. He couldn't hear it, but he could see it vibrating as it idled in the road. The machine would be just fine while the road dried.

"Jack." Gordon fixed his tan eyes on him, clear like the wind sweeping over a ripening wheat field. "You need to know how your mother lost her land."

"She always told me Dad lost it in a card game."

"He never gambled that night."

"What night?"

"The night he died," Herm said. "He gave up gambling when he married your mother. I know that for a fact."

Jack caught himself gaping at the man's words. His mother had always told him his father had fallen into his old habits of gambling and drinking. There was something strange about her story and that old man Kolcinivitch would end up owning his dad's 4,000 acres of grape fields over a card game.

"Tell me, Mr. Gordon. Was my dad drinking the night he died?"

Herm tapped the document. "Read the police report and decide for yourself what he was doing."

Jack slowly lifted the report. "What does this all have to do with me selling the combine today?"

Gordon tightened his lips. "You're a lot like your daddy, Sugar, you know?"

"No, I don't know."

"I've watched you play, Jack. You're good."

Jack had seen him at some of his games, watching from the top of the bleachers. In a town with little entertainment, it wasn't unusual to see farmers, kids, and families satisfy their love of sports watching where they could.

"You have the tools to be good, Jack, and you know it. You're so much like Sugar at times it takes my breath away watching you."

"He was a gambler. He lost everything."

"Farming is the biggest gamble of all time, young man. Every farmer in the valley risks a dollar to make a nickel. He was a good man. A real good man. He tried to stand up to what's been going on in the valley a long time now."

"What about his card playing?"

"It was a gift. You should be so lucky."

Jack scoffed at that and turned to the window. This old man had a loose tile or two. Jack opened the door a crack edging over to leave. Herm gripped Jack's damp arm and held him tight.

Gordon narrowed his gaze at Jack. "Just take a minute and read this police report. It'll clear up some stories you've heard about your father."

"Let go of my arm." Jack didn't fear for his safety, he could break this old coot in two if he had to. With the door open, he could hear the combine's motor purring strong. He tried to twist away, but the old man's grip was solid.

With his free hand, Herm Gordon opened the case and then slammed it shut. "Here's what you need to get back your land." He slapped something down on the case but kept it covered with his hand. Jack ceased struggling, eyes glued to the case.

Gordon slowly removed his hand and released Jack at the same time.

A deck of Bicycle playing cards. "They're Sugar's."

More clouds rolled in and the day turned gray, a low mist lingering on the road.

"What do I do with those?"

"You'll know soon enough."

Jack gave him a hollow smirk. "You're crazy."

"Give me your baseball cap?" Herm said, his eyes now bits of coal.

He hesitated, but the old man fixed him with a hard stare until Jack handed it over.

Gordon took the cap then set the cards in Jack's lap. He tapped the report. "Read the first couple of pages. It's a long report. They interviewed a lot of folks. Then you can be on your way. The sun is out. It's better you waited. You'll make good time to Delano."

Jack slammed his door shut. The quietness returned. The air thickened with the closeness of something he always feared, knowing the truth. Herm eyed him. Jack scanned the first page. Under the logo of the SFPD was his father's name and address. His pulse quickened. Why hadn't he ever seen this?

"Jack, this'll take just another minute," Herm Gordon said. "I have something in the trunk to give you before you leave. I'll be right back." Herm's door opened and slammed shut.

Jack leafed through the thick report. So many details here from the night his father died. The trunk popped. A commotion of thuds and clangs sounded like Herm throwing junk around looking for something. What did he have in there?

He stared at the cramped writing on the first page. He held it up to his window to read it. By the second page, hotness seeped out of his gut and settled in his upper chest. By the third page, it smashed upward into his throat and face, flushing his cheeks.

If this was true, she had been lying to him for the last ten years. His father hadn't been gambling. The night he died, he had given a speech that made people angry. The report wasn't clear why they were angry.

A fight broke out. Someone had punched his father, who fell. The hotel staff called the cops.

What followed was page after page of eyewitness accounts. His father had been seen leaving the conference hall in a heated conversation with a group of men. What men? It didn't say. There were no reports of gambling or drinking as Jack had always been led to believe.

He took a deep breath and closed his eyes for a moment. All the baseball games Dad had missed. Why? A sharp pain filled him as if he had opened the door to a room he dreaded entering.

Who were these men? He didn't know how long he sat in the darkness, eyes closed in a rigid fear. Why would his mother keep all of this from him? What was that speech about that bothered so many of the men? Peering through the front windshield, he caught the tail end of green and yellow smudge far down the road on its way to Delano.

He scrambled out of the car just in time to see the combine, faded green and yellow, disappearing into the swirling mists of the billowing Tule fog that swallowed the road.

Yanking the driver's door of the Cadillac open, he reached to start the engine. No key in the ignition. Frantically he searched the floor, the glove box, in the crevices of the seat, everywhere he could think. It took him another minute to realize even his coat from the front seat was missing. He climbed out and stared up and down at the empty road. Not a sound. Man and machine had disappeared into the mist. Jack could chase him for days and never find him. The county was a spider web of innumerable farm roads, spreading in every direction. But he had to find that combine.

He stooped to pick up something on the road. A suit jacket. Herm Gordon's jacket. What was that guy up to? Why would he take Jack's sopping jacket and hat and leave his suit coat? He dropped it in the mud. How did he explain this to his mom?

"What have I done?" he said loud enough so that the black and white mottled-faced Holsteins by the wire fence lifted their heads and stared at him with their milky eyes.

Chapter 2
Lost

JACK STOOD IN THE middle of the road, too shocked to move. This had to be a practical joke. Herm would come busting through the thick Tule fog that had rolled in, hugging the ground in a band that obscured the horizon in every direction. He would laugh so hard, he would be holding his side, and hand over the combine. When there was no sign of him, Jack circled the Cadillac a few times to gather his wits. Why would Herm take off with the combine? He stared at the papers in his hand, then up at the empty road. The old man wasn't playing games. He folded the papers in his back pocket, then trotted down the road, looking for distinctive tire tracks in the rain-washed road. The hard rain had turned the packed dirt into a squishy mess.

At an intersection, he checked the north side of the intersecting road; he immediately spotted wide tracks heading north. He knelt—a trace of a heavy machine had pushed a bald tire deep into the mud. On the opposite shoulder, right up against a field of sprouting alfalfa, stretched another ten feet of a bald tire track. But it didn't look fresh; it could have been here before the last rain.

He stood still, not even breathing, ears perked to the sounds carried in the shifting air. A faint echo of a machine brushed by him on the moist breeze. But what direction did it come from? The metallic sound bounced off the damp mist that swirled around him.

He did a slow spin. He was hardly able to see thirty feet in either direction, the thick air filled with cold shifting webs of fog.

He crossed the intersection to the road heading south. Tracks were there too, but it was hard to say what—one of the big farm trucks, a tractor hauling heavy trailers; they could be from anything. He jogged back to the middle of the intersection. If Herm had gone straight ahead, he would end up on the Delano city streets. He wouldn't steal it just to drive it into town, would he? Jack shook his head. If he went south, farther into the labyrinth of narrow dirt roads separating fields and vineyards, he could hide the combine inside a barn or a shed, or behind a stand of trees. The time to find it before the old man hid it ticked away. What would that old man do with a combine?

He faced north again—away from Delano—that way just made more sense, if Herm was trying to get away. He trotted north in the chill. Herm could be anywhere. Jack studied each farmyard as he passed. Was the old man going to cut it up for parts and sell it piecemeal in another part of the state?

He stopped again, holding still to listen. Nothing. Had he made the wrong turn? He passed narrow side roads that branched off into vineyards and farmyards. Guessing Herm would go straight he plunged ahead.

Why would his father's friend steal their only hope of saving their land? The whole scene around the Cadillac tumbled over and over in his mind. It made no sense. Then there were the papers in his back pocket. His father, Sugar, had not been gambling the night he died. Neither had he been drinking. And the playing cards in his pocket. Was this Herm guy insane? The longer Jack waded through the fog, the more he felt lost in a labyrinth of conflicting versions of the past.

He came to a major intersection. Now there were more choices. Did he go straight, or left, or right. The road gave him few clues. Only distant sounds came on the wind. He kept straight, thinking Herm would want to get as far away as possible. Every so often, he stopped and listened. Nothing but the songbirds attempting to make a dour morning bright.

Behind him, he heard a motor. Not the growly lope of the combine. He turned as two headlights pierced the fog.

Ella's gold El Camino pulled up. She flung herself out the door, her long nut-brown hair fluttered as she ran.

"Where have you been?" Ella hugged him. "What happened to the combine?" She rattled on. She had waited at the meeting spot. When he didn't show, she drove to the tractor dealer and called his mother.

Jack groaned.

"I thought you might have turned around because of the rain."

Jack pushed her toward the door. "Let's go. We have to keep looking."

Jack recounted meeting Herm Gordon on the road. Ella covered the dirt roads north of where Jack had left the Cadillac parked in a ditch.

About noon she pulled into the driveway by the Victorian. He braced himself, not sure what to tell his mother.

"I'll go in with you and tell her what happened. We'll just tell her what Herm did."

Jack shook his head. He was still trying to form the words to describe what had happened. He closed the car door and peeked his head in the window.

"Are we still going to the lake tonight?" she asked.

He scanned the yard, hoping to see the yellow and green combine sitting in the drive and his mother and Herm chatting on the porch like old friends. Parked by the barn sat her white and green Olds. No combine. Something had been cut out of him, coming home without the money or combine.

"I got to find that combine."

"It'll show up."

"Yeah, but in what condition?"

"It'll be okay." She touched his hand. "Call me later."

"If I'm alive." He hadn't told Ella about the police report. He hadn't told her about the playing cards. They both felt like ticking bombs in his pockets. He couldn't explain them to himself. How did he expect to explain them to her?

His mother came out onto the porch, then down the rickety steps to meet him as he strode toward her. Her arms were crossed and mouth set as if she were holding back a storm.

"Are you all right?"

"Yeah."

"What happened?"

He told her about Herm meeting him on the road, talking him into climbing down off the combine so they could talk.

"I told you not to stop for anyone."

"He's Dad's friend. What was I supposed to do?"

"You were supposed to get that machine into town."

"Did you call the sheriff? He's got to be close by. His Cadillac is still off D Street. They can't miss it. He's gotta come back for it sometime."

"Why did he stop you?"

"He had stuff to show me. Said it was important."

"What stuff?"

"A police report from the Frisco PD."

She rolled her eyes. "That man's crazy. We've been around and around about that. There's nothing to be said for his theories."

"He said Dad wasn't gambling the night he died."

Her straight gray hair clipped back in a ponytail riffled in the breeze. He saw no flicker of truth or lie in her eyes, only a tightness to her body.

"I told you not to stop that thing for anyone." She pulled him toward the house. "Come on. You need to get out of these wet clothes before you catch a chill."

"Is it true?"

She walked him up the steps and into the front door in silence. At the foot of the stairs, she turned to him. "Go up and change. I'll call the cops."

Jack rested one hand on the balustrade. "He can't be far."

"Go now." She scooted down the dark hall into the kitchen. Upstairs he changed into dry jeans, shoes, and a work shirt. He unfolded the police report from his back pocket. The San Francisco PD masthead was dated November 13, 1958. Jack had just turned eight years old. No wonder he didn't remember anything.

The report appeared to be genuine. Ten pages of neatly typed script and more pages of handwritten reports, all detailing eyewitnesses' accounts. He slipped them into his back pocket. The pack of Bicycle playing cards lay on his desk. He slid them into his front pocket, without any notion of what he would do with them.

From the top of his closet, he reached for an old cookie tin. Opening it, he unrolled a wad of bills and leafed off a couple of fives.

In the kitchen, his mother fussed over making him lunch. "A deputy will meet you at the car so you can make a report. I'll drive you over."

He stood by the table. "I need to get going."

She kept spreading mustard on a piece of bread, staring at it as if she needed every ounce of her concentration.

"Would he sell it out from under us?"

"Never."

"Then what's going on?"

"Sit down." She turned and set a sandwich on the table.

He had seldom defied her. He folded his arms the way she would and stood over her tight-lipped. She slipped into a chair and waited, lacing her fingers together.

"What did he show you?"

Jack unfolded the police report and spread it out on the table. She ran a finger over the cramped handwriting.

She took a breath and exhaled. "Your father went to San Francisco for a meeting. When he didn't come home, I called the San Francisco PD. They didn't find him, but they talked to people who had seen him get into a fight at the hotel. Someone slugged him."

"Who? Over what?"

She pointed to the report. "Doesn't it say?"

Jack leafed through the first few pages, scanning for names. "It names the witnesses, but no one says who he fought with."

She stood, wiping her hands on her jeans. "That's why I don't want you to get involved."

She turned to the sink.

"Involved in what?" he said to her back. "Why is it all a secret?"

"All the growers were at that meeting. They knew who hit him. But not one of them would say a word."

Jack considered that for a moment. Then scooped up the papers. "Why does Herm think this had anything to do with Dad's death?"

She gave him a look of exasperation as if she really didn't want to explain herself. "He was your dad's best friend. He thinks he knows what happened."

"What was that speech about that Dad gave and upset everyone?"

"Jack, you need to just let this rest." She reached for the police report in his hand.

Jack pulled it away and pushed it into his back pocket. Parents had their secrets, and he'd always suspected she had many of her own. In the past, he had asked her questions about the land, but she had only given him bits and pieces of their history. He had learned to trust that in her time she would tell him more. Then it occurred to him—it was okay to tell him as a child that Santa Claus was real, but if she insisted on feeding him that myth now, then it would cross over into a lie. Perhaps the way she stared at him now meant she was trying to figure a way out of a lie she could no longer manage.

"Herm knows something you haven't told me, doesn't he?"

"Jack, look around you." She spread her arms. "This is all we have left. And that bastard next door has our land."

"That's why I gotta find that combine."

"Looking for the combine and digging up old squabbles involving your father are two different things." She had a set look on her face. "Do you know the difference?"

"What if they're the same?" And that's what bothered him. Herm hadn't stolen the combine to cut it up and part it out. If he had come to the house, his mother probably wouldn't even allow the man to come inside. So Herm had come up with the insane idea to kidnap the combine to drive home his point. As soon as he found Herm, he'd wring the answers out of him.

She took a step toward the door. She reached for the car keys on the rack, but Jack beat her to them. He clutched them in his fist.

"Look, Jack." She pulled open the back door and pointed. Twenty feet away a chain-link fence separated their overgrown backyard from rows of grapevines on trellises that stretched out as far as he could see. "Your father built that. I fought for years to keep it. We've lost everything except this house."

He gritted his teeth, more determined than ever to get on with his search. "I'll meet the cops, and then I'm going to look for Herm."

"Talking to Herm will only—"

"Will only what?"

"I'll go with you."

Jack glared at her, and she stepped back. He felt time grinding away. He didn't want to hear any more family myths. He strode alone through the door and stomped to the Olds. He couldn't stop looking, but he was unclear what he was looking for besides an old combine stolen by a friend, who was either a complete head case or the only honest man Jack knew.

Chapter 3
The Lake

Saturday afternoon, Jack stood by the Caddy that angled into the ditch off D Street as a deputy with a skeptical frown took a report. The tall officer asked his questions slowly, rolling his eyes in disbelief when Jack told him about the old man jumping onto his combine and driving off with it. His questions sounded accusatory, insinuating weakness because Jack couldn't chase down an old man on a creaky machine.

Jack stared into the waterlogged pastures.

"We'll let you know what we find," the deputy said with an air of finality as he slapped closed his metal writing case. Jack had the dark feeling that was the last he'd hear from the cops about the matter. Except for making the theft official, it had been a waste of time. He would probably find it before the police.

A wrecker clattered up in a clamor of chains and gears. It backed up to the bumper sticking into the road. With the car hauled from the ditch, the driver cinched the chains tight, winched it up, and took off down D Street, heading for the police impound.

After the deputy drove off, Jack drove to Lacy's Tractor. Had old man Lacy set this up by tipping Herm off about him driving the combine into town?

Jack found Mr. Lacy in his office. The big man with puffy gray sideburns, a full head of gray hair swept-back, leaned forward in his captain's chair and listened open-mouthed as Jack detailed what Herm had done earlier that morning.

"Listen here, Jack, I had no idea he would do anything like that. He and your Pa were tight." He held up two crossed fingers, "Like this. So I just figured he wanted to help. Jeesh." He shook his head mournfully. "Sounds to me like he's gone off his rocker."

Jack wasn't certain how to take Lacy's words: Herm's stopping him was either an act of genuine friendship or a man so steeped in grief at the perceived misdeeds of the past that he couldn't let it go. To Herm, was his father's death no accident—he had been killed over a speech? It sounded too bizarre to believe. He wanted to know more about his father, but that mystery would have to wait. He had to find that damn combine.

"Tell you what I'm going to do." Lacy picked up the check already made out to his mother. "I'm going to put this right here." He slid open the top drawer of his desk and dropped in the check. "When that machine shows up, and I know it will, you can come get it."

Jack left the tractor dealer reassured on one point. Lacy talked as if she was genuinely stunned that Herm Gordon would do anything to hurt the family of Sugar Duncan. And Lacy had done one practical thing to help. Before Jack left, he pointed out on a large wall map the exact location of Herm Gordon's house. It was far out of town, on the other side of Lake Woolmoes, in a section of isolated farms and fallow acreage.

Waiting for the signal light to turn, he checked his watch. It was already late afternoon, and he'd promised Adrian long ago he'd double with him and take their girlfriends out to the lake for a picnic and campfire. There wasn't time to go to Herm's place right now.

Besides, he couldn't do much by himself. If the combine was there, he didn't plan on calling the cops; he would drive it directly to Lacy's. But then he'd have to leave his car. If Adrian was with him, he could follow him in the Olds. Jack figured he'd have a better chance of surprising Herm in the dark.

Before the traffic signal flashed green, Jack imagined himself finding Herm sleeping in his bed. He'd put his hands on the man's throat and just squeeze tight. A honking horn stirred him, and he plunged the gas pedal to cross the intersection on the green. He didn't think he could ever kill a man. But from what he'd been through today, he sure felt a boiling inside that could easily spill over into something nasty—if he let it. He took a deep breath and eased his way through traffic toward West Delano to pick up Adrian.

➤

THE DAY HAD BRIGHTENED, the afternoon sun burned away the morning fog. The wind swept the dark clouds toward the Pacific, turning the sky that stretched out to the Sierra a pale blue, the air cleared of the usual haze of dust whipped up off the fields. Jack drove in the warm daylight to Adrian's house in West Delano. The neighborhoods west of the Southern Pacific tracks were a warren of narrow, potholed streets where Filipino and Hispanic field workers, laborers, farmhands, and recent migrants had settled into box-like homes. Jack pulled into the driveway. Adrian's squat tract house was always neat and clean, the only green yard in the neighborhood. But since Adrian's father had been out on strike, the lawn had turned brown, and dirt patches showed in places. Mr. Sanchez's primered '54 Chevy pickup took up one side of the drive. The flat front right tire rested on its rim.

Adrian in jeans and a T-shirt bounced out of the house. He tossed his backpack into the backseat and slammed the door.

"Let's go," he said. He punched his friend in the arm. "Man, who died, your pet dog or something?"

Adrian, brown skinned and lean with an aquiline nose, had a constant sparkle in his dark brown eyes. He kept his black hair short during sports, which for him lasted all through football and baseball season.

"Man, it's worse than my dog dying." Jack couldn't remember when the dog joke had begun between them, but it had become the easy way of dealing with a bad game or a bad situation. Jack told his friend about what had happened this morning with the combine on his ride into Delano.

Adrian fixed his dark eyes on Jack until he finished. "You couldn't catch him? That's bad, real bad. I thought you could outrun anyone, except me. How fast could that old thing go, five, six miles an hour?"

Jack pursed his lips, his jaw muscles flexed. He backed hard out of the drive, then shoved the automatic shifter into drive and tore out on the gravel road.

"Hey sorry, man. Don't kill me for pissing you off."

Jack slammed on the brakes at a stop sign. They both jerked forward then back.

"It's gone."

"The combine?"

"What else? I searched everywhere for it. It's gone. You know why I needed to sell it." Jack had told him about his mother's pending tax sale.

"Yeah, but why'd you stop in the first place? He was just an old guy, right?"

Jack swung the Olds into a Vallarta Supermarket parking lot. He cut the motor. Jack explained the entire episode from the time he stopped on the rainy road, to running through the fog searching like crazy, and then filing a police report. It had just disappeared into thin air.

Adrian stared out the windshield into the bright daylight after Jack finished his story.

"Did he tell the truth about your dad, or was he just trying to get your machine to make a few bucks?"

Jack shrugged. "He was telling what really happened, but I don't know—," he turned to his friend. "Right now I need the combine back."

"And you know where this guy lives, this Herm guy?"

Jack nodded. "But let's wait till later tonight. We'll surprise him."

"Don't worry, man. This won't go down, it won't stay this way. You'll see. We'll find that *lardón*, that thief, and give it to him." Adrian pushed his fists side-by-side and twisted them in opposite directions as if strangling a length of rope.

"Hey, it's almost four. The girls are waiting for us." Jack fired up the car and turned out of the lot into traffic.

Adrian slumped low in the seat, appraising the road ahead. "Don't worry, man. Your dog won't be dead long."

Jack laughed for the first time that day. The tightness in his shoulder blades released, and he felt a new surge of energy. He pushed the Olds harder, toward East Delano and the girls.

The day he and Adrian first met was one of Jack's clearest childhood memories. They must have been five or six when his father took him to see his first baseball game at a park in Delano. He didn't remember much about the game, who won or lost, except for a stringy kid his own age who caught his attention. Brown skinned on an all-white team, he whacked the ball so hard the outfielders on their little legs were running all over the green grass. Then there was the screaming in Spanish that erupted from the stands every time the boy hit the ball or made a play. Jack caught himself cheering for him too; he ruled the game.

After the game, Sugar held Jack's hand as he talked to the boy's father. It was Isidro Sanchez, his father's field supervisor. Adrian stood beside his father. As the two men spoke, Jack admired Adrian's uniform, reddish-brown stains on his chest from sliding into bases, and green streaks from catching balls while sliding on knees, badges of his achievement and fun. Jack wanted his own uniform.

Jack didn't remember a day they didn't play ball together, behind their barn, in the street in front of Adrian's house, in the park, in schoolyards, before school, during recess, and after school. They played together through every grade, on nearly every team.

If Jack could choose his own brother, it would be Adrian. At school, kids always wanted to know why Jack was best friends with a Beaner, a Mexican, a wetback. They both wanted to play the game as long as they could, to ride the wave of their enthusiasm as if it would never give out. Jack worked hard to make it last, and when he flagged, Adrian pushed him harder with a dare. Jack often returned the favor. That's what brothers did best.

After a ten-minute drive, Jack turned into the Terrace neighborhood where Darcy lived. Here the houses were wider and bigger, with emerald green grass year-round. The town's wealthy and connected lived here, and Darcy's house lay in the middle of a street of expensive ranchers. Her home stretched out along the width of the property. The pale yellow paint gave the home a soft glow of prosperous ease under the afternoon glare of sunshine.

Jack cut the motor by the curb.

"You want to stay here? I'll go get them." Jack offered.

Adrian opened his door, his foot already on the curb. "No, man, I'm going."

Jack grabbed his T-shirt sleeve. "You sure."

Adrian turned to Jack with a determined stare. "I'm not afraid of him."

"Yeah, but—" Before Jack could finish, Adrian strode across the grass toward the front door. He hustled out of the car and trotted to catch up. "Hey, I'm just saying, the last time you came to the door, her old man blew up."

"He can blow a gasket if he wants. I haven't done anything wrong." After a couple of large strides across the spacious concrete drive, he slid between a Cadillac and a Lincoln parked in front of the house, and up onto the covered porch. Colorful beds of Lenten roses stretched along the front of the house, carefully cultivated, expertly trimmed.

Adrian knocked on one of the double mahogany doors.

Jack leaned an arm against the jamb, and Adrian stood with hands in his back pockets, waiting. They heard heavy footfalls across a stone floor. The door lurched open with a sudden burst.

"Whadda *you* want?" Mr. Lovitch's voice dripped with insinuation. A squat man with a full head of black hair and a broad face, he stood with feet apart as if blocking the door. He wore Bermuda shorts, a madras shirt, and a very unfriendly grin.

"How are you today, Mr. Lovitch? Just stopped by to pick up Darcy," Adrian said, his voice cheerful and firm.

"And Ella," Jack said, chipping in to make sure the grower knew he was here. Maybe with him and Ella close by, the man wouldn't go off on Adrian like he had been doing lately.

"I told you how I feel about you coming around here, young man." Lovitch's dark eyes narrowed.

"Darcy and I—"

The round man plunged an index finger toward Adrian. "As long as your father is trying to organize a friend of mine's fields, I don't think you should come around here."

"I hear what you're saying, sir, but I just don't see how what my father does has anything to do with me and Darcy"

The red-faced grower stepped to the threshold and folded his arms across his chest. "Tell me something. Is your father trespassing in Kolcinivitch's fields, actually going into the vines and getting workers to leave?"

"Why don't you call him up and ask him yourself? He'll tell you what he's doing. He'll probably tell you why he's doing it too." Adrian stood languidly, his hands resting in his back pockets.

Mr. Lovitch gave Adrian a hard glare as if a fireball was building inside him.

"Mr. L, look," Jack said, still leaning on the jamb, thinking he could defuse the situation, "we're just going on a picnic."

The man turned from Adrian to Jack, then stabbed the air with his index finger. "You, you are standing on very thin ice yourself."

Jack held in a smirk. Adrian, still smiling, didn't budge.

Lovitch gathered himself, puffed out his chest, and rubbed his thick hand through his black hair. His voice calmer now, he said to Adrian, "I hear rumors about you I don't like."

"Mr. Lovitch, I don't really know what people are saying, but Jack and I did not rob that bank downtown last week."

Lovitch pursed his lips and slowly nodded. "This is all a joke to you. But when the dust settles, and mark my word it will settle, we'll still be here." He lifted a thick finger and poked Adrian's chest. "And only the Lord knows where you and your kind'll be." He stepped back then slammed the heavy door.

Adrian stared at the door, unmoving. Jack took him by the arm and pulled him away. "Let's wait in the car." They strolled across the lawn to the car and sat in silence for a moment.

"Your dog okay?" Jack asked.

"My dog's fine." Adrian flashed him a wan smile.

"Hey, don't pay attention to that guy. He's just full of hot air, like a lot of the other bigwigs around town."

"I hope that's true." His voice lowered as if to carry a heavier weight. "But, you know, deep down, guys like Lovitch—they mean what they say."

"We're leaving this place anyway. They can have their damn grapevines. What do you think Lovitch heard that he would go off on you like that?"

Adrian shrugged. "I've been helping my pop when I can, driving him here and there so he can do his work. Man, I just can't leave him out there alone. You know how strikers are getting hurt."

"I don't know how he would hear about something like that."

"They got eyes and ears everywhere. But I'll tell you one thing, I'm not going to skulk around like I'm a criminal. I'm not doing anything wrong here."

It had been tough for Adrian and Darcy lately. They had been together as long as he and Ella. And now if Adrian wanted to see her, he had to go through this embarrassing grilling from her father. None of this made much sense to Jack. Adrian was the same stand-up guy even if his father had joined the farmworkers union. Still, whatever strife tore apart the town, they still had their mutual understanding. Baseball was their way out of here, so they didn't let anything bother their game. They would both graduate in a few months, and the game was their ticket out of this land of grapes.

"Here they come," Jack said.

Both girls hurried down the driveway in their cutoffs and tank tops. Darcy with her sinewy stride and her soft cheerleader smile, and Ella with her long brown hair riffling in the breeze. She seemed to float on her white-skinned legs, and a question always seemed to be forming behind her intelligent eyes.

Adrian opened the door, letting Ella in the front seat. He climbed in the backseat with Darcy. Jack fired up the motor.

"I thought for sure your dad wasn't going to let you go," Ella said, as Jack slowly drove away from the curb.

"He wouldn't dare," Darcy said.

In the rearview, Jack watched his friend. Adrian had a wide grin. If he was breaking some law, some code, with his arm around Darcy, it didn't matter to either of them.

Jack raced down Highway 23 and headed to Lake Woollomes southeast of town. A half hour later, the four of them carried a cooler and towels down a trail to the sandy beach sheltered by spreading oak trees. The lake glistened in the afternoon sun as it sank toward the rim of the water.

Adrian and Jack in their cutoffs and the girls in their bikinis swam in the cold water. Adrian built a fire on the beach, and they roasted frog legs and washed them down with beer. By sunset, pink and purple in the distance, they sat on their towels as the flames licked the twilight air. Sparks flew up in tangled streams.

"Did you talk to the cops about the combine?" Ella asked.

"They filled out a report, but it's not a priority for them."

"Combines don't just disappear." Adrian threw a stick on the fire.

Jack stared glumly into the fire. "This one did."

"What are you guys going to do about the house?" Ella asked.

"I'm not going to let it go to a tax sale, that's what I'm going to do."

"What tax sale?" Darcy asked.

"Jack's mom is going to lose her house," Ella said, "if she can't pay her back property taxes."

Darcy let out a low sigh and leaned back into Adrian's arms. "Jack, what're you going to do?"

"I'm going to find that combine." Jack told them about his plans to stake out Herm Gordon's house tonight. "He's gotta come home at night. I'll strangle it out of him if I have to."

"Why would he steal that old machine?" Darcy twirled a strand of her long black hair.

Jack shook his head. He took another swig of beer and swallowed hard, staring deep into the fire. He didn't want to get into any more of the story about his father, a story he only understood in bits and pieces.

Ella rubbed Jack's back in sympathetic circles, trying to force a smile from him. Ella's comfort seemed vague to Jack. He stared at the glowing embers, then stirred up the flames with a stick.

"Have you guys heard from the UCLA scout?" Darcy's voice was cheery as if trying to turn the conversation upbeat.

Jack shook his head. "Coach said he's coming this Monday for the Arvin game, to make his final decision."

"The biggest game of the year," Darcy said, raising her arms in an excited cheer motion.

"We play them the last game of the season," Adrian said. "That'll be a big one too."

"Maybe my father will come out for that one," Darcy said. "I'm talking to him."

"Did you hear that crap he gave me at the door today?"

"We were in the other room listening," Ella said.

Jack tossed another stick on the fire. "You went over there all the time, and he was really friendly, and now he thinks you're a criminal or something."

"Yeah, well, things change." Adrian tossed a couple of sticks in the fire.

"We just about died laughing when you said you didn't rob that bank!" Ella said.

"This whole strike thing is pretty serious," Darcy said. "I just don't think Cesar Chavez is your friend in all this." She nudged Adrian with her elbow.

"He's a friend to my people." Adrian didn't want to start an argument. She had no idea what his father was going through. At times he wondered if she could ever understand what they endured.

"They could just go back to work."

"Is that you speaking or your father?"

Darcy sat up, her lithe body turning suddenly rigid. She turned to Adrian. "My dad says Chavez is a communist, and he's trying to take the farms from the owners."

"And you?"

Darcy pushed her hair away from her face. She pulled her knees to her chest and wrapped her arms around them. In the firelight, the tortured look on her pretty face was evident, as if even considering a different opinion from her father would be impossible. He seemed like a guy who could easily sniff out if she was even thinking traitorous thoughts.

Jack picked up a stick. "Look. Lots can change quickly. They could settle this next week. Then everything will be back to normal. In a few months, this will all be behind us. Even if I have to help my mom for a while, I'm getting out of here. So is he." He pointed the stick at his friend.

"You better. You'll both get drafted if you don't go to college," Ella said. "Like my brother." Her older brother had dropped out of college two years ago and lost his deferment. His letter of greeting from the president arrived a month later. He had shipped off to Vietnam two months ago. "He's going to get his ass blown off, and he doesn't even care."

"We're going to college. We just have to find a way to pay for it, that's all." Jack stirred the embers again with his stick. He didn't want to get Ella started on Vietnam. She hated that war the way the growers hated strikers.

"I'm not going to let my mother live in her car."

"She's not going to live in her car," Darcy said. "She has too many friends."

Jack lifted his head and stared at her, turning over the prospect of his mother sleeping on friends' sofas or in spare bedrooms. He shook his head slowly.

"Did you hear about Tom Jenks and Harvey Collins?" Ella said. "They're going straight into the Marines after graduation."

"They only thing those guys talk about in PE is killing gooks," Adrian said.

"What a waste," Ella said. "They're just going to get chewed up by the machine and spit out."

Jack saw the disgust on her face. Ella had a vision of horror about that war—boys her own age being blown apart by bombs and bullets; limbless, speechless, blinded, and forever crippled—for what? That's what stirred her anger the most, the vague danger that justified such sacrifice from boys she knew.

"That's the only thing they're intelligent enough to do," Darcy said.

"Digging ditches is better than shooting people," Ella said.

"You can't fight patriotism around here," Adrian said.

"I can." Ella stiffened her back. "We have to find a way to put our bodies on the gears of this messed up place. Or the government's going to do everything they can to screw us."

Jack could feel an intensity ripple through her body. He put his arm around her shoulders and pulled her closer until her frown melted into a smile, and she laid her head on his shoulder.

Adrian stoked the fire, and they talked and laughed as the stars poked through the growing darkness smothering the valley. Embers flared up on the breeze, and for a few moments, they lived in a circle of illumination, leaving the rest of the world to itself.

➤

JACK TURNED INTO THE narrow dirt lane that led up to the clapboard house at the far end. They had dropped the girls off before eleven, and it had taken another hour to find this place stuck away at the end of unmarked dirt roads.

"I don't see any lights."

"Let's go." Adrian motioned him on.

Jack flicked on his brights and rolled up the lane leading to a clapboard house. His headlights splashed the yard and the square house at the far end of the drive. The run-up to the front porch, on both sides, was a morgue for dead tractors, combines, seeders, cultivators, graders, a couple of rusted out harrowers, pickups, farm implements of all shapes and uses, all rusted, many cannibalized for parts. Tarps covered a few of the pieces. A waxing moon had risen, and its faint glow cast deep shadows over the field of machines.

"Look at all that junk." Adrian scanned the yard.

"It could be in there, for sure." Jack parked by the small covered porch. The motor ticked off its heat. "Let's see if he's home first. I don't see his car."

All the windows were dark. Stepping onto the creaky porch, Jack knocked several times but got no answer. The doorknob twisted in his hand. No one locked doors around here. The boys walked around the outside of the house to see if it was empty, then pushed the front door open and checked out all of the rooms. There was no sign of Herm.

Jack pulled the Olds forward, then turned until his headlights faced the largest section of the field of machines. A narrow path ran down the middle of the clutter. He cut the engine, and they sat in the quiet darkness, scanning the broken down equipment. Jack sipped his beer. Midnight ticked by while starlight lit up the weedy fields around them.

Adrian tossed an empty beer can out the window and leaned into the backseat for another one. He snapped it open and laughed.

"What's so funny?"

"Do you remember the first time we drank a beer?"

"That's so long ago." Jack had taken a beer from one of the coolers during an end of the season barbecue in Adrian's backyard. He and Adrian snuck behind the garage and polished it off. "Junior high, wasn't it?"

"Man, my dad thought you were drunk."

Jack laughed. "I felt so strange."

"You still are." Adrian peered out the windshield. "From the looks of this guy's front yard, he probably makes a living parting out old equipment."

They both got out and stood in the cones of light from the headlamps. Jack squinted into the half-lit field. So many carcasses of disassembled tractors, graders, and other junk lay in rusted piles. It was as if a metal-eating vulture had descended and gorged himself leaving only the prickly spines of the steel monsters to rot. Something threatened to snap inside him. That old fool probably had all the major parts of his combine already stripped off and sold. Cash in his hand so he could go do whatever old men did with their stolen money. Was that story about his father just a ruse? A big lie to get him to trust him? Brutus came to mind, the traitor sticking the knife in the back of Caesar, his friend, and the two men's eyes meeting as Caesar's life drained out onto the ground. Jack closed his eyes for a moment. If his mother didn't get that money, she was sunk, and he would sink with her.

"I don't see anything that looks like your combine," Adrian said. "Just rusted out hulks."

Jack opened his eyes. "He had to know the cops would come by looking for it here. But we may as well look." Jack went to the trunk and fished around for a flashlight. He played the beam over his path. They picked their way through the carcasses, climbing over rusted harrowers and plows, teetering on fenders, their feet jamming into dark crevices, squeezing between tractors and old trucks until they reached the end of the junk pile.

Adrian's foot punched through a rusted-out motor cowling, and he had to pull it back carefully. "Let's get out of here."

Jack stood on the fender of a nearly rusted-through tractor and swept the beam of his flashlight to the edge of the shadows. "It doesn't look like he's moved anything in years."

"Where is this Herm guy?"

"Good question."

"Strange, isn't it?"

"Very."

They weaved their way back to the small path running down the middle. Back at the car, they both popped beers and leaned against the car. Jack took a pull and swallowed it slowly.

"He said my dad didn't die the way I had been told."

"Then he rode off into the sunset, right?"

"The fog, actually." Jack shook his head. "I don't know what he was up to, telling me the truth just to try ando get me distracted." He stood, hands on his hips, trying to figure out his next move.

"You've looked here. You've searched the roads. You called the cops. What else can you do?"

Jack shook his head. "Let's go." Shaking his disappointment was hard. After Mr. Lacy had given him Herm Gordon's address, Jack knew if he could find the old man, he could unravel this mess.

He made his way back to the car. He opened the door and settled behind the wheel. Through the windshield, he watched the quarter moon slung low over the fields brightening the night, leaving heavy shadows. Jack took the last gulp of his beer and held the empty can.

Sitting in the deepening shadows, he felt strange, a wooziness mixed with disgust at his own stupidity for stopping on the road today. If the guy was so concerned about him finding out about his father, he could have met him at the tractor dealer later in the morning. The two of them could have gone to breakfast and talked as long as he wanted. No, the guy had to waylay him in the road, convince him to get off and get in his car. It had to be a trick to get him out of the combine. A flood of chagrin floated through him at his own stupidity. He crunched the empty can in his hand then tossed it out the window.

Jack stared out the windshield at the field of dead machines. His friend slumped in the seat next to him, dealing with his own mess. His dog looked down, real down. "Mr. Lovitch looked like he was going to haul off and hit you, especially when you gave him that wise-ass answer about not robbing banks."

"They're the guys in charge. They're not going to do the dirty work, believe you me. I just didn't want him to get started on what he might have heard."

"He heard something?"

"You know, man. I've told you already. I help my dad sometimes when he goes into the fields. That's probably what he was talking about."

"You go into the fields with him?"

"What am I supposed to do, man? If they find him, they'll beat him until he can't walk. He's too old for that."

If Jack's dad were alive now, he would do anything he could to help him, wouldn't he? He turned to his friend.

"You're doing the right thing, just don't get caught."

Adrian nodded but didn't say anything.

Jack fired up the motor. "There's nothing else we can do here."

Jack rolled down the drive, the crunch of gravel under his tires echoed in the night air. The car itself seemed heavier with all the trouble they both carried. Jack turned into the dirt road leading away from Herm's place, and as his car kicked up a wake of dust, the old house and junkyard dissolved in the darkness.

➤

ALMOST ON EMPTY, JACK pulled into a gas station by an off-ramp of Highway 99. It was the only twenty-four-hour station in the area. As Jack rolled up to the pumps, the double ding of the island bell echoed in the empty station. A fella strolled slowly out of the office, rubbing his eyes. He brushed his unruly black hair into place with a swipe of his hand as he made his way to the car.

"Hey, it's Eddie," Jack said.

"Sure is, man."

At Adrian's window, the young attendant stuck his head in the window. "What're you guys doing out so late? We got a big game tomorrow." Eddie Carasco, their right fielder, leaned into Adrian's window with a sleepy smile.

"What're you doing working graveyard?" Adrian said.

"Got hooked into it. Another guy got sick, and Mr. Ellis said he didn't have anyone. Someone comes in at six. Don't worry, I'll be rested up."

Jack got out, unhooked the nozzle, and slid it into the fuel spout. He clicked off two dollars. He replaced the nozzle, and across the driveway, one of the two roll-up bay doors was open. The fluorescent lights lit up the racks of tools along the walls and other equipment.

"You know how to work that tire machine, Eddie?"

"I'm a champ at working that thing. Why?"

"How much to fix a flat?"

"I'll just charge you a quarter for the plug. I'd give it to you, but Mr. Ellis counts them every morning."

Jack leaned into Adrian's window. "Let's go get your dad's flat and get it fixed."

"Nah. That tire can't be repaired; it's worn out."

"Put the spare on it and bring it down," Eddie said. "I'll see what I can do."

"That is the spare. The other tire's shot too."

"Bring 'em both in. I got some tires in the back I took off a nice truck a few days ago I can fix you up with. Old man Ellis won't miss those."

In less than an hour, Jack returned to the brightly lit station with both flat tires. Both of them were bald, with holes that couldn't be patched.

Eddie went through the tall pile of discards in the back until he found two that fit and still had a couple of thousand miles of tread. He mounted them on the pneumatic tire machine. In no time, both tires and rims were in Jack's trunk. Adrian bought a couple of sodas out of the vending machine by the door, and they stood around talking about their next game, about their girlfriends, and about school, until they'd finished off the drinks.

"We gotta go." Jack tossed his empty into the trashcan.

"Thanks, man." Adrian shook Eddie's hand warmly.

"Just be ready Monday. It's going to be a war." Eddie smiled.

At Adrian's house, Jack pulled into the driveway halfway. He cut the motor and left the headlights on. In the wash of lights, Jack rolled a tire up and mounted it on the lugs.

"Pump the jack one or two clicks higher," Jack asked. Adrian worked the jack by the front bumper and clicked it higher, so the inflated tire slid easily onto the lugs. Jack screwed all the nuts on finger tight, then tightened them with the lug wrench.

Jack then backed his car into the street until the headlights illuminated the rear of the truck. Jack rolled the second tire to Adrian, who slid under the truck and mounted it in the rack. After he'd screwed it tightly in place, he scooted out, and the two brushed off their clothes.

Jack pulled his car into the drive, and Adrian leaned in the window.

"Your dad will be surprised in the morning, that's for sure."

"Thanks for the help. He was going to borrow some money from my uncle to get two new tires, but these will last a couple of months, for sure." He gripped Jack's arm as if ready to say something, but for some reason, the words didn't come out.

"You know, if we don't help each other, who will?"

"Yeah," Adrian said, a melancholy shifting across his dark eyes.

"Hey, you ought to play your dad, just don't let on for a while that you know how the tires got repaired."

Adrian smiled again. "Yeah, cool. My mother would claim the Virgin of Guadalupe had blessed her with a miracle. She's been praying for a new stove forever, and if Papa got his new tires before she got her new stove, she'd have a thing or two to say to the Virgin." Adrian laughed.

They both laughed, their voices carrying in the quiet of the early morning.

"Hey, we better cool it." Jack lowered his voice. "But don't burst her bubble. Have her pray for our game on Monday."

"If we don't get some sleep, we're going to need a big-ass miracle to beat Arvin. Good night, amigo. See you later, man." Adrian straightened and ambled across the field of light, hands in his pockets, and up to the porch.

Jack backed up, shifted into drive, and rolled slowly out of West Delano toward home. Despite the sharp fatigue slowly seeping in from the beer-soaked edges of his mind, he kept his eyes focused straight ahead. His day had been long and full of disappointment at his own gullibility, but if it ended with only memory, it was a good one—there was someone in this world he could count on, and there was one person who could depend on him.

Chapter 4
Sheriff Grant

JACK OPENED HIS EYES with the taste of sour beer in his mouth. He lay crunched up on the lumpy front seat of his father's old Ford F-150 in the car barn, his knees against the stick shift, his boots tight against the driver door. Something sharp stuck him in the rib and hurt like hell. The air smelled of spiders, dust, and bird poop. Pigeons, roosting in the frayed rafters, murmured satisfied coos, luxuriating in the fresh morning air before the day's heat licked them to a boil.

Every time he moved, something sharp jabbed him. Then there was the *thud, thud, thud* of a bass drum right behind his eyes. He had been dreaming, but the pounding pushed the images beyond his memory. Faces he might know, places he could have been were phantoms cavorting along the borders of his memories. Every time he attempted to focus, the pounding began again.

"Jack, you in there?"

His mother's voice vibrated in his brain. He clamped his eyes shut. The barn door creaked open. A shaft of light tumbled across the windshield. He closed his eyes again. "Jack." Her voice closer now. She rattled his leg. "Jack, wake up."

He groaned.

"You smell like a brewery. Is that why you slept in the barn?"

"I don't know." He couldn't think too clearly. It came to him that when he rolled into the driveway early this morning, he had imagined the combine was parked in the barn. He came in to have a look. When his head began swimming, making it too difficult to walk, he had crawled into the truck.

"The sheriff's here. He wants to talk to you."

"Great." He pulled himself up by the steering wheel.

"He wants to talk to you about what happened yesterday. He's inside, waiting."

"Give me a minute." He rubbed his eyes.

The door creaked when he pushed it open. He stumbled toward the sunshine. His mother took his arm.

"Hold up." She put a hand on his shoulder to steady him. "Kauffman's here, too."

"What's he doing here?"

"Came with the sheriff. So, behave. I don't want any more heat between you two. We need their help finding our combine. Just answer his questions. Sheriff's in the kitchen eating like he's the fatted calf."

Jack pushed the barn door open and stepped out into the sunshine. Shielding his eyes, he spotted a Kern County white-and-green sheriff's cruiser snugged up tight against the barn. A few yards away a stiff-backed deputy in a crisp tan uniform stood next to his mother's Olds parked by the chain-link fence.

The deputy turned slowly. He stood tall and fit with a square jaw. His black hair neatly parted, with the corners of his mouth turned down in an angry smirk and an open traffic citation book in his hand.

"Hey, Earl."

"If it isn't the farmer boy who lost his tractor. I was just leaving you a love note from the county, but since you're here, I'll give it to you. You need new front tires on this crate."

Jack nodded at Earl Kauffman, now Deputy Kauffman, who wasn't but seven years older than him. Earl had dated Ella's older sister, Kathy, the San Joaquin Valley beauty queen a couple of years back. So, Jack used to see Earl regularly at Ella's. Since Kathy had broken up with him, Earl had been sore and edgy every time Jack saw him, as if Jack somehow was responsible.

Shirley stepped between Deputy Kauffman and Jack. She wore Levi's and a chambray work shirt, tucked in with sleeves rolled up. Her gray hair up in a ponytail gave her a cowgirl look, fit and lean for a woman of sixty. "Better go, Jack. Sheriff's waiting."

The deputy stepped around Shirley and handed a citation to Jack. "And don't 'hey' me. It's Deputy Kauffman."

Jack took it from Kauffman's outstretched hand, but the deputy held it tight. "You know, most folks on Sunday morning are on their way to church, but you're holed up in a rats-nest of a barn sleeping off a bender." He let go of the citation with a sneer, shaking his head with disgust. "Get your butt inside. Sheriff's a busy man."

Before Jack could say a word, Shirley pulled him toward the house. Sheriff Stanley Grant had just finished a slice of peach pie when Jack slipped into a chair next to him. Grant had heft and roundness of the cheeks, thicker all down the middle and legs, pillars that carried serious weight.

Shirley set a cup of coffee and a plate of scrambled eggs in front of Jack.

"You say ole Herm stopped you in the road?" Sheriff asked. "Why'd he do that?"

Deputy Kauffman sat across from Jack jotting notes.

"He wanted to tell me something."

The sheriff rested his sunspot mottled hand on the table. "Tell you what?"

Shirley stirred behind Jack. "What's it matter what he said? Are your boys out looking for our combine?"

Sheriff Grant pushed up the brim of his white Stetson and eyed her with an official air. "I'm just doing my job here, gathering the material facts."

"Have you sent a deputy by Herm's place, Stan?" Shirley asked. "He wouldn't dare try to sell it from under us."

Sheriff glared at Shirley then fixed his investigative glare on Jack: "Now, what did Herm Gordon tell you?"

"He said my father wasn't drinking the night he was killed."

Kauffman stifled a laugh, and a severe glare came over Sheriff Grant's face.

"I investigated your father's death from every angle. It was an accident, plain and simple," Sheriff Grant said. "Roads around here can be dangerous when you've had too much to drink."

"Smells like his son is going down that same road, doesn't it?" Kauffman said.

Jack used to like Earl before he had become a jackass. Since he had pinned that badge on, he had begun talking to Jack as though he had some specialized knowledge about people. His disgust suddenly turned to curiousity. How could Deputy Kauffman know anything about his father?

"Did Herm give you anything?" Sheriff Grant tapped the table.

Did he show the police report to them? The sheriff would likely take it with him if he did. He pulled out the deck of cards and set it on the table.

"That's what he gave you?" Grant raised his bushy eyebrows. "He said these were Sugar's?"

"Probably marked," Deputy Kauffman said.

Grant picked them up, undid the flap and shook the cards out. Deputy Kauffman separated them with his pen.

"If you thought the combine was parked in Herm's yard, you'd already have been there, wouldn't you?" Shirley asked.

"It's not there, Mom," Jack said. "I already checked."

The sheriff kept his eyes on Jack. "What were you wearing when you left for Delano yesterday morning?"

Shirley slapped her thighs and let out a sigh of disgust.

"Coat, baseball cap, Levi's, work boots."

Sheriff Grant leaned in toward Jack. "Did you give Herm Gordon your coat and cap?"

"I was waiting out the storm in his car. I put my jacket in the front seat, and he took it."

Shirley stood by the sheriff now. "Stan, where do you think he took it then?"

"How'd he get your cap?"

"He demanded I give it to him."

Sheriff Grant scratched the side of his face slowly. "Was he trying to look like you?"

"I figured he just wanted to keep the rain off him."

The sheriff took off his Stetson and brushed back his gray hair.

"Damn you, Stan, will you tell us what's going on here?" Shirley stepped closer, hands crossed over her chest.

The sheriff ignored her and lifted a brown paper bag from the floor. It read EVIDENCE in black letters. He snapped open the top and retrieved a muddy baseball cap and gingerly set it on the table. "Is this your cap?"

Shirley reached in and flipped it over. Across the sweatband written in her neat printing, DUNCAN. "So if you can find Jack's tiny baseball cap, Stan, why can't you find a 10,000 pound combine?"

"That's the one I gave him, Sheriff," Jack said. "Where'd you find it?"

"Next to Mr. Gordon's body on the road to Delano."

Shirley sucked in a breath and put a shaky hand on Jack's shoulder. Jack blinked and waited, thinking he might have misheard. Sheriff Grant's eyes shifted from one to the other. Leaning close, Jack observed a drop of dried blood streaked across the white thread of the Delano logo. A tremor ran through his right leg.

"We found him face down in the mud. He's got four broken ribs, a broken wrist, and a cracked skull. He's at Mercy Hospital." Sheriff rubbed his chin. "I don't know if he's going to make it."

"Damn that Kolcinivitch." Shirley stomped her foot.

Everything turned fuzzy for Jack, and the sight of that combine disappearing into the mist came into view, Herm wearing his coat and hat.

"You can't go accusing him of being involved," Grant said. "Robberies happen, and these roads can be dangerous."

"Kolcinivitch has been after our land for years. Now it's happened again. When is this going to stop?"

"Now, Shirley, I can only investigate the facts—we have a missing combine and an injured citizen. I can't arrest someone based on hearsay."

This conversation about Kolcinivitch had probably been going on for years between his mother and Sheriff Grant. He rubbed his hands over his face, wishing this would all go away. He had enough and rose to his feet.

"I'm not done yet, young man."

"I am."

Shirley backed away. Kauffman rose and stood tall, resting his hands on his duty belt.

"I'm sorry for what happened to Mr. Gordon," Jack said, "but we need that combine back, Sheriff. And we need it back now."

"Just sit back down here for a minute." He held out his mottled hand to steady the situation.

Jack and Kauffman eyed each other.

"Let's not get ahead of ourselves, Jack. The tracks disappeared down the road a way," he said, talking right at Shirley. "Could be the rain washed them away, or could be—."

"I combed every road I could find between where Herm left me and town. I didn't find anything," Jack said. "Someone had to have trailered it away or hid it on one of the ranches."

"Could be either one." Grant rubbed his wattle. "We got tractor thieves in this county like they got car thieves in the city."

"What does Kolcinivitch got to do to get your attention, come in here in broad daylight and steal our dishes?"

Sheriff Grant folded his hands and stared up at her. "Shirley, he's one of Delano's most outstanding citizens. It's not going to sit well accusing him of robbery and attempted murder without concrete evidence."

"He's wanted this property for years." Shirley stood over both of them, arms on her hips. "He's already built a road right up to our back fence, just waiting for the tax sale."

"There couldn't have been a worse time to drive that machine into Delano," Grant said. "Not with the grape strike going on." He took off his hat and brushed down his gray hair.

"Don't go blaming this on the labor dispute, Stan."

"Shirley, you know I'm going to run hard on finding this combine of yours. Trust me on that. But we're staffed thin, awful thin. Blood's going to run in this valley if I don't keep every deputy on the road." He slowly shook his head. "Strange, old Herm stopping you on the road and giving you playing cards." He slowly rose. "I'm just glad you're all right, son. I better be getting off to church now."

"Best you should," Shirley said.

Sheriff Grant hesitated by the kitchen door and pointed his hat at her. "Don't go taking matters into your own hands. If I find you on their property, your situation could get worse. Leave this to us. And, Jack. You better be careful. Deputy Kauffman here is particularly vigilant about spotting underage drinkers."

He watched the two men file outside. After the screen door slammed closed, his mother came up beside him. "That could have been you for sure."

Jack stared at the back door. "They think we're just drunks, don't they?"

She turned to the sink, fiddling with the dishes as if cleaning them had taken on a new urgency.

"You've got to tell me what's going on here," he said to her back.

"They're after you, too, Jack."

"Who? Why?"

She turned to him, her eyes filled with a determination not to let herself go. She spoke slowly and calmly but with the full force of her will. "This is why I tell you to stay focused on baseball. You're going to college soon, and you'll be out of this." She swept her wet hand through the air. "None of this will matter, Jack. None of it."

Jack stared at the door, then at her. Herm Gordon in the hospital. The combine missing. The sheriff and his mother's long history of griping at each other. What the hell was going on here?

"You have a big game tomorrow. You'd better get upstairs, get a shower. You need your rest if you're going to pitch your best game. You can't let anything throw you off."

"Yeah." If his fatigue found his way into his fastball at tomorrow's big game, and it became fat and slow and easy to smack around, Coach Dickey would spit nails. His teammates would harp at him for not being ready. And his mother would call down fire on his head. He turned and dragged himself up the stairs.

Chapter 5
Hospital Visit

Later Sunday afternoon, Jack stretched out on his bed, hands behind his head, mulling over the sheriff's visit. The sheriff hadn't hidden the fact he didn't think much of Jack's father, driving drunk after a night of playing cards. But the visit had left him more confused than before. Why would someone beat an old guy near to death just to steal a combine? If Jack had been driving and those men had tried to hit him, there would have been a fight for sure. He would have put a few of them in the hospital.

The house was still. He slid off the bed and stepped out into the hall. He could hear his mother's sewing machine whine away on the second floor. He grabbed a few books off his desk and headed downstairs. He poked his head into his mother's workshop. Hunched over her work, she fretted a piece of fabric under the yammering needle.

"Mom."

She stopped and turned.

"I'm going to meet Ella at Roscoe's for a soda. She's going to help me with my algebra."

She furrowed her brow in disapproval. "You have a big game tomorrow."

"I'll be home early, don't worry."

She glared at him with narrowed eyes.

"I'll be okay."

She turned back to her work.

The lobby of Mercy Community smelled antiseptic. The receptionist, in a pink pinstripe uniform, pointed him to a hall on the left. "Mr. Gordon's in 193."

He stood outside Herm's room. A nurse hurried out carrying a tray of medications. She hesitated and eyed him. "Are you lost?"

Jack nodded toward the door. "I'm looking for Herm Gordon."

"Are you family?"

Jack tilted his head.

"I'm sorry, Mr. Gordon's only able to see family members right now. Besides, I just gave him his medication. He won't be awake for long."

"Is that you, Jack?" Herm called from inside.

"How you doing, Mr. Gordon?"

"Nurse, let that young man in here right now."

She rolled her eyes and stood aside. "Five minutes, buster. He's had a serious head injury and needs to rest."

Herm looked like a casualty of war. White bandages covered his head down to his eyebrows; his cheeks were scabbed and bruised, and both eyes were black, with one swollen shut. Jack grimaced. Why would someone do this just to steal an old harvester?

"Jack, come closer so I can see you, son."

Herm squinted through his one good eye and reached out a shaky hand. Jack took it, clammy and weak, and held it.

"I'm sorry, Jack, I tried to get that combine into town for you," he said, so softly Jack had to lean down to hear him. His lips were chapped and dry.

"You knew someone was after me, didn't you?"

"I wanted to help you, Jack."

"Help me do what?"

Herm closed his one right eye.

"Mr. Gordon…"

"Herm, it's always Herm."

"Were they after me?"

"They were upset when they found out it wasn't you. They dragged me down and beat me harder."

"Who were they?"

He gave a tired shrug. "What'd you do with those papers I gave you, Jack?"

"I showed them to my mom."

Herm's head lolled back. The painkiller must have kicked in.

"Okay, young man, that's enough." The nurse stood in the door. "Between you and Sheriff Grant, you're going to be the death of him."

Jack held Herm's hand. The man lifted his head with great effort. "One more minute."

Herm motioned for him to come closer. Jack leaned over the bed railing. "Water rights." His words came out breathy.

"What water rights?"

Herm's eye flickered open. "The old spring...by the road."

That old spring by the road? Would it still have water? How would stealing the combine get them water rights attached to Duncan land? "I don't understand."

He stared up at Jack and gripped Jack's hand. "Take your father's truck; drive it out of this place. Don't leave it behind. Just pitch and get out of here. Please, Jack, do it."

The old man drifted off. The stale air made Jack fear Herm had slipped into more than sleep. He rushed past the nurse, down the hall, and outside into the dusty winds whipping off the fields. Jack slid behind the wheel and keyed the ignition. He slapped the steering wheel several times until his hand hurt.

If Herm hadn't run off with the combine, that could be him in that hospital bed getting morphine shots. His season would be up in flames, his dream of pitching gone forever. Or he'd be dead like his father. What kind of sick bastards would do this for water rights? If that spring weren't all dried up, their little bit of land would be valuable. Valuable enough to steal and maybe kill for.

What had Herm meant about taking his dad's old truck? That thing hadn't run for years. The old man wasn't making too much sense, except about pitching himself out of here. He could win that scholarship if he put his mind to it.

Jack started the car. A dusty wind scraped over the windshield. There wasn't any future for him in this city of grape hawkers. If he stayed, he could end up looking like Herm. People treated their dogs better than that.

Johnny Cash blared on the radio. Jack flew out of the lot with the words of raspy-voiced Cash in his ears. "I shot a man in Reno just to watch him die."

There seemed to be a lot of good reasons to shoot a man. Would that make it less of a crime or no crime at all?

Chapter 6
Ash Wednesday

Monday at lunch, Jack and Ella settled on the grassy school quad. The morning haze, a gray dullness, hung over them. Ella in a long skirt and T-shirt printed with her favorite saying played her guitar. Jack ate slowly, as Ella gently strummed a Joan Baez song.

She let the last chord vibrate in the air. "You look far away today, Jack."

"Just thinking."

"Worried about the big game?" She strummed a C chord.

"Not really. I'm ready for those guys." As crucial as the Arvin game was to his chances for a scholarship, his head spun with Herm, the sheriff, and lost combine. He needed to set all that aside. But how?

"You're worried about losing that combine, aren't you?"

He shrugged and glanced off into the haze. Herm's beat-up face filled him with too many questions, ones he would rather not ask.

"What do you think happened to it?"

Jack did his best to suppress a frown. He spent the next twenty minutes explaining how Sheriff Grant found Herm Gordon face down in the mud and how their combine had gone missing. Short of stealing someone else's machine and selling it to pay the taxes, he didn't have too many ideas about what he could do to save his mom's place.

"Jack, you have to protest. Write to the newspaper. Make noise until the sheriff finds your combine. Someone knew you needed that money to save your property."

Ella's sense of urgency hovered over her, an impending sense of doom that required her to stand up and shout to drive it away. She had been this way since he first met her, always ready to protest. Vietnam had taken up most of her attention. But it was their trip to Berkeley a couple of years ago that had set her on fire, and had almost got Jack arrested in front of Sproul Hall.

Two years ago, their sophomore debate team had joined the junior and senior team on a field trip to UC Berkeley to observe a statewide competition. They left Delano before dawn and talked for the entire four-hour bus ride. That was something he had never done with any girl. They sat across from each other, an aisle between them. Her darting green eyes held his interest. Life shot out of them, beautiful and intelligent in the same instant.

They debated the war in Vietnam, who killed JFK, the likelihood of a gunman on the grassy knoll, the Selma march, the Freedom Riders, Malcolm X, the Black Panthers—she had an opinion on everything. Mostly, she made sense. The girl's intensity at times unsettled him, but it mostly intrigued him.

During the debate competition in a Berkeley auditorium, shortly after the lunch break, Ella leaned into him in the dark. "Meet me outside on the steps in a few minutes."

Without waiting for an answer, she rose and disappeared. Jack stewed in his seat, trying to figure out what she was up to. He wouldn't miss much if he left. Besides, her sense of adventure piqued him. A few minutes later, he found her outside the glass doors on the steps. In the breeze, her brown hair, straight and long, riffled across her mischievous smile.

"There's an FSM rally on the other side of the campus. Go with me. We'll be back in plenty of time."

"A what?" he asked.

"You know, the Free Speech Movement. *Please,* go with me," she pleaded with her green eyes. "Mario Savio is going to speak."

From the way she threw out his name, he was someone Jack should know. He had never heard of the Free Speech Movement, or Savio, whoever he was. Jack glanced back to the doors.

"They'll be in there for hours." She took his hand. He marveled at her warm grasp. He liked it.

They made their way through a maze of buildings. She must have had this all planned out. She led him directly to a large plaza packed with students milling about. Some sat, most stood talking and smoking, and clouds of strange smelling smoke wafted over the crowd. A line of cops stood on the fringes of the crowd. They fidgeted with their batons.

The two of them were so far back, they could hardly make out what the speaker was saying. Ella pushed her way toward the front, and Jack held on. Had she done this before? She stopped when they were about twenty feet from the speaker, who read a list of students who were being expelled. People were booing.

A new speaker came to the microphone, a tall wiry-haired student in a white shirt and sheepskin-lined jacket. Electricity seemed to shoot right out of his hair. The crowd around Jack murmured, likely wondering what this guy was going to say. Ella squeezed his hand tighter. He didn't dare let go of her, afraid they'd get separated in the jostling crowd.

The crowd hushed when the man with the electric hair started to speak. He had a machine-gun delivery. His message burst from him with so much energy the entire crowd leaned in for more. His lips moved like waves, every word coated with fire.

I ask you to consider if this university is a firm...we're the raw materials.

And we don't mean to be made into any product...to be bought by anyone.

We're human beings!

The crowd applauded, and Ella loosed her hand to clap and shout.

*There's a time the operation of the machine becomes so odious…
you can't take part.*

*You've got to put your bodies upon the gears…upon the levers…
and you've got to make it stop.…Unless you're free, the machine won't
be prevented from working.*

The crowd broke into more applause. Kids were yelling their agreement. Jack wasn't clear what machine the guy was talking about, or what freedom he didn't have, and what gears needed to be stopped. Then the speaker introduced Joan Baez, and the crowd went crazy with chatter and clapping.

She started singing a Bob Dylan song, and a hush fell over everyone.

How many times can a man turn his head
And pretend that he doesn't see?
The answer, my friend, is blowin' in the wind…

Ella hopped up and down on the balls of her feet.

Baez started up another song, "We shall overcome…," and everyone joined in, the crowd swayed with the words. Something great, something powerful was about to break open here. He took Ella's hand, and she gave him a complicit smile. She held him tight as if she feared she would float away in the euphoria of the moment.

When the song ended, she pulsed forward. Jack dared not let her go as they slipped between applauding students who hovered around the famous singer. Ella ascended right up to the great Joan Baez, her long black hair draped over her shoulders, her guitar slung over her neck.

Ella tried to talk calmly, but she only stammered.

"Did you want an autograph, honey?"

Ella had a confused look as if the question she wanted to ask had slipped away.

"Do you go to school here?"

Ella shook her head. "Delano High School."

"Look," Baez pointed over Ella's shoulder. "You guys got to get out of here. There's going to be trouble."

At the far end of the crowd, cops were forcing students to move. Cop cars with lights flashing swarmed into the quad forcing students toward them. Panicked voices, screams, and shouting rose in the quad. Police vans rolled into the quad, lights flashing, the short squawks of their sirens stirred up the crowd.

The man with wiry hair grabbed the microphone beside Baez. "Everyone sit down. Resist them. Don't let them take you. You have a right to be here."

Baez fished in her purse and pulled out a black pen. "Here, let me sign something, then you two split." She hovered her pen looking for something to write on while Ella stood motionless. Finally, the singer reached up and scrawled her name in big looping letters on Ella's forehead.

"Go!" Baez pointed off to her left.

Jack led Ella down the side of the steps, away from the surging crowd. Students were shouting as the cops swung batons, pushing and shoving them into the center. Jack ran along the front edge of the students sitting cross-legged on the ground. Several cops ran toward them from their right. Jack, with Ella in tow, sprinted away from them across the open plaza, heading for the shelter of a building.

"Hey, you two, stop!" Heavy footsteps gained on them.

Jack clutched her hand, nearly dragging her. He desperately wanted to reach their seats in the auditorium. They ran full out down the side of a building, between another two into a smaller plaza. They dodged students, dashed around a fountain, and then behind another building.

"That way," Ella said, pointing over his shoulder to a long hall. The footsteps were still behind them. They made their way down the side of the long hall, into a parking lot where they ducked between two cars, then down a lane.

"There! There!" Ella said. Jack saw the auditorium in front of them. If they could just make the doors.

"You two stop now!" Jack ran with everything left in him through the lot, across a small plaza, up the steps, and into the lobby. They blasted through the double doors into the darkened auditorium.

"Oh, no!" Jack said, stunned. It was empty.

"The buses are right outside. Over there!" Ella said, pointing to a side door down by the stage. They hustled down the aisle, both breathing hard, and turned to the door. Just as he reached for the crash bar, a shaft of light flooded in from behind them. Jack held up. A silhouette stood in the open auditorium door.

"As soon as I open this, he'll see us," Jack whispered to Ella, who was crushed up against him.

"We can make the bus." Her breath was hot on his ear.

The door closed, plunging them into darkness. A beam of light flashed and began sweeping the seats, steadily moving toward them.

Jack pushed the bar, and they burst into the sunlight. A line of yellow buses, motors idling, were strung along the curb. Halfway down, Jack found the Delano High bus and pushed Ella up, then he jumped up the step. The two stood in the small aisle by the driver. Every eye on the bus stared them down. Every eye wanted to know where they had been. Heat seeped into his cheeks. He calmed his breathing.

"It's about time you two showed up," Mr. Thompson said. The only two seats left on the bus were in the front row next to him. Jack took the window, and Ella sat between them.

"Sorry, Mr. Thompson," Ella said, demurely. "I was in the bathroom. I got lost, and Jack showed me where the buses were."

He sighed and shook his head. "You can roll now, Howie," Thompson said to the bus driver.

The bus door soughed close, and the driver revved the motor. Jack closed his eyes, letting all the tension out of his body. He wanted to laugh, but he dared not.

Just then someone banged on the door. It opened, and a cop stepped up into the bus.

"I'm looking for two demonstrators who ducked in here."

"All of our students are accounted for, officer," Mr. Thompson said. "We have to get on the road."

"These two." He pointed at Jack and Ella with his Billy club. "They look familiar."

"They're with us," Thompson said.

The officer squinted and inched closer, staring at Ella. "What's that on your forehead?"

Mr. Thompson leaned over to have a look.

Before Ella could answer, Jack asked, "Are you aware of what day it is, sir?"

"What?" The cop had an angry look.

"It's Ash Wednesday."

"Yeah, so?"

"We were at the church this morning." Jack pointed vaguely behind him. "And that's how they anoint now." A few months before, Jack had seen a TV special on the changes in the Catholic Church.

"They don't do ashes like that."

"Everything changed with Vatican II." Jack had been learning about the power of rhetorical questions in debate. Now would be a good time to test one out. "Are you at peace with your religion, officer? Is that why you're singling her out?"

The officer looked as if he was gagging, trying to get an answer out of his mouth.

"Officer," Mr. Thompson urged. "We have to get on the road."

He backed out of the bus, the door closed, the motor revved, and with the grinding of old gears the bus haltingly rolled forward, gained speed, and headed home.

Darkness had fallen. Jack let his mind wander as he stared out the window at the passing cars trying to understand what had happened between them today. Holding Ella's hand was like being captured by a tornado. He had to admit he didn't want to let her go.

She rested quietly beside him. Mr. Thompson snored. They were still an hour away from Delano when Ella squeezed Jack's hand. She leaned close and kissed him on the cheek. She put her mouth to his ear.

"I'm a Presbyterian. But for one moment I was a Catholic. I will never forget that."

Her words made him smile. He wasn't Catholic, but that didn't matter. He wouldn't forget today either. When her parents heard about her meeting Joan Baez and hearing Savio speak, they never allowed her near Berkeley again.

After they arrived back at campus, Mr. Thompson took him aside. He said he'd let this episode slide, but only if he showed the same initiative and creativity in debate for the rest of his high school career. He felt himself in a squeeze. Ella was a top debater. This was her territory.

He'd be in her whirlwind. Then there were the ramifications of getting caught leaving the debate. He had far less to fear from a cute girl.

"Sure," he told Thompson. They shook, and no one talked about it again, except for Ella just about every time they kissed.

➤

THE AFTERNOON SUN BROKE through the lunchtime sky, and the Delano High quad became too hot to sit in. They moved under the shade of a large oak in the center of the lawn. After they settled, Ella went back to prodding.

"Did the sheriff say how bad Herm Gordon was hurt?"

"I saw him last night. He's in bad shape."

"What did he have to say?"

Jack admired her alluring face. He stared into her soft green eyes for a moment. "He said it had something to do with the water rights on our property. I have no way of knowing if that was true."

"Did he hide the combine somewhere?" She rested her guitar on her lap and tuned a string.

"Adrian and I checked out his place on Saturday night. It wasn't there. He says someone stole it from him."

"Why would they do that?"

Jack shrugged. "I don't know. This whole thing is…" His voice cracked. "It could be anywhere."

A bell rang.

"I have to get to calculus." She began to collect her books. "I'll see you at the game today."

"If you don't get detention for wearing that T-shirt," Jack warned.

She puffed her chest out. On the black T-shirt, white letters read "Put your bodies on the gears…" A wry smile broke out on her face. "Teachers don't even know what it means. Besides, I wear this over it in class." She took up a jean vest that had wide collars and slipped it on.

"Have you found any gears to gum up yet?"

She gave him a sly, knowing look, one full of something he didn't quite understand. "Jack, your problem, you know, is that you don't see them. The gears are everywhere."

He wanted to laugh. She always had the suspicion that a grand conspiracy existed; secrets she should know had been hidden from her. That's why she had taken up the cause of free speech. She had convinced the principal the best way to keep peace on campus was to set aside a corner of the quad for open discussions as they had done at Berkeley and other colleges. Every Friday at lunch, students could speak for five minutes each. Ella often spoke out against Vietnam, drawing boos and catcalls from students in the quad. She was seen around campus as unpatriotic, outspoken, a rebel. Next week she was starting a new campaign for pants. Girls should be able to wear jeans to school the same as the boys. She had determination written all over her face.

He leaned over and kissed her.

Chapter 7
Red Stains

Jᴀᴄᴋ's ꜰᴀꜱᴛʙᴀʟʟ ᴡᴀꜱ ᴀʟᴡᴀʏꜱ faster in the heat. He would need every bit of that today.

Monday afternoon the Delano High team bus turned into the sun toward Arvin for the third game of the season. The Central Valley town lay just ahead in a low swale where the heat festered in the late afternoon stillness. The road bore potholes, bumps, and dicey edges—thin strips of asphalt slicing through rows of grapes. The fields rode up to the ragged, narrow shoulders that seemed to say stay away, go home, unless you want to get your brains beat in. These Arvin guys had knocked them out of the league title the past three years with their aggressive play.

That wouldn't happen today if he had his best game.

Jack leaned close to the window, letting the hot air wash over him. He closed his eyes and imagined the sun exploding into a white heat. He'd throw bullets, strike out every damn one of them. The crowds would shake their heads in awe. Arvin cheerleaders, growers' daughters in short skirts, would faint right to the ground.

That coach from UCLA would never stop smiling. He'd write out that scholly on the spot and slip Jack a pale blue *Bruins* cap. He'd pull it low over his brow like a pro, fix that coach with a stare of steel, and they would shake hands like men.

Ella would sprint from the stands and jump into his arms, her body firmly against his, kissing him and not even caring about the vice-principal and his detention slips. This was Jack's destiny, his ship of golden treasure in the bay of dreams-come-true.

"Wanna play, Jack?" Marty Kolcinivitch, the grower's son, shouted over the creak of steel and thumping tires. Jack turned to the team's star catcher, a boy of broad shoulders and sharp cheeks of his Slavic ancestors. He slumped on the backbench with three other boys playing seven-card stud. They held their cards to their chests. Jack shook his head. They had been over this too many times. He didn't play cards, any cards. After all the agony his mother had been through, he just didn't have any appetite for gambling even if it was just for fun.

"Okay, okay, you don't play. But you're looking sad, Jackie boy," Marty said. "We need you big-time today."

Adrian, in his tan uniform, sat across from him, a set of cards fanned out in his hand. "He's just getting his dog on."

Jack laughed under his breath. "Yeah, just getting ready." He wanted to stand up and remind everyone they had their brains beat out coming here the last three years. Everyone heard the Arvin players' talk. They were hunting for a fourth championship with their noses in the air. Playing cards wouldn't help him get ready for battle. But every kid had his own way. For Jack, he had to see in his mind the ball spinning through the air for a strike. He leaned back, closed his eyes, and willed the ball to go fast.

The chatter on the bus turned to Arvin. Jack opened his eyes. In front of him, through the hazy dust off the fields, Arvin's stucco buildings, only four streets wide and five deep, lay arched up against Bear Mountain purpled in the distance. Two left turns later, the bus rolled down Varsity Avenue. Parked along every inch of curb on both sides of the avenue were old Chevys, Fords, beat-up wagons of every make and model. Most were covered with a dense layer of dust from driving the farm roads. Hanging limply from antennas were flags—a black eagle centered on a white and red field. The black eagle flag of the United Farmworkers. Why the black eagle here? The UFW had become notorious for stirring up trouble in the oddest places.

Adrian, across from him holding a fistful of cards, notched his head in recognition. "UFW flags." Adrian had a wry smile on his lips. He leaned forward to get a better look.

Marty cursed under his breath. "We don't need no UFW trouble here."

"What's going on?" Jack asked, concern tightening his voice. "Why are they here?"

Adrian shrugged. "Is your dad here, Marty?"

"Yeah, he wouldn't miss this game for anything."

"I thought he'd be too busy firing people," Adrian said. His father used to work for Marty's dad until he fired him last year for joining the UFW. Off the field, the two boys weren't that friendly. But the team couldn't win without either of them.

"Shut up and play cards," Marty said, his face flushing red.

"You guys." Jack stood in the aisle. "This is our biggest game of the year. We don't need any of these people hanging out here."

The boys studied their cards, poker-faced.

"And what about our agreement? The team first."

"Okay, Jackie boy, we're cool," Marty said. "Aren't we, guys?"

Adrian rolled something around in his mouth. "We got a game to play. That's all that's going on."

Jack slid into his seat, his back against the window, eyeing his teammates. He had worked his butt off to get noticed by college scouts. This strike nonsense was a distraction. He took a breath to calm himself—he had to stay focused.

The bus entered the Arvin High School lot where cars were doubled parked in the lanes. The lot was full of clean, shiny Fleetwoods, freshly washed Devilles with fins and fancy two-tone paint jobs, a few black Lincolns, and several shiny Mustangs with chrome rims. Some yo-yo in a candy-apple red Eldorado had pulled up on the sidewalk blocking the way to the ballfield. The driver had to weave through them to his usual spot.

"Must be some party going on around here," Marty said. "Hope we're invited."

"We're the guests of honor, don't you know," Adrian said.

Coach Dickey stood in the aisle, his tan uniform with brown piping snugging his lean frame. If it weren't for the jiggle in his right hand, he could take the field and play with anyone.

"Listen up. Everyone knows what happened on this field last year, and the year before that, and the year before that. We all know what's going through the minds of those Arvin fellows out there." He motioned with his head toward the ballfield. "And then we got those UFW flags. I know you all saw them. Feelings are running hot around here. Growers are coming out to watch us. I don't know what's going on out there, but I'm warning you, stay focused." He moved down the aisle, poking a finger at them. "The only way we win here is if we don't see or hear anything outside those chalk lines. On that field we're brothers. You got that."

Guys nodded.

He put a finger to his temple. "You let anything get inside here but baseball, you're going to stink up the field."

All eyes were fastened on him.

"The times demand our best efforts. You got that."

Heads nodded.

"Let's go play ball."

They strode to the field, sweaty and rumpled in their tan and brown Delano High uniforms from the hour's ride in that yellow jolting oven. Jack pushed his brown cap back to cool his head. They had the grass greened up really nice, the outfield crisply mowed, the base paths a blood red diamond in the freshly dragged infield.

Arvin had just finished batting practice, and the team gathered around the backstop glaring. They were well-fed guys in prissy white uniforms that were so crisp they must have been ironed. Not even a sportsman's greeting, they peered from behind the mesh.

Jack trotted out with his teammates for his warmups. As Jack straddled the mound for his practice throws, Adrian jogged by and tossed him a ball.

"Lots of big white guys in white uniforms," he said, a smirk on his lips.

Jack laughed. Their uniforms were so bright they almost glowed. As Jack threw his first practice tosses, the visitors' wooden bleachers vibrated with people. Parents, friends, cheerleaders, and girls were everywhere. School brass always came for this game. People moved about, finding seats, getting cold drinks from the snack bar.

Then there were the Mexicans and Filipinos in jean jackets, denim work shirts, and colorful bandannas around their necks. There were women in straw hats, familiar in the fields. They milled about, filling the high seats in the stands behind both dugouts.

Jack usually didn't see this many fieldworkers at his games. But then this was Arvin. A small burg surrounded by fields, not even a movie theater in town. This game was a big deal.

His mother in a home-sewn pink and blue sundress, a straw hat with a pink feather, and large sunglasses sat next to Ella, in her flared jeans, a yellow peasant blouse, and sunglasses. They were both in the bottom row of the bleachers right behind their dugout. Those two never missed a game.

The Arvin home stands, a little larger and just as full, held a party in the making. Kids in red T-shirts waved school banners, and ladies in summer dresses and wide-brimmed sun hats unpacked baskets. Several men wore planters' hats; one of them wore a madras shirt and sat in the front row, smoking a cigar. Jack recognized Mr. DiGorda from his madras shirt and his fat cigar. His son batted fourth. Marty's father, Ethan Kolcinivitch puffing on a thick stogie, sat next to Mr. DiGorda. Friends and big-time grape growers, and they hated Cesar Chavez. Did the UFW plan on a picket line somewhere nearby?

It didn't surprise Jack to see Kolcinivitch sitting on the Arvin side. The grape grower would never sit near his mother. Those two would light into each other the moment they came close. His mother didn't have any kind words to say about that man.

After warmups, the umpires yakked about proper conduct and rules and such. The school band played the national anthem with a possibly drunk trumpet player missing every note. It set the whole team to laughing. Marty urged the guys to stand and clap in mocking adulation, an endearment the Arvin boys noticed. The air was already at broil.

With Delano up first, a string bean of an Arvin pitcher twirled through his act, making a big deal of throwing strikes and getting grounders for his three outs.

Bottom of the first, Jack trotted to the mound, tugging on the bill of his brown cap. The heat bore down on his shoulders. He squeezed the ball, squared his shoulders, then leaned over and stared the first batter down. The eager look on the guy's face told Jack to throw strikes.

The first two outs came on ground balls to third. The third batter swaggered to the box, bat on his shoulder. Jack wound and let loose. The pop off the bat, solid as a gunshot, echoed in the silent heat. The ball carried in a giant arc. Jack held his breath. On this team with Adrian in centerfield, if it wasn't over the fence, there was always hope.

By the time he turned to centerfield, Adrian's back was to him, already in a dead sprint across the green expanse, his head up, tracking it in the bright sunshine. The ball dropped fast out of the glare, no doubt a home run, but Adrian ran on, his legs a blur. Near the wall he leaped, landing with his foot halfway up the plywood, the boards clattered as if they were on the verge of collapse. His body stretched out, the ball caught in the tip of the mitt's webbing. He clenched it and dropped onto his back on the grass. A second later he shoved his glove in the air and held the ball up with his other hand.

The ump jabbed his fist toward the ground for the third out.

Before his teammates could reach him in the outfield, before a moan could escape the Arvin fans, the stands exploded in a rhythmic chant.

¡Huelga! ¡Huelga! ¡Huelga!

Strike, strike, strike.

Jack froze in astonishment. *Huelga* was the despised slogan of the farmworkers, calling pickers in the fields to join the strike. It was so hated around Kern County, a local judge had decreed anyone shouting it near a grape field could be arrested. And now they stood chanting in one slab of voice, *huelga, huelga, huelga*, as the team trotted in.

Black eagle flags danced in the air, fluttering in the breeze. In the top row, men unfurled a white banner with blood-red letters—*Kolcinivitch is Unfair to Farmworkers.*

When Marty reached the top steps of the dugout, the chant took up again.

Kolcinivitch is unfair.

Kolcinivitch is unfair.

Kolcinivitch is unfair.

Jack and Adrian took seats close to Marty

"This is garbage," Marty said.

"Why are they here?" Jack nudged Adrian. "Why today?"

"Calm down," Adrian said. "I didn't know about this today. But this is the only place they can legally protest, thanks to the county judges."

"Your dad's here, isn't he?" Marty's said, accusing him.

Adrian gulped down some ice water then wiped his mouth with the back of his hand.

"Your dad fired everyone who asked for a quarter more an hour. A free game is all they got."

"That's double baloney," Marty said.

"Why now? Why today?" Jack said, holding his hands apart. "We're just here to play ball." The chanting behind him grew louder. With these clowns protesting anything could happen.

Adrian fixed his dark stare on Jack as if he should know why they were protesting.

"That's enough," Coach Dickey yelled down the bench. He strode toward the boys. "You guys block all this noise out. It's not your business." He pointed to the field. "That's the only thing going on here today. You got it."

Jack stifled his disgust. Marty shrugged and moaned something. Adrian put a towel over his head, rubbing the sweat out of his hair. The chanting became a soft repetition:

¡Huelga! Strike!

¡Huelga! Strike!

¡Huelga! Strike!

The Delano stands seethed. On the Arvin side, the women in sun hats sat stiffly, their carefree smiles given way to puckered faces.

After three quick outs, Delano took the field. Jack leaned in to take a sign. His eye caught sight of the man standing behind the backstop. A tall, lanky fellow, clipboard in hand, watching him intently. A powder blue cap on his head. *The UCLA scout.*

Jack gripped the ball along the seams and added to his concentration. Arvin's first baseman stepped into the box, tapped the plate several times with his bat. His gaze was brutal. Tall and hefty, it was Arvin's slugger, Ed DiGorda, son of the largest grape grower in the long valley.

DiGorda's unfair!

DiGorda's unfair!

DiGorda's unfair!

Tension rose on DiGorda's fat face as he stood at home plate, and Jack stared down at him, taking the signs. His first two curveballs missed to the outside. Marty yapped away at the batter as he flashed the signals, calling for a fastball, low.

Jack wound, pitched, and heard the thunk of the bat on the ball. At the top of his throwing motion, balanced in the air on his left foot, the white orb of the ball appeared a mile wide, hurtling at his head. Jack lunged to his left. The ball nipped his right shoulder and caromed toward short. Jack landed on the side of his head, dust billowing into his eyes.

He heard the Arvin crowd cheer, which couldn't be good. His vision blurry, he rubbed at the sting. He felt Coach's firm hand on his arm. "Settle down, Jack." A wet cloth pressed down on his eyes and the pain ebbed. Someone put a towel in his hand, and he dried off his eyes.

"Can you get up?"

Jack steadied himself on his feet and blinked in the sunlight.

"Let's take a look at that shoulder." It was Doc Barton, Jesse Barton's father, who came to every game. Jack waved him off.

"I'm all right." He stretched his arm up and a stinger shot through his shoulder, but he didn't flinch. No way he'd come out with a chance to pitch a tough game in front of the blue-hatted man. "I'm staying in."

Coach didn't argue. "If you can't get him out, I'll pull ya." Coach jogged to the dugout.

DiGorda stood on first, and Jack ignored him. He was too flat-footed and round-bellied to be much of a base stealer. A wiry kid stepped into the batter's box. The scoreless game wasn't out of hand despite the hurt lacing through Jack's shoulder.

When Jack leaned forward to take a sign now, a wall of tan uniforms stood on the other side of the chain-link backstop behind home plate. A skirmish line of Kern County Sheriffs, batons drawn, stretched from the home bleachers to the visiting bleachers. Their riot helmets made them look like bobbleheads.

This was his day to pitch, his day to shine, and these damn farmworkers were messing it all up. He wiped the sweat from his forehead with his shirtsleeve.

Blocking the noise out, he set to work. He threw sinkers that sank. Curveballs that dropped. Fastballs that shaved the right corner of the plate, punching out three straight batters. The last player kicked at the dirt, and the chant resumed.

Kolcinivitch is unfair.

Kolcinivitch is unfair.

Kolcinivitch is unfair.

Field hands raised another banner high at the top of the bleachers. Two deputies pushed their way up the stands, shoving folks who refused to move. They ripped both banners out of the workers' hands and tossed them over the side where deputies gathered them.

On the bench, Marty covered his ears and stared down at the dirt.

The top of the fifth, Delano got two baserunners on. At bat, Sanchez took two strikes not even moving his bat.

An Arvin player on the top of the dugout steps yelled. "Hey, Sanchez, we heard you're a genius." Laughter rippled from players behind him. "You can work in any field you want. We got cotton fields, grape fields, tomato fields. Lots of picking for you."

Adrian didn't turn or frown. He twisted the handle of the bat in his hands and stared off into the distance as if he had no idea what those guys were quacking about. He kicked the dirt with his spikes, took a few practice swings, and stared down at the pitcher. With a smooth stroke, Adrian grooved the next pitch over the first baseman into the right corner. Two runs scored and the Delano bench rose in an energizing cheer. The stands behind them went wild.

Even Coach Dickey grinned from the far end of the dugout as he cracked sunflower seeds between his teeth. He put his foot on the top step of the dugout and leaned toward the game.

Jack strode to the mound. The crazy shouting, the chanting, and the sour-looking cops made the world close in on him as if the valley's destiny pivoted on this one game. A divide ran down the center of their lives, between teammates, friends, and even families. A conflict that had no place on the baseball field. Why were so many cops here? Who were they here to protect? The misery of the heat and the anger in the crowd exhausted him.

Jack walked a player, and another got on base with an infield hit. His next offering floated high in the zone. The solid thud of the ball off the bat meant it would carry far. The left fielder ran to dig it out of the corner. He fired it to the waiting second baseman as the Arvin hitter slid hard, taking Barton's legs out from under him even as he jumped to avoid the sliding player. Jesse flipped a half circle in the air and came down on his head, slamming into the dirt infield. He lay on the ground while two runs scored.

Players on both benches shot out of their seats. Coaches in both dugouts calmed them down.

Jack knelt beside Jesse. Other players gathered around, and finally, Jesse sat up. He rose slowly and ambled off the field. Folks clapped, and a new Delano player ran to take his place.

Before trotting off, Coach told Jack, "Don't back off. The game's in your hands." The score was now tied two, two.

Coach took his place at the top of the dugout and made his signals. He wanted fastball, down low, then move it in, move it out, move it up, get him to work. Jack hit his corners, and the player lifted a fly ball to center where Adrian closed on it for the third out.

¡Huelga!

¡Huelga!

¡Huelga!

The deputies waded into the crowd and pulled out a couple of the chanters. One of the field-workers wouldn't stop chanting, so a deputy threw him to the ground. As he lay in the dirt, the cop swung his baton down on the helpless man's head, and the chanting stopped. Trotting in from the mound, Jack hesitated at the edge of the dugout. Just feet away on the other side of the chain link, blood oozed from a gash in the man's forehead, and a tremor rippled down his body.

A red stain blotted the earth. Jack didn't need more reasons to hate this town. All this fighting was one more reason piled on top of all the others. In the dugout, Jack hung two wet towels over his head and covered his ears with his hands. Still, the commotion sifted through. Would they have all this racket when he pitched for a college team? If he didn't keep his fastball down, there would be no college. He wanted to stand up and tell everyone to leave—the cops, the workers, the fans, everyone—and just let them play. Angry words boiled up inside, and then he heard Coach calling him to get on the field.

He threw off the towels and grabbed his glove. When he took the mound and stared down at Marty, he glimpsed faces, bloody ones, with pale skin and death in their eyes. He shook his head and stepped back. He didn't see the man in the blue cap anywhere. He used pure adrenaline to get the first man out, and the second, but the third boy stroked a double to left field. With the crowd cheering for more, Marty jangled out to the mound in a tired jog.

"You're losing concentration. You got to block all this crap out."

"I'm trying."

"Trying's for Little Leaguers." Marty's face appeared half-angry, half-sympathetic. Jack took the ball and faced centerfield. Adrian motioned with his mitt in the air and nodded as if to say, *Just pitch your game.*

Jack steadied himself and studied the batter's face. The fear he had seen earlier in the Arvin players had disappeared. They didn't respect his fastball anymore. He focused on Marty's glove, his target. He wound and threw, and the ball zipped into the catcher's glove with a thud, as the Arvin player swung, twisting his body in futility.

"S-t-r-i-k-e," the ump yelled, stretching out the word out. With his head down, the Arvin player shuffled back to his dugout. The Arvin boys took the field for the top of the seventh inning.

Jack smiled in relief that he'd pitched out of that mess. He jogged in and took his seat with his teammates. Marty stripped off his gear and strode to the plate.

"Come on, Marty, let's go," Jack yelled. Down to their last three outs, they had to get a baserunner. On the first pitch, Marty took a fastball right in his gut. Jack lept with his teammates to the edge of the dugout.

Coach called out, "Sit down." Marty trotted to first holding his side like a wounded hero.

Before Sanchez left the dugout, Coach said to him, "This is your time. Put an end to this garbage before bad things break loose."

Adrian nodded, shouldered his bat, and swaggered to the plate. Marty stood off the bag, hands to his knees. The pitcher whirled and torched a strike to first base. Marty flung himself to the bag, but not before the first baseman swung his mitt across Marty's outstretched hand.

"O-u-t!" the ump called, punching the air.

The Arvin bench broke into cheering, and laughter erupted in the stands as a red-faced Marty trotted in. Coach didn't yell at him, but Jack had a mind to. Coach never yelled. He just stared at that empty space above a boy's head as if he were wondering what kind of torture would produce one ounce of common sense in the teenager's brain.

Sanchez rested his bat on his shoulder and let the first strike pass. Catcalls and jibes flowed from the Arvin team.

"We got a field you can work in."

"Too lazy to even swing, Sanchez."

"You could pick grapefruits with those gorilla hands."

Adrian's neck and arms were taut, eyes focused. The next pitch came in at his knees. Adrian lifted his lead foot, and with a milky fluidness strode forward, swatting a solid hit between two big fielders, who turned and chased.

Every bench emptied. Jack shouted until his throat hurt but still couldn't hear himself in the frenzy. In a flash, Adrian tagged first. Rounding second, he churned toward third while the ball arched high toward the second baseman. Delano's third-base coach waved his hands in a frantic sign to stop, but Adrian tagged third and blew past him, willing himself to reach home.

Adrian's full effort, a headlong glide, neck straining, arms jabbing, legs in full sprint, mouth-sucking air, Jack had seen many times. The second baseman caught the throw from the outfield, pumped once in disbelief, and fired a hotliner home. The catcher, astride the plate, held his glove chest high, outstretched and waiting.

Just before the ball reached the catcher, Adrian dropped into a feet-first slide, facing in, spikes high. The ball thudded into the mitt, and the catcher swung it down, but the teeth of Adrian's cleat bit into the boy's bare wrist. The catcher's arm and glove slammed hard against his knee. Adrian's lower foot rammed the catcher's left shin guard, taking his feet out from under him as Adrian hurtled on. Dust rising, Adrian slapped home base, and the catcher pounced on top of him, belly to belly. Their bodies disappeared in a spur of dust.

The ball dribbled onto the ground and rolled away.

"Safe!" the ump yelled, his arms outstretched.

A gasp went up from the stands. Adrian rose, bent over, and extended his hand. The catcher raised his arm slowly. Adrian reached farther down. The catcher flung a fist full of dirt into Adrian's eyes. Jack leaped to his feet, followed by the team. Coach Dickey yelled at them to sit down.

Then DiGorda charged out of the Arvin dugout, his face mangled in rage, the Arvin team following. Jack jumped out of the dugout and raced toward home plate. By the time he reached Adrian, DiGorda's raised fist loomed over him. Jack didn't think about Coach's handbook of rules that didn't adequately cover friendship and duty. In full stride, Jack unloaded on the grape baron's son with a fist to DiGorda's nose. Bone crunched; blood squirted.

Players around him swung and kicked, yelled and cursed. Jack couldn't say how many blows he rained on DiGorda, whom he gripped by a fistful of jersey before deputies and coaches pulled the players apart. In the melee Adrian knelt in the dirt, his eyes ringed with dust, cradling the catcher's bleeding arm in one hand, and pressing his palm to the wound with his other. Red stains mottled the earth.

AFTER THE TEAMS HAD been separated, Coach gathered them in the dugout and inspected every one. Marty was getting a shiner, but somehow it looked good on him. Adrian's jersey had blood all over it. So did his hands and arms, but after cleaning him up, Doc Barton determined none of it was his. Barton examined Jack's hand and said it wasn't broken, so he wrapped it in a towel, telling him he'd look it over closer on the bus. Coach didn't yell or curse, but kept his words calm and direct.

The deputies were wrestling with the crowds in the stands, who were still shouting and chanting. The cops waded into the bleachers, pulling folks out, and throwing them down. Coach told Jack his mother and Ella had been escorted away by cops as soon as the fight broke out.

Coach corralled two deputies who led the team to the bus, making them walk in a single line. No one said anything even though they won the game on a technicality since Arvin had another turn to bat. But after their catcher threw dirt in Adrian's eyes, the umps called the game in Delano's favor. They strode like victors with their heads up.

Adrian and Jack marched behind Marty. Just before the catcher stepped onto the bus, his father, Mr. Kolcinivitch, a tall, well-built man with an angular face and a tough skin, appeared right beside Marty, a deputy at his shoulder.

"You okay, boy?" He raised his son's chin and gave him a wry grin. "You gave it to those morons, that's for sure. That's what it takes to win here."

Marty shrugged and disappeared inside the bus.

The big man nodded to Jack and Adrian. "Good game, boys." His voice was firm.

Jack imagined his own father would be about the same age. His eyes were calm and confident, dark brown, experienced, friendly. Not what he expected.

He spoke to Adrian. "I'm sorry about what happened to your Papa. He worked for me for a long time."

Adrian stared at him, speechless.

"If he ever gives up running with those red commies, tell him to come see me. He's a good man."

"My dad's not a communist."

"Didn't say he was. Just saying, if he stops working with those who are Reds, I'd like to see him work for me again."

Adrian stood frozen. So Jack stepped forward. "We gotta go, Mr. Kolcinivitch." Jack had seen the man before but never spoken to him. He seemed nice. His mother's rants about the man didn't appear to jibe. He didn't yell at Marty for fighting. That was definitely cool.

Jack stepped up to board when the grower caught Jack's sleeve. "I knew your daddy well."

Jack felt suddenly connected to something good. He turned to the grower.

"If you ever need anything, give me a call." He smiled and handed Jack a business card. Jack took it and boarded.

All the way home someone played his transistor, and everyone relaxed, listening to the sour whine of Haggard and Owens and that Jerry Reed song he was getting sick of, the one about the man thrown in jail for gambling. Adrian brooded next to him.

Jack mused on what had happened at the end. He had expected to speak to the UCLA scout, but Coach Dickey had said the UCLA scout had taken off as soon as the deputies showed up, so he hadn't seen Jack fight. That was good. He would have earned a scholarship for sure if the man had stayed and Jack had been able to pitch a complete game. Those damn strikers had messed up his future.

"I don't believe a word that man says," Adrian said, sitting beside him.

"You have to admit, kind of him to come over," Jack said.

"The devil can smile too, *Hermano*."

"He just sounded reasonable, that's all."

"Don't go betting on that. The man cheats everyone who works for him."

"I don't know about that."

"Look how he treated my Papa. He worked for him for seventeen years. Calls him a red commie and up and fires him. Then he pulls this crap that he knows your daddy," Adrian said. "All that means is that he'll give you the special shaft. You don't even know what's going on around here. You were born with your head in the sand."

His friend's words stung. Jack understood his anger. His father had been thrown off his job by that man. But just because the man had been nice to him didn't mean he didn't know what was going on. His mother hated Kolcinivitch, Adrian hated Kolcinivitch, and many people hated Kolcinivitch. Maybe he should hate the man too, but when the grower mentioned his father he had felt himself warming to the man. Jack would like to know what the grower knew about his father. He felt a sudden craving for details about a man he should know well. And when he allowed himself to indulge his hate, Kolcinivitch didn't come to mind. But the UCLA scout being run off did. Was his scholarship gone with him? Jack had to admit he did hate. He hated this place, this valley, this idiotic riot of events that were holding him back.

"All I know is if those strikers hadn't shown up, we would have got our full rides out of here today," Jack said.

Adrian stared out the window and didn't say much. The vines, row after row, flicked by in the dry and dusty fields. The afternoon haze had moved in, swaddling the land. The highway ahead stretched up the valley.

"Some days," Adrian said, staring off into the air, "I don't think any of us are ever getting out of here. And there's nothing we can do about it."

Chapter 8
The Shotgun

DARKNESS HAD FALLEN BY the time Jack walked up the driveway to the Victorian. The house stood dark. He dropped his gym bag in the laundry room. In the kitchen, he leaned against the table wondering what he'd eat for dinner. Then the thumping began. Upstairs someone was moving heavy boxes and letting them drop. He climbed the stairs to the second floor.

The noise came from above. He took the stairs to the third floor. Down the hall, the attic ladder extended down. Climbing to the top, he stepped into the dusty attic. A bare bulb illuminated the far end of the narrow room. Dust motes floated in the stifling air. His mother leaned over an open cardboard box, taking out old clothes, hats, shoes, and pots then dropping them on the floor. Her grayish disheveled hair fell in long strands over her face.

"What're you doing?"

"Looking for something." A pile of old clothes, coats, and sweaters stacked up next to her.

"Can I help you?"

She closed the flaps of the box. "I'm going to find it myself."

"Find what?"

"That combine."

Jack stared at her. Had she lost her senses? How would she find the combine up here?

"It's up here somewhere." She fixed her gaze on a tall stack of boxes in front of her.

He moved closer. "Are you okay, Mom?"

"No…I'm not okay. I'm not okay with having this place stolen from me. I'm not okay with you having your chance at a scholarship stolen from you because of those damn growers who won't settle anything. I'm not okay with you fighting with a grower's son, and having the cops break it up." She caught herself and brushed her hair off her face. "That scout left early, didn't he?"

Jack nodded.

"Glad he didn't see you punch that kid in the nose." She heaved an exasperated sigh.

"The punk had it coming."

"They all have it coming, Jack, that's the problem. But if you're the one giving it out, they'll gang up on you. That's why I gotta find that gun."

"Mom, why don't you come downstairs, let this go—"

"Your father's old shotgun is up here someplace." She rubbed her forehead with the back of her wrist.

"You sold that a long time ago."

"One of them. But there's an old Browning. It's not worth much, but it shoots just fine."

"Whatta you need a shotgun for?"

She moved a box into the light and opened it. "I broke it down after—," her voice trailed off. "It's up here somewhere."

She stood over an open box. "Mom. What's going on?"

"I know where that combine is, and I'm going to go get it."

"You know?"

She eyed him, then turned to the stairs. He followed her down to the third floor and into his bedroom. She stood in front of his desk, opened the drapes, and pointed to the Kolcinivitch Ranch. The grapevines lay in silvery darkness lit by a sliver of moon.

"See those lights off to the east?" Jack squinted into the darkness. "Those little ones. Those are the sheds Kolcinivitch uses to store equipment and supplies. There's a whole row of them. The combine's in there."

"You know that for a fact?"

"Where else could it be?" She folded her hands across her chest. "He's the only one who would benefit from us losing this place. He had every motivation to keep us from selling that machine. Herm must have known something was going to happen, so he figured out a way to get you off it, thinking they wouldn't bother him. But they're not the type to care about an old man."

Jack peered at the dots of light off to the east. She could be right. And if she was right about them beating Herm, then she could get herself killed barging into those sheds with a shotgun.

"You just going to drive over there and search them?" He had seen those sheds before, driving along the county road that bordered the property on the north. There was a double row of them. The farm labor camp lay west of them, hidden behind a row of eucalyptus trees.

"I'm not going to sit here and do nothing."

Her eyes grew redder as she stared off into the night. Had she been crying?

"I don't think it's a good idea to go over there, particularly with a gun."

"If he shoots me…well…then you'll know."

What would Jack know? "Is he after the water rights?"

"Where did you hear about them?"

"Herm."

"He gave you these, too." She picked up the deck of Bicycle cards off his desk.

"Said they were Dad's."

"He going to teach you to gamble now?"

If Jack let her go off on the subject of gambling, there'd be no end to her rant. "Where's the water?"

"Under the oak tree. After I lost the land, I tried to sell the water to Crawford across the road, but Kolcinivitch sued me. I can plug it and store the water in the ground. But since his land is downstream, he has rights to some of it—if I unplug it. He won't buy the water from me. He wants me out or nothing."

Water was the golden key that unlocked the treasures of the land. Without water, this land would revert to fields of needle grass. Valley farmers guarded their water rights better than they watched over their firstborns. Any water that ran over property was permanently attached to the land and could never be sold or transferred. They were riparian.

That spring by the oak would make his mother's one acre valuable. Worth fighting for. But barging into a man's domain armed would get her killed. People got killed all the time on farms—run over by tractors, keeled over from heatstroke, accidentally shot by farmers trying to scare off varmints. Then there was the hatred of trespassers picking fruit that didn't belong to them. It happened enough to know it could happen to her if she went on Kolcinivitch's property. No grower would ever be arrested for protecting what was his.

Jack followed her gaze to the distant blips of light—the sheds. If he found the combine in one of them, he could solve a lot of problems.

Chapter 9
Organizing

THE NEXT MORNING, HOURS before dawn, Adrian crouched under a lemon tree in the early morning dark, across the road from Kolcinivitch Ranch. Cold pierced his clothes and skin, but it didn't penetrate deep enough to freeze the anger swelling inside him. He should be home in his warm bed, blankets pulled over his head. But he dare not sleep, not with Papa out here in the fields.

His legs stiffened, waiting for the signal to race into the rows of grapes across the way. Behind him, more *campesinos*, all of them strikers, hid under branches. One of them shuffled his feet on some leaves. Papa squatting just ahead half raised his hand: *Stay quiet. Stay low. Don't be seen.*

Adrian wanted to add what they all knew—*If they find you in the fields, they'll bust your head, stomp you into the ground, then drag you off in handcuffs.*

Papa's warning rolled through him: *Never fight back,* mijo. *Do not strike any of the grower's men even if they hit you. It will bring shame to* la causa, *what we work so hard for.*

He had met Cesar Chavez many times at Papa's house meetings. A saint in Papa's eyes, a man with steel in his bones; power in his words. He would have nothing to do with violent people. Papa believed in this nonviolence of *la causa* the same way he prayed the rosary.

Shadows moved among the vines. Adrian squinted into the darkness, searching the far shoulder of the road. Guards! Their cigarettes glowed, and their laughter lingered in the air. They loafed among the vines, waiting. He imagined they held their sticks cocked. They wanted to bust heads. The guards were big, carried clubs, and didn't care about anything but the grapes. Adrian had no intention of getting caught. He had school, baseball, Darcy, and his future giving him the strength to outrun any of those *gordos*.

Adrian doubted Chavez's talk about turning the other cheek. Could Adrian do that if one of those goons caught him and beat him? Could he *not* strike back? Where would it get him in the end if he didn't defend himself? So far it had earned his family charity food, used clothes, and an ache in his belly.

Papa, in jeans, and a dark jacket pulled over a sweatshirt, kept his hand half raised. He kept his dark hair, sprinkled with gray, short, and his sideburns high. It was almost time. The buses full of scabs would be here soon. The strong smell of lemons brought on his hunger with a fury. For too long, he'd eaten nothing but beans and rice. Not even a leg of chicken or a piece of fruit. He could care less about vegetables, but damn, it wasn't right he couldn't choose *not* to eat them. Did a boy have to be rich around here just to eat vegetables? Fruit and vegetables grew out of the ground like weeds here, right there for the pulling. But his whole family only ate union hall handouts. Everyone had to make sacrifices for *la causa*, Papa would say.

A dagger of light searched the dark. A brown and white sheriff's cruiser rolled by. Adrian huddled lower, his face near the dirt. They had parked their cars far off the road between the trees. If the deputy found them, he'd unleash his dog. They had to be gone before full daylight.

The courts had forbidden picketing the Kolcinivitch Ranch. If Mexicans and Filipinos dared even walk the shoulder of a public road, they'd get arrested. Damn *gringo* courts. They didn't care one bit about what happened in these fields as long as the growers got their grapes picked. Adrian fought a rising bitterness.

Gears ground in the distance, then a rumble of diesel. Adrian gave Papa a furtive glance, catching his eye. He nodded toward the west. *The buses are here.*

Peones from Mexico who didn't know squat. They didn't know they were stepping into a war. For three years strikers had been getting arrested, beaten, harassed, and treated like dirt. Neither did these scabs know they were being treated as less than a piece of trash, sleeping on the ground like homeless bums, hunching over pits to take a crap, and cooking over a fire some moldy beans and rice they had to pay for with their own sweat.

They wouldn't know they were walking into a bad situation. They were told they were going to well-paying jobs in America. Any work that paid fifty or sixty cents an hour was a rich man's wages for a *peón*.

Having nothing rode a man hard—no land, no work, no way to get married and have a family, no way to buy even one lousy beer. When growers dumped them back across the border after they had picked the fields clean, they would go home with some dollars in their pockets. They would buy some necessary things and sit around their tables eating like rich men in a city of shacks. They would hold their heads high as men did who had money. That's what Papa said they were thinking. That explained why they would traveled so far from home to work a strange field in the early morning freeze— because they were hungry.

It is your job, Chavez had said at one of his father's house meetings, *to teach them. To organize them, to make them understand they must speak up for themselves.*

Brakes squealed, and buses turned into the farm road. This northern section of the grape ranch across the way needed trimming and bundling. Before spring the vines needed to be trimmed and tied up to the trellis or clusters would grow scrawny and thin. They would then clear away the trimmings and throw them into the burn pits. Hard work, but work that required some skill and training so the grapes would ripen, sweet and liquid. Or else who would buy them?

Headlights flickered as shadows passed in front of the parked buses. Workers lined up in the road. Papa squinted, tight-lipped, peering into the vines. This had been his job, training pickers on this very ranch. First, for Sugar Duncan, whom Papa nearly venerated, then for old man Kolcinivitch, an irascible *cabrón*, who had fired him. Twenty-seven years of hard labor all ended three years ago. Now Adrian went to school with the bite of hunger in his stomach. All for la causa.

A thin voice carried in the still morning; someone instructed the scabs how to trim and bundle the vines. Papa would spend all day with a group of workers, taking them by the hand, pointing out where to make the cut—fast and clean to the branch. Then he would check their cuts, teach them to bundle and tie the vines. What kind of work would these scabs do with so little knowledge of the grapes?

Papa rose on his haunches to peer into the fields. How could he be so calm, watching these *burros* do his job? In the ultramarine light, the scabs filtered into the vines, ready to work. Papa signaled for the men to spread out. Some went left. Others to the right. Adrian and Papa scooted straight ahead. He patted the bundle of the flyers under his jacket.

He was to give the scabs flyers about a union meeting where they would learn about their rights. Some would never see a dime of their wage before they were dumped back across the border. If they were sprayed on, they would get sick. When they coughed up blood, they would need medicine. They would need something to eat to keep up their strength.

Papa spoke to him with his eyes: Be careful, mijo. Those eyes—confident and resolved—settled him.

"Remember what we have talked about." His voice was low and cautioning.

Adrian nodded.

"Two hours only to convince them of la causa, then you must go to school."

A vision flashed through Adrian's mind—*Papa lying in the dirt, a trickle of blood curling down the side of his face, bruises under his eyes, and the dull pallor of a man on death's doorstep.*

Adrian shook it off. They edged cautiously out from under the branches. Adrian squirted across the road, light steps on the asphalt, soundless in the morning echo, close behind Papa as the shadow of a cat, sleek with cunning. It rose in his heart why he came here—*I'll kill anyone who hurts Papa.*

Chapter 10
The Search

BEFORE FIRST LIGHT, JACK rose in the hopefulness of the bright moonlight, everything a flimsy silhouette. He dressed in jeans, slipped on his father's old heavy coat he found in the hall closet, and pulled on a slouch hat. He stuffed his Instamatic in a pocket, stashed his books and glove under his bed. He had another glove in his locker at school. On the kitchen table, he dropped a note, "Off to school for an early practice. Adrian picked me up."

He had called Adrian late last night, who had agreed to meet him on the South Road at lunchtime and drive him to school. Outside, he followed the fence to its farthest corner and scaled it in one lunge. He jogged through the vines, and in the tawny dawn, he made the farm road.

He was far into Kolcinivitch Ranch by the time the sun bled over the Diablo Mountains in the east. A fine mist lifted from the vines. In the rows workers stooped, swinging their hoes high over their heads, cutting at the Johnson grass, turning the earth. The road went on for miles straight into the heart of the sprawling grape ranch. Only a few puddles of chocolate-colored mud remained, and Jack stomped hard in them, splashing his shoes and Levi's, even up to his shirt and jacket, to blend in with the *picadores*. Some Filipinos, many Mexicans, all bent over in the faint light, swung hoes in a voiceless rhythm, chopping at the earth.

Shadows dogged him as he ran. A man in a straw hat raised his head above a vine and shouted: "*No más trabajo.*" He desperately waved his hands as if encouraging Jack to flee. Jack nodded, his legs heavier, breathing harder, a stitch in his side beginning to pulse. Field hands busied themselves everywhere. He'd blend in, unnoticed. He'd find the combine and be back at school by third period.

A clearing came into view. He jogged past workers lined up while a man in a planter's hat passed out hand tools. Jack kept on, as if on an urgent errand. His jean jacket flapped in the wind. The mud flaked off his work boots as he flew.

At a long row of sheds, Jack turned a corner and stared down a dirt lane, ten or more corrugated metal sheds on each side. This could be an all-day job. Lots of places to hide a combine. Some were far too small for a combine. At the far end, a man dropped something heavy in a pickup bed and then slipped into the cab; a motor fired up, and it rolled toward him. He needed to get out of sight.

To his right stood the largest metal shed with an open door in the center of a larger overhead door, one wide enough to drive a combine through. He clutched his camera in his jacket pocket. If the combine was inside, he could get in and out and get home. He stepped inside.

The heavy clanging of a hammer on metal echoed from the darkness. When it stopped, he heard men talking in Spanish. Moving deeper inside, squinting until his eyes adjusted, he passed rolls of wire, bundles of wooden stakes, all stacked to the ceiling, but no machines.

He worked his way up one of the parallel rows. The Spanish voices were just ahead. Closer in, he made out they were debating about something.

Rapid hammer blows on metal drowned out their words. He came upon them working in the yellow circle of a bare bulb, two men fixing hand tools at a workbench. Both were stripped down to their muscle undershirts.

"Have you seen the tractor they brought in here?" Jack asked in Spanish, standing in the shadows.

They stared at him. The man with a wild Fu Manchu and a hammer cocked in his hand peered at him. "¿Dónde está?"

"Salinas."

They both laughed, then spoke too rapidly to one another for him to understand.

"Are you a *Chavista* here to organize us?" the mustached man asked.

"The foreman sent me to look at the combine they just brought in."

The two men eyed each other as if smelling something bad.

"We grow grapes here, *güero*." They both laughed again. "There's no combines here."

They had called him a güero—an Anglo-looking Mexican. His Spanish must be convincing. With quick jerks, both men returned to hammering and fastening as if Jack had disappeared.

The rancid odor of stale beer warned Jack he was not alone. Then a movement in the darkness behind unsettled him. When he turned, someone slapped him across the side of his head sending him sprawling on his back. A beast of a man stepped toward him and raised a giant foot over his leg. Jack scrambled away. In the seconds before he rose, the two laborers stood over him, blocking his escape. The three surrounded him. One of the men held a hammer.

"What are you doing in here?" the big man shouted.

In the pale light, Jack made out his attacker. His shoulders were broad and bulky, his belly wide, his cheeks sagged; his eyes were menacing.

"Who sent you?" the big man demanded.

"Carlos. He said you needed workers." Jack threw out a name. There had to be a Carlos working on the ranch.

"Are you for Chavez?" the big man asked.

"I need to eat. I'm looking for work."

With his thick arms, the man yanked Jack up by his jacket collar. "You look hungry." The man's breath stank. He grabbed Jack's hand and rubbed his palm with his thumb. "You been working with the women or are you a college boy?"

The two Mexicans behind him snorted. One of them told the fat man about his questions.

"Gomez says you asked about a tractor."

"I can drive anything on a farm. Just looking for work."

He gave Jack a lopsided smile. "I have work for you, güero. But if you try to organize any of my workers, I'll cut your balls off, ¿comprende? I'm telling you this now if you wanna go home to your mama."

Jack had the terrible sense that if he ran, this brute would set his hounds on him.

"I need work." Jack used his most convincing Spanish.

"We'll see, amigo." He grabbed a fistful of Jack's collar and pushed him along, the man following with a fatigued shuffle. With all the tensions in the fields, Jack now understood how he could be mistaken for an organizer.

Outside, the man shoved him toward a stake-bed truck packed with campesinos. Jack lifted himself up and leaned against the wooden side. The big man shoved him all the way in against a girl.

"He's on your crew." He nodded at her. "If he talks about Chavez." He made a cutting sign with his fingers. "Use your clippers."

The workers broke into laughter. Everyone wore hats and bandannas around their necks. The girl had long black hair, smooth olive skin, and dark, almond-shaped eyes. She'd be pretty if she smiled. The truck swayed over uneven roads, crossed the highway, and headed to a remote section in the center of the ranch. If he jumped off here, they would be convinced he was a *Chavista*. They'd send men to chase him down.

Adrian had agreed to pick him up before the third-period break on Boltin Road that skirted the far side of the Kolcinivitch property.

He'd drive up and down it three times; if Jack didn't show Adrian promised to return during lunch. Jack was scheduled to pitch today and needed to attend some classes, or he couldn't play. Coach's rules.

It was still early, so he had time to make it out of here. The truck turned east, then west, and again until he had no bearings. He searched the horizon as they rumbled over dirt tracks. A moving speck in a sea of green vines. The truck halted suddenly, and everyone lurched forward.

A supervisor in a broad-brimmed straw hat appeared at the back gate. "*¡Rápido! ¡Rápido!* Get moving! Get moving! *¡Rápido!* Go, go, go."

Everyone piled off and spread out. Jack followed the girl into a row. She pulled the bandanna over her nose and began working on a trellis, trimming off branches. Another worker came behind her and tied up the branches on the wire trellises. She worked methodically down the row, trimming off branches till the thickest ones were bare and straight. Then they were bundled at the top by workers attaching the healthiest branches with thin wires to the thick trellis wire.

"You," she called to Jack. "*Vamos.*" He hustled over. "Take these branches." She pointed to the cuttings scattered on the ground. "Cut them smaller, then pile them up at the end of the row."

Jack held out his empty hands.

"You come to work, and you have no clippers." She gave him a disgusted sigh.

Jack shrugged.

She called to someone. A worker in another row handed a pair of worn clippers through the vines. She gave them to Jack, and he examined the blunt-ended tool.

"You've never used them?"

"I'm all right." He watched her cull through branches, cutting the smallest ones, and stripping them away.

Jack threw cuttings into a pile, scooped up the bundle, and carried it to the end of the row. The crew thinning and bundling worked faster, tossing vine clippings everywhere, leaving him farther behind. Every time he checked, there were more branches to pick up.

The girl shouted at him from far down the row. "We're paid by the crew, so hustle. The way you work, we'll make two cents an hour." She pointed at the branches strewn on the ground.

Jack bent over and clipped, stacked, then scooped up armfuls and ran to the end. He dumped and returned running, sweat pouring down his face. Damn if he'd let this girl outwork him. He moved faster, clipping, stacking, and running. His back ached, but he kept at it—again and again. Still, he couldn't keep up.

Sunlight slid across the vines, chasing the shadows, heating the air.

"Work faster, or we'll get fired." She and her crew had crossed a small lane into the next row, leaving him behind.

He forced his hands to work faster but felt himself fumbling. He could only stay steady if he worked at an even pace.

"We have to clean this up." The girl jogged to him. "We can't be behind like this or we'll get nothing from Chuey."

"Chuey?"

"Chuey Lopez, the big man who pushed you into the truck." She shook her head. "The labor contractor. The *hombre* with the money. Piss him off, and he'll call *la migra* and have you shipped back home. He does it all the time. But you're *Americano, sí*?"

"Yeah, just trying to make some money to live."

She mumbled something. The morning dragged on, his shirt soaked through, and a burning rolled down his throat into this belly, settling like a hot coal. His throat felt like a worn-out piece of leather, and his eyes itched.

"Where's the water?" Hours to go before his pickup on the road. Today's game wasn't until three. If he worked much longer, he'd be too tired to pitch.

"They don't give us any until we have three rows finished."

"Bastards."

"Get moving."

He hitched a large bundle of branches on his shoulder and hauled it down the row, half running.

"Don't think. Work faster." She returned to her trimming, leaving him alone.

He had enough. After he carried the next bundle to the dump, he intended to slip away.

He had become disoriented, not sure where he was on the ranch, but roads ringed the ranch. If he ran long enough, he could reach one.

At the far end of the row, a man wearing a red ball cap walked by, came back and peered at him down the long stretch of vines, then disappeared again. Jack knew that man.

"What are you always looking at?" She yelled at him. "You aren't afraid of *la migra* too?"

Behind him, a voice boomed. "What's this? Why aren't you working?"

She ran down to him, pointing at Jack. "This gringo doesn't even know what a grape is? Why'd you put him with me?"

Chuey Lopez stood with his hands in his pockets, shirttail untucked over his bulging belly, a sly grin across his mouth. His laugh turned into a snort.

"You owe me for two weeks now." She pointed her clippers at the fat man. "I need my pay."

"I have some other work for you. It might even pay better, *puta*."

"You pig." She spit at him.

Lopez moved swiftly toward them. Belly jiggling, he slammed Jack against a vine as he passed and backhanded her across the face. The olive skin of her cheek turned crimson. She didn't put her hand to her face or cry, but her black eyes glared hate.

"Work faster," Lopez warned them, then turned and ambled away.

The girl returned to trimming. She worked slowly now, all of her self-assurance appeared drained from her. The men in her crew wouldn't even look at her. A couple of rows down Lopez yelled curses at someone.

Jack stood tall, trying to see over the vines. There had to be a way back to the sheds. With Lopez busy here, he could search a few of them before Adrian showed up.

He hefted another load of clippings and made his way to the dump spot. A tractor pulling a trailer came by, and he helped load the clippings. He could follow the tractor out of the fields, but that would take too long. He'd be seen.

He watched her work. He had never seen a man hit a woman like that. He felt sorry that she had to labor so hard in the fields. There was little he could do for her; there were a thousand like Lopez in the valley. Jack noticed the field hands duck into the vines across the way to pee. As soon as he finished loading the trailer, he would dash across the road to take a piss, and not return.

Ready to go, he grabbed his jacket and heard the girl talking to someone. Had Lopez returned? No, it was the man in the red baseball cap. The two of them were halfway down the row. The man looked familiar. He jogged to them.

"I can't leave here. *Sin papeles*." She had no papers.

"¿Sin papeles? It's okay. We can help," the man insisted. "Come picket with us."

"The minute I go outside, la migra comes and I'm gone." She motioned with a sweep of her hand.

The man froze when Jack neared. Their eyes met. It was Adrian's father. Isidro Sanchez had a pleading look as if asking Jack to remain quiet.

"¡Chavista! ¡Chavista! ¡Chavista!" Lopez yelled from behind Jack. Heavy footsteps pounded in the dirt toward him. Isidro Sanchez's eyes grew large, then he took off in the opposite direction. Lopez shoved Jack as he passed, forcing him against the thick vines. The girl stepped out of the way, but with her foot, she pushed a big branch in his path.

The fat man swore as he flopped on his belly with a dull thud. A cloud of dust puffed up around him. He scrabbled in the dirt trying to rise, but she kicked his arm out from under him, and his face hit the dirt. Lopez grunted. He swept a large arm out, grabbing her ankle, and he swooped her to the dirt. She screamed and landed hard on her butt. She kicked viciously, but Lopez worked his way up her body, grabbing her thigh, then her shirt, pulling her toward him, then her arm, a great white shark swallowing a helpless fish whole. He yanked her hair, snapping her head back, then put his hand on her neck.

Jack dropped his jacket. He searched around for something, anything. Somber faces from a gaggle of men crowded into the row stared back. No one moved.

"Help me," Jack yelled. Some turned away, others lowered their eyes.

Jack remembered a grape stake that lay under the vines. He grabbed it and sprinted to her. Lopez had both hands on her throat and crushed her under him. She gagged and choked.

Jack loomed over the fat man. Lopez looked up open-mouthed. Jack's first blow caught his left ear. Lopez swore and struggled to push up with his knees, but wouldn't let her go. Jack's coolness drained and in a smoothbore rhythm, he pummeled Lopez with staccato blows—to his head, to his neck, to his turned-up cheek. Red welts formed across his cheeks.

Lopez rose on a knee, and Jack slammed the soft back of it hard until he collapsed. Lopez shot out his hand and clenched Jack's ankle, twisting it. Jack stifled the pain and struck the man's arm, elbow, his beefy forearm, until his hand dropped. His other hand loosened around the girl's neck. She squirmed out from under him.

Beyond thinking, Jack struck harder, a man hacking weeds, removing filth, eradicating a blighting evil until Lopez's body shuddered and collapsed unmoving to the ground.

Jack stepped back, breathing heavy, his entire body drenched in sweat. Lopez's back rose and fell in shallow breaths. Jack helped the girl to her feet. She hesitated in the sunlit row, massaging her neck. Her eyes were bloodshot, her throat red, her long hair disheveled. She stood in the bright day, a child's fright in her eyes.

Men were talking fast. "*Patrones* are coming. Vamos, vamos."

She didn't cry, and that made Jack admire her. She motioned for him to follow. "You can't be here when they come."

She led him through fields, over narrow paths, across farm roads, jogging along rows of vines to reach the farm housing on the far side of the ranch. They slipped between a row of frayed shacks, many with cloth on the windows, through trash-strewn alleys, past beat-up jalopies, deeper into a labyrinth of weathered huts ripe with the stench of urine, of stale lard, of rusted dreams, where the shadows swallowed them whole.

➤

HER SHACK WAS ONE room with no running water. A gray-haired woman, thin with deeply weathered nut-brown skin lay on a cot, her eyes half open, wearing only a filthy nightshirt, wheezing as she breathed. Her chest rattled with every cough. The place was neat but sparse, like camping in an oven. The girl threw down her hat and stripped off her scarf.

Jack didn't feel the throb in his ankle until she left the shack for some water. The pain came back with a rush. Lopez had twisted something.

When she returned, she filled a cup, sat next to the old woman on the cot, and lifted her feeble head. The wheezing stopped for a second as she sipped. The woman clutched the girl with thin arms. Heat sifted in through the tin roof, the temperature set to broil.

"What's wrong with her?"

"She breathes the pesticide. They don't say anything when the plane comes over. It makes her asthma worse."

The woman had a slight tremor in her left arm.

"She should see a doctor."

The girl stared at Jack with weary eyes.

"Do you have any medicine?" Jack asked.

"Lopez owes me *dinero*. But he will not pay me now."

"You don't have to work for him."

"I cannot leave here without her." She nodded toward her mother. From a table, she picked up a glass tube with a squeeze ball on it. "We ran out, and he hasn't paid me in two weeks." She dunked a cloth in the basin and wrung it out. She sat on the edge of the cot and laid the towel on her mother's forehead.

He picked up a box from the table. "Is this her medicine?"

She nodded. "It helps her breathe."

He stared at the label. It must be for her asthma. He had never heard of it, but drug stores in town should have it. "I'll see what I can do." It was almost noon. "I have to go."

She went back to wiping her mother's face. The woman coughed, deep and rumbling.

"She could die."

The woman had to be about his mother's age, but with her thin and weather-beaten face and sunken cheeks, she looked much older. His mother was but a mile or two from here and was healthy and full of life. If she needed medicine, she would know what to do, who to call. And if she didn't, he'd do something. He wouldn't wash her face and watch her die.

Nobody cared what happened here except this girl.

"What's your name?" he asked.

She pressed the towel to her mother's cheek. "Sabrina."

"Jack."

"You must go now before they come looking." She stood and wiped her hands on her jeans. She told him how to find the main road through the fields that would take him to the north county road. He headed out the door and turned to her for a moment.

"*Vaya con Dios.*"

He stepped into the narrow dusty lane. Furtive, and limping, he moved through the fields, hoping that Adrian would wait for him.

Chapter 11
Fish Story

"COACH, JACK'S HERE," MARTY yelled out in the bustling locker room. The last period of the day had begun when Jack limped in. The joshing and sparring stopped, stretching ended, one boy gave out a low whistle, and Jack slumped onto the wooden bench in front of his locker. The boys crowded around, their faces set in silent concern. Jack stared into the darkness of his open locker, not willing to meet anyone's eyes.

He heard Coach Dickey's office door burst open. The group around Jack parted and Coach, dressed in home stripes with brown piping, appraised him.

"You look like you been wrestling pigs." Coach Dickey was a wiry man with a weather-scarred face, gray-flecked black hair trimmed militantly short, with a slight tremor in his right hand. A jiggle, he called it, injured during a fight, one he didn't talk much about. It had sealed his baseball dreams after seven years in the Cardinal's minors.

Coach Dickey turned and strode away, and Jack followed.

Behind a closed door, they stared at each other in a weighted silence across Coach's metal desk.

"I've had a rough day." Jack sheepishly stared at the floor.

"I can see that." Coach leaned back in his squeaky chair, waiting.

Jack had considered keeping back specific details, like hitting Lopez so many times, but there was just no way of keeping anything back from Coach's dead man's stare. Coach winced when Jack described the popping sensation in his leg when the labor contractor had grabbed his ankle and twisted it. When Jack finished, Coach gazed at him for a long while, tapping his chin with his finger.

"Sounds like you killed him."

"He was breathing when I left."

"That's small consolation, son, too small." He took a breath and crossed his arms.

"You've got to have your ankle taken care of." Coach rifled through his Rolodex. "It'll be better if you have it looked at here." Picking up the phone, he called Dr. Barton. "He'll be here in about an hour."

Coach swiped his brow with his shirtsleeve.

"Do you have any idea what you've put at risk here?"

Jack rubbed a throbbing kink in his calf. "I didn't think it would turn out this way."

"You're right, you weren't thinking. I doubt your mother put you up to this. What if this fellow dies?"

Jack shook his head. "That's not...possible."

"I know your swing, buddy. When you get mad, you let loose. If he's not dead, he's at least in the hospital, which means the sheriff will be involved. If he files charges, you're in a heap of trouble."

"But he was strangling the girl."

Dickey leaned forward now, talking low. "Did she report it to the police?"

Jack could not forget the sick woman and Sabrina seated on the edge of a cot, stroking her forehead. He shook his head.

Coach Dickey lifted his cap, brushed back his hair with one hand and resettled his cap.

"Jack, you're one naïve young man." He leaned forward, elbows on the desk. "Growers are busing illegals from Mexicali. Scabs are lower than migrant workers around here. And you know how low farm workers are. When the harvest is over, scabs are deported. No one's going to believe anything that girl says. To cover his ass, that fellow you hit will claim you attacked him. Whatever a grower says is gospel."

Jack studied the pattern in the linoleum. In all his times getting chewed on by Coach, he had never noticed the black swirl on the white flecked background.

"There's a war going on out there. You have a team that's counting on you, and your college career is right around the corner. This is no time to play the hero."

Jack understood. "What if I tell Sheriff Grant what happened?"

Coach put his palm on the calendar on the wall. "That girl and her mother are on their way right now to Salinas to pick lettuce. I doubt anyone around here will ever see or hear from her again, buddy. Besides, I don't believe for a second Grant will care about your story. Everyone wants to fix blame on the UFW."

Jack rested his head in his hands.

Dickey had a look of disgust as he shook his head slowly. "If you were a grower's son, your situation would be different. But you're not. So, you have to look out for yourself."

Jack wanted to bleed right out of his body and settle down in a puddle on the warm floor.

Coach didn't say anything for a full breath.

"Is Adrian the only one who knows where you were?"

Jack nodded.

"You can't go around talking about this, Jack. Not even your girlfriend, you hear?"

He nodded again.

"I don't care what you tell people, but you better keep this episode under your hat, you hear?"

Jack nodded. He had no idea what he'd tell his mother, cutting school on his pitching day.

"You know what your problem is?"

Jack didn't want to answer that question.

"You don't want this bad enough." Coach leaned forward. "You have the tools to be the best ballplayer in the Central Valley, compete for state honors, but you aren't focused."

He was right, but that could have been his mother searching those sheds. He had to try and find that machine. He felt caught in a pickle, a rundown between third base and home. Either way he ran, he was going to get tagged out. "I agree. I've been lousy about everything."

Coach Dickey leaned back. "I want more than words from you, fella." His chair squeaked as he leaned back. "Cutting school on game day and getting yourself hurt shows me you don't care about the team. Until I see the level of desire and commitment I expect, you're on the bench." Coach laced his fingers together in front of his face and waited.

Something heavy dropped on Jack. Would he get another chance to pitch? His scholarship. Ella. Everything. He studied his feet for a few seconds. Then looked sheepishly at Coach, meeting his eyes. "I want to pitch, Coach. You know that."

"We'll see."

"What do I need to do, Coach?"

"You need to put the team first every time." He stood. Meeting over.

➤

A STRONG ANTISEPTIC SMELL filled the training room as Dr. Barton examined Jack's leg. He had showered and now lay on his stomach on the treatment table in his underwear. Dr. Barton examined his ankle, prodded his thigh and calf, and pronounced Jack healthy enough to live at least another eighty years. He was to ice his ankle, then spend a half hour in the whirlpool every day followed by a tight wrap. Barton left him with a packet of anti-inflammatory tablets and a solemn warning to stay away from playing hooky on game days. And no running for a week. The ankle would take that long.

Next Monday he could test it. Before he left, Dr. Barton squeezed Jack's bicep and reminded him the team was in the hunt for the league championship, and kids were counting on his fastball. Now wasn't the time to spearfish in the irrigation canals with his friends and risk needless injury.

Jack had worked out the fish story himself. Coach left it up to him. He just didn't want to hear anything about ranches, unions, combines, or migrant workers. Fishing and swimming in the canals and irrigation ditches that crisscrossed the fields were about the only fun they could enjoy on a hot day that wasn't indoors. Brown trout washed down from the Sierra and multiplied in the concrete-sided rivers and their puzzle of sluices. Running along the edges of the canals, they speared them using small knives wired to thin poles tied to a rope.

Sometimes lousy stuff happened like stepping in a hole while running to spear a prized trout. Kids broke limbs; others fell into the rushing water and had to be rescued. Once a kid drowned, pinned by the force of the water against the iron grates that kept refuse from the pumps. Jack agreed he would be more careful next time he fished. All the while, he wondered about Sabrina, the terror he saw in her eyes, and what it must be like to be run off from a place you called home, even if it was just a ratty old shack.

Cutting classes cost Jack five days of detention in the library during lunch. That week during a morning snack break, he sat with Ella in the shade of the olive tree in the quad and kids pestered him to know whom he went fishing with. A rumor circulated that he'd been fishing with some players from their archrival Arvin, and one of them had tripped Jack. He smiled at the attention. But he politely refused to elaborate on the details of his mishap.

What hurt him most was telling Ella the fish story. She had wrinkled her nose, brushed her hair behind an ear and frowned at him, not saying a word. He couldn't tell if she believed it.

Holding Ella's hand around campus, he couldn't help but hope Sabrina was somewhere safe, that her mother hadn't died. Was she picking lettuce now? What if she hadn't moved away as Coach said? He had promised to find her some medicine. It was the decent thing to do. He would drive over to Harrison's Drugs after practice today.

His first day of detention on Wednesday, he picked over the *Delano Record* looking for any mention of an injured man at Kolcinivitch Ranch.

It wasn't until right under the obituaries, a page that truly bothered him, where he found a small article, one he'd miss if he weren't looking for it.

LABOR CONTRACTOR ATTACKED
BY UFW ORGANIZER

Delano, CA—A labor contractor was beaten on Thursday morning while inspecting his crews on Kolcinivitch Ranch. Chuey Lopez, a longtime area labor contractor, confronted a trespassing United Farmworkers organizer trying to recruit one of his workers. When Lopez tried to restrain the trespasser, he was jumped and beaten unconscious by another organizer, according to eyewitness accounts.

Sheriff Grant is investigating this as a criminal beating. "We will find the coward who did this," Grant said, in response to questions about possible suspects. "We have a list of known agitators who have a history of violence. We plan to track each of them down. Mr. Lopez was just going about his business, and was beaten for no good reason." Grant went on to say that…

Jack dropped the paper. They were quick to place blame where the sheriff wanted it put. There was a sickness spreading in the valley, and the germ of its unease settled in Jack's stomach. Coach Dickey had figured correctly.

Chapter 12
Ella

JACK'S DETENTION LASTED A week, missing another turn to pitch, which was a steep price to pay for cutting classes. He did his penance with great attention, making sure that Coach Dickey understood his commitment to the team.

Yet, as he went about classes, practice, and study, he never forgot the sight of that sickly woman, and a girl nearly strangled to death. He carried the empty box of medicine with him, not leaving it on his dresser or desk at home for his mother to find. It would mean more questions he didn't want to answer.

Jack could kick himself for going into the fields on a school day. If he had waited until Saturday, he might not have come home empty-handed. He could have stayed and worked all day, and made his way back into the sheds later in the evening. Now it was too risky to go over there unless he had proof they had the combine.

His mother had taken on a new frenzy looking for that gun. He doubted she would find it. She most likely had already sold it and just didn't remember. She had stripped the place of nearly everything valuable to keep the lights on. In the last few days, she had gone into town to meet with a lawyer who might help her. Jack didn't know how she could afford one.

➤

HIS MOM HAD FOUND out about his cutting school from the attendance office. He had given her the same fish story he told everyone else. If she knew about his failure to find the combine, she would do her own search of their neighbor's ranch. She appeared to believe his fish story, but to keep her from prying too much, he accepted a two-week grounding.

That's why on a Saturday night, instead of taking Ella dancing down at the Rainbow Room in Bakersfield, Jack sat at his kitchen table with Ella across from him, studying.

Ella wore a copper-colored peasant blouse, tight with a ruffled neckline, trimmed with lace. His mother had helped her with it, and she wore it tonight not only because Jack liked it, but because his mother made such a big deal over Ella's stitch work.

"Are you still planning on going to UCLA?" She fingered his class ring as it dangled from her neck.

"What makes you think I've changed my mind?"

"That stupid fish story."

He rubbed his forehead. He worried about this since the day he agreed with Coach on a pact of silence.

"I was fishing." His words didn't even sound convincing to himself.

"Do you think for one minute I believe that?"

Jack tapped his pencil on the table. "Why wouldn't you believe it?"

"Darcy told me she knows Adrian wasn't with you, even though he says he was."

"Have you asked everyone in the entire school?"

She eyed him quizzically, her hair sliding across her cheek. "Do I have to?"

He opened his algebra text, flipped through the pages to his assignment.

"What's going on, Jack?"

Her green eyes pierced him. She had his ring pulled away from her blouse, holding it in the air, as if she were thinking of taking it off and throwing it at him. His lie was spinning in an unexpected direction. He rose quickly, his chair screeching back, and turned to the refrigerator. He opened the door and stared at the nearly bare shelves. If he told her everything and it got back to Coach, his ass would get blisters from riding the bench for the rest of the season. He closed the door and turned to her.

"You were gone nearly a whole day." Ella's intensity rose. "It was your day to pitch. And your mother doesn't know where you were either."

He sat and spoke in a low voice. "Does your mother know everywhere you go and what you're doing?"

She blushed. "That's beside the point."

He flipped through the pages, losing his place, tossing around the inevitabilities—she'd find out soon enough, anyway.

"Were you with another girl?" The blood had risen under her nails as she gripped his ring.

He rubbed his bottom lip, trying to pick his words carefully. He slung an arm over the back of his chair. "Yeah, I guess I was, sort of."

Her face flushed a deep red. Her fingers tightened on his ring. Her eyes opened wide.

"How can you just sit here, and…and…?"

"It's not what you think."

She tightened her lips and stared.

"I was trying to help someone."

"With what?"

He leaned forward whispering, "A sick friend."

"Is that why you've been asking people around school to help you get some medicine." She tugged harder on the ring and leaned forward. "Someone said you needed penicillin."

There was only one way to kill off the rumor. He closed his book. His mother was upstairs watching TV. "Is what we talk about just between us?"

She pursed her lips. "Of course."

"Are you done writing your speech?" Jack asked, loud enough to be heard down the hall.

She wrinkled her forehead. "Not quite, but I need a break anyway."

"Good." He reached across to touch her hand, but she pulled it back. He rose and motioned for her to follow.

He led her outside. It was a warm night under the stars. They stood in the shadows of the barn while he told her about jumping the fence to look for the combine, about getting caught in the sheds by the labor contractor, about working in the fields, and about saving Sabrina from getting strangled by Chuey Lopez. Then the fight and meeting her sick mother.

Jack pushed his hand deep into his pockets and retrieved the empty medicine box. "I went to nearly every drugstore in town, but I need a prescription. Dr. Barton wouldn't help me without seeing the woman."

She was silent in the dark. Then she moved closer and hugged him.

"I'm sorry for doubting you."

"I'm sorry I lied to you."

"We can't do this to each other again." She moved close and touched his chest.

Jack held her for a moment. "Can you look at what she needs? Maybe you know where I can get some."

She let go of him and read the box. "My father uses that for his asthma."

"I didn't want to ask you."

"Were you planning on taking it to her?"

"She's only getting worse without it."

"I'll help." She held his hand. "But then you need to find a way to get back on the team. You can't let this missing combine destroy our plans."

"I'll take care of that Monday." Jack hugged her tight. "But I don't know if you want to go with me to bring it to her."

"Oh?"

"Your dad. He's friends with all these growers."

"Yeah, so?"

"You might think differently of growers after you see how these people live."

She smiled at him confidently. "Thinking for myself isn't something I'm afraid of."

No, Jack really didn't think it was. It took a while to convince Jack's mom he was finished with his homework, and Ella needed to go home because she left some notes there to complete her anti-Vietnam speech.

At Ella's house, Jack talked to Mr. and Mrs. Carter while they watched *M*A*S*H* together in the den as Ella gathered some notes from her room. She sneaked a bottle of medicine from her parents' bathroom. Mr. Carter always stood and shook Jack's hand when he left. Jack always promised he'd take care on the roads.

After an hour of maneuvering along back roads to avoid patrolling deputies, Jack rolled the Olds onto the shoulder across from a small gate on the north side of Kolcinivitch Ranch. Jack wedged his car as far off the road as he could under some eucalyptus trees. He and Ella squeezed through a gap in the chain link and strode down the dark track.

Ella stiffened at the stench of rancid food, trash in the dirt, and the rundown shacks the workers called home.

"I've never seen anything like this," Ella whispered as they moved cautiously down the narrow lane between two rows of shacks. Jack found the door and knocked. No one stirred. He knocked again. A man's voice asked in Spanish, "What do you want?"

"I have medicine."

The door opened quickly, and several curious faces greeted him. Sabrina stood under a bare bulb in the center of the room. The wheezing sounded more profound, more desperate than the last time Jack had been here.

Inside, he introduced Ella to Sabrina, who stood by a cot in faded and patched jeans and a worn navy blouse. A suspicious smile crept across her face, then her dark eyes brightened when Ella handed her the medicine. Several adults and children sat on the floor along the wall.

Sabrina prepared a dose and sat on the edge of her mother's cot. She gently lifted the woman's head in the dim light. Ella placed the tip of the glass tube in the woman's mouth and squeezed the rubber ball. The raspy sound of clogged lungs eased. Ella gave another squeeze, and the sun-spotted hand, weak and thin, clutched hers.

Ella knelt and with a wet cloth cleaned the woman's sun-parched face, and she opened her eyes. With a brief sparkle of energy, the old woman stretched out her thin arm, mottled with purpled veins, and clutched Ella's wrist, as she breathed the medicine deep into her lungs. In moments, a relieved look surfaced in her ashen smile as if her breathing suddenly eased.

Ella turned to Jack, looking up at him with sympathetic eyes. Jack had always admired her independence, but tonight her courage to come here, and her compassion for this stranger, made him appreciate her even more.

Chapter 13
House Meeting

Dusk fell swiftly, leaving a thin band of scarlet across the horizon. Adrian stepped on the gas, barreling the old truck down the narrow county road, the engine wound full up in a raspy growl. The old truck twitched like every bolt wanted to unfasten and fly off. The faster he drove, the more he remembered his friend, Emilio. Adrian hadn't been there when Emilio died. What would he have done if he had been?

Already his friend's wide grin began to dim in the fog of his memory. No more Emilio at his house, begging Mama for more of her tamales while telling his stupid jokes about fat cops in his fake gringo accent. What a crackup. Mama always said it was good to remember what he liked best about a person. It helped their spirit to stay with us. Did Emilio tell a joke as that gringo jerk struck him so hard his skull split open? All because he was on a grower's land trying to convince scabs to strike. Nothing funny about dying, but Adrian could see him trying to make a joke of it. Life around here was a joke. No, living like a peón was the joke.

Adrian pushed the gas pedal of Papa's Chevy to the floorboard, roaring down Road 33, skirting the edge of Kolcinivitch Ranch. His father had warned to drive safe, not to attract attention to himself. If he was caught this close to a ranch, he'd be beaten, too, like Emilio.

Out of the corner of his eye rows of vines clicked by. What about Papa? What if one of those bastards broke his head open? He'd have to quit school, go to work, and help Mama. He couldn't leave for college and play baseball knowing Mama and his sister needed help.

They had to win this strike. He was tired of being hungry, yet there was something worse than hunger. There would be no family without Papa holding them together. He always smiled and cheered them up, even when they had nothing but warm tortillas and some beans to eat. He had a way of solving problems. He knew what to do when men came to the door with their troubles.

Coming up to the lemon grove he and Papa had hidden in earlier in the week, he backed off the gas. The five scabs were to wait under a lemon tree off the road at dusk so they would be nothing but another shadow. He shifted into neutral and let the truck coast, idling the motor so he could roll up in the quiet darkness. He doused his headlights. They were to hop into the bed when he drifted by.

As he neared, five figures rose from the deepening shadows among the vines.

¡Imbéciles! They were to be on the lemon grove side of the road. Not on Kolcinivitch land. He tightened his grip on the steering wheel and slowed. As he neared, one of them started across the road. Before others could follow, men jumped out from between the vines, grabbed them by their shirts and dragged them back. One, her long hair twisting in the air as she struggled, fought hard.

A girl!

Santa mierda. Papa had warned him not to get out of the truck. Pick them up and hustle back for the meeting; that's all he was to do. He didn't dare get caught on this road helping scabs attend a house meeting.

He slowed to a crawl. The man threw the frantic girl to the ground. Adrian braked the truck, jumped out, and collared the man by his jacket, then swung him violently around until he faced the vines. He shoved his boot into the man's butt and kicked him headlong to the blacktopped road. The man landed with an *ooof*.

She ran across the road and tumbled into the bed of the truck. Adrian sprinted to the open door, revved the motor, and jammed forward, letting his door slam closed on the fly. While the others disappeared back into the vines, big men with sticks ran toward the road too late.

Studying his rearview mirror, he spotted the outlines of men in the middle of the road, waving their clubs. He prayed they didn't recognize him or the truck

No headlights followed as he sped off down the dark road.

➤

THE SMALL HOUSE ON Hadley Street was nothing more than a box, just like the other houses in West Delano. The tight living room was crowded by the time Adrian showed up with the girl. Votive candles flickered on the altar to the Virgin of Guadalupe by the kitchen door. Even with the lamps on the room felt dark, as if this were a place of secrets. Men and a few women, scarves still around their necks from their workday, filled every spot on the carpet. They crowded the worn sofa, even on the puffy arms, and two crunched into Papa's old rocker. The rickety kitchen chairs dotted the living room.

Adrian squeezed inside and motioned to the girl to find a place on the floor. Papa stood in the kitchen door talking. He nodded at Adrian, who remained by the front door. Papa relaxed his shoulders and spoke with a renewed vigor when he stepped into the room.

He talked about how strong they were when they worked together. And the power they had when they spoke to the growers with one voice about their wages.

"What about toilets?" a woman asked. "The growers don't want you peeing on their land, but the toilets and water are so far away from where we work we lose an hour's pay to get back and forth."

Several men glared at the woman who had spoken up, and she shrunk back into her seat.

Papa told them about la causa. They needed to speak as one to get that changed.

"What about the huelga?" a man asked. "You say we should leave the fields, but how do we eat? How do we feed our families?"

"Yeah," another one mumbled. That question rippled around the room. Papa was about to answer when the back kitchen door opened. Adrian felt the rush of fresh air cut across the room, thick with the smell of cigarettes and sweat.

A short man, Indian brown, with carefully combed black hair, dressed in work clothes and dusty boots, stood in the doorway next to Papa.

"Hello, brother." Chavez greeted Papa warmly then moved to the side. Cesar Chavez turned to the group. Adrian had often wondered about this man, why Papa followed him so closely. He didn't look like much when he walked into a room. He didn't at all appear like anyone who would pick a fight, much less against the patrones.

"You ask, how you are to live if you huelga?"

"Sí." He nodded, as did many others.

"How do you live now?"

A few laughed, then the room fell silent.

"Are you eating well? Did you eat steak and potatoes tonight? Did you have a little wine with your dinner?"

A ripple of sardonic laughter again. Men began to shift in their seats.

"Do you bring us here to make fun of us?" a big man on the sofa asked.

"Tonight, I want to help you understand something essential. There is nothing more shameful than the man who offers to work for low wages—to cheapen oneself is a crime against human decency." Chavez stood straight and pointed right at the man. "Work is a sacred thing, and so are your wages. You are endowed with dignity. That's why, even as a farmworker, you merit a just wage."

He scanned the room now, pointing at each one. "Listen to me, poverty does not make us saints. Neither does it makes us immoral. We are men and women who have suffered and endured much. Not only because of our abject poverty, but also because we have been kept poor."

The room was silent.

"We eat chicken necks," a girl said in passable English, heavily accented but still clear. It was the girl Adrian had brought. She had dark almond eyes and long raven hair. Her mouth was set as if she had a lot to say and she intended to say it. "Old, moldy chicken necks."

"Women should not talk," a man on the sofa said.

"Women can speak in this union," Cesar said, sounding stern. "This is a democratic union. Women work the fields right beside men. So, women need to speak up just like men."

"My six-year-old hijo works the field, too," one man said. "Does he get a vote?"

"Your hijo needs to be in school, hermano. It's against the law in California for six-year-olds to work the fields. If our children don't go to school, they will be poor like us for the rest of their lives."

Cesar turned to the girl. "*Señora*, what is your name?"

"*Señorita*. My name is Sabrina."

"Señorita. What about the chicken necks?"

She sat with arms folded around her knees on the floor by Adrian's feet. "In Mexico," she said in fluid Spanish, "we feed chicken necks to the dogs, along with the guts. Here we are the dogs."

"And where do you sleep?" Cesar spread his hands to the room. "Tell me. Where do you sleep?"

"Sometimes in the fields," a man said from the rocker.

"All the time on the floor," another one said.

"In the cold," another man said. "*Muy frío*. Some nights I think I'm going to die."

"We live like dogs." Sabrina spit out her words.

"A lot of times women are closer to the truth," Cesar said. "If you are being treated like dogs, then someone must think you are a dog."

"I'm tired of being treated like that," a man spoke up. Others glanced around as if testing the air to see which way others were leaning.

"Only when you decide that you must be treated as a man will will you have the commitment to go out on huelga," Cesar said. "Listen to me," he said pointing at the man, "being a man isn't getting drunk on Saturday night and coming home to push around the wife and kids. Being a man is standing up for the union, signing an authorization card, standing up the foreman, making a better life for your family."

"Still, you have not said how we will eat." The big man on the sofa folded his arms and stared up at Cesar.

"You may eat no worse than you do now," Cesar said. "But you will eat with dignity when you are able to choose to eat or not eat." He pulled a stack of cards out of his coat pocket, and he held them up. "All we have is our lives. If we want to be treated as human beings, then we must be willing to suffer. It takes courage to be nonviolent."

Men stiffened, but no one spoke.

"These are authorization cards. Fill them out and designate which ranch you work on. We're putting pressure on the ranchers to hold fair and free elections. When we have a union of our own, we will ask for a wage that you can feed your family on. No more chicken necks. No more sleeping on the ground like dogs. You will have health care. They will stop spraying poisons on you."

"What about toilets?" The woman spoke up again.

Cesar smiled at her, apparently glad she dared to speak her mind. "In no other industry in America does the patrón force his workers to go in their pants to keep working."

No one laughed.

"On the ranches with union contracts, portable toilets are brought close to the workers, and no one loses time because they have the same human needs as the patrones. All we ask is to be treated as humans. Nothing more."

"As soon as we sign these cards, the patrones will know," the big man on the sofa said. "They will threaten to send us back to Mexico. They sent others back without even paying them. They just call la migra and let them do the dirty work."

"How many of you have green cards or are citizens?" Cesar asked. Many raised their hands. A few studied their shoes. Sabrina held her chin high as if she had fought off every bit of shame, and raised her hand. There was much to like about this girl.

"I have to tell you, my friends, whether you have a green card or not, if you cross picket lines you are strike breakers. You have to understand you are being used by the growers to defeat our cause for justice."

"What about Emilio?" a man asked. "Will that happen to us?"

Many stared down at their shoes.

"Let me tell you this one thing more. La causa is harder than you think. Ours is a nonviolent huelga." Cesar eyed everyone in the room carefully as if searching out dissent. "Our brother Emilio was killed last week organizing a ranch. Immediately the desire for revenge comes into our hearts against the monsters who would destroy a life over a few dollars of wages. There is talk of finding those men and striking back. I can tell you this violence will destroy la causa. We will never win with violence against men who have the law and guns and courts on their side. They will grind us into dust. They have done this for nearly a hundred years in this state. If you pay back evil for evil, you will shoot our movement right through the heart. We will never achieve our goals of equality and fairness. So, if there is anyone here who cannot abide by that rule, then la causa is not for you."

"What? You want us to fight like a *chica*."

"Speak for yourself, muchacho," Sabrina said. The other women giggled, and a couple of men laughed out loud.

The man on the sofa glared at her, then broke into a smile. "Maybe this *mujer* can negotiate for us. She can fight with her tongue better than anyone."

"This is a democratic union. You elect your own leaders. Our best negotiator in the union is Dolores Huerta, so why not Sabrina?"

A couple of the men laughed uproariously, then suddenly fell silent when they saw that Cesar meant his words.

Sabrina held the card in her hand. "I want to sign, but if I do, they will kick me off the ranch, and my mother's very ill. She was sprayed on a couple of weeks ago and has not been able to breathe well. They promised me medicine, but I have not seen any. If we are sent back to Mexico, she will die for certain."

Cesar wove his steps through the crowd on the floor and came right up to her. She stood to meet him. "We can help you get medicine, señorita," Cesar said. "Whether you are a green carder or not, we will help you as a fellow human."

She took a card and a pencil from his hand. "If you will do that for me, I will sign it. All we have is our lives. *Viva la causa*," she said with passion.

Cesar had this impish grin on his face as if he had just struck a rich vein of gold. He turned to the rest of the room. "It takes courage, it takes sacrifice, to stand up for what's right. We may be poor, but we have the wealth of our own lives to give. It's up to you. Do you want to continue being a slave, treated like a farm implement? If you do, you'll be tossed out on the garbage heap when they don't need you anymore. If you want to be treated as a human, then you must be willing to sacrifice for what's right."

The cards began to circulate, and heads bent as they read them. Papa collected the cards. Cesar stayed and spoke with each person who came to him, asking him for help. It must have been another couple of hours before everyone was done.

Adrian understood now why his father admired Chavez. He spoke with great strength. His words rang with truth and deep conviction. He was willing to help anyone who asked. It didn't matter what that person could do for him.

Cesar spoke to Sabrina, asking her to hang around until some of the other women returned. It was late in the evening before the last visitor straggled out. Sabrina had fallen asleep on the sofa when the women returned with a paper bag. Cesar brought it over to her and woke her. They talked for a long time. Sabrina clutched her medicine. It was late when she asked Adrian if he could take her home.

Before he left, Adrian went up to his father, who was now speaking to Cesar in the kitchen, where they both sat at the table.

Cesar shook Adrian's hand. "Your father tells me you are very good at baseball. And your grades are excellent."

Adrian felt a sudden warmth run through him.

"You go to the same school as my daughters, yes?"

"Yeah, I've seen them around."

"Cesar just told me they're threatening not to let his daughters graduate if her father continues with the strike," Papa said.

He knew Linda and her younger sister. They were nice girls. She had growers' kids in her classes, just as he did, who could make life rough for anyone they didn't like. He wondered what the girls had done to get the school so mad at them. Were they not doing their work? "What did they do?"

"They are my children," Cesar said. "That is their only sin. Their schoolwork is tops, but a grower on the school board doesn't want any strikers' kids to get ahead."

Papa looked at him with those knowing eyes of his as if to say, *That's the world we live in, and you must be realistic in your expectations.* Adrian's education was everything to his Papa. He would be the first in his family to attend college.

"I'm not going to get expelled," Adrian said.

"It's a risk you must weigh, young man, to live for la causa," Cesar spoke in his quiet yet confident way. "It's a risk you must consider if you want to change the world."

Chapter 14
Trouble on the Road

A FEW DAYS LATER, on the road just outside Delano, the team school bus with all the players, coaches, and the entire cheerleading squad rolled to a stop.

Jack leaned his head out the window, wondering why they had stopped in the middle of nowhere. Waves of heat intense enough to simmer prunes rolled off the leafy vines stretching out to the horizon on both sides of the road.

Two sheriff's patrol cars blocked the way. A deputy strode to the door, and Coach stepped down to the road. From the back of the bus, Jack couldn't hear them, but he could read them. He knew Coach's antics well. Coach punched the air with his finger in the direction of Hanford, and the deputy pointed back the way they had just traveled. Coach set his hands on his hips, just as he did when getting ready to tear into an umpire, and inched closer to the lawman. The deputy's barrel chest puffed out. His badge glinted in the sunshine and motioned for the bus to turn around. Coach, with his hell-no-you-don't swagger, pointed his index finger in the direction of Hanford, *That's where we're going.*

The deputy shook his head. The two almost bumped chests.

The slant of Coach's body and his insistent pointing spoke of urgency. The game started in forty-five minutes, and they were still a half hour from Hanford. The long way around to Hanford would take at least an hour. For Coach being late to a game was a full-blown moral dilemma, one that injured his sense of sanctity about the rituals at the heart of baseball.

Traffic jacked up behind them, horns blared, and the minutes flicked by in ounces of sweat.

"Why'd we stop?" Adrian asked.

"There's trouble in the road ahead," Jack said to his friend.

"What trouble?" Marty asked.

Jack turned to the boys behind him. The usual guys had started up a card game. Lined up like three pinballs on the back bench, Marty, Michael Retuda, and Doug Barton. Adrian, next to Jack, leaned in from the aisle seat in front of them. Each boy held their two hole cards in their hands, and between Marty and Retuda, three thick textbooks laid end to end served as a table. On top of them lay a pile of coins and four cards face up.

A wide-eyed Marty set his cards face down to his lap and gaped at Jack. "What trouble?" he asked again.

The road to Hanford took them over county roads that ran for miles through Kolcinivitch fields, past rows of trellised Thompsons, Emperors, and Almeria grapes. Grapes that Jack's father had planted on land now owned by Marty's dad. The land was a tension between them that never rose to the level of a conversation, but it colored every interaction. And now Marty's demand to know dripped with expectation as if he knew someday the land itself would rise up against him.

What kind of trouble was he expecting? Jack stuck his head out the window to get one more look. The road beyond the sheriff's cars narrowed in the distance, clear and unhindered. He considered telling Marty a giant fire burned in the fields, maybe his house on the far side of the ranch. But Marty could be a landmine waiting for the slightest pressure to explode.

He turned back to his friend, "It's probably just a truck overturned or something. I wouldn't worry about it."

Marty relaxed, and his taunting smile returned. "Hey, Jack, you wanna play this hand? We need a fifth player."

Jack shook his head.

"What a wuss."

Adrian playfully slapped the bill of Marty's baseball cap, forcing it over his eyes.

"Maybe he's the smart one." Adrian nodded toward his friend. "He keeps his money in his pocket. It's your deal. Get going or we'll send you to sit with the girls."

Marty licked his lips. "I'll sit right next to Darcy."

"She'll kick your butt if you get near her," Adrian shot back.

Marty smirked and collected the cards, shuffled them up, and then dealt out two each.

Jack had watched them play cards for years. The game had certain rhythms, but he wasn't clear on all the rules.

He didn't see playing cards as more than a game of wits. If he did play, he didn't doubt he could take their money. But his mother's talk about the family curse plagued him. But after talking to Herm, that fortress in his mind began to crumble. His family had some kind of curse on them, but he was coming to believe it had nothing to do with gambling.

All that still, he didn't recognize the game they were playing. He nudged Adrian and signaled his interest. "What's this game called?"

"It's Hold 'em. It's more fun than five-card draw." Adrian nodded toward the cards spread out on the seat. He explained that two "hole cards" were dealt down to each player, and then five community cards were dealt out in three rounds—two cards on the flop, one each on the turn and the river. The player with the highest five-card poker hand won. Then you had the button, the small blind, and the big blind. These rotated around the circle of players to the left; each player took turns dealing and starting the betting.

"That doesn't sound too difficult," Jack said.

"We'll see, lover boy. This game takes major skills," Marty said, chiding him. "You in for a hand?"

Retuda tossed in his small blind, then Barton his big blind.

"You're under the gun," Marty nodded toward Adrian. He explained to Jack the first one to bet can call, raise, or fold. "A dime to stay in."

Adrian tossed in a coin. The betting continued around.

Marty dealt the three-card flop: a five of clubs, six of clubs, and nine of diamonds. As he watched, Jack studied their tells. Everyone had them. He'd noticed them for the past couple of years. Marty always flinched his mouth when he got a lousy hand. And he just did it again. Adrian rested his hands motionless and became downright chatty when he had aces or kings, never when he had queens. Jack had observed these tics for years. It wasn't much different from what he did every time he stood on the pitcher's mound, staring at the batter, trying to read his eyes, the wiggle of his bat, the way he stood in the box.

Adrian held his two cards close, and by the way he clutched them, they were good. The betting went around, more dimes gathered on the seat. Retuda bit his lip thinking up a strategy, then hesitantly tossed in another dime. He didn't think much of his cards, or he had vacillated on purpose, trying to bluff his way through. Did he have two more clubs or a pocket pair? He'd never seen Retuda play the bluff the way Marty and Adrian did. Either Retuda had good cards, or he didn't.

Everyone tossed in their dimes.

On the turn, Marty dealt a nine of spades. With a pair showing, Adrian sighed. Barton chipped in a nickel. Everyone called.

Jack couldn't say how he knew, but the same way he could sense if a batter would bite on a curveball down two strikes, he could sense what these boys had. How could this knowledge be a curse? No one had ever said that about the way he read a batter's stance or the tepidness in a boy's eyes.

The way Retuda bet like a spooked cat, either he had a nine or the makings of a straight and was slow playing them to build the pot, he was hoping for his card on the turn. The odds in the same hand could float in your favor, depending on how you played your cards.

"Here we go, boys." Marty flopped an ace of clubs, the river card, onto the seat. "Okay, who's got the flush?" Marty asked.

Adrian sighed again, acting like a loser. The boy was really playing them. If there was one person who possessed coolness down to his bones, it was his best friend. He wouldn't give himself away—if he didn't want to. Jack figured he had a winning hand.

Retuda puckered his lips, holding still. He held his breath so long, a sure sign he had something good. He raised fifteen cents.

A quarter to stay in.

Barton sighed. "I'm sick of your bluffs." He tossed in a quarter.

Adrian ceased his happy patter and rubbed his chin, then called, chipping in his quarter. Then raised a quarter.

"Hot damn," Marty said, rubbing his cheek as if he'd been stung. "You're playing us, aren't you?" He tossed in fifty cents.

Retuda hesitated.

"Gonna fold 'em, huh?" Adrian said.

Retuda eyed the center fielder across from him and pitched in two quarters. "I'll pay to see your cards. You're probably nursing a couple of deuces."

"You and those deuces," Barton said and dropped in two quarters. "You're always trying to strangle us with nothing."

"Let's see 'em," Marty bellowed.

With a Cheshire smile, Retuda laid down his four and six of clubs. "You can't bluff your way out this time." As he reached for the pot, Adrian spoke up, a knowing smirk on his face.

"I thought you might like these cards." He laid down two aces. "Full house beats a flush."

Retuda slumped in defeat as Jack tapped the edge of the seat with his palm. How he knew, he couldn't say. But it was a game that was no more mysterious to him than playing ball. And that hadn't cursed his life in the slightest. He turned to the fields, green and lush against the windswept sky. He knew what made winners and losers.

He turned to his friends. "Hey, guys, deal me in."

They all stared at him.

"Bitchin', we've corrupted Saint Jack." Marty shuffled the deck.

"You sure?" Adrian questioned his friend.

"Don't worry. I'll teach you everything I know." Marty handed the deck to Retuda, who dealt them out, two to each boy.

"You'll lose for sure now," Adrian said.

Jack fanned his cards in his hand.

"You boys gambling?" One of the assistant coaches, Mr. Thomas, stood over them. "You know that's against school rules."

Marty, looking downright cherubic, stared up at him. "No, sir, we are not. We are having us a church service before the game. We're asking Jesus and Mary to help us win the league."

Thomas crossed his arms and frowned. "What're you talking about, Kolcinivitch?"

"You see, we're telling Bible stories with our cards."

The coach pursed his lips and shook his head.

"Look, Mr. Thomas, Adrian here has a queen of spades." Marty leaned over the seat, pointing. "That symbolizes the Virgin of Guadalupe. That means she'll be on our side while we're beating back the atheist dairy boys."

A hint of a smile ran across Thomas's face.

Marty then reached over and pulled down Jack's cards so all could see. "See here, a pair of Jacks. That's Jesus and Joseph. So we got the Holy Family all in one here. We're going to win for sure."

Thomas shook his head, a definite unbeliever. "So what's that?" He pointed to the pot of nickels and dimes Retuda had just won but left piled on the seat. "An offering for the poor?"

Marty nodded solemnly. "Just trying to do the right thing."

Thomas rolled his eyes.

"Besides, everyone knows Jack doesn't gamble."

The assistant squinted at Jack, looking him over then tugged the bill of his cap. "Why don't you boys try gin rummy?"

"Great idea." Marty gathered up the cards.

After Mr. Thomas disappeared up the aisle, Marty broke out in a big smile and slapped Jack's arm. "You can play with us anytime."

Before they could start their game, the bus door opened and a sheriff's deputy followed Coach inside. Coach stabbed the air again with his index finger, speaking directly at the deputy. Finally, the deputy threw up his hands and stepped outside. The door shut, the bus driver hunkered over the wheel and shoved the stick into first with a determined thrust, as if he were preparing to ram a barricade.

Coach stood in the aisle and announced that fieldworkers were demonstrating in the road. Company thugs were there too. The sheriff said there was a good chance of some violence, but they had to get through, or they might forfeit the game.

"So, put your windows up and keep your heads down." He pointed to the open windows by the cheerleaders. "No use seeing all this." He sounded upset that local events would interfere with the playing of serious games.

"Damn Mexicans." Marty blurted.

"I wasn't talking about you, Sanchez." Marty gave him an apologetic nod.

"Of course you're not talking about me." Adrian turned to Marty behind him. "I'm just a Mexican, not a damn Mexican, right?"

Marty's little eyes blinked in a flurry. Sanchez turned forward.

Adrian went back to gazing out at the fields as if he was looking for someone. Around his neck, the pewter medal of Saint Jude caught the sun. He fidgeted, striking the dark center of his worn mitt with his fist. He used a tired Roger Maris fielder's model; the webbing was so old he had to restring it to keep it from falling apart.

Guys eyed each other but didn't say much. Some put their heads down. A few stared outside. Up ahead the way bent north. Someone in front said the strikers were invading the fields, trying to talk scabs into joining the strike. Jack knew growers had court injunctions against UFW organizers entering their land. But then just last week, he saw Adrian's dad trying to talk Sabrina into leaving the fields. So that's probably what the strikers were doing.

The road straightened into a long strip that shimmered as the rising heat peeled up in waves. On the west side of the bus, rows of Kolcinivitch grapevines stretched into the distance. The heads of campesinos bobbed up and down among the vines as they worked their way toward the road, trimming, tying, and bundling.

A long line of tough muscled men, unshaven with wide shoulders and broad chests, stomped up and down the edge of the fields, a fence of flesh against defectors. They shouted, hooted, swore, and raged at the strikers who milled in small clumps on the opposite shoulder of the road.

One Teamster in a tan shirt, jeans, and work boots strode nearly to the middle shouting obscenities at the UFW strikers standing on a flatbed truck.

A line of riot-helmeted deputies stretched down the middle of the road.

From the back end of the flatbed truck, a priest prayed into a bullhorn, and women who gathered close by held green authorization cards as they knelt in the dirt and prayed.

"What's going on?" one of the boys asked Adrian.

"The UFW wants the workers to sign authorization cards." Adrian explained the activity outside their windows. "Free elections can't happen until pickers sign the cards. But ranchers won't let organizers on their property, and they brought in thugs to block workers from leaving the fields."

A field hand took off running between the vines, shot past a Teamster, who cursed and chased. The two scuttled across the road. Only feet in front of the bus the thugs held up, but the picker sprinted on. The bus lurched to a groaning stop, barely missing him.

The man skidded into the group of women kneeling in prayer and joined in on his knees. The praying women were now right under Jack's window. One of the women handed the escaped picker a card.

Adrian half rose and leaned over Jack to get a better view.

Marty smirked. "What a bunch of idiots, praying."

"Not even the courts can stop people from praying." Adrian kept his attention glued to the action. The women calmly fingered their rosaries as the chaos swirled around them. The UFW had begun to have prayer vigils instead of full strikes as a way of getting around the court orders barring them from showing up on county roads across from a grower's fields. Not even Sheriff Grant would break up a prayer meeting.

Marty leaned over the seat, practically next to Jack's ear. "God doesn't care about grapes."

"Maybe not. But I hope he cares about people." Adrian kept his eyes focused on events unfolding outside. "Or we're all in deep trouble."

Marty gave Adrian a smoldering glare.

"As long as the grapes are trimmed," Adrian said, "it doesn't matter if workers are poisoned?"

"No one's died on my dad's ranch, Sanchez, and you know it."

"I know. He fires the sick so they must go somewhere else to die."

Marty's face blanched. "You bastard." He grabbed Adrian by the front of the shirt, pulling him up. "Take that back or I'll shove it down your throat."

Adrian didn't flinch, his hands calmly on his thighs. "I'll take it back when your father stops spraying workers."

Marty swung, Adrian turned his head, and the fist hit him square on the jaw. Adrian snapped back and sprawled on the floor. Stunned boys stared down at him, as Adrian held his jaw.

"That's enough." The voice was smooth and firm. Coach Dickey stood in the aisle close by. "We got enough going on here, trying to play good baseball." Dickey strode down the aisle, in front of a standing

Marty. "We're teammates. Remember. We fight for one another, not against each other. How many times have I told all of you, keep this conflict outside here—" He pointed toward the window, "Outside our team. Is that clear to everyone? Get in your seats and put those cards away. We got a tough game today, and we gotta be ready." He pointed at his temple. "Up here. You got it?" He gave them all a hard stare, then turned to the front and strode to his seat.

Marty sat slowly. Jack helped his friend up. Everyone took seats and stared ahead in silence. The distinctive marks of Marty's knuckles were outlined in the red blotch on Adrian's cheek. Jack forced himself not to stare at his friend, who held his chin up and mouth tight, eyes straight forward as if he had no fear of what lay around him.

Outside, a deputy yelled for the bus to move, to get out of the way.

It rumbled through its gears, gaining speed, and then it suddenly slowed. Jack leaned close to the window. Two lines of marchers, escorted by helmeted cops marching at their side, filed by, silent and peaceful, led by Cesar Chavez himself, a man whose photo ran regularly in the *Delano Record*.

The columns stretched out, and the workers strode briskly forward, intent, holding their signs, waving their flags. Shouts of "huelga, huelga" went up from the lines as they passed by, but no one fell out of order, or threatened, as they flowed on, past the bus.

"Communist bastard," Marty said under his breath.

The bus continued on, an uneasy quiet inside. Jack rose in his seat and turned to watch the receding line of marchers disappear down the road. The wind had kicked up, and a pall of dust drifted over the fields, turning people in the street into dark figures, running back and forth, gathering in knots—mere shadows in the obscuring air.

A sharp crack came from behind. The boys ducked as if to dodge a bullet; the girls screamed. Jack strained to see what had happened. Adrian rose in reflex.

"Get down, you two. Get down." Coach motioned with his hand to sit.

Jack stared down the thin aisle at Coach, concern written all over his face. Marty smirked, arms resting on the top edge of the seat. Adrian stood solid, staring pensively out the back window, his black eyes on fire.

➤

JACK SMELLED HANFORD BEFORE he saw it. Welcome to dairy land. Pastures full of black and white Holsteins lined both sides of the road as their bus rolled into town. Arriving after four thirty, the Hanford team waited impatiently on the field. The boys hustled to warm up. Taking the mound, Jack felt like a man reprieved of a terrible sentence, getting out of that bus. It took him an inning to locate his fastball, but soon he found himself in a groove.

In the third inning, Jack spotted the lanky man in the powder blue baseball cap behind the plate. Coach Kish from UCLA, with his stoic mouth, charted his every pitch. It was time to bear down.

The bottom fell out of his curve, and the big Hanford boys swung at air. Before dark, they were in the seventh, and Jack's fastball took to floating up into the strike zone where the milk-fed sons of Hanford dairymen began swatting it hard. He despised not finishing games, and their lead had been trimmed to one run thanks to the heroics of his center fielder. Adrian had a spark in his swing today. He had hit a home run, doubled in two runs, and saved a few more with his masterful glove work.

After the last white-cheeked Hanford player zinged Jack's curveball-that-failed-to-curve into left field for a double, Marty trotted out to the mound, his equipment jangling, his mask pushed up onto his sweat-plaited hair. Jack raised his cap and wiped his brow with the sleeve of his arm. The thermometer had retreated a degree or two from its high of ninety-nine. Heat sifted through his uniform, wanting to bake him dry as it did turning grapes into raisins.

Marty warned him to keep the ball low.

Jack nodded, positioning his cap to shade his eyes.

"Look, Talbert's up. This guy's a fat oaf. His farts smell like cheese. But he's big."

Jack sized up the raw-boned teen swing three bats in the on-deck circle. He was tall and muscled with a dull look in his eyes.

"If you keep pitching like you're his mother," Marty said, "he'll hit the ball so hard it'll make it back to Delano before we do. Keep it low, and we're out of this mess." He jogged back home.

Coach rose and gave Jack a steely look. Jack signaled he intended to finish. Coach flashed Marty a series of signs.

Talbert stepped into the batter's box and dug in his back foot.

Marty took up his chatter. "Okay, batter, smelling like rotten Gouda back here."

Jack dropped the resin bag and set himself. As he leaned in, he could see Kish standing, eyes squinting his way. Jack checked the tying run on second. Now was the time to end this. Jack wound and threw a heater that slipped out of his hand early and hung over the center of the plate.

Talbert swung so hard he stood on his heels, popping it a mile up until it disappeared in the waning light. The crowd rose to its feet. Coach and the entire team stood and searched the sky. The second baseman ran in a bewildered circle, desperately searching. The shortstop pointed to Adrian, sprinting full speed out of the heat haze of deep center, head up tracking the ball. Leaning forward, he caught the ball at the top of his shoes, clutching it one-handed in his mitt. Still running, he threw a strike to second base for the game-ending double play. His teammates jumped up and down then ran wildly to him.

Jack raised his arms with a shout. He had watched Adrian make catches like that for the past four years, and he felt lucky having him in center field. Jack pitched a gutty game for not being on the mound for almost two weeks, so he hoped he had impressed Kish. But

Adrian had played with an unusual concentration today. For sure, he was going to earn himself a scholarship somewhere.

Shortly after the game, Jack slumped in his seat in the rear of the bus, staring out the window. The bus idled in the twilight. Everyone was on board except Adrian, who leaned against the bus by the door as Coach Kish from UCLA spoke to him. Jack could see the back of the tall, lean coach and Adrian's profile. He nodded at whatever the coach was saying. Then they shook hands, and Adrian turned to the door.

Jack didn't need Adrian to tell him he had been offered a scholly. It was written all over the boy's face as he strode down the aisle and took a seat next to Jack. Adrian glowed as he sat taller than usual. Boys slapped him on the back. Even Marty gave him a hearty slug on the shoulder. Coach made his way down the aisle and shook Adrian's hand, giving him a few words of praise. Jack took this all in as he leaned against the window, happy for his buddy who had earned every dollar of that scholarship but confused at the UCLA's coach's disinterest in even speaking to him.

Had his opportunity passed with that school? All his work and effort on the ballfield had come to nothing. A bleakness came over him. Wasn't he good enough to pitch for a college team? Had he been fooling himself all these years? Afraid of sinking into a joyless stupor, he leaned over and squeezed Adrian's bicep.

"You did it, man." Jack playfully tugged down the bill of Adrian's cap. "You deserve it."

Adrian nodded thanks, a glow of satisfaction on his face. Darcy came down the aisle, her short cheerleader's skirt swishing with the rhythm of her hips and asked to sit with Adrian. Jack rose and stepped all the way to the back of the bus, squeezing onto the rear bench next to Marty. Jack stared out the window. Marty elbowed Jack in the side. The big catcher leaned closer to Jack and spoke softly.

"You know, my dad's not a dickhead." Marty's serious look was something Jack hadn't seen before.

"Of course not," Jack blurted. Then images of Sabrina and her mother living in that tiny shack, the bleakness of the labor camp, and that fat labor contractor running after Adrian's dad, all on Marty's father's land. But these things were happening everywhere. Besides, who wanted to think poorly of his own father? All the way home, Jack stewed in a bumpy silence on the backbench over the dust-up between his two friends. The feud was unsolvable, a fistfight that was bound to go on forever until one of them just dropped dead.

Chapter 15
Dangerous Roads

THE NEXT DAY ON his way to history class, Jack stopped by his locker to drop off a book. At mid-morning, Adrian usually stood at his locker shuffling his books at the same time. Jack expected he'd be all smiles about his new scholly. But there was no Adrian. He hadn't seen him before first period either. He didn't see him in the halls between classes. Darcy was just stepping into a class when Jack caught up with her. She didn't have any idea where he was. He hadn't shown up where they usually met before first period.

Strange. Adrian would show up even if he had a broken leg. Had he stayed up late celebrating with his family?

At lunch in the cafeteria, Darcy saved a seat for Adrian. It remained empty the entire period.

"Maybe he's sick." Ella tried to calm everyone.

"He usually calls me before school if he isn't coming," Darcy said.

"He was great yesterday." Jack glanced around the cafeteria. He wouldn't sit anywhere else and not at least say hi. He had to be sick.

When Adrian didn't show for practice either, Jack became concerned. He wasn't the only one wondering what had happened. His teammates peppered him with questions. All he could do was shrug. Marty was the only one who didn't ask him anything about Adrian. Coach Dickey didn't say a word about Adrian's absence until boys pestered him. After practice, he gathered everyone and told them Adrian would be back tomorrow.

"What happened?" one of them asked.

"He'll be back tomorrow." He wiped his mouth. "Listen up, we got a heat wave coming, so for a few days, we're going to early morning practices. You all know the routine."

After practice, Jack drove over to Adrian's house. He lived in West Delano, a dark neighborhood of tiny homes and potholed streets. Adrian's father's truck wasn't in front of the house when he pulled up and cut the motor.

Adrian opened the door warily after Jack knocked. An angry surprise stitched his face.

"What're you doing here?" Adrian searched the street behind Jack.

"That's what I'd like to know. Why do I have to come here to find you?"

Adrian stepped onto the porch. Dressed in a T-shirt and jeans. "I would've been in school if it wasn't for that dick-head Marty."

"You guys get into another fight?"

He shook his head. "I would've killed that bastard."

Adrian told Jack how Principal McGrew had called his house before school to tell him not to show up on campus today. McGrew suspended him one day for fighting. Adrian had tried to explain that Marty had struck him, and he hadn't hit him back. Didn't matter. Adrian figured someone had told Marty's father what had happened. He must have called his friends on the school board. The board is made up of growers. They must have put pressure on McGrew to do something.

"Marty was at practice today."

"Knew he would be."

"Thought you had to knock someone out to get suspended."

"If you're white, yeah. If you're Mexican, you just have to get hit."

His friend's glumness bothered him. After yesterday's high, today's Adrian was a different picture.

"Look, you shouldn't be here right now." Adrian searched the street over Jack's shoulder.

"Why?" Jack had always felt welcome at the Sanchez's.

"Just not a good time to be around."

"Let's go for a ride then."

A minute later, they tooled out of West Delano toward downtown to a favorite drive-in for a Coke. They pulled into Roscoe's Drive-in on Cecil Boulevard. He ordered two sodas and two French fries.

Two Kern County Sheriff's cars roared by on the street behind them.

"Wonder where they're going in a hurry."

Adrian watched them pass. "Probably my house. That's why I didn't want you around. They'd harass you too."

"Why they going there?"

"They're accusing my dad of beating that labor contractor."

Jack stared at his friend. "The one I beat?"

"'Fraid so."

Jack slapped his steering wheel.

"They're coming to the house nearly every night. They say they have a witness who saw him on the ranch talking to a girl about going out on strike. When Lopez approached, he beat the guy."

"But why blame your father?"

"They want him off the picket line," Adrian said. "If they destroy the leadership, they think they can kill the strike."

"That explains why McGrew suspended you. You're the son of a strike leader."

"The cops have been over to my house three times in the last week." Adrian's voice turned glum. "Asking me where I was. Who I was with. Where my father was. What was he doing on the day of the beating? It's bad, man, real bad. They threatened to arrest him."

He studied his friend. "I'll explain to the sheriff what happened."

"They'd say you're just trying to stand up for your friend. They believe what they want to believe."

"Sheriff Grant would know. He was over at my house. He warned me not to go into the ranch looking around on my own."

"You're not even living in the same town as I am, Jack."

"I'm sorry, Adrian. I didn't think this would happen—"

"If that Lopez guy dies, they're going to pin the murder on my father."

Jack cursed and stared out the window.

"Why'd you have to hit that guy so hard? You knew my father was there."

"That fat slob was going to strangle that girl. Should I just let her die?"

"I guess it doesn't matter. They're going to do what they want."

"That's BS, and you know it," Jack said, "The cops need to do what's right."

The waitress roller-skated up with a tray and attached it to Jack's open window.

"BS is getting blamed for something you didn't do." Adrian's face flushed. "They don't care about what's right."

Jack handed him a full cup of soda. "They can't just go around pinning crimes on whomever they want."

"What planet are you living on?" Adrian slapped the cup out of his hand, spewing soda all over Jack.

"Hey! What the hell?" The drink splashed in his face and down his shirt. "What's wrong with you?" He reached for something on the tray and grabbed the French fries and heaved them at Adrian.

Adrian slugged him on the arm, again and again.

"Damn you," Jack yelled. A sharp pain shot through his pitching arm. He yanked the door open, his foot caught, and he tumbled onto the blacktop. The soda and fries from the tray drenched him. Wet and sticky, he rolled on his back, his feet hung up in the car.

A short burst of siren blasted. Red and blue dots whirled over him. A pair of headlights stopped inches from Jack's bumper. Before he could scramble up, an officer stood over him. He held the beam of his flashlight in Jack's eyes, blinding him.

"You find the oddest places to sleep, you know that," a familiar voice said.

Jack shielded his eyes then groaned. What a time for this idiot to show up. He rolled over and pushed himself to his knees. On his feet, he leaned against the car, holding his shoulder.

"You been drinking again?" Kauffman flashed his beam in Jack's eyes.

"Just soda."

"Yeah, right." Kauffman surveyed the ground, and then leaned into the open door, running the beam of his flashlight on the seat. "Doesn't look like you're actually drinking any of it." He focused his light on Adrian. "Is that you, Sanchez? We've been looking for you. Get your ass out here."

Adrian came around and stood next to Jack.

"He hit you?" Kauffman asked Jack.

"Nah."

"Why you holding your arm?"

"Banged it when I rolled out?"

Kauffman eyed him suspiciously, then studied the mess by the open door. He searched the front seat with his light. "There's an empty cup down by the gas pedal. The seat is soaked on the driver's side." He then ran the light down the front of Jack's clothes. "You're soaked, but he's not." He nodded toward Adrian. "It appears to me that Sanchez threw a cup of soda at you. Probably started hitting you. Then you tried to get out of the car quick, but because you're such a clumsy oaf, your feet got stuck. You fell out instead. Look at this mess you made here."

"I spilled it on myself." Jack quit rubbing his arm. "I wanted to get out fast, and I fell."

"I say there was a fight." Kauffman ran the light in tight circles on Jack's face. He got real close to Jack. "Now, I can arrest your friend right here for assault and battery or you two can tell me what you were fighting over." He flashed the light in Adrian's face, who glared back at him with angry eyes. "That's what I want to know."

Kauffman splashed the light from one boy's face to the other, back and forth.

"It was that Lovitch girl, wasn't it?"

"Actually, we were debating about your mother." Jack had to find a way to distract this idiot.

"You've got a mouth, you know that." Kauffman held the light tightly against Jack's face. "I'd watch it."

He moved to Adrian, and with a malicious smile, he pointed the light in his face: "He wanted to screw that Lovitch girl, didn't he? That's it, huh, Sanchez. And you didn't like it." He held Adrian's glare. "Are those fists? Go ahead, are you man enough?"

"He was saying your mother was an ape, that's why you got all that curly hair. But I said she had to be part pygmy. That's why you got such a small dick."

Kauffman moved the light back to Jack's face, a mean look contorting his grin. "You better shut up while you can still talk."

"Everyone in town knows you got the short end of it when the dicks were passed out. That's why you go around acting like a big one to make up for it."

Adrian snorted a laugh, trying to hold it back.

Kauffman pulled his Billy club from his belt, and stuck it in Adrian's cheek, pushing his face away. "You get your brown ass out of here and run home. You got visitors wanting to ask you questions." When Adrian hesitated, he yelled. "Get!"

Adrian turned, and Kauffman struck him across the thigh with his baton. He didn't yell, but took off limping through the lot into the dark street and disappeared down the road.

"These are dangerous roads." Kauffman stood close to Jack. "Anything can happen in the dark."

"Nothing better happen to him."

"Or what?" Kauffman pointed his baton in Jack's face. "You talk big for a punk. Now get in the cruiser. I have something important to show you, moron."

Kauffman opened the back door, and Jack slid in. Kauffman took his place behind the wheel. "See that coat beside you on the seat?"

"Yeah."

"Recognize it?"

Jack held it up to the light. Something froze inside. He reached into the pocket and pulled out his Instamatic. The film cartridge was empty. He took this one into Kolcinivitch Ranch.

"You left that somewhere didn't you, idiot?"

"Someone must have stolen it."

"You were trespassing."

"I don't even know what that word means."

"You're a fool and an idiot?" He flicked something over the seat. "Recognize those guys?"

"Yeah." Three Mexican farmhands, with the vines behind them, stood stiffly for the photo. "They look like the farmworkers I saw at the grocery store in town yesterday."

"They said they recognize you as the man who almost killed that labor contractor."

"You must have beat them with your baton to confess. I can see the marks on their souls."

"Attempted murder with great bodily harm gets a couple of years in county jail, Jack. For you, probably more."

"Isn't there some law against cops talking out of their ass in public?"

Kauffman turned and handed him a photo. "What about her?" It was an unsmiling Sabrina. The wall of her cabin in the background. "She says she saw you on the ranch."

"Why didn't you include her dying mother in the picture? It would have made a great family photo."

"So you do admit to trespassing?"

Jack sighed. "What do you want, Kauffman?"

"It's not what I want, Jackie boy. It's what you want." He flicked another photo into the backseat. Jack picked it up. It was the combine. Two men with blowtorches stood beside it, the flames of their torches a bright orange.

"You want this back?" Kauffman glared at Jack. "You come to the office and sign a sworn affidavit that you saw Sanchez's old man try to kill the labor contractor, Chuey Lopez."

"You wanted Adrian to hit you, didn't you? You didn't want to take him in for assaulting me. You wanted to arrest him for assaulting you."

"You're not a half-wit after all. They don't belong here anymore. They've worn out their Delano welcome. It's a big country. They can go pick somewhere else."

Jack gathered the photos and reached for the door handle, but it had been removed. "Hey, let me out of here before I puke. You're making me sick."

"Hand over the photos, and I'll open the door."

"Open the door, you punk cop."

Kauffman stuck a .45 revolver over the seat, the barrel just a few inches from Jack's face. "This can go off accidentally, or I can pull it trying to defend myself. The only regret I'd have is that it would mess up my backseat." He clicked the hammer back. "Now hand them over."

The round barrel stared him down. A fire kindled in his gut. This close to death, the image of Sabrina's mother gasping for breath came to him. Everything in him told him not to give in, to spit in Kauffman's face. Then the barrel loomed larger. Death was just a couple of inches away.

Kauffman's smirking glare had a look of resolve. Slowly Jack handed the photos across the seat. The deputy took them. "And the jacket." Jack pushed it over the front seat. "Now, you got five days to come in and sign. You got that, Jackie boy. After that, you go to jail."

Kauffman lowered the gun, got out, and opened the back door. "Now get."

Jack strode to his car, every nerve on fire. He hated the smallness of his surrender. He spun around at his car door. "You're not the only one who has a gun."

Kauffman crossed his arms across his chest. "You threatening a deputy?"

Jack shook his head. "I'm threatening Eric Kauffman, the jerk. These roads can be dangerous. Better watch out." He jammed into the driver's seat and slammed the door. He fired the motor. The headlights behind him sped backward, and the cruiser screeched away.

Jack sat for a moment, his heart racing, his mind flitting between what he could do to make this right, and what he should do.

Chapter 16
Sugar's Truck

THE NEXT MORNING JACK woke to the remnants of a bad dream floating through his thoughts. He had stared down the barrel of Kauffman's gun. Forced to plead for his life, he had begged the crooked cop to spare him. The memory of the deputy pulling the trigger lay somewhere on the foggy margins of his memory. Jack sat up and shook his head to clear his mind. He shouldn't have threatened Kauffman. He would find a way to make Jack eat his big words.

He rose and dressed, grabbed his books, and made it downstairs to the kitchen. Today's practice started early, and Coach penalized players who were late. He had heard her downstairs while he dressed. In the kitchen, a cold chill swept in from the open back door. Was she outside? They didn't have any more chickens to feed or eggs to gather.

Slumped at the table, he ate a bowl of cereal. Kauffman wasn't the kind who let slights off easy. Besides, Jack didn't even own a gun. But other ways came to mind. He could run the cop off the road and into a tree. He could sideswipe him on one of the desolate county roads, or push him off the road into a canal. Let the bastard drown. He could run him over when he got out of his patrol car to give out a ticket. All of that was nonsense.

Kauffman would come after him some time, somewhere on some dark road. An accident would happen, and no one would know the truth.

He needed a gun.

Digging beyond his ill ease at pissing off Kauffman lay the real root of his anxiety—a ticking bomb that would explode in five days. He had to make a decision by next Tuesday. Turn against Adrian's father, and his mother gets her combine back. Or jail, or worse.

Would the sheriff actually hand over the combine if he betrayed his friend? Even if he did, Kauffman could find a way to sabotage the deal. He had personal reasons now. Jack finished eating, grabbed his backpack, and lifted the car keys off the hook by the door.

Standing on the back porch, Jack didn't see his mother in the garden. He wanted to remind her that he was taking the car for morning practice, and he'd be home early. He stepped across the dirt yard toward the car. The reedy looking clouds, pink and thin at the margins between land and sky, said today would be another scorcher. In the still dry air, the aromas of grapes were strong as if the vines were under his nose.

His mother in a sweater, jeans, and her uncombed gray hair peeked her head out of the barn door and spotted him. He waved to her, but she slipped back inside. He barely had enough time to get to practice. Yet, the way she was skulking around, he had to look.

He slipped through the open barn doors. The air was musty and warm in the dark. Slats of light poured in through the spaces in the weathered boards. She stood by his father's Ford pickup, leaning in the passenger window.

He rested his arms on the open driver's window frame. He followed her eyes to the gun rack in the back window.

"Where'd that come from?" He was astonished to see a shotgun in the rack. It hadn't been there before.

"It's your father's old Browning five-shot. I found it in the attic." A thick coat of dust covered the tooled oak of the worn stock and his father's initials.

"You put it together yourself?"

"Yup. Sugar kept shells in here."

"They'd be pretty old."

"If the powder's dry they'll still kill a thief."

"What're you going to do?"

"Get my combine back."

Did she already have a plan? Jack reached in and ran his hand over the stock. It was grimy and dirty. He doubted if it would even fire. If she went next door with this thing, it could end in a disaster. He opened the creaky door and slid into the front seat. He had to find those shells first. She yanked the other door open.

He put his hand under the bench seat and ran it along the bottom reaching under the passenger side. Nothing. He reached deeper, feeling up into the springs. His hand hit something hard, a case or a container wedged up in there tight. He wiggled it until it dropped loose and pulled it out. A dust-covered sandwich container, it was old and faded, and the plastic so clouded he couldn't see the contents. His mother grabbed it out of his hand and shook it.

"My old Tupperware. You're father always took his lunch with him." She shook it hard, and it didn't rattle as shells would. "Don't open it unless you want to stink out the place." She tossed it on the floor and then leaned over the back of the seat.

Jack retrieved the Tupperware and shook it. Didn't sound like a sandwich, which would have rotted into crumbs. This sound was solid. And it was heavy. Holding it up to the light seeping through the windshield, something inside covered the bottom—paper or cards. He worked at peeling off the lid. A corner of it finally came up, and he pried it the rest of the way off. He slid out of the cab, to get a better look at the contents in a shaft of light.

It was packed tight with cards. Baseball cards. The photos were black and white, bright and unfaded. There were two stacks, side-by-side. A piece of folded paper lined the bottom. Probably to hide the cards. He rifled through them. Most were names he didn't recognize, players from the forties and fifties. Then he came to a Willie Mays rookie card, then a DiMaggio card. He lifted it out. It had an autograph across the back. He tamped down the stacks and stared at what he held in his hands. His father loved baseball, too. Herm Gordon's words in the hospital came to mind: *Take your father's truck with you. Don't leave it behind. Drive it out of here.*

Did Herm know Jack would find these cards?

His mother pushed the seat forward and now burrowed behind it, making a racket throwing old junk around. She mumbled, but he didn't pay attention to her.

"Jack?" She pushed her head out of the driver's side window, calling to him.

He kept his back to her. She'd sell them to buy ammunition. He snugged the Tupperware top back on.

"Jack, you listening to me?"

He spun around.

"Jack." Her hand rested in the air, reaching toward him.

"What?"

In her palm rested two shells, brass and red. "I found two whole boxes hidden back here."

He stuffed the plastic container in his backpack. He opened the door and moved quickly across the rotted seat, forcing her back.

"What're you doing?"

He unracked the Browning and backed out of the cab, grabbing a box of shells off the seat. She reached for the barrel, but he eluded her grasp.

"Bring that back here."

He hustled out of the barn and locked himself in the Olds. He threw the gun and ammo in the backseat. By the time he fired up the engine, she was banging on the driver's window, yelling for him to open up.

He shifted into reverse, but she slid around to the back, standing by the trunk lid, blocking him from backing. He rolled forward and turned around by the barn. He tried to edge by her, but she jumped on the hood, banging on the windshield, her wide eyes right down against the glass. She pounded on the glass with desperate fists, shouting: "Give me back that gun."

He took his foot off the brake, and the car rolled toward the street. He turned slowly into the county road so as not to knock her off in the ditch. At the end of his turn, he pressed gently on the brake pedal, and she slid off, landing on her feet on the road.

She banged on the driver's side window as he eased away, shouting that he'd regret losing this place. He pressed ahead, ignoring her. He gradually picked up speed.

He watched her in his rearview diminishing into a speck and every possibility rushed through him. She would have stormed next door and shot her way into those barns if that was the only way to save the land. He already had a load of regrets—losing the combine, getting himself into a jam with the sheriff and his favorite acolyte, Kauffman. If he hadn't taken the gun, and his mother ended up in a pool of her own blood on Kolcinivitch land...land that was once hers...her death would bury him, too.

People were being killed around here all the time. It better not be her. And it wouldn't be him either, now that he had a way to protect himself.

➤

DURING THE EARLY MORNING practice, Jack worked off the chill, but he couldn't block out the wild look in his mother's eyes, holding out those shells. He doubted they would fire anyway out in the damp all those years. Then again, he didn't understand the first thing about guns, so how would he know?

He pitched on the sidelines, then shagged balls in the outfield during batting practice. If he brought that gun home, she'd find a way to unlock the trunk and steal it back. He worked up a sweat, running and throwing, pushing his focus onto baseball, and the game he would pitch on Sunday afternoon, an audition for his future.

During batting practice, Jack met Adrian behind the backstop as they waited for their turns. They both stood, fingers in the mesh of the wire fence, watching the batter take swings. Finally, Adrian broke the silence.

"Sorry I threw that drink at you."

"Don't worry about it."

"I wasn't trying to hurt you, hitting you and stuff."

"If I thought you were trying to hurt me, I would have beat your butt."

Adrian laughed. "Not likely, amigo."

"Kauffman was sure digging for you last night. He wanted you in jail."

"They want all the Mexicans in the fields or in jail."

"Or out of the county."

Adrian nodded. "I saw him put you in the car last night."

"You didn't go home?"

He shook his head. "I hid across the street. No way was I going home so those cops could treat me like scum."

"Kauffman put a gun in my face."

"What?"

Jack leaned close and told him about Kauffman's threat to arrest him unless he became a witness against Adrian's dad.

"Bastard."

"Hey. You guys going to stand there yakking or what?" Coach Dickey yelled at them from over by the dugout.

"I wouldn't do that in a million years." Jack shook his head.

Adrian nodded and stepped into the batter's box. Jack watched as he swung smoothly, spraying balls all over the field. Jack admired how he could shut off the world and focus on one thing—hitting a baseball. Maybe that was the only way to survive around here.

Later in the morning, Jack worked his way through the crowded hall. Kids squirmed around each other, racing the bell, rats running for darkness. He passed Adrian as he stood talking to Darcy. He gave

Jack a friendly nod. Jack thought to reassure his friend he would never betray him. Somehow, Jack didn't think Adrian needed more words. There wasn't a need to make a bunch of promises to a person he was already bound to by friendship. There wouldn't be much between friends if it could be undone by hatred and half-wit cops. Jack gave him a nodding smile in return.

Jack was sitting in history class when he felt something slipping away like the sand in an hourglass, drawing down relentlessly toward a deadline. Every minute hurtled him forward toward a future he couldn't control. That crook Kauffman would find a way to arrest him. He spent the whole period staring absentmindedly at the teacher. Her words sped right over and around him. He needed someone to talk to; someone who knew what was really behind all this crap.

Herm had started this whole chain of events by stopping him on the road. He knew more than anyone what was going on. Then there were those baseball cards. Herm had wanted Jack to find them. His mother had said Herm was out of the hospital, and it looked good for the old man's recovery.

At lunch, he and Ella sat on the lawn in the shade of the old olive tree. She had a curious look in her eyes.

"What's going on?"

He told her about Kauffman's threat.

"That's the work of that slob Sheriff Grant." She was her indignant best, spots of red high on her cheeks, firm confidence in her voice. "He was over our place the other day too, talking to my dad."

"About what?"

"I assume the strike. Daddy closes the door to his office when one of his grower friends or the sheriff comes over." She took her guitar out of its case and strummed a few chords. "If I knew something, I'd tell you."

"I know."

"Honestly, Jack, I can't get that girl's mother out of my mind. She's going to die in that ugly place."

"The way she coughed," Jack said. "It sounded like she wasn't far from death."

"I talked to Mrs. Paulson. She runs the compassion pantry at St. Andrews. She's setting aside a whole bunch of clothes and food. She said we can pick the stuff up tomorrow. I've collected more medicine, and we could take everything tomorrow night."

"I'll help you."

She lowered her head over the guitar, hair hiding her face, and strummed it lazily.

"You upset about something?" Jack said.

She had a distant stare for a second then went back to tuning a string. "I just kept thinking about that woman. She's probably already dead. All of this effort to end a useless war our president wants to fight, and not five miles from me, people die because they don't have medicine. Stuff that we have in our drawers."

"Doesn't seem right, does it?" Life shouldn't be such a struggle to stay alive, to just take a breath of clean air.

Chapter 17
A Good Man

O**N HIS WAY TO** Herm's house, he passed by a shop he had seen for years: Robert's Guns. The shotgun he took from his mother this morning didn't look in good shape. Would the thing even work? He parked nearby and took the box of old shells out of the trunk along with the shotgun. Inside the shop, he laid them on the glass counter. An old man, easily in his seventies ambled slowly over and lifted it off the counter.

He looked it over thoroughly, rubbing his fingers over the carving in the stock. "Where'd you get this, young man?"

"It's my father's. He's dead now. Does it still work?"

The man, gray hair and reading glasses resting halfway down his nose, looked Jack over. "You Sugar's boy?"

"You knew him?"

"I sold him this gun, oh, gosh, twenty, twenty-five years now." With one hand on the barrel and the other on the stock, he turned it over, inspecting it. He then slid the bolt back to check the chamber. "It's not in good shape."

"How do you know it's the same one?"

He raised the butt of the stock so Jack could see it. "I carved those initials for him."

An ornate "S" and "D" with curlicues and squiggles were carved right in the middle of the stock. "It was a real beaut new."

"My dad had it stored. I just found it."

"I'm glad you brought it in. The barrel's not seated correctly, and it needs a good cleaning. I'm Sol Roberts." He offered his hand, and Jack shook it. "It's a real pleasure meeting Sugar's boy."

"Did you know him well?"

"Well enough to know he was a good man."

"What was so good about him?" Jack was beginning to wonder why Herm and his mother and now Sol Roberts said the same thing about Sugar.

Sol laughed. "Take my word for it. He was a good man."

"Like what?"

A glint appeared in Sol's eyes. "He was just one of those guys who stood out."

Jack didn't know what to say. He laid the box of shells he brought on the counter. "I found these shells. Are they still good?"

Sol took one from the box. "If you're going duck hunting."

"I'm interested in shooting bigger game."

"Deer?"

Jack nodded. "As big as deer or bigger."

Sol eyed him, then took a couple of boxes of shells from a shelf, and laid them on the counter.

"You'll do better with these."

Jack reached for his wallet.

"Don't worry about it right now. Take these." He slid the shells toward Jack. "Give me a couple of days, and I'll have the gun ready for you." He took the Browning off the counter.

"Is it going to cost much?"

"We'll talk about it when you come in next." The door chime dinged, and he moved on to help another customer.

Jack scooped up the boxes and left the shop.

It didn't take him long to reach Herm's house, which sat at the end of a long rutted drive. He only had a hunch that Herm could help him, but he felt drawn here. He was the only person who had shed any light on the Duncan family circumstances.

The morgue for dead tractors and rusted out farm implements of all shapes and sizes was more extensive in the light.

Jack wondered if the hospital dropped Herm out here to die alone. In such an isolated place, Herm could die, and no one would know it. Stepping onto the creaky porch, he knocked several times, but no answer. The doorknob twisted in his hand. It swung wide with a loud squeal.

In the half-lit hall, he peeked around into the narrow kitchen. Herm, dressed in flannel pajamas and a robe, sat at the breakfast table, legs crossed, a cigarette between his fingers as if expecting friends for coffee. He flicked ash into a glass dish on the table.

"It takes more than an iron bar to the head to kill me, Jack."

Herm had a single bandage around his forehead, and his gray hair was neatly combed. The puffiness around his eyes had receded. The wanness in his face had disappeared, and blushes of health marked his cheeks.

"You sure look better than the last time I saw you." Jack came into the kitchen.

Herm took a drag and blew out a long stream of smoke. He motioned for Jack to sit at the gray Formica kitchen table.

Jack took a seat. He pulled the Tupperware from his backpack and set it on the table.

"Your father was a real fan."

"Did you stick this under the seat?"

He nodded. "When I saw what direction it was going with the land, and your mother's money, I knew there wouldn't be much left, especially when she sold her piano. I knew someday you'd want these."

"Why did he collect so many?"

"He loved the game. You two had a lot in common." He pushed the plastic container toward Jack. "Keep these safe. They're some valuable cards in there."

"I'd like to ask you a few questions."

"Sure. As long as I don't have to get up, I got all day to talk."

Jack told him what happened with Chuey Lopez on the Kolcinivitch place when he went looking for their combine. And how Sheriff Grant had sent Kauffman around to force him to turn on Mr. Sanchez, and about his mother's blossoming anger.

"She thinks she can march in there with dad's old shotgun and force Kolcinivitch to cough up the combine."

"Tough deal with Adrian's father. A real tough deal for Shirley. It should never have come to this." Herm scratched his chin. "These shenanigans between the growers and the law have been going on around here a long time."

"That doesn't make it right."

"You look like your Pa when you talk that way, you know that?"

Jack didn't say anything, but stared back at the man, trying to understand in what way he was similar.

Herm tapped the table with his index finger and then pointed to something on the table. "You're more like him than you think." Centered on the table were a pair of glass salt and pepper shakers, a plastic napkin holder with *God bless this home* emblazoned in yellow over a pair of praying hands. Next to them lay a deck of red Bicycle playing cards. They were new except the paper seal had been broken.

"You play?"

Jack shook his head. "In my house, the devil carries a deck in his back pocket."

"The Devil's good at sleight of hand." Herm took the deck out of its package. "But he's far too impatient to be a good card player." He pointed at a cupboard and asked Jack to fetch a rack of poker chips. Herm parted out fifty chips each in neat stacks of ten, shuffled and dealt, two down. "One game, that's all."

Jack tapped the two cards face down then slid them to the middle of the table. "I need help figuring out what to do."

He slanted his head a bit as if he were trying to remember. "You need a lot of help, Jack. You just don't know how much."

"What do you mean by that?"

"Play one game of Hold'em with me, and I'll spill the beans." Herm pushed a pile of chips into the center of the table. "Hold'em's new to the valley, but its gaining popularity real quick."

"I've heard about it."

"It's deceptively simple, but it takes real skill to be good. A game I think you'll like."

Jack took up his two cards, the ace of clubs and king of clubs. He placed them face down and covered them with his palm. "Mom told me about the water rights and how badly Kolcinivitch wants that water. But everything else is a secret."

Herm studied his cards. "Your mother also says that gambling is the family curse, and that's the reason you've lost your land because Sugar was a betting man."

"Any truth to that?"

"He was a good man."

"People keep saying that."

Herm smoothed down his sparse gray hair. "It's a big story. I guess if you knew it from the beginning, you could decide for yourself what you want to do." He laid his cards face down on the table.

Jack eased back in his chair while the old man unwound. Sugar's father was a dirt-poor farmer in Vermont. When the Depression hit, Sugar wanted to go to Ag school, but there was no money. He found he could work his way through school playing cards.

"He had a gift, I've heard."

"Indeed." Herm shuffled the deck. "After college, he came to the valley to farm. He had little money but a ton of ambition. He won a small parcel in a card game and bought more as he was able. He built up quite a stake, and the land was cheap then."

"So he won the land playing cards."

Herm nodded. "He quickly turned from growing wheat and row crops to grapes. Growers from Eastern Europe had the expertise, and your dad learned quickly."

"What about his gambling?"

"After he met Shirley, he put that all behind him. He made his living from the land from then on. When you were born, his gambling days were far behind him."

"He didn't lose his land in a card game?"

Herm shook his head, becoming suddenly pensive.

"Why does my mom insist he did?"

"Because she doesn't want you involved in a fight that probably cost your father his life."

As much as Herm's statement took his breath away, it also clarified his mother's anger, her insistence that he not get involved. But with what?

"Does this fight have anything to do with that police report you showed me?" Jack tapped his cards.

Herm nodded. He reached across the table for the Tupperware container, pried it open, and carefully took out both stacks of cards. Inside was a folded-up piece of typewriter paper. He slowly unfolded it and handed it to Jack. The type had faded, but the words were clear and legible, a letter dated the year his father died and addressed to the membership of the Associated Farmers of the Central Valley.

"Who are the Associated Farmers?"

"Growers in the Central Valley who banded together to defeat every attempt by labor to organize. They were formed in the early thirties. You have to understand, back then there was a great social upheaval in California and the West. Farms were changing, becoming more corporate. The smallholders were being driven off their land by the Depression, and consolidation set in. The large growers worked hard to keep their labor under control. Immigrants were always abused by low wages and horrible working conditions. That's when communist organizers came into the valley to agitate.

"Growers were faced with a crisis created by their own greed. Instead of solving the labor problem by treating fieldworker's decently, they turned to tactics the Associated Farmers picked up in Europe. The leader had toured Germany in the 1930s. He watched as a demagogue political leader dominated opposition to his program through street brutality."

"What leader?"

"Hitler used the Brownshirts, a paramilitary force, to violently put down political opponents."

"What's that got to do with this Associated Farmers?"

"He organized the Associated Farmers along the same lines. He fired up the fear in local authorities, convincing them the communist organizers were on the verge of overthrowing the government in California once the labor strikes were successful. In 1933, Associate Farmers successfully broke the back of multiple strikes all over the Central Valley by deputizing thousands of civilians. They used violence to instigate a violent response. As soon as strikers fought back, cops came in and cracked down, arresting the strike leaders. It always ended up in a bloody mess. Of course, the growers won out. Communist agitators were arrested and run out of the valley. Some were given long prison sentences."

"I still don't get what this has to do with my father."

"The Associated Farmers weren't as strong in the '50s as they were in '30s, but the growers used similar tactics. Fomenting violence to drive out the strikers."

"What about communist agitators? The farmers claim all these unions are run by communists."

Herm shook his head. "Communists always gravitate to the injustice and exploitation of the workers. They see the exploited as fertile ground for their cancerous message. Farmworkers are treated miserably, and that always attracts radicals with ulterior designs. Communists have evil intentions for our nation, no doubt." Herm leaned over, earnestness in his eyes. "There would be no communist agitators in the valley if workers were treated fairly. There'd be no reason to agitate, and that's a fact. Your father had another solution, one that would disarm the radicals and bring true labor peace to the valley."

Jack perked up. "How would he do that?"

"It's in that letter." Herm pointed to the typewritten paper laid out on the table. "He mailed that out to all the farmers in the Association."

Jack read it over again.

"That's when things began to turn sour for him. Death threats—"

"What?"

"Threatening calls in the middle of the night. Vandalism on his ranch, that sort of thing. Shirley became unnerved. They wanted him out of the valley. But your father became more determined. At the next Association meeting up in Frisco, he read that letter to everyone. Called them out. He wanted them to put the field-workers on equal footing with all the other workers in the state. Give them their rights."

"That's when he got in that fight?"

Herm nodded. "He got a lot of big men mighty pissed at him, enough that a few would take some swings."

"All he's saying here." Jack swept his hand over the faded letter, "is that growers should take a new approach to labor. Treat them decently by building better housing, giving them better pay, open clinics for them, that sort of stuff. Give them the same rights as any other worker in the state. It's the same benefits they're asking for now.

"They were pretty much treated like disposable parts. When the grower was done with them, they'd discard them."

"Like cogs in a machine?"

"You could say that. Look, there's a lot more to Sugar's story. But right now we need to finish our game, and you need to figure out what to do about Adrian's father." Herm picked up all the cards and dealt a new hand. "Now, the best five-card hand wins."

"I know the rules," Jack said, taking up his two cards, an eight and deuce of hearts.

"Then you know it's your turn to bet."

Jack slid in a matching stack of chips.

"The first three community cards are the flop." Herm swirled out an ace of spades, eight of hearts, and a two of clubs.

"It's to you." Herm nodded at Jack. He threw in two chips. Herm called, but his hesitation stood out to Jack. Why would he hesitate to play two chips?

Herm flipped over the turn, an eight of diamonds.

"Pair of eights on the board." Jack now had two pair. One card away from a full house, the same hand he'd watched Adrian win with the other day. If Herm had an eight, three of a kind beat two pair all day, and that would lower the odds of Jack getting another eight on the river. Jack tossed five chips into the pot. Herm slid in five chips and raised it five more.

Betting hard as if he had something, Jack called. Herm floated the river card onto the table. A four of clubs.

The tension of the unknown thrilled Jack, a head-to-head competition of outwitting, out figuring, and being plain audacious. If that were real money on the table, there would be even more pressure. Like a big game where you won more than bragging rights.

Jack studied the up cards. He had two pairs, aces high. With three clubs on the board, Herm could have a flush or three of a kind. Either of them were winning hands. Jack rubbed his chin, figuring the odds. Herm carefully turned up the edges of his hole cards, considering his hand. The way he held his hands confused Jack. One laid on the table, palm clenched, while the other covered his mouth. Was that uncertainty? Was he just bluffing?

Jack checked. Herm slid in two stacks of chips. Jack looked around the room as if the solution he sought was written on a wall. He felt the same way he did when an opponent stole home in the ninth inning to win a game. He folded his cards.

"Flop your cards, Jack."

Herm laid out his five highest, nothing but an ace high. The old man sifted through Jack's cards. "You folded two pairs?"

Jack shrugged. "I knew you didn't have anything, but I couldn't be sure."

"The bluff will kill you every time. You have to believe what you see." Herm dealt another hand. "Trust what you know."

They played several hands, Jack learning to forgo his caution when he saw the signs. He had seen all of this for years on the back of the bus, watching his buddies play cards: bluffing, calling, and betting. They played on, Jack getting better at sniffing out a bluff, at figuring out Herm's cards, at seeing the patterns. His last hand he pulled in a large pot.

Herm gathered the cards from the table. "If you're so good at figuring out players' down cards, what hand is the sheriff playing? What's he got in the hole?"

Jack leaned back. "He said he'd arrest me if I don't turn witness against Mr. Sanchez."

"That's powerful for sure. But what does he have in the hole that would tell you he could actually do that?"

"He's got a witness who says I beat Chuey Lopez."

"Chuey Lopez is a labor contractor, a human parasite. He's an affliction upon the goodness of the land, skimming the sweat off his own people and selling it dearly. He wouldn't dare show up in court to testify he was beaten up. He's cheated half the laborers in this valley. If he's a hole card, he couldn't be more than a deuce, maybe a three."

"That still doesn't mean that the sheriff can't throw me in jail for a week or two just on a trumped-up charge. I'd be off the team and UCLA wouldn't offer me for sure. He's done it with so many farmworkers to keep them from striking."

"Now you understand firsthand the power of a strong bluff. How a man handles the bluff, Jack, determines the big winners and losers around here."

A point of pure insanity if that's all the sheriff was doing. "But how do I know for certain that's what he's up to?"

"Let's finish our game. Maybe you'll figure that out."

Jack considered his chips, just two short stacks. He hated losing, and this would be his last hand if he didn't figure things out.

Darkness filtered in the kitchen windows.

Herm dealt and started betting heavy. The old man loved to bluff, but Jack couldn't bring himself to put an end to Herm's charade. Caution taught patience, but caution also had its sharp edges. And it was cutting him open from the inside out.

As Herm dealt more cards, another pattern emerged. He could see the signs of a man's greed, bluffing to steal a pot. If a man were bold enough, he could own everything he set his eyes on. Bluffing was a game to Herm. Easy money lay on the table. Why not bet aggressively and take it home? But a voice of reason drummed in Jack's head.

Jack had to trust what he saw in front of him. The signs were everywhere—in his eyebrows, in the flick of a finger when he viewed his hand, in the roll of his eyes as he surveyed the board, in the folding of his hands, trying to appear calm. This wasn't anything Jack had to work at. But to trust that sense with his money would be hard.

Jack was down to his last ten chips when Herm called him all in. He had a pair of tens. With what he saw, Jack had the winning hand. Herm's bet was a desperate way to show him up. But a shrill voice told Jack if he went any further this would inevitably lead to the death of his dreams, of playing baseball, of attending college, or possibly his life. His mother's voice sounded like an army of boots marching through his brain.

Jack stared at Herm. The old man didn't even twitch a finger. A bead of sweat trickled down Jack's forehead. He wiped it away with the back of his hand. It was just a damn game, he told himself. But he hated to lose.

"Sometimes," Herm said, "all a man can do is go with his gut."

Jack took a deep breath and pushed in his remaining chips. Herm flipped his cards. His pair of sixes couldn't beat Jack's tens. Jack grinned as he raked in the entire pot.

Herm gathered the cards and stacked them neatly in front of him. "So do you think Sheriff Grant's bluffing you?"

"He had that bastard Kauffman show me the jacket and camera I left in the fields. He knew I trespassed on the Kolcinivitch's place and the fight. Kauffman also had a photo of our combine. He said he'd have it cut up for scrap if I didn't do what they wanted."

Herm folded his hands in front of him on the table. "So he's playing you."

The sheriff's game clarified. "I've got to find Sabrina."

"What good would that do?"

"She'd tell the truth. I know she would if she had a chance."

"You know where she's at?"

"We've already talked to her once. Ella and I brought her some medicine." He told Herm about the clothes and medicine they were going to take her tomorrow.

"If you can find her, take her to the police," Herm said. "The cops won't turn her over to the Border Patrol if she's a witness to a crime."

"I can't take her to the sheriff's office."

"Go to the Delano police," Herm said. "They are more sympathetic about investigating a crime. Make sure you have them write a report. I have a friend over there you can talk to." He scribbled a name on a piece of paper and handed it to Jack.

"That would get Adrian's father off the hook." Jack stuffed the paper in his pocket.

Herm grinned. "And you, too, my friend. It's one big game the sheriff's playing. So you have to have a plan if you can't find her by Monday."

"I don't know what I'll do if I can't find her. But if I do what Grant wants, I'll be in his back pocket like the growers around here have the sheriff in their pockets."

"Your father was his own man. He didn't let the local politics sway him. That's why I've always thought of him as a good man." He pointed across the table, raising his finger chest high at Jack. "Those are big shoes to fill if that's what you choose to do."

➤

AT HOME THAT NIGHT, in the upstairs farm office on the second floor, Jack slipped into the wooden office chair and rested his hands on his father's old desk. This is where his father must have written that letter. He leaned back in the squeaky chair. That letter must have surprised them, made them angry. Then the truth of what had happened to his father gripped him like an ancient curse. Those sons-of-bitches had found a way to silence Sugar.

Had they killed him?

Did they make it look like an accident?

He stood, pushing the chair back. He turned to the wall of old photos behind him. His smiling father reached out to him. He had never given much time to these old memories. But now they meant something to him. Then he spied the planter's hat on a hook above the photos.

He climbed onto the desktop, then reached across and grabbed the hat. Standing on the desk, he settled it on his head. Jack kept his hair short, so it fit a bit loosely. He climbed down and settled in the chair and surveyed the desk and old plat map of their land.

Sugar had built this place with his own hands and ingenuity. It may be gone now, thinned down to one acre and a house, but much of his father remained. People remembered him for who he was—a good man. Jack pulled the hat down over his brow and leaned back until the chair touched the wall. Were these memories enough to fill the empty spaces, the mean spaces, the gaps that haunted his life?

Chapter 18
Empty Roads

THE NEXT AFTERNOON AT St. Andrews, Mrs. Paulson, a short, put-together woman in a gray suit, who spoke with the force of iron, greeted Jack and Ella.

"Follow me."

In her office, she set herself up in her oversized leather chair and picked up a paper off her perfectly arranged desk. She read the letter from the elder board. It laid out the obligations the church had to its members and the broader community of Delano, "So at this time it could not allow any of its donated items to be handed over to migrants."

"It's just old clothes," Ella protested.

Paulson laid the letter down. "It's not the issue of the clothes, dear girl. I hope you understand that."

"Last week you said I could have whatever clothes and food I needed."

"Under normal circumstances, I would have been able to follow through on that promise." She shrugged her bony shoulders. "But there are larger issues that have been taken into consideration."

Ella looked over at Jack, who shook his head.

"What's changed, Mrs. Paulson? I don't understand." Ella cocked her head.

She pointed to the letter. "It's what the elders have decided is best for the members and for the community."

"How is not feeding and clothing migrant workers good for the community?"

She took off her glasses and set them on the desk. "That's the point the elders are making. They're migrants."

"They'll take the clothes with them when they leave."

"I'm positive that's the outcome the elders' desire."

"Are you saying you hope they do migrate?" Jack asked.

"The community hopes they leave." She touched the temples of her glasses.

"I don't understand." Ella's impatience grew on her face. "We just came for the clothes, that's all."

Mrs. Paulson cleared her throat. "What's become apparent in our church community, and is of significant importance to our larger community, is that if the migrants become too comfortable, they won't do what they're supposed to do."

Ella looked at Jack, who studied the older woman's face, trying to figure out her intentions.

Jack cleared his throat. "So what you're saying is because they aren't migrating you can't help them because it would make them too comfortable. And that's against your church's policy."

"That about sums it up." Paulson leaned forward, her arms resting on the desk. "They're supposed to migrate." She fluttered a hand in the air, "Like the birds."

"But these are people." Jack was having great difficulty understanding the issue.

She raised her eyebrows and stared at them across the desk with a steely smile, then rose.

"I see." A tightness crept across Ella's face. She looked down at her hands for a moment, then stood. It was apparent to Jack that she fought to control herself. He touched her arm and felt a tremor.

Jack didn't rise. "I have one question. Are most of the elders growers?"

Paulson sniffed. "Farmers, growers, businessmen." She dipped her head toward Ella. "Your father has been on the elder board in the past. They are all very responsible men who have the interests of the larger community to consider."

Jack rose. He followed Ella to the door. She turned to Paulson, who stood rigid, with a bony finger to her cheek.

"Didn't Jesus say to treat people the way you want to be treated?"

The woman tightened her wrinkled mouth. "Possibly we misunderstand the context of those remarks." After a moment's hesitation, she added, "I'll pass that question along to the elders. Maybe they'd be willing to clarify for you whom the 'people' are that passage refers to."

"That's not necessary." Ella's voice was clipped, certain. "I'm not certain I'll be coming back to hear what they think. Their opinion couldn't possibly be constructive…to the larger community. It would only salve their self-serving, penurious consciences."

Jack nudged her down the hall. If she stood there much longer, she'd get thrown out of the church before she could resign. In the car, Jack keyed the ignition and turned into the road toward the outskirts of town.

Ella stiffly stared out the window. In that woman's office, she was angry. Now she had an entirely different look to her, more focused and determined. "We still have the medicine you collected."

"Yeah. Wanna deliver it?"

"Damn right."

Jack drove slowly, letting the night creep over the land. The fieldworkers would be settling in, and the Teamster guards would retreat to their air-conditioned motel rooms for a Friday night of TV and beer drinking. The roads would be quiet.

Just after dark, Jack pulled onto the shoulder across from the gated dirt track leading to the migrant camp. He cut the engine. A dog barked somewhere.

"I know you're upset, but you can't let that old witch get to you."

"I've gone there my whole life, Jack." There was something final in her words. "I'm not going back."

"I wouldn't either. I'm sure you'll find a nice church somewhere."

"I mean anywhere."

He took her hand. "Maybe that's something you could think about tomorrow."

"Don't patronize me, Jack Duncan."

He held up his hands in a sign of surrender. "We'd better go. I don't want to be out here too late. We can talk about this later."

The gravel crunched under his boots, but she didn't move. He slid around to her side and opened her door. She stepped out. He grabbed a paper sack from the floor.

Under a faint glimmer of starlight on the two-wheel track, he led her down the dusty path into the migrant camp. The barking ceased when they entered the narrow lane between the first row of shacks. The odors of frijoles, lard, fetid beer, and urine thickened the air. Men covered in shadows shifted about in the night, slowly passing by, and some leaned against the worn planks of their hovels. The red butt of their cigarettes glowed as they passed. Jack felt their eyes on him.

Someone dumped a bucket of water in the dirt behind them. Jack wrapped his arm around Ella's waist and pulled her close. A high-pitched yowl of a singer's voice, the squeezing of an accordion, and the energetic strumming of guitars filled the night. Outside the door of Sabrina's hut, Jack noticed a shirt covered the window, and a yellow glow illuminated the fabric. He knocked.

"Who's there?" A gruff voice spoke in Spanish from behind the door.

"We're looking for Sabrina?"

A bare-chested man abruptly opened the door, the outline of his head visible in the amber light shining behind.

"Sabrina doesn't live here anymore." He spoke in rapid Spanish.

"Where'd she go?" Jack leaned around the man to peer into the hut. The stench of sweating bodies pushed him back.

He shook his head and waved his hand. "She left days ago."

"We need to speak to her. Does anyone know where she went?" He half-heartedly turned to the men inside then shrugged.

Jack held up the paper sack. "I have medicine for her mother."

The man grabbed the sack. "I'll take it to her." He slammed the door.

Jack cursed and slapped his open palm against the flimsy wood. Ella pulled hard on his other arm, and Jack turned. Men with slumped shoulders had come out of the shadows and moved around them in a half circle. A few pulled hard on their cigarettes, the butts turned angry and hot. The hardness of the day shone in their eyes. The accordion playing ceased. Ella clutched him, and he felt the beating of her fear right through her hands.

"Maybe you should leave, gringo."

"I was just trying to find the girl who used to live here." Jack motioned toward the closed door of the shack. "We brought her some medicine. Does anyone know where she went?"

"Maybe she went to pick cotton up in Tulare." A few of them laughed.

An older man, with a grizzled beard and weathered skin, stepped forward. "We don't know. A truck came for her the other day. They both went off. Maybe to the doctor, huh. We just don't want no trouble, okay."

"We're leaving." Jack held Ella's hand tight and moved through them toward the road. Behind them, someone squeezed an accordion, guitars played, and the strains of Ranchero music drifted in the air as he led Ella back up the lane. The night had turned to pitch. Clouds rolled in blanking out the moon and stars. Hand in hand, they stepped along the tire tracks, and gravel ground under their shoes. Only a hint of music reached them in the stillness.

This mess made him want to pack up and leave the valley right now. He didn't want to be around when his mother flipped out and did something stupid. As much as he didn't want to play the sheriff's game, what choice did he have? Grant had found a way to hide the girl. Herm had said he needed a plan. Jack had nothing.

Ella stopped and pulled him to her in the darkness. "Don't you dare think of giving up, Jack."

The two hugged on the dark road.

"Sometimes I wonder if I'm going crazy. The sheriff is always one step ahead of me."

Ella laid her head on his shoulder. "He's been doing what he wants for years. You can't let him stop you from doing what you want. It's the only way we can get out of this place."

Ella always excited him. Her obvious beauty. Her constant struggle to be heard. Her adventurous spirit. But today it was her refusal to be intimidated by that churchwoman, and tonight her strength of action. She wasn't at all afraid back there.

She lifted her head. "You'll figure it out. There's always a way."

He kissed her. She kissed him back. He held her tighter against the darkness. The two stood in the empty road kissing. Holding her warm body against his warded off the growing cold sweeping in from the fields.

Chapter 19
West Delano

WEST DELANO WAS THE rough side of a piece of sandpaper—streets of grit and potholes, trash overflowing in cans at curbs. Dead lawns if they had grass, old cars stacked four to a front yard, a tired looking place.

Early Saturday morning Jack parked in front of Adrian Sanchez's box of a house on Hadley, deep on the west side. Mr. Sanchez, an open-faced man, answered the door. He was cheery most times they'd met, but now he appeared drawn with fatigue. His work shirt and jeans were clean and faded.

"Adrian won't be back for a couple of hours."

"I didn't come to see him."

The man let him in. Jack sat on a sofa that had been old when his father was alive. The place smelled of beans and fresh tortillas, reminding him he hadn't eaten before leaving the house this morning. Mrs. Sanchez, a large woman in a brown housedress, ambled in and asked if he had eaten yet. Jack hesitated to answer.

"Why don't you get him something, Carlita?" He gave her a weak smile, and she returned to her kitchen.

Mr. Sanchez eased back in a threadbare rocker across the tight but orderly living room. Lace doilies covered a coffee table in front of him. Family photos were everywhere. Blue and red votives in front of an image of Our Lady of Guadalupe flickered, surrounding her serene face with an aura of red and blue in an otherwise dark corner. At least someone in the room was smiling.

In between bites of food, Jack told Mr. Sanchez how he had beaten Chuey Lopez and rescued Sabrina.

"This happened right after I saw you in the fields that day?" Mr. Sanchez asked.

Jack nodded.

"Adrian told me you were looking for your combine. But you wouldn't find it in the fields."

Jack told him about what happened in the shed, and his fear of being beaten. "I thought the Chuey guy was going to kill me. He had me on the ground. I said I needed work."

"Then later when Lopez chased me in the fields," Sanchez said, "that's when the girl tripped him?"

"Yeah." When Lopez tried to strangle her, that's when Jack jumped in and beat him.

Mr. Sanchez rubbed his stubbled face. "I outrun that Lopez burro all the time, so I expected this time would be no different."

"I'm in a situation I don't see how I can run from."

"And you think I can help you?"

"I need your help finding Sabrina."

"That girl you helped in the fields?"

Jack told him about the Sheriff Grant's threat to arrest him. "He knows I'm the one who beat the labor contractor, but he wants me to blame it on you."

"And if you don't?"

"He's threatened to arrest me for assault and battery. An arrest could risk everything I've worked for."

"And how will a scab help you? No doubt, she was bused here from the border. Whenever they want to turn her in, she'll be arrested and deported as an illegal. That's how gringo justice works in this county."

"If I can find the girl, I'll take her to the Delano police. There's a cop who'll take a police report. I'm hoping that will stop the sheriff from putting me up on false charges."

"Sheriff Grant is a snake who eats little lambs for spite. Snakes have ways of knowing things. If you know where she is, then so does he." He rubbed the back of his neck thoughtfully. "You say her mother's sick. The girl won't leave her. They must be together. I'll see what I can do."

"Thanks."

"Don't expect much, my friend."

The man's dour face spoke of more than fatigue.

"I didn't realize this would happen when I beat that guy."

His hard glare eased up a bit. "You did what you thought was right. That's all God asks of us. You told the cops the truth. That, too, is of God."

Did God care one ounce what he did or didn't do? Surely if God were concerned, he would have beaten Chuey Lopez himself. Maybe he could save a lash or two for Sheriff Grant.

Sanchez leaned back, rocking his chair. "I will make calls. Many of the ranches are filled with scabs from Mexicali so it will be difficult. But a sick woman with a daughter…" He shrugged. "We will see. And if Tuesday comes and you do not know where this girl is, what will you tell Sheriff *Loco*?"

Jack stood. "I'm not going to jail, Mr. Sanchez, and neither are you because of anything I will tell Sheriff Loco."

Mr. Sanchez stood and extended his hand, and there was a flash of gratefulness about his eyes. "It takes courage to be a man of truth." Mr. Sanchez rested his hand on Jack's shoulder. "I have prayed for you, my young friend, that Satan would not sift you as he has so many around here. And I see my prayers have been answered."

Jack left with a more confident step, something he hadn't brought into the Sanchez home. He didn't feel his usual impulsiveness to run on to something else. Resting his hand on his car door, he looked back at the pale yellow of the porch light. Is this where Adrian found his calmness?

➤

LATER THAT MORNING ON the Delano High baseball field, Jack warmed up his arm, throwing to Adrian. He followed the ball as it arced through the air and landed in his mitt. The field, his teammates, the ball hurtling toward him, appeared as an old newsreel, a record of events in someone else's life—two boys playing ball and the world around them, fuzzy on the fringes, enjoying the game. It didn't matter who sat in the stands, their color, or their clothes.

Then beyond the outfield fence, he spotted the tall stand of corn, softly waving green stalks brushed by a lilting breeze. The plants looked innocent and alive, but the men who grew them and those who picked them were at war.

"Hey, where's your brain, Duncan?" Coach yelled at him from across the field.

His attention snapped back to Adrian, standing arms akimbo, a look of frustration on his face. He pointed beyond Jack to the ball lying in the grass. Jack hadn't even noticed it fly by him.

Coach Dickey trotted over and stood beside him. "What's going on?"

"Nothing. Why?"

Coach eyed him with a narrowed look. "You're mind's not here, Jack. That's going to cost you tomorrow. It's your big day." He retrieved the ball from the grass and held it out to Jack. "See how small this is?" He held up the small round orb.

"Yeah."

"That's your planet." He dropped it in Jack's outstretched glove. "Live on it."

Jack dwelled on every throw, focused only on the moment, pushing out everything else.

After practice, he drove to Ella's house. He worked the man's hay field in the spring. Jack steered a tractor through the recently cut hayfield, his chest bare to the sun. The bailer bound up the dry stalks, cinched them tightly with wires, and spit them out in straight rows. He worked until just before dark.

He ate dinner with Ella and her folks. They were talkative, but Jack couldn't bring himself to laugh and chat at the table. He watched a movie with Ella but lost interest in it soon after it started. Ella sensed his unease. She knew he had a big game tomorrow. She sat beside him, holding hands, not saying much.

Before he left around ten, her father paid him in cash. He folded the bills into his jean pockets. Ella walked with him to his car. He knew she wanted to talk, but he kept to himself. They both leaned against the fender under the waning moon that loomed yellowish and silent over the fields. He held her slimness close to him, and they kissed.

"You seem somewhere else tonight." She laid her head on his shoulder.

"Thinking about tomorrow."

"It'll go fine. You'll see."

He drove off, his window rolled down, letting the warm air caress his face. He rode through town, slow and deliberate. Tired from his day's work, he could feel the fatigue in his body. It felt good. He needed to sleep. He wanted to sleep. He tried to forget.

He reached home after eleven. He was hoping his mother would be asleep. He didn't want to answer any more questions about what he did with the shotgun. He never told her about leaving it at the gun shop. Or how it would have probably misfired if she had tried to use it.

Shirley heard him come in and called to him from the living room. Slumped on the sofa staring at the TV, she watched scenes from the day's battles on the roads around Delano.

"You're so late. You have a big game tomorrow."

He stood behind the sofa, staring at the black-and-white figures as they flitted across the screen.

"How was practice today?"

"Bitchin."

"Jack, please."

The camera to panned the road, people milled about in a confusing melee behind a reporter. Then the camera focused on a teenager lying in the road in a pool of blood. "What's going on?"

"A striker was shot on a picket line today; another one was run down by a truck. It looks like he's going to be crippled."

"They're killing kids now?"

She looked up at him. "You need to get rested up for tomorrow."

"Who's that?"

The camera had switched to a gas station outside of town. A short Mexican man stood behind the building, surrounded by field-workers.

"That's Cesar Chavez. He's starting a fast."

"Why's he doing that?"

"He prays and fasts to get people to stop the violence."

Jack stared in fascination. Fasting wouldn't prevent growers from doing what they do best—provoking a violent response from the strikers. They wanted strikers to be angry. He didn't see what fasting would accomplish.

"He's sure got guts." Shirley stared at the TV.

"He's going to have to give up eating for the rest of his life to get people around here to stop shooting each other."

She turned to him again, the concern in her slender face palpable in her eyes. "I don't like that look you have, Jack."

He ground his teeth as he watched Chavez being interviewed, talking about peace and fairness and justice. It seemed to Jack that the man lived in his own world of unworkable dreams.

Chapter 20
Masterful

ABOUT NOON ON SUNDAY, Jack slipped into the front seat of Adrian's truck. The sun stood over them in a white heat. He thanked Adrian for driving out from town to pick him up, and his friend nodded with a sure smile. The game wouldn't start until late afternoon, but they both liked the early silence to prepare. As the truck bumped along, Jack closed his eyes, and his mind roamed wide over all that lay before him—another chance to play before a crowd and a scout from UCLA, Ella, and his mother. His life felt contained within the boundaries of a game he loved. One he had a mastery over.

Then there was the other game playing out in the fields surrounding him, one with uncertain boundaries and rules of greed and power. When he allowed himself to dwell on that game, he felt a smallness creeping over him. He had ribbed Ella, asking her if she had found where to put her "body on the gears of the machine." He hadn't thought any such machine existed. All her protest over being bit cogs in a larger mechanism that used and disposed of people in brutal anonymity was just Ella's mythmaking. He had to admit, she wasn't far off in her thinking. But who were these people with their hands on the levers?

"Oh, great!" Adrian said, studying his rearview mirror.

"What?" Jack turned to see what Adrian had spotted behind him. A Kern County Sheriff's cruiser made a wide U-turn, kicking up dust on the shoulder. It fishtailed briefly then its lights blared, and its siren blasted as it sped toward them.

"Were you speeding?"

"No. He passed us going the other way. When he saw me, he slammed on his brakes."

Adrian pulled to the dirt shoulder.

"Just play it cool." Jack slumped in this seat and watched the cruiser in the side mirror as it nosed up to the truck, gravel crackling under its tires.

"You play it cool," Adrian said. "Don't piss these guys off. We got a game to play."

"Don't worry. I'm Mr. Cool, man."

Adrian glared at Jack, and Jack returned an innocent smile.

A tall, lean, Stetson-wearing deputy strode toward his window.

Deputy Kauffman stood at Adrian's window. "Well, if it isn't the two French-fry brothers. What're you two up to this beautiful day?"

"Gotta game this afternoon," Adrian said, nonchalantly.

"Is that so? Well, we got some business to take care of before you guys get to have all the fun." Kauffman strode to the front of the truck, meeting the other deputy by the front bumper.

"What're they doing?" Adrian asked.

Jack shook his head, watching through the windshield as the two conferred. "This doesn't look good."

"Keep calm, okay," Adrian said, flashing Jack a nervous smile.

The tall, thin one came around to Adrian's side, and Kauffman strode over to Jack's window.

"Step out of the vehicle." Kauffman stood with one hand on his revolver.

"Why?" Just then, Adrian slapped his arm. Jack turned to his friend. He nodded for Jack to go. He opened the door and stepped into the dirt. Kauffman motioned to follow him to the rear of the truck. The two stood in front of the idling cruiser, under the blanching sunlight.

"What do you want, Kauffman?"

The deputy tugged his hat down over his forehead to shield out the bright sun.

"I was just on my way out to your place to deliver some bad news, Jack."

"Yeah." Random insults floated through his mind, but he promised his friend he would play it cool.

"The labor contractor has taken a turn for the worse."

"This world will be a much nicer place without him, I'm sure."

"I'm not going to dick around with you today."

"That would be hard for you to do any day."

Kauffman looped his thumbs over his duty belt and pursed his lips. "You seem fixated on the size of my manhood. That about right?"

"That's because I've never seen you do anything a real man would do."

"You know all about such things?"

Jack glanced down at his shoes and kicked at the dirt. He didn't want this moment to spin into something it shouldn't.

"I'm talking to you."

Jack glanced up at him. "I'm learning how things work around here, and I'm not sure I like it, that's all."

Kauffman squeezed his lips together as if he were thinking over Jack's words. He pushed an index finger against Jack's chest. "Here's how things work—you got till Monday at noon to testify against Mr. Sanchez in the assault of Mr. Chuey Lopez, or you'll face severe consequences."

Jack felt his pulse quicken, blood rushing everywhere. If he picked a fight, today's game would be shot. Coach Dickey needed him. His team needed him. Adrian would probably get beat up right here, too, if he got into it with this jerk. He calmed the throb of war rising in his stomach.

"Deputy Kauffman." Jack used his most placating voice. "Can I ask you something?"

The deputy seemed to relax, settling back on his heels, half-smiling. "Sure."

Jack looked him square in the eyes. "Have you ever done one decent thing in your life?"

The fist caught Jack in the stomach, doubling him over. The next punch to his left cheek twisted him around, sending him sprawling to the hard dirt. Lying on the ground, his knees up against his chest, he gulped air.

"Get up." Kauffman stood over him. When Jack didn't move, the deputy leaned down and grabbed him by the hair. Icicles of pain shot down his skull. Jack forced himself to his feet. Kauffman rudely shoved Jack toward the truck, pushed him through the open door, and slammed it shut.

The sun blazed through the windshield, and Jack slouched in the sullen heat of the cab. He held a hand to his throbbing cheek. If he stayed perfectly still, it wasn't so painful.

The other deputy probed Adrian from a long list of personal questions as he filled out a detailed form. It was a local practice of the sheriff to harass every farmworker they stopped. It took over an hour to answer the questionnaire. The sheriff compiled a cross-referenced, alphabetical card file on every farmworker in the valley—farms they worked, where they lived, cars they owned, family members, and affiliations. If the occasion arose, they rounded up any union member, or arrested any picket captain or organizer for any purpose they concocted. Information for their machine.

A sudden wave of nausea overwhelmed Jack. He leaned out the window and vomited.

➤

"What's going on?" Coach stood at the end of the row of lockers.

The two boys were alone in the locker room. Jack lay stretched out on the wooden bench, a sweatshirt under his head, and a wet towel covering his face. Adrian stood in front of his open locker, bouncing a ball in and out of his mitt.

"Just getting ready, Coach." Adrian tossed his mitt into his locker. "It's really hot. Just wanted to take a cold shower before the game."

Coach did not pay any attention to Adrian. Jack heard his heavy steps come toward him. He stood over Jack. "You taking a bath?"

"Trying to keep cool, that's all." Jack folded his arms over his chest.

He lifted the towel off Jack's face. Coach's dark eyes fixed on the purpling bruise on his left cheek. "What the hell happened to you?"

"We were out fishing this morning, and Jack fell. Almost lost him in the canal."

"Adrian saved my ass, Coach."

"No one can save your ass, Jack." He shook his head slowly, displeasure in his voice. Coach gave Adrian a disbelieving look. "Don't give me another damn fish story."

Jack pulled the cloth back over his face. He heard the usual sigh Coach gave when he wasn't happy.

"UCLA called. They're sending a man up." Coach pushed his ball cap back on his head, and folded his arms, looking like a hard crust of bread.

"Someone else besides Kish?" Jack asked.

"Kish likes you. What you gotta do is like yourself enough to stay out of trouble."

"I like myself just fine. It's the folks around here causing trouble who don't like me."

"You can't let losers get to you. Just pitch lights out today, and you're headed to LA in a couple of months. This'll all be behind you."

Coach paced for a minute beside him. He whipped his cap across his pants leg in frustration. "With so much going today, how could you get in another fight?"

"Honest, Coach," Adrian said. "We were minding our own business this morning, driving to school early to get in some extra work, and the cops stopped us."

He turned on Adrian. "A cop did this?"

Jack sat up slowly, drawing away the towel. "You got it."

Coach rubbed his bottom lip. "What did you say to him?"

"You're assuming I did something wrong," Jack protested.

"In your case, I got a right to assume."

Jack hesitated, then said, "He was hassling us, and I just questioned his decency, that's all."

Coach folded his arms over his chest. He glanced at Adrian then back at Jack, looking like he was thinking over his words. "Did he piss you off?"

"Yeah," Jack said. He told Coach about the hour Adrian spent answering all those stupid questions.

Coach put his arm around Adrian and nodded to Jack. "You both had a right to be pissed off today. Now you boys take it out on those poor bastards coming in here to play ball. You got it?"

Jack grinned. "Yeah, I got it."

"All right," Adrian said, smiling for the first time that day.

"Winners know how to channel their energy. And you guys are winners." Coach spun and stormed down the row toward his office. At the very end, he stopped abruptly and turned to the boys. "What you did today, Jack, probably wasn't such a bad thing."

"Oh!"

"You gotta have some decency to know when others don't. And being decent isn't a crime—yet." Then he disappeared around the corner.

Adrian laughed and grabbed his mitt off the bench. In a moment of levity, Jack laughed, too. He found his glove and Adrian tossed him the ball. Jack lobbed it back, and he felt a surge of something good run through him. They both stood in the aisle and backed up, tossing it harder and harder.

"You did good, Jackie boy." Adrian flashed a broad grin of satisfaction.

"You did even better, Adrian, my boy." Jack felt strong as if every bit of energy on his best days flowed through him. He tossed the ball harder; his arm, loose and fluid, came alive. Today was going to be a good day.

With a couple of hours to go, Jack and Adrian talked and laughed and let the outside world disappear in its meaningless stupidity.

An hour later, Jack and Adrian dressed out. Kauffman, the sheriff, and the combine were over the horizon. He took a baseball from his locker and worked it hard in his palm, practicing where to place his fingers for a slider, for a fastball, for a curve. He studied the stitches, feeling the pattern over the leather surface. He concentrated on how to make it curve or sink; how to make it do his will. That is what mattered today.

He ran in the outfield, limbering up as he jogged. He played toss with a teammate, feeling the magic in his arm. In the dugout with the pitching coach, he went over the Corcoran team that had just arrived. They had played these guys already this season, so he knew the players reasonably well. They had a few decent hitters, but their guys were suckers for the sinker and sissies when it came to his inside heaters.

A familiar voice called to him from the bleachers.

"Jack." Ella stood with her fingers looped in the chain-link backstop. He trotted over and twined his fingers in hers. "I saw the UCLA coach." Her brown hair riffled in the breeze.

"He better have a scholly with him."

"Did you get in a fight?" She stared in concern at the bruise on his cheek.

"Nah!" But he didn't say more.

She fixed him with her green eyes. He could see her restraining her skepticism. "You're going to pitch lights out today."

He stood tall. "Lights out, babe."

"Jack, get over here and get warmed up," Marty yelled from the top dugout steps.

Jack hustled over and began throwing to Kolcinivitch. His mother stood by the chain link bordering the bullpen and called him over when he finished. She wore a flowery sundress and wide-brimmed floppy straw hat that hid her face from the sun. They talked through the wire.

"Good luck today." Shirley had a gleam of excitement in her eyes.

"What's going on?"

"Sheriff Grant found our combine. It's safe, thank God. He sent Deputy Kauffman to tell me. But before he returns it, the sheriff wants to talk to you."

Jack hitched a deep breath. "Just tell him to hand it over. It belongs to us."

Shirley wiped the corner of her mouth with her index finger and glanced away. The look in her eyes told him she worried about his ignorance of how things worked.

"He's the law." Jack rested his mitt hand on his hip. "Tell him to do his job."

"They're going to arrest Mr. Sanchez anyway."

"How do you know that?"

"Deputy Kauffman just—"

"Kauffman's a born liar. I can't believe you listened to that butthead."

Shirley narrowed her eyes at him. "Deputy Kauffman will drive it down to Lacy's himself tomorrow night. If you show up and talk with the sheriff."

"I spoke to Kauffman this morning. I already told him to go to hell, so he left me with a beauty mark." Jack pointed to the bruise on his cheek. He stared into his mother's eyes until she broke away.

"Jack," Marty called to him. The team was lined up on the foul line for the national anthem. He trotted away. He was not going to play the sheriff's game, so he would just have to see how it sorted out with the cops.

A sophomore girl sang the national anthem without reaching any high notes. The teams, hats over their hearts, stood in the sunshine under a blanket of hot light.

As the Delano team ran to its positions, Adrian gave Jack an encouraging pat on the shoulder. "Take it to these chumps."

After throwing his warm-up pitches, the ump called for the first pitch. Jack stared down at the batter as he stepped into the box. Marty flashed him the signs. Jack stood tall, the mitt and glove to his chest. The bleachers were packed. People milled around on the grass, their chattering settling over the field in a hovering buzz while the stifling breeze whipped banners and flags.

What existed across that chalk border became a foreign land. Jack took a calming breath. Leaning into his stretch, he let loose as the hitter waggled his bat impatiently. The ump signaled a strike with an emphatic pump of his fist. Before his second pitch, he caught the sight of the powder blue cap of the UCLA coach. The man stood behind the backstop, directly in line with home plate, clipboard in hand, staring right at Jack, a look of ragged skepticism on his face.

For the next five innings, Jack displayed every pitch and strategy he had worked to master since little league, striking out six and inducing harmless grounders that were vacuumed up by his infield. He set up batters with his inside pitches that made the weak jerk away; he flirted with every corner of the plate, low and high, with curves and sinkers that made the Corcoran boys lurch and twist. Yet it still was a scoreless game. Several times, he spotted Kish smiling after he charted a pitch. The man stood for every throw, then crouched low to see the movement of the ball.

As his teammates batted, Jack watched the opposing pitcher closely, intent on the game. The Corcoran hurler made one great pitch after another. A commotion broke out in the stands. Some shouting. Maybe a huelga or two, but he didn't care. He locked his mind on the ball, watching the opposing pitcher, noticing where he placed it, keeping it out of the reach of the Delano hitters.

In the sixth, Jack set up the three batters with a flurry of fastballs, some inside, some away, then came back with slow pitches that dipped and curved to confuse their timing. It only took thirteen pitches to finish them off. As he trotted to the dugout, he saw an unfurled banner at the top of the bleachers. Cops lined up, and he heard the chanting.

He stepped over the foul line and took a spot on the bench next to Adrian. He placed a towel over his head then held his hands to his ears. Only the game existed; only pitches in the strike zone mattered; he lived on the clay mound.

Jack cheered on every Delano batter even with his head covered. The game stood locked in a scoreless tie until the bottom of the sixth when Marty looped a hit to shallow center, and Adrian followed with a double off the plywood fence. When Marty crossed home, he pushed the catcher out of the way instead of sliding under him.

The Corcoran bench rose, and a few fellows shouted, but Coach gave the team the eye, so none of the Delano players stirred. The boys shook Marty's hand as he strode down the bench, taking a seat by Jack.

Coach patted Jack's back as they headed out. "Three more outs and your deal is sealed."

With Delano up one to nothing, Jack took the mound for the top of the seventh inning. He could end it right here.

Marty called for a pitch, and Jack nodded. Working fast he delivered a high one out of the strike zone right at the batter's chin, close enough to shave him. The boy jerked back. The ump came around and stared Jack down but didn't say anything. The next two were at the kids' belly, making him twist like a pretzel. The ump trotted to the mound. Coach hustled over, and Marty followed.

"You hit him, I'll kick you out. You're pitching too good to buy in to this nonsense."

Jack held the glove by his mouth and listened. The ump jogged off.

Coach trotted to the mound, took the ball from Marty and handed it to Jack. "Show Kish your command here. Strike this guy out."

The heat worked into his muscles. Sweat dripped down from under his hatband. His world smelled of dryness, grapes, and victory.

Here it was, the day he had dreamed of, and the next victim stood sixty feet away, waiting to be put out of his misery. Fear floated in the batter's eyes, uncertain what Jack would do.

He hurled a fastball, the hardest one of the day. The boy's bat didn't even move. Then he fed him a curve that dumped down at the plate. The boy twisted with his swing but came up empty. Jack could hit a gnat at sixty feet today. Focusing on a speck of air above the narrow plate, he wound and threw with a focused rhythm. His confidence put a harder spin on the ball. Folks cheered with every strike, and his power came on stronger.

Corcoran was down to its last strike. Jack leaned in, watching Marty move through the signs. He nodded, tugged on the brim of his hat, and settled his feet. This was his party. He wound up and blew it by the Corcoran player who stood slack-jawed at the ump's call then tossed his bat in the dirt in disgust. Jack clenched his fist in jubilation and jumped up and down. The home crowd cheered, the bench erupted; Adrian wrapped his arms around him from behind and hugged him tightly.

"Great game," Adrian shouted over and over.

The celebration continued on the field with his teammates and the Corcoran boys shaking hands. Just before he trotted off to the showers, Coach Kish stood before him with a broad smile and held out his hand, and Jack gripped it.

"Masterful."

If the man said anything besides that one word, Jack didn't hear it. But that one word crawled inside him and carried him up, he floated around, shaking hands. Ella found him in the crowd and hugged him.

His mother came over and kissed him on the cheek. "Good job," she said, forcing herself to smile. "You have what you've always wanted."

Chapter 21
Long Night

JACK TOOK HIS TIME in the locker room, shaking hands with teammates and their fathers, taking his time dressing, letting the players filter out until Coach called him into his office. Kish wanted updated transcripts. If everything checked out, the offer would come in the mail—a full ride.

Coach cracked a broad smile, rehashing the highlights of the game. Jack let the conversation drag on as Coach rehearsed his pitches, pointing out the good and the bad. He nodded, encouraging the man to give a full blow-by-blow analysis. He wanted to cross an empty lot to Adrian's truck.

He would deal with his mother and her disappointment when he got home. Right now, even Sheriff Grant and his threats existed in another world. Jack was going to LA in a few months, and nothing would change that.

As far as he could see, arresting him for beating Chuey Lopez was something that wouldn't stick. Local courts rarely convicted white guys of assaulting Mexicans. It just didn't happen. All the witnesses to the beating were in the country illegally. They wouldn't dare testify against him. Grant and Kauffman's threats were nothing but a big bluff.

By the time Coach had finished scrutinizing his game and congratulating him, a couple of hours had passed. Adrian would be sitting in his truck waiting. When Jack crossed the empty lot, he spotted Adrian by the front bumper talking to a girl. Was that Darcy? What was she doing here? Right after the game, in the crush of excitement, Ella had found him and invited him and Adrian to her house for dinner. She and Darcy would be home now getting ready.

"Hey, what's up?" He called to her, but the girl didn't turn. He dropped his gym bag and moved beside Adrian.

"Hey," he said. Her face was hidden in shadows so he didn't recognize her. In the tick of silence that followed, she raised her eyes. He stood speechless in the twilight.

"I didn't think you would remember me." She wore the same jeans and blouse as the day he met her in the fields. The hard edge of her voice brought everything back. "Sabrina." Her tight smile reminded him of the girl who defied Lopez.

"You are looking for me, muchacho?"

"We brought some medicine for your mother the other day, and they said you'd gone away."

"That sheriff made me lie. That I see another man, a UFW hombre, beat Lopez," she said, standing beside him with her hands in her pockets.

"That was Adrian's father." Jack nodded toward his friend.

"Sí, I know that now."

"Why did you do that?" Adrian asked.

"He tells me we'd get medicine if I say things. So I did. Then they moved us to another ranch. The place is worse than a pigsty."

"He knows where you're staying?"

"He knows since the day you nearly killed that *cholo.*"

"What did you tell the sheriff?"

"That Lopez attacks me, and you come over and hit him. He said I'm lying and need to go back to Mexico. But I tell him my mother will die if we have to get on that bus. And he says he can get her medicine if I help him." She shrugged, and a sad frown wrinkled her forehead. "What do I do?"

Jack rubbed his neck

"You don't just lie about people." Adrian said. "My father wanted to help you."

"I'm sorry, amigo." Her look turned sad. "My mother is very sick. It has been a week since she had medicine. The sheriff promised more, but he is a liar."

It all began to turn red around the edges of his mind—Kauffman's threats, his father dying on a highway, and Grant's game of toying with fragile lives.

"Where's your mother?" Adrian asked.

"When I hear there is medicine at the old place, I pay someone to drive us back. When we come, it is gone."

Jack figured that would happen. "Don't worry, I can get you more."

She smiled for the first time. "The patrón has your tractor."

"You've seen it?"

"I saw it with my own eyes yesterday when I work in the sheds. They are cutting it up. The welders in the shop slice it up like *carne asada*. Soon it will be scraps for the dogs." She told him about the shed where they stored the grape lugs in the warehouse next to the big shed where the welders work and seeing it driven into the large shed early on Saturday.

Everything tightened inside. The lies, the threats, the pressure on his mom formed into an unforgiving knot. He had what he wanted, but letting those men get away with stealing the combine would be the same as spitting on his father's grave.

"You must take it tonight."

"Tonight?" Jack squirmed inside.

"How can we do that?" Adrian looked from Sabrina to Jack.

"Sunday they drink like *pescado* all day and gamble like *tonto* all night. They come home before dawn. Once they are asleep, nothing will wake them." Sabrina leaned against the truck, a weariness in her eyes. "I need the medicine rápido."

"I'll call Ella, and we'll get more." Jack wiped his mouth. He could reach the large shed by the north road, which would be a long drive into Delano for the combine. He had to get started soon. It wouldn't take all night if he had help hauling it away.

"Can you take me to it?"

She nodded. Once the combine was safe, he could tell that lackey Kauffman exactly where to go. He'd like to drive that damn machine right over that self-righteous prig's back and send him there.

➤

THEY DROPPED OFF SABRINA at a café in Delano. Both the boys scrounged through their pockets and came up with enough cash so she could buy a burger and drink while she waited for them to return with her medicine.

"It's too dangerous, Jack." Adrian drove away from the café, toward Ella's house on the east side of town. "I can't get caught on growers' property."

"Look, if we do it right, we can put to bed everything Sheriff Grant has against both of us. Sabrina won't lie anymore, as long as she has medicine. That takes your father off the hook. And Kauffman won't be able to hold the combine over my head."

Adrian heaved a heavy breath. "It'll take all night to drive that thing into town."

"Not if we trailer it. But we need a big one." Jack rubbed his chin thinking.

"Barton's father has one," Adrian said.

"Yeah, but we'd have to find him, explain everything, and get it out of the yard without his old man seeing us."

"Yeah, that won't work."

"I know where one is." Jack cracked a mischievous smile.

"Where, on the dealer's lot in town?"

"Herm's place. I saw a big one at the far end of his junkyard."

"He'll let us use it for sure."

"Why ask?" Jack patted the dashboard. "We'll eat with the girls, then get away early and get this done."

They stuffed themselves at Ella's but begged off staying late, complaining about their exhaustion. Jack had taken Ella aside and told her that Sabrina had shown up. Before Jack left, she gave him another box of medicine and promised she would find more. They picked up Sabrina at the café, then shot out to Herm's place to hitch up the trailer.

Within the hour, they had backed up to the trailer that had been custom-made for hauling wide loads. While the boys hitched it up, they expected a light to go on in the house just fifty yards away. But all the windows remained dark. If he was home, he was sleeping soundly. If he saw them, he was letting them be.

"We have to be off the roads way before dawn," Adrian said. "This load will attract attention."

Adrian drove the long way around, so they turned into the county road that bordered Kolcinivitch Ranch heading east. They dropped off Sabrina with her medicine at the entrance to the migrant housing. She assured them she left the back door to the large shed unlocked. Inside Jack would find his combine.

Farther down the county road, Adrian eased the truck and trailer into the shadow of a lemon grove and doused the lights. About a quarter mile back, they had passed the dirt farm road leading directly to the row of sheds.

"I know exactly where it's at. You stay here. I'll get it and drive it out."

Adrian had to stay in the truck. Jack told Adrian if he saw a ruckus going on, he had to assume his friend had been caught. He was to light out. Jack would find a way to talk himself out of trouble. Besides, his house was a mile or so on the other side of the vines. He could just hightail it through the fields. They'd never find him.

"When you hear me coming down the road with the combine, pull the trailer to the middle of the road. I'll ride right up, and we'll take off. This won't take long."

"Just hurry. This thing's an eyesore. If anyone comes along, they'll see it for sure. Who knows what'll happen."

"I won't be long." Jack quietly slipped out into the night.

At a loping run, he made his way through the vines. Under the dull glow of a quarter moon, he crouched by a grapevine, deep in Kolcinivitch property. Between the branches, he could make out the roofline of the sheds. Staying close to the farm road, he worked his way through the vines. He stopped often, listening for guards, but only heard crickets and frogs.

He shimmied under the last row of vines and squatted beside a wall of corrugated metal. The farm lane went down the middle of the row of sheds. The largest one sat at the far end. It was the same shed where he had met the welders and encountered the labor contractor weeks before.

After scrabbling through the vines, he stood by the back door of the largest shed. An inkling that Chuey Lopez hunched inside, waiting, crossed his mind. He doubted Sabrina would set up an ambush, but then she was desperate to get her mother medicine. Maybe the labor contractor bent on revenge had induced her to lie again. But the girl hated Lopez. She would never trust him. She promised the back door would be unlocked. He turned the knob. It opened.

He stepped inside and closed the door slowly. Submerged in darkness, he held still, listening. His eyes adjusted to the pitch dark. A shadowy outline of a boxy machine appeared. He took a step, nearly tripping over something. It rolled away, clanking metal on metal. He halted and breathed deeply to calm the thumping inside. Retrieving his flashlight from his back pocket, he flicked it on. Irrigation pipe lay strewn everywhere. He played the beam in the dark space ahead until he illuminated a slab of dull green metal—the combine.

Working through a maze of pipe, sprinkler heads, valves, and wooden crates, he reached the welder's workstation. He didn't like what he saw. The combine hunched in the darkness, its rotary thresher blade in pieces in the dirt. Not unbolted so it could be sold for parts, but blowtorched off. Two steel nubs protruded like severed limbs. Jack could have turned in Cesar Chavez himself for trespassing, and Sheriff Grant would never have returned this machine.

He spit in the dirt.

He climbed into the cab, choked it up, pumped the brakes, and checked the gear setting. He flipped the ignition; it turned over then died. He pumped the gas and tapped on the gas gauge. He prayed it would be enough to get it to the road where he'd trailer it out. He flicked the ignition again; it stuttered then turned over. It was drivable if he babied it out of here. Jack shut it down, slid to the ground, and turned to the sliding doors. When he played his light over the path to the double doors that led to the overhead door, he groaned in defeat.

Directly behind the combine were tall bales of heavy trellis wire. Behind them and all the way to the door were stacks of grape gondolas stacked to the ceiling. The lane was blocked entirely. A slow burn flamed inside. It might take him all night to move this stuff, but he was leaving with this contraption if he had to tear the entire shed apart.

Already 1:00 a.m., he figured it could take a couple of hours to clear the path. The fastest way he figured would be to push the wire to the side. After wrestling the first wire bale off its flat end, he rolled it away. Its momentum carried it off, stopping with a thud. He pushed over another one so he could roll it away. He leaned hard into it; they drove it forward until it cleared out of the way.

The hard, plastic gondolas were a big problem. They were stacked at least twenty feet high. If he shoved a stack and it fell, the racket would wake the dead. He found a folding ladder and placed it beside a stack. He tried lifting the top five feet, but he couldn't balance them as he descended. There had to be a simpler way. The trays were arranged in eight rows across the dirt path and six rows deep: It would require a huge effort to move them section by section.

He would have to stack them on top of equipment that lay to the right of the gondolas. He could push the piles over one at a time. Any of the plastic tubs that remained, he could run over. It would be noisy, but he had to get out of here. He hadn't seen any guards, but that didn't mean they weren't around. He couldn't think of any other way that wouldn't take all night.

He'd already been at it for over an hour when he positioned himself alongside one stack and reached his hand between gondolas. He froze when he heard the back door open then shut softly. Jack flicked off his light and stood motionless. The pipes by the door rattled as someone walked over them. He slowly reached down for a short-handled hoe just in case.

"Jack," came a whisper.

He flashed his light at the visitor. "Adrian. You're not supposed to be here."

"I saw Kolcinivitch's Caddy come down the road. He was swerving all over the place."

"He's supposed to be playing cards."

"He must have left the club early. He was driving all crazy. What's taking you so long?"

"Did he see the truck?" Jack knew the risk his friend was taking even stepping on Kolcinivitch property, but here he was.

"I don't know how he could miss it. But he's so drunk he probably didn't think anything of it. Down the road, he braked hard then swerved onto a farm road. He's probably home in bed. What's taking you so long?"

Jack flashed his light on the stacks of gondolas. "I moved the wire. But this could take hours."

"Give me the light."

Jack handed it over.

Adrian searched the gondolas, up and down. He slid beside them to the front of the shed by the door. The beam flitted around. Jack heard a creaking of metal wheels rolling in the dirt.

"Over here," Adrian called.

"What is it?"

Adrian handed the flashlight to Jack.

"A pallet jack." Adrian rolled the jack over. "Shine it on the very bottom."

Jack illuminated the wooden slots at the bottom of the first tall stack. Adrian expertly maneuvered the pallet jack, sliding it under the first tall stack of plastic containers. In a couple of minutes, he moved six pallets out of the way. Adrian stowed the tool while Jack mounted the driver's seat. Adrian stood next to the combine.

"Don't start it until I check the road. I'll flash the light once to let you know it's clear. Then bring it out."

Jack heard the door rolling away then starlight twinkled in the opening. The light flashed. Jack turned it over, gunned it once, then slid it into reverse and eased off the brake, letting it roll back. Outside in the middle of the lane, he halted and pushed the gear into drive. It jerked forward threatening to stall. Jack feathered the gas until it crawled. Even then it jangled and jerked on the rutted road, hankering and creaking as though it knew its age. It was so noisy inside the cab, it would wake someone for sure. When he opened the throttle, the motor sputtered, so he backed off, but it gained a head of steam on the flat lane. Once underway he knew the sudden lightness of achievement. Already he could see himself striding into his mother's kitchen and slapping a check on the table. It would change her world.

Adrian trotted beside him, painting the thin beam onto the dark road. They cleared the row of sheds. The county highway lay a quarter mile or so ahead. He blinked into the inkiness, hoping to see the road.

Tensed with all the jiggling and jarring, he jerked when a dark figure jumped out of the vines. Adrian pulled himself up onto the step. Straining forward, Jack searched for the county road. Low on the horizon, the moon gave the farm road a faint silvery glint.

The fields lay silent. A shallow pool of light glimmered on the blacktop dead ahead.

"I'll get the truck."

Just then headlights passed on the road then taillights flashed by, heading toward town. Adrian froze. Jack slipped it into neutral.

"Could you make out the car?" Jack asked.

"It's just a passing car," Adrian said. "Let's keep to the plan." He jumped off and sprinted away, disappearing down the paved road. By the time Jack reached the road, Adrian would have the trailer parked with the gate down so he could drive it up and in. Then off for Delano.

The cold moonlight shimmered on the pavement. He gripped the wheel. A few more rows of vines and they'd reach the shoulder of the road. He needed more speed to make the rise. He throttled it up, but the motor coughed, and the machine vibrated. He backed off then coaxed the throttle forward. Jack could only imagine the rage on Kolcinivitch's face when he found the combine gone.

Out of the corner of his eyes, he glimpsed movement on his right. Probably Adrian coming back to tell him something. Jack plunged the throttle full open, willing the metal hunk to move, but it hesitated, jerked, and then caught. The shadow reached the combine and jumped. Jack leaned forward, urging the machine on, his heart a piston surging toward an explosion. Reaching the incline the combine slowed just as thick, work-hardened hands squeezed his throat. Jack lost his grip on the steering wheel as he struggled to breathe. He grasped the hands clenched to his throat, willing to tear them away. The machine lost momentum and began to slip backward. He gasped for air. A heavy body pulled him off the seat; he plunged out of the cab and slammed to the ground.

Splayed on his back, dizzy and breathless, a field of bright lights sparkled in his vision then dissolved. Jack smelled the alcohol before he spotted the outline of a man blocking the moonlight. The man raised something over his head. Jack, the fuzziness of his brain slowly clearing, struggled to move. He rolled over, slid against a vine, and something hard whipped across his back. It struck from shoulder to kidney, awakening every nerve, a bruising stampede of pain stormed through him. Jack curled up, covering his head with his hands. The rod lashed his back, sometimes missing and hitting the dirt beside him, then lashing him repeatedly. Then it stopped.

Shivering in a tight ball, he heard a struggle.

"Hey, you, let go," the man with the stick yelled.

Jack uncurled and behind him two men struggled, shadows wrestling over something, grunting, swearing, and scrambling about. The fighting stopped, and footsteps took off up the farm road and turned onto the blacktop.

"You punk, come back here!" The man sounded clumsy, his steps halting, but he pursued, grunting and swearing. Something clanged on the blacktop and bounced away.

That must have been Adrian! Fighting the throbbing ache, Jack pushed himself to his feet. Limping and breathing hard, he made it to the pavement, but both men had disappeared into the darkness. Adrian must have led him off into one of the groves. The putrid stench of alcohol lingered. If the man were as drunk as he smelled, he would never catch Adrian. That boy could fly.

This guy wasn't Chuey Lopez. He hadn't spoken with an accent. He doubted that Kolcinivitch himself would come out into the vines. Not on a Sunday night after drinking and playing cards. Jack took a few steps and kicked at something. It scooted away with a clatter. A thick grape stake, the one used to beat him. Adrian must have wrestled it away from him, and then taken off. He picked it up and gripped it, thick and powerful in his hands. A grape stake with a sharpened end. Just the thing to run through that man's heart if he came back.

The combine. Where was the combine? Jack ran back onto the farm road and found it about twenty yards down the lane where it had veered off into the vines. The motor had stalled. He reached for the handhold to lift himself up, still clutching the stake. Uneven footsteps pounded toward him. The man weaved and huffed, but his steps were dogged.

That guy had already yanked Jack out of the cab once. So Jack stepped into the shadow of a grape trellis, crouched and waited. He gripped the stake like a lance. The big man trotted up beside the combine and clumsily climbed into the cab, his back to Jack. His wide shoulders, neat khakis, and a shirt too nice for a field worker said he wasn't the labor contractor. He could be a Teamster guard.

The man began a slow hoist up to the cab. If Jack allowed this guy to drive it off, he and his mother would join the homeless. Gripping the stake hard, he rose on his haunches, burst down the row in three bounding steps, and caught the thief in mid-stride just as he stepped into the cab. Jack stabbed the man's outstretched arm holding the steel grip.

He cursed wildly and flew around. The man's broad face, receding hairline, and red-rimmed eyes of greed seemed familiar. His thick body twisted, hanging in the air by his fingers on the grip. Then he steadied and lowered himself from the combine's step. Feet apart, as if ready to take charge, he shook his right arm, flexing it up and down. Jack clenched the stake and pointed at the man.

"I'll kill you if you come here again." The edge to the man's gruffness sent chills through Jack. He backed farther into the darkness. He couldn't bury the niggling fear that mean-fisted ranch hands were sneaking up behind him. He could take off; he could easily outrun this guy, but he'd never see the combine again.

"Come on, punk, let's see what you got." His voice taunting, and his words slurred, the big man struck his breast with his fist, a grape-growing gladiator, and lunged forward. Jack thrust the rod at the man's legs, but he grabbed it in midair, ripped it out of Jack's hands, and flung it away. It rattled against the combine behind him. In a wrestler's crouch, the man attacked and Jack back-pedaled, dodging sweeps of his long arms in the narrow lane between the trellises. In the shadows between the vines, he tripped Jack, hurling him onto his back on the hard-packed earth. The man stomped Jack on the stomach, a spike of pain shot through his chest, and he fought to catch his breath.

Just then, the combine's motor turned over several times then fired up. Someone gunned the engine and put it in gear. Jack's attacker turned and ran, cursing as he went. Jack inched up on his elbow and breathed deep, an ache shooting up into his ribs. The combine had disappeared from the end of the row. He forced himself to rise and hobbled after them. He tripped over the grape stake. He steadied himself, grabbed the stake, and jogged up the farm road. The machine rolled slowly up the dirt lane. In the moonlight, he caught the outline of the big man leaning into the cab.

He was attacking Adrian. Jack sprinted, coming even with the back tire of the combine. He pushed harder, ignoring his pain until he reached the man. He whacked the intruder hard on the side of his head with the thick stake. Jack continued to strike him hard. The man lost his grip. Fending off the attack, he tumbled backward and thudded on the hard earth. He struggled to rise, and Jack laid into him, beating him as crawled across the dirt toward the vines. Jack kept striking until a firm hand seized the grape stake. Adrian stood behind him. "That's enough."

The man's head lay against the end post of a grape trellis, and he wasn't moving. Jack dropped the stake.

They both stood over the prone body lying face down, unmoving. The man groaned. The combine's engine idled down the lane.

"We've got to get out of here," Adrian said. "That's old man Kolcinivitch."

Jack wiped his forehead with his sleeve and looked the big man over. He searched the man's features carefully. Adrian was right. It was Kolcinivitch himself. Marty's father.

"We'll rot in a gringo jail forever if he dies."

"He's fine. Just plastered. Let's go before he wakes up. He probably won't even remember what happened." Jack ran to the combine and mounted the cab. He throttled it and let it labor up the incline to the macadam, and he steered it into the empty road. A part of him wanted to kill the man for stomping him like that. He would have gotten away with it, too. No way, he was going to get caught stealing his own machine. Around here, justice existed in the hands of the strong.

Adrian's truck idled in the middle of the road with the trailer gate lowered. Jack guided the combine up the rails and onto the bed. He shut it down. They cinched it in with heavy chains, folded the gate up, and drove off into the night. Jack leaned out the window letting the cool night airplay on his face, wondering what would happen if he had killed a grower. He was thankful for Adrian, for risking so much to help him tonight. And for him stopping him. He could have killed the old man. Jack tasted bitter redness in his mouth. Blood seemed the only remedy for so many problems around here.

➤

AFTER BREAKFAST ON MONDAY morning, Jack handed his mother a check. She stood by the back kitchen door, searing him with a look of skepticism as if he toyed with her. She turned it over, examining it. When she realized it was real and what it would buy, she slumped into a kitchen chair and sobbed. Jack knew her tears were the sighs of relief from the months of worry and anger. Lines around her eyes softened. She wiped her eyes and drummed the tabletop with her fingers. Then she jerked her head up at Jack, who leaned against the kitchen sink, sipping coffee.

"What did you tell the sheriff?"

"I don't have anything to say to that useless windbag." He wore Adrian's jacket to cover up his shirt. He didn't want her making a fuss over the bloodstains.

"If the sheriff didn't give you the combine, how did you get it?"

"When I found it, Kolcinivitch had cut off the rotary blade. They were tearing it up for scrap."

Jack had slept in the cab of the combine after Adrian had dropped him at Lacy's Tractors. Mr. Lacy wouldn't give him top dollar since the rotary blade was missing. When Jack told him where he could find the pieces of the blade, Mr. Lacy looked away and mumbled something. He hustled to cut Jack a check and had a lot boy give him a lift home.

"How did you find it?" his mother asked.

He set his coffee cup on the counter. "I have to take a shower, and get back to school. I can still make third period class." At the doorway, he paused. "I hope you're up to writing me a note for school, so I don't have to do detention for cutting class. Just say I was up all night on family business killing thieves."

She smoothed back her gray hair and moved to him. Hands on his shoulders, she said, "Your father would be proud of you, Jack. You're every bit the man he was."

Jack didn't smile or nod but moved off stiffly to the stairs.

Chapter 22
Lunchtime Visit

A T NOON, THE DELANO High cafeteria filled with the high chatter of eight hundred kids eating meatloaf and mashed potatoes. With Adrian and Darcy across from him and Ella beside him, Jack jabbed at the brown slab of ground beef. Sitting eased his pain. After showering earlier this morning, he had used the mirror to check what he could see of the bruises. One big one had drawn blood but had begun scabbing while other long stripes were purpling. He had swallowed a couple of aspirin, and the throbbing had settled into a steady drumbeat. Amazement at what he had pulled off made him smile. Right under the sheriff Pinocchio's outsized nose.

He wouldn't pitch for a few days, enough time to heal.

"You boys are sure quiet." Darcy nudged Adrian, who shoveled food into his mouth.

"You must have partied late last night." Ella searched Jack's face. "You left my place early."

Adrian nodded at his friend.

"As a matter of fact," Jack quipped, "we got quite a bit of celebrating in last night. I was a real hit."

His friend eyed him.

"What'd you do?" Darcy asked.

Adrian shook his head slowly.

"They're too tired to say," Ella said.

Jack couldn't contain his giddy grin. His mother had her money in the bank by now, and that made him sit even taller. She planned to get the taxes paid today, and that would end her struggle and give her a couple more years to figure a way out of her financial mess. He didn't mind his tiredness at all. His back hurt less thinking of Sheriff Loco and his empty threats. Even if that creep Kolcinivitch came after him, the combine was sold. The taxes were paid. His letter from UCLA was on its way. Things were settled.

Marty sauntered over and patted Jack on the back. He held back a wince.

"Congratulations, college boy. Going Hollywood on us."

"UCLA's offer's in the mail." Ella smiled proudly.

Jack flashed on Kolcinivitch's look from last night when he had him pinned to the ground. The man intended to do him in. Marty wasn't anything like his father.

"Long night?" Marty said with a salacious grin, tapping Jack's shoulder with his fist.

"Longest one of my life." Jack wondered what Marty's old man said about getting beat-up. Was it just another episode in a drinking man's life? Something he endured by becoming the class jokester?

Marty hooted. Ella looked at him quizzically. Adrian rolled his eyes while he shifted the boiled vegetables around on his plate. Jack heard the double doors slam open then the hard stomp of boots marching toward him in a martial rhythm. Adrian looked toward the doors, and his gaze turned to dread. He lowered his forkful of limp broccoli from his open mouth. The boots stopped behind Jack. Wordless and hard-breathing men stood behind him.

"You're under arrest for assault and battery." Kauffman, in his most officious tone, shouted loud enough for everyone to hear. He sounded like a carnival barker. Jack would have laughed, but the solemnity and alarm on Adrian's face were an ominous sign. Arrested for defending himself. Another Central Valley joke. He had the bruises to prove he had been attacked. It would take a bunch of kangaroos to send him to jail for stealing what he owned. He slowly rose, doing his best not to smirk. Showing Kauffman up in front of all of these kids would be hilarious.

"Sit down, Duncan, before I beat you down."

Another one of Kauffman's jokes. Jack stepped over the bench. "What's this about?"

Kauffman unholstered his gun, pointed it straight armed, hand on hand, at Jack's head. "I said sit."

Jack stared down the shadow of the barrel. More menace than usual in this little boy's voice. He bit his cheek and returned to his place. Deputies surrounded Adrian on the other side of the table. Adrian rose slowly, shock and horror on his face. The khaki boys with badges roughly yanked his arms behind him. A deputy clamped handcuffs on him, cinching them tight. Adrian's body jerked.

He shot Jack a questioning glare, one fringed with humiliation but also with a searching inquiry, *Are you going to let this stand?* Jack pushed himself up, but Kauffman forced him down.

"I beat Kolcinivitch," Jack shouted to Kauffman. "Not him. He'd never do anything like that."

"Brave words, Duncan, but we got a positive ID on this perp. Just more UFW crimes."

The deputies led him down the row and around toward the doors.

Jack tore up out of his seat, forcing Deputy Kauffman back.

"Jack, please." Ella reached for his arm, but he shrugged it off.

"Can't you hear me? That old coot attacked me, and I beat him with his own grape stake."

"Stand back." Kauffman puffed out his chest out.

Jack untucked his shirt and undid the buttons. "Look at me." He stripped his shirt off and turned to the deputies. "This is what Kolcinivitch did to me."

"You're sick, Duncan." Kauffman shook his head, giving Jack a look of pity. "You need psychological help."

Barton clutched his arm. "Jack, come on."

Jack threw down his shirt. "Listen to me."

Kauffman marched up, inches from his face. He tapped Jack's chest with his finger. "It's time for law and order to prevail in this county." Stiff shouldered, the deputy led the hard men in khaki toward the hall as they dragged a handcuffed Adrian with them, the metal door slamming behind them.

Chapter 23
Night Raid

"D O YOU HEAR ALL of this, Jack?" His mother rustled the newspaper, shaking it hard. "This is no time for you to be out on the roads."

Jack ate his dinner slowly, as his mother read to him. For the past three nights after Adrian's arrest, she had turned family dinner into battle reports straight from the pages of the *Delano Record*.

Reports of growers repulsing efforts by organizers to lure workers from the fields grew more urgent as the cultivation of the vines continued in the run-up to a bumper harvest.

When she read the story about the young Filipino field hand bludgeoned to death by a deputy on a sidewalk when he disobeyed an order to leave, Jack set down his fork, his appetite suddenly gone.

"Why'd that cop kill that guy?"

"If he didn't, they're going to overrun the town."

"He didn't have to kill that guy."

She shook her head. "He must have felt threatened, don't you think?"

"These guys just want to work."

"You don't know the whole story. Are you listening to me? You need to stay off the roads."

"I hear you." The roads were hell for sure. Police cruisers raced up and down the highways. Thugs in vans and trucks scoured the back roads hauling over anyone flying a black and red union flag, breaking windshields, slicing tires, yelling in the faces of frightened drivers. Caravans of strikers in tired and worn cars were riding heavy on their springs, loaded down with workers, lumbering down farm roads, searching for scabs picking the fields.

"I can't stop living."

"School and home, that's all." She folded the paper to another article. "Don't get caught in the middle of any of this. It's not your business."

He didn't tell her that after practice he had been venturing into West Delano to the Sanchez home. The first time, Adrian's mother, with streaks of tears down her cheeks, only mumbled that Señor Sanchez was out, probably at Forty Acres, the UFW headquarters outside town, or on a picket line. When Jack had stopped by today, Mrs. Sanchez answered the door, her wordless grief etched on her face. He had opened his mouth to ask about Adrian, but she waved her hand and closed the door before he could get a word out.

"Listen here," his mother said. "You need to hear this. This is from the opinion section."

The Central Valley growers, the ones who till the fertile valley that feeds the mouths of nearly every American, are fighting on the front lines, holding back an invasion of socialists, communists, anarchists, and the collectivizing hordes seeking to subvert freedom and enterprise. The boundaries of this battle form precariously along the uneven and potholed roads circling Delano, where the stalwart growers and their faithful friends, armed for self-defense, are staving off an imminent takeover of the fields.

If Chavez succeeds in his attempts to unionize farmworkers, according to the plans laid out by UFW organizers, they will move on to collectivizing all farming operations across the nation. Their ultimate goal is to wrestle control of the nation's farming operations out of the hands of those who have financed and own them. If this plan is allowed to come to fruition, then America will lose control of its source of foodstuff across the nation. Our food stocks will be under the control of foreigners.

Freedom itself is in jeopardy. The livelihood of so many of Delano area growers who have worked hard to create our thriving agricultural industry will evaporate.

Chavez and his union must be stopped at all costs.

We urge Governor Reagan to veto the pending SB 4091 authorizing farmworkers and itinerant labor to receive Workers' Compensation benefits and other employee privileges.

To extend employee benefits to workers who are showing no loyalty to our nation's security would be a travesty of justice.

She rested the paper on the table. "This is horrible. The communists are ruthless. No wonder the sheriff has to be so tough."

"I've never met any communists," Jack said.

"Jack, they're everywhere. You need to read this." She slid the paper across the table.

Jack didn't want to start an argument. He knew what he knew. Adrian was not a communist; neither was his father. He didn't think Cesar Chavez was either, but he didn't know the man. But how could the man be evil when he was helping so many people?

He took up the newspaper and folded it next to his plate. "I don't think *you* see the whole picture. Don't you remember the letter Dad wrote to the growers? What was it, about ten years ago? About how they mistreated the workers."

"Jack, your father would have nothing to do with communists."

"Don't you see? He was talking about the same issues the strikers are upset about today. If the workers had the same problems back then and they weren't communists, why are they communists now?

How can they be plotting to take over the ranches? Dad wouldn't have anything to do with that."

"If your father were here, he would know exactly what's going on. But he's not. Truthfully, I don't know what's going on. But I know this." She pointed at Jack. "You need to stay out of it. You get drawn into this, taking sides either way, and it will get you off track."

"You know how the growers control things around here. What if those articles are all lies?"

She looked up at him. A glimmer of disbelief crossed her eyes. She took back the paper, unfolded it and perused the pages.

"There's an article here about Adrian, why he got arrested."

"What's it say?" Three days now, Adrian had stewed in the county lockup in Bakersfield. No one at school—Principal McGrew, Coach, any of his teachers, all folks who had universally praised Adrian's work ethic and character and untapped potential—would help him. They all raised their arms in frustration or shrugged their shoulders in disbelief when he asked them about helping Adrian. Jack appreciated their sympathy for his friend's predicament, but they believed what they had been told: Adrian had struck a prominent grower. It didn't matter what Jack admitted, no one listened to him. No one hit a grower and got away with it.

Principal McGrew went as far as to reprimand Jack, asking him why he'd go to such great lengths to risk his scholarship and future by saying that Adrian didn't hit the man.

Yesterday morning Jack had told Coach the details of what had happened in the field. The coach had shaken his head for a long time, then rested his chin on a palm and stared at Jack like a man ready to pull his hair out. He asked Jack not to say anything. He hoped that Adrian's family would be able to help him with bail. Once Adrian was back in school, life would calm down. But Coach reminded Jack—if it was Adrian's word against Kolcinivitch's, his friend didn't stand a chance of getting a fair hearing.

What about Adrian's scholarship? What about his graduation?

Coach leaned back in his squeaky chair and rested a finger on his lips, pondering. He agreed to reach out to Coach Kish. Adrian hadn't been convicted of anything yet, and he promised to assure the UCLA coach of Adrian's innocence. Coach wouldn't take sides. If he did, he'd lose players.

His mother folded to the story about Adrian. "This sounds serious."

"What's it say?"

She read how Kolcinivitch had been assaulted in his own grape fields while preventing a union organizer from vandalizing one of his farm pickups. "In trying to thwart the crime, he had been thrown to the ground and had hit his head, knocking him unconscious. This was no standard Central Valley crime but one full of the rage and malice driven by the unjust labor demands."

Jack folded his arms on the table and rested his head on them. To hear these accusations framed in such spectacular lies forced the breath out of him. He felt a hollowness expand inside, as if every effort he made to shape his future, every step he took to help his family, had all evaporated into nothing. He opened his eyes at the empty pie dish in front of him. His friend was probably eating cold mush and stale bread right now. Jack raised his head.

"Are you all right?"

Jack scraped his chair back and moved to the door. "I need to go."

She folded the paper on the table. "Are you hearing this, Jack?"

He opened the back door. "Doesn't it bother you that Adrian's in jail for something he didn't do?"

She tapped the paper laid out on the table. "That's not what they said happened."

He closed the door and faced her. "Who do you think helped me get the combine back? He wasn't vandalizing a pickup. He was helping me steal back the combine."

Slowly he unbuttoned his sports shirt and peeled it off. He snapped his T-shirt over his head and swung around.

He heard her quick intake of breath. "What happened?"

"Kolcinivitch did this when he caught me driving our combine off his property."

Jack told her all about Monday morning, discovering the nearly dismembered combine, driving it out, the fight among the vines, and Adrian's saving Jack from getting beaten even more.

"He tried to kill me."

She covered her mouth with both hands, slowly shaking her head; her blue eyes wide and unbelieving. She stared down at the paper then up at his back.

"I need to talk to Mr. Sanchez," Jack said.

She went to him and touched his skin. "Please do that after school tomorrow," she said. "In the light."

"The sheriff wants two thousand and five hundred dollars to make bail."

"Won't the union help? They have lawyers."

"Adrian's father is a member, but not Adrian. He helped us save this place. Don't you care?"

She touched his back above a bruise. "Of course I care, Jack, but—" She seemed unable to say more.

She had told him the money from the sale of the combine had gone fast. Taxes had been paid, and a leak in the roof repaired. She had also put aside some for her seamstress shop. But something, anything would help. He felt her finger run over one of the stripes on his back, a welt that ran from his shoulder to his hip.

"Jack! Please stay off the roads," she said, her voice nearly trembling. "You're going to get—." Her touch made his bruises ache, and the angry redness of his wound seeped into the deepest part of him.

➤

"THE UNION CANNOT HELP my son." Mr. Sanchez sat on the edge of the seat of his worn rocker. The lights were off in the house, and the close living room was dark except for a few flickering votives in front of the family shrine. It looked disheveled, as if they were hastily rearranging what little they had. Mr. Sanchez explained that even though he's being called a member of the union, Adrian never joined. Besides, the UFW refused to bail out any member caught using violence. Even after Jack explained that Adrian had not struck the grower, the gray-haired man, his shoulders slouched from years of stoop work, only hung his head and slapped his knee in exasperation.

"That is what you told Carlita on Monday," he said. "I told David Briscoe, our attorney, and he promised to see what he could do. But it may not be much right now with so many of our people in jail." He rose and strode from the room into the darkened hall where he spoke to his wife in animated Spanish. Jack wondered if they were moving, but didn't want to pry.

"I must go soon." Mr. Sanchez returned, flitting his eyes to the windows then the door.

Carlita pulled a heavy suitcase into the room, and Sanchez's young daughter had a backpack over her shoulder. They stared at Jack until he rose. They wanted him to leave, but he had to know. "Is he going to lose his scholarship?"

"I spoke with UCLA. Coach Kish thinks Adrian will be okay if he isn't convicted of a felony. But if he is, then—" Mr. Sanchez shrugged, and they moved to the back door. "But if he doesn't graduate, then none of this matters."

Jack stood.

"It is not okay for me to see him," Mr. Sanchez said. "Please, go to him. Now I must go. It is not safe for me to even sleep in my own home." Mr. Sanchez flinched when a beam of light pierced the front window; two more followed, searching the dark room. Several bright shafts shot in through the kitchen window. Mr. Sanchez held out his arm, shielding his family. Carlita scooted across the room and snuffed out the candles.

Heavy rapping on the front door rattled the windows. "Open up, Sanchez, we know you're in there."

"*Madre de Dios, nos ayude*," Carlita whispered. Mr. Sanchez pushed the women toward a back bedroom.

"Police. Open up." The front door shook until it smashed open. Dots of blue and red flashed through the windows, crawling over the walls, the furniture, the Virgin of Guadalupe.

"Quick, quick," Mr. Sanchez waved for Jack to follow down the hall. They all crowded into a back bedroom. He watched stupefied as Mr. Sanchez pushed his daughter under the bed. He searched the room for a place to hide. Heavy boots pounded down the hall. Jack turned to the black-vested cops storming through the bedroom door. Before he could scream, a riot-helmeted deputy roughly grabbed his shirt by the throat and shoved him to the floor.

"Down, down." Handcuffs roughly clasped his wrists. Two strong hands grabbed his feet and dragged him on his belly down the hall, into the living room, dropping him. They pulled Mr. Sanchez next to Jack. The cops tromped up and down the hall, in and out of the rooms, rummaging through closets, tearing through kitchen cabinets, tossing dishes and glasses on the floor. Weeping sifted in from the hall.

Something substantial crashed to the floor nearby, startling him. It tumbled up against his shoulder. He stretched around and in the sallow light the Virgin's head lay on her ear, facing him with her peaceful smile through painted lips. Her eyes were full of pity.

A couple of hours later they rough-handed Mr. Sanchez away, cursing and threatening him. By jailing strike leaders, Sheriff Grant was determined to destroy the strike, a strategy endorsed by the growers. But every minute Jack spent with his nose in the carpet, breathing dust and humiliation, he felt a little less human, a little less of a person who could have a better life, and more like the dirt under a strong man's boots.

Two deputies lifted Jack to his feet and pushed him outside. They commanded him to kneel, and they shoved him face down into the wet grass. A deputy uncuffed him, then squatted by his ear. Red and blue flashes tumbled over everything.

"Time for you to leave," the deputy said. "And don't come back here."

Jack held his breath. Car doors opened then slammed, loud voices trailed off, tires squealed, and colored lights dissipated into darkness. The street fell quiet until he heard nothing but comfortless wailing that drifted through the broken front door.

Chapter 24
The Gas Station

WHY HAD JACK COME here to Forty Acres? Clots of people surrounded the California Mission–style gas station with the red tile roof off Garces Highway. Cars lined both sides of the road. Tents dotted the grass field behind it. Small groups gathered on the lawn, eating, talking, singing, and waiting. Some were praying. Smoke from barbecues and food stands smelled of carne asada. The breeze carried Ranchera music with the spicy smell of grilling beef.

Jack joined the crowd who appeared to be waiting. Folks wandered around the two pump islands so cars couldn't pull in. Most were farmworkers; a few were nervous men in suits who looked like politicians.

For five days now, Cesar Chavez had fasted to end violence. Jack figured there would be a few people here tending to him, but it was a festival. Had they all come to speak to the labor leader too? Someone here had to know who could help Adrian. Now that his father was also in jail, Jack couldn't think of anyone else he could talk to.

"You look lost." A man with long blond hair in a rumpled checked cotton shirt approached. He had a friendly smile and seemed interested in listening. Jack explained Adrian's situation, the arrest of Isidro Sanchez in his own home, and Adrian arrested at school for something he didn't do.

"You are not good luck to the Sanchez family." There was a humorous lilt to his voice.

"I need to find a way to help them."

"Let me talk to some people. Stay right here."

Jack stood on one of the pump islands. To his left were two mechanics' bays, the glass and steel doors rolled down. Next to the bays, the station's office was jammed with people sipping coffee and talking. The blond-haired man in the checked shirt disappeared into a jam of people in the short hallway that bisected the two. From what he heard, Chavez had holed up in a small room down that hall. Nothing more than a closet with a mattress.

The man in the checked shirt worked his way through the crowd back toward Jack.

"He says you need to speak to David Briscoe, our attorney."

"Where do I find him?"

The man pointed to a set of squat brick buildings across the lawn behind. "He's in Reuther Hall. But he's busy right now." Jack squinted into the distance at the complex of brick buildings that served as the UFW headquarters. He didn't want to get shunted off to someone who couldn't give him any answers. It wasn't likely he could speak to Chavez himself, but really, who else could help at this point?

"I need to speak to Cesar," Jack said.

"It's not likely, Champ."

"My friend's dad works for Cesar. His son is in jail for something he didn't do, and it's because of the union. I need to talk to him." Jack stared the check-shirt man down.

"Give me a minute." He disappeared down the hall. What seemed like an hour later, he returned followed by a husky Mexican man with a wispy mustache. He asked Jack a few questions and patted him down. He nodded for Jack to follow.

Jack stood in the doorway of the small room. Cesar Chavez lay on a small mattress on the floor reading a book. Rosary beads were wrapped around one hand. A crucifix was affixed to the wall above his head. He looked like his photos—dark complexion, jet-black hair parted on the side, and the hawk nose of an Indian. But after drinking only water for a week, he looked healthy and eager to talk. He greeted Jack with warm, brown, sympathetic eyes. A banner of the Virgin of Guadalupe hung on the wall.

"Hello, brother," he said. He set down his book and motioned toward a plain wooden chair in a corner. "How can I help you?"

Jack told him about Adrian's father getting arrested.

"Yes, I heard about Isidro. David will get him out. We need him back to work. But that is their strategy, you know, to strip the union of its leaders. It is illegal, but not beyond the growers to do. So we must help him, and we will."

Jack told him about his stolen combine, the sheriff pressuring him to testify against Mr. Sanchez, and how he had refused. He rehearsed the tale of the combine and how he and Adrian had retrieved it when being attacked by Kolcinivitch, getting beaten when he fought the grower, and then Adrian's arrest at school.

"You know what it is to fight for what is yours," Chavez said.

"But he's not the one who beat Kolcinivitch."

"They will never arrest a gringo when they can blame the son of a strike leader."

"But it's not right."

Cesar considered for a moment, rubbing his chin. "Do you know why I am fasting?"

"I suppose. Because of all the violence."

"But what violence?" Chavez turned on his side with a painful grimace. "There is nothing we can do about the violence of the growers and their thugs. The courts and the police are in cahoots with them, so that is how they operate. But the reaction of the poor workers is to strike back. That is what I must stop. Some men who have sworn themselves to nonviolence are now bringing guns to the fields. The anger is in their eyes and in their hearts. I see it every day.

They want to hurt the growers the way they have been injured. If they do, we will lose everything. So that is why I am fasting. To quell the anger in their hearts. Do you see?"

"Sure. I saw a cop tempting Adrian to hit him."

"And he didn't?"

Jack shook his head. "I sure wanted to."

"We all have a struggle, Jack. You must work through your struggle and find your own way."

Jack looked at the labor leader quizzically.

"You don't understand yet, do you?"

"Not entirely." Jack felt on the spot. Cesar wanted him to understand something that just wasn't clear.

"What do you see all around you? Every day it happens to the poor. What do you call it?"

Jack stared at the ceiling for a moment.

"If you don't know what it is, then how do you defeat it, Jack? How is your friend Adrian being treated?"

"He's not going to get any justice."

"So now you see it, don't you?" Cesar propped himself up on one elbow. "The problem is justice, equality, fairness, isn't it?"

"Yes." Jack brightened with a sense of relief.

"And if you see the problem, then you have to do something about it. But if you use violence, then any change you seek will not last."

"But what can I do about the cops? They do what they want."

Cesar laid back down with a sigh. "That is what you must find out. I have discovered what I can do about the injustice I see. We are not treated as other American workers are treated, so I demand justice. Yet, we're as American as any grower. But we're treated like farm implements and discarded when they don't need us. There is no dignity in that."

"So you're saying that there is nothing you can do to help Adrian. He's going to rot in that jail. He's going to lose his scholarship."

"No, I'm not saying that at all." Cesar raised himself up slowly on one elbow. "I'm sending the best man for the job to solve this difficult problem with your friend."

"Oh, great! Who?"

Cesar smiled mischievously. "I'm sending you. You must figure it out, what to do. That's the nature of nonviolence, Jack. It requires we use the creativity God has given us to solve our problems. It doesn't take a genius to use your fists. Violence is the easy way out. It takes courage, brains, and hard work to be creative. To find another way."

Jack took a heavy breath. He wasn't as much confused as he was frustrated.

"Jack," Cesar said softly, "do you know that two years ago senators from Washington came and held hearings into the violence in the valley?"

"I'd heard about it."

"Senator Robert Kennedy came and listened. During the meeting with Sheriff Grant, he told him he needed to take a break and read the Constitution of the United States. That how he was treating farmworkers, arresting them for no reason, was illegal and unconstitutional."

"I didn't know that."

"Yes, and Sheriff Grant, I am told, was so mad he went home and tore up his copy."

"What a jerk."

"You know, I only have an eighth-grade education. But I have read the Constitution. I know what it means. I am accused of being a communist, an anarchist, a threat to American freedom, and much more. But do you know what I am, Jack?"

"I have heard all those things."

"So you have questions, too?"

"Yes," Jack said. He heard so much about this man's communism, he wanted to know.

"I am a Catholic. A Christian. And I am an American. That's what the Constitution of the United States calls me. I'm as American as any grower. Kolcinivitch's parents were born in Slovenia. DiGorda's are from Italy. Mine are from Mexico. We are all the same, born here as children of immigrants. I believe in our democracy. It is the finest country on earth. It gives us the greatest chance to live as free men."

"In fact, I am as American as any of these growers, and I want equal justice under the laws of this country. I want to be treated like a human being with respect and dignity. That is what I am promised.

"They want a dictatorship of the rich. The Constitution doesn't guarantee them that. Neither does it say they can treat me differently than they would treat their other workers. It says we are the same. But their actions keep us poor, and they think we are too stupid to know their game. That is why I am sacrificing my own life for the poor. It's one thing to be poor. It's another thing to be forced into poverty by men who don't care that we're human beings. But I know who I am." His voice suddenly grew weary, and he laid back down. He rested a hand on his forehead.

"I'm sorry to take so much of your time."

"Time is all I have, Jack. I have no money. But I have the life God has given me. If I can help you with what I know, then I am glad."

A woman with a stethoscope around her neck stuck her head into the room. "How are you feeling, Cesar?"

"I am in the hands of God, and that's enough."

She gave Jack a hard look of warning.

"I'm all right, Linda. Leave us for a few minutes so I can help my friend."

"You can't wear yourself out, Cesar."

He waved a hand, and she closed the door. Then he eased himself up on an elbow. He held out his calloused hand, palm up. "This is a fast of penitence. I won't eat until my people recommit to nonviolence. I'm doing what I can do. I can't carry the entire load. It's necessary, Jack, that you do what only you can do."

A knock at the door. It opened, and the nurse came in. "Cesar, you need to rest now."

"Yes, yes."

Jack rose and stood over the tired man. Cesar extended his hand, and they shook. The man held Jack's hand in a firm grip. "We all have paths to take, Jack. I chose to take this road to Delano. No one forced me to be here with the poor. This is where I live, and where I'll die. You must make your own decision. And take your own road."

"Yes," was all Jack could think to say

"Go now and do your work."

Jack slipped out of the room as Linda entered. She told the labor leader in concerned tones that he was jeopardizing his health. Jack left the hall. The crowd had thinned as the evening set in. He strode toward his car. He wasn't any clearer how to help Adrian. But he was more convinced that he could find a way.

He drove slowly through town. Mario Savio's saying on Ella's shirt about putting your bodies on the gears flitted through his mind. Gears of the great machine were grinding everywhere. Men in high places were relentlessly turning them. Cesar Chavez refused to be a product of that machine, spit out and discarded like so much trash. So he volunteered his body upon the gears, gumming them up, allowing himself to be chewed to pieces to stop the machine. For what? To make a better life for other people.

Jack could never do anything like that.

Chapter 25
Growers, Gamblers, and Men of the Land

A FTER PRACTICE THE NEXT day, Jack guided his Olds up Herm's narrow, potholed drive and parked close to his chipped and peeling porch. He cut the engine, and it ticked in the dying day. He felt castaway here, washed up to the edge of this clapboard house, listing in a sea of wilted stubble by strong tides of circumstance.

Jack had collected nearly two hundred dollars from his friends. Ella had helped the most. Raising another $2,300 for Adrian in a town where growers were heroes would be like prying pennies from the palms of Scrooge. Even if he worked every day after school and baseball practice bucking hay for Ella's dad, it would take him nearly three months to earn that much. Adrian would lose everything by then. All week between classes, Jack had walked the campus with his head down not wanting to answer any more questions. Adrian was the one boy who should have never been caught sneaking onto a grower's land. He had far too much to lose. Everyone knew that.

Herm opened the front door and stepped into what remained of daylight, hands in his jeans pockets, smiling. He descended the porch and stood by Jack's open window.

"I'm sorry to hear about your buddy." With his bandages removed and his hair neatly combed, Herm looked almost the way he had when Jack had first seen him on the road on that rainy day weeks ago. Herm leaned into the open window. "Let's talk."

Jack followed him inside and slumped into a seat at the kitchen table.

"What's the word on Adrian?"

"He'll flunk out and lose his scholarship if he doesn't get out of jail."

"What're you thinking to do?"

Jack related his conversations of the past week and Mr. Sanchez's arrest the previous evening. And his visit to Cesar Chavez. "He said I needed to figure out for myself what to do."

Herm nodded with a grin as if appearing to know all along it would come to this. He reached around and retrieved a deck of cards. "I'd give you the money if I had it. But I'm pretty confident you can raise that much if you put your mind to it." He looked up at Jack as he dealt out a hand of Hold'em, "Of course, you'll need a little coaching."

"Are you saying I should gamble to raise his bail?"

"Just play. Then tell me what you think."

The cards came fast and continuous, a never-ending stream—two of a kind, flushes, three of a kind, straights, followed by weak hands, raising and calling, bluffing and folding, winning and losing. The night rolled on, Jack feeling the power, the will to win with each turn of a card, each hand played out to its end. Combinations appeared like bright constellations in the night sky, unmistakable and universal. They had always been there, he just had to learn what they meant. It was almost eleven. Six hours of playing had snapped by. His mother would be furious at him for not calling. She'd be phoning the hospitals by now. Despite the wrath he'd get for walking in the door so late, he smiled, counting the chips in front of him. He could bail out his friend right now if these were worth money.

"It's not going to be that easy. So don't go thinking you can just waltz into a card room and win that kind of money."

Jack smirked. Herm slapped the table hard, and the chips rattled. Jack dropped a stack.

"What was that for?" Jack asked.

"You got that look of easy money. Your dad would never fall into that trap. This is a thinking man's game. A game of skill. You gotta keep your wits about you."

Jack's cheeks warmed under Herm's steady glare. He picked up the cards and shuffled them.

"There're players out there who are ten times better than either of us." Herm collected the cards. "Your strategy changes when you have a full table."

Wiping his top lip, Jack leaned his chair back on two legs. The old man was right. It didn't make sense to be too cocky right now. "What do you think I ought to do?"

"Spend every minute you can over here. Sunday night you might be ready to try one of the Mexican card rooms in West Delano. They play mainly five-card draw in the front tables. But they always have a game of Hold'em going somewhere. They're small stakes, dollar- and five-dollar tables so you won't lose your shirt. Play there, then we'll see what's next."

Driving home, he felt the minutes ticking away toward midnight. Morning would come too soon for another day of school. The clock ticked on Adrian too probably lying on a cold concrete floor after a dinner of slimy beans with only a blanket to keep him warm. In those lonely moments, he must fear his dreams were slipping away.

On Friday, Jack pitched to a strong Turlock team. Delano's center fielder didn't help Jack when he couldn't reach a few balls Adrian could have tracked down with his eyes closed. The score veered back and forth, making Coach spit out his sunflower seeds faster than usual. He even gnawed on a fingernail at one point.

By the fifth inning, Jack was pitching well, but he didn't care if he won or not. On the bench, he wiped his face with a cold towel. *Just pitch. Just pitch. Just pitch*, he told himself. In the last inning, Marty hit a soaring home run into the orchard beyond the fence; the pop off the bat brought the entire team to their feet. Everyone oohed, clapped, jabbered, and slapped backs as they trotted to the gym, their hopes of a league championship intact.

In a joyous and steamy locker room, happy boys snapped each other's butts with towels, threw pilfered underwear over the fluorescent fixtures, and razzed each other about the size of their packages. Jack dressed quickly and ducked out, ignoring Coach's booming voice from his office. Coach wanted to review every pitch of Jack's less than inspired performance. Jack keyed the lock on his car.

He had cards to play.

Before leaving campus, he told Ella he'd be busy most weekends until Adrian was free. She gave him a slanting look and said she understood. He heard her words of encouragement but her reluctant tone concerned him. She had asked all of her friends for help, even approaching her father. Mr. Carter had launched into an hour-long rant about Cesar Chavez and the death of their way of life if the grape boycott continued much longer. Ella and her father weren't on speaking terms right now.

The grape boycott had pinched the small growers particularly hard, making it near impossible for them to market their table grapes. The Seafarers Union's members working the docks in San Francisco refused to load any table grapes from Delano area growers. Supermarket chains nationwide wouldn't touch Delano grapes. Mr. Carter, like most of the farmers in the area, had been forced to stuff his harvest into cold storage lockers, an expense that chewed up his precious cash. Some growers had even put their properties up for sale. No wonder Ella's father was so angry.

Still, none of the growers would even sit down with Cesar Chavez to discuss the issues that had launched the strike. The large growers put pressure on smaller landholders not to negotiate, not even to meet with anyone from the union.

That evening Herm had a plate of tacos and beans waiting for Jack. He wolfed them down, following them with coffee strong enough to make a dead man dance. Jack dealt and learned from

Herm's every move. The old man lit cigarettes and settled them burning in the ashtray until the cramped kitchen filled with thick smoke that made Jack's eyes water. Around nine, Herm clicked on a radio on the counter and tuned to a Bakersfield news station, letting the yammering voice of the newscaster drag on and on as he dealt, called, bet, and folded. The combinations, the pairs, the trips, the flushes, the straights all came clear even amidst the confusion and stink in the air.

Saturday morning Jack snuck out early while his mother slept. He spent the day at Herm's, bluffing and betting, acquiring confidence in his ability to read a man's tells by slogging card by card through a couple of dozen games. They played through lunch, eating cold turkey sandwiches and drinking more black coffee.

They played through a dinner of warmed-up refried beans with rice and spicy carne asada. After dinner, he caught Herm exchanging cards under the table. Herm told him he did well, but professional cheaters were much harder to detect. A professional could hide cards, use spotters, pay dealers to feed them certain combinations. Some cheaters were impossible to notice, especially the slick dealer who had a polished sleight of hand. Some were so good they went their whole careers undetected.

Around nine, Jack went on a losing streak that continued for a couple of hours until he was down to a single stack of chips. Losing to a pair of aces he hadn't seen coming, he threw down his hand and scraped back his chair.

"Just because you know you can beat a fellow doesn't mean you will." Herm gathered the cards, shuffled and dealt a new hand. "You have a gift, but you have to stay vigilant."

"I'm trying."

"Trying's for the penniless." Herm leaned over the table and pointed an arthritic finger at him. "Watch everything everyone does. Start with the dealer."

He stood. "It's eleven. I'm tired."

"One more. Sit." Herm swept in the cards and shuffled them up. He had almost finished dealing when Jack bent over the table and covered the deck with his hand.

"You just dealt from the bottom."

Herm leaned back. "I've been doing that since nine. I'd own your undershorts and the tires on your car if we were playing in West Delano. Over there they'll wager for your dentures." He gathered the cards, shuffled and dealt out a few cards, expertly spinning one off the bottom.

"See this bottom card sticking out just a tiny bit?" He flipped the deck upside down. "That's called a 'hanger.' They're hard to detect, but they always indicate a card has been dealt off the bottom. A good sleight of hand man won't make this mistake, but you can spot the 'hanger' if you're looking for it."

Herm talked about second dealing, false shuffling, and colluding players who work together to bet a weaker one right out of the game. It all made Jack think there had to be a far easier way to make a buck.

Herm slapped the deck down. "Look here, there's a million ways to cheat a man if someone's set to do it. It doesn't matter what game you play, play hard, but play fair." Herm pointed a finger across the table. "And watch everyone else, because a lot of folks don't live that way."

➤

SUNDAY MORNING STARTED WITH chorizo eggs and black coffee for five. Three of Herm's unshaven friends sat around the kitchen table shoveling in eggs smothered in Tabasco sauce, slurping down coffee that had the flavor of raw earth. Herm introduced them as a few of the better cardsharps that plied the gambling rooms of West Delano. The men grinned through scruffy beards; one had a front tooth missing. Another had a silver incisor that caught the morning light. It appeared knife sharp when he smiled. The last had an unkempt Pancho Villa mustache that drooped past the bottom of his chin.

The speed of the seasoned players—the bluffing, the rapid-fire Spanish, a lot of which flew by Jack, made him wonder if they were ridiculing his play. At first, he didn't even recognize the game, it moved so quickly. After he had folded his hands a couple of times, the movement settled into a detectable rhythm.

The meaning of the sly grins, the ticks, the scratching of the face, the folding of the hands, and the rubbing of the chin at an unwanted combination all clarified. The game turned to him. His stack of chips rose incrementally, but so did the older Mexican across from him. The men smoked, knocked back shots of tequila, and stuffed warm corn tortillas into their mouths without slowing the pace. The stench of smoke and alcohol soaked into his skin. Around noon, he had a large stack of chips and that old smirk of his surfaced again. He noticed Herm on the other side of the table frowning hard.

"Let's take a break, boys." Herm scooted his chair back. The men laid down their cards, rose, their chairs scraping on linoleum. The smell of carne asada and fresh coffee livened Jack up. He lounged on the porch, leaning against the wall, eating a plate of food.

"Don't start getting cocky." Herm rocked slowly in a cane-back chair.

"I was just smiling."

"That's a tell that'll cost you the farm. Keep a straight face."

"I got to go soon. I have a game at three."

"Can you be back here by six?"

"I think I'm ready to play for real."

"The tables don't heat up over there until around nine anyway. Let's play a couple of games for cash, see how you do."

"Fine." Jack wiped his mouth with the back of his hand and turned to the kitchen. They played for another hour. Jack refused even a hint of a smile when he raked in the largest pot of the day, cleaning out two of the players. The silver-toothed player apparently didn't know that he telegraphed his weak hand every time he tapped that fake incisor with his tongue.

"Gotta go, boys. Time to play ball."

Herm's glare lightened up for the first time all day as he followed him out to his car. He leaned in the window as Jack let the Olds idle. "During that last hand, I saw Sugar." He patted Jack's arm. "Bring your money next time."

Jack rolled out of Herm's dusty drive and headed west into Delano. The afternoon heat had settled hard and burned away the grayness of the valley, bleaching the sky a burnished pale blue. With his windows down, the rush of air cooled him. Now he understood the meaning of that photo on the wall of the old farm office. The one with Sugar and Herm Gordon, young and prosperous, both in planter's hats, standing in freshly turned furrows up to their ankles. Neither of them smiled, only stared straight on as if they could stare down fate and misfortune. They were growers, gamblers, and men of the land.

Chapter 26
Black Diamond

THAT AFTERNOON STODDARD PITCHED for Delano, and Jack
moved to center field, Adrian's spot. He had to force himself
to pay attention to the game, his mind wandering back to the card
games. Despite his forced attention, he felt odd, as if he floated
outside the game and his friends. When his name was announced
over the PA playing centerfield, his teammates glanced down the
bench at him. Jack usually played left field when he wasn't pitching,
but with Adrian out, he moved over, and Sam Taylor took his
place in left. Neither of them could run like Adrian, but they could
catch fly balls. Neither of them could hit like Adrian, but they were
good enough.

Since Adrian's arrest, his teammates had been cool toward Jack.
A rumor floated around that Jack and Adrian had been together
when the fight went down with the grower. His teammates suspected
it was more than a rumor. The race for the league crown was tight;
both Delano and Arvin had only one loss. The last game of the
season, the Arvin boys were coming to town aching for revenge. To
make that game meaningful, they had to keep winning. And without
Adrian, their chances of winning everything were slim. Jack couldn't
mistake the meaning of their glances. He kept his chin up, ready when
his moment came. That's all he could do. Jack caught everything that
came his way, and had a couple of hits, but nothing timely. Taylor

played well but struck out four times. It was excruciating watching Taylor bat.

Down to their last at-bats, Barton doubling down the left field sidelines, driving in two runs, notching another win. The game over, Jack hustled to the locker room. While the others were showering, he dressed and then ran to his car.

By sunset, he took his place in Herm's smoke-filled kitchen. Two empty bottles of Don Julio tequila were on the counter, and empty beer cans filled the trash. They had played right through the afternoon, only taking breaks to piss, and now they were lousy with red eyes and loquacious ways.

The game began with a ten-dollar buy-in. Jack rolled off five ones and a five from the wad of bills Ella had given him on Thursday. Herm collected the cash, laid it on the counter, and set an empty tequila bottle on the stack of bills. It didn't take long for Jack to realize that even half crocked when these boys saw greenbacks every bit of their wit and vigor came alive.

A couple of hands in and half his chips had disappeared. When it came Silver Tooth's turn to deal, he had a grin as if he had something to hide. The men were restless, some smirking and passing under their breath asides in Spanish followed by spurts of laughter as though they had an inside joke. Maybe they were just drunk. Jack worked his hand, checking his cards, giving off false tells, chatting them up, wanting them to think he didn't see their antics.

On the fourth hand, he had a pair of pocket aces, and another one came on the flop. He bet strong, thinking he would induce at least two to fold. Only the toothless man tossed his cards to the table. Pancho Villa with the bushy mustache called and raised, forcing Jack to bet the rest of his chips if he stayed in. He considered folding, but with aces, he wanted to at least see the river card. He felt good. Mustache's brazen wager surprised Jack—an eight of diamonds, a six of clubs, the ace of hearts, and two of clubs showing on the table— at most he could have only a trip of eights, sixes, or twos. None of which would beat his three aces. Mustache man was an enigma with his bloodshot eyes and sallow skin. Jack pushed in the remainder of his chips. With the others out, it was just him and Mustache now.

Mustache dealt the river card: a two of spades. Jack pinched his bottom lip. He could have four deuces, but that was doubtful. He was all in, so Jack flopped over his pair of aces, confident with three of a kind. His opponent, stern-faced, turned his down cards over showing a pair of twos.

It wasn't the ten dollars he just lost, it was the snickering and going on among the three of them. And the fact Mustache was smiling the way a man did when he just stole something. Jack didn't like that at all.

The Mexican reached for the pot. Jack clenched his jaw and grabbed the man's wrists, stopping him from sliding the chips away.

"¡Hombre!" Silver Tooth said, "¿Que haces? The others scraped back their chairs. Herm sat by silently, ticking his bottom lip with a finger.

"What's going on here?" Jack eyed Herm, then the Mexican straight across from him.

"Ask him to stand." Herm motioned toward Silver Tooth.

"¡Levantate!" Jack said.

Jack let go, and the man slowly rose. A card fell out of his shirt, and another one lay on his seat. The three Mexicans started laughing. The men brushed several more cards out of their shirts, convinced this was the funniest trick they'd ever played. It took Jack a minute to realize this was more about having fun than cheating him; they just wanted to rough him up a bit. Jack pushed all the chips toward the Mustache, who promptly shoved them back. Jack waved him off.

"You deserve it. You almost got one over on me."

Even Herm smiled. "You picked that up, Jack." Herm patted his shoulder. "But if you think someone's cheating, call the pit boss."

"What if there isn't one, like here?" Jack scooped in the cards and shuffled them up.

"Ask for a new deck. Make sure they unwrap it in front of you. You won't catch guys sticking cards in their shirt like this."

"What if none of that works?"

"Whatever you do, I wouldn't grab a man like that unless you're among friends."

"I hate cheaters." Jack couldn't give a fellow a pass. He'd grab a cheater every time he caught one.

The rest of the evening everyone mostly played by the rules. There was a lot of friendly ribbing when Jack made a bonehead bet or bit on a ruse. He went on a winning streak, figuring out how to play these guys. It was a little before nine when he noticed he had almost cleaned them out. So he pushed his chair back.

"I'm going to take off." Jack rose. "You got any suggestions where to go first?"

"Whatever you do, don't go to Black Diamond by yourself," Herm cautioned.

"Sí, sí," They all chimed in.

Jack counted out the bills. He had won eighty-five dollars playing fives and tens. He rolled all $320 into a wad and stuffed it into his jeans pocket. And these guys were good.

"Don't go getting cocky." Herm looked him over with his dark eyes.

Jack buried a smirk. "No way. Just going to play cards, that's all." His boot heels clicked on the linoleum as he strode to the door. He peeled out, whipping up a tail of dust in the dry dirt. He clicked on the radio as he made the highway, heading toward the neon-lit card rooms that lay on the barren flatland adjacent to the Southern Pacific tracks in West Delano.

➤

JACK HESITATED UNDER THE blinking neon sign of the Black Diamond Card Club. The sign, a high black ace of diamonds outlined in garish pink tubes, lit up the front door. Herm had warned him to avoid playing here. He had already tried a few other places along the railroad tracks, but husky bouncers at the first two card rooms had turned him away, asking him for ID, claiming they just been raided. "Come back tomorrow," they said.

The Black Diamond was his only option tonight. He was too psyched up to go home without playing a few games. He remembered Herm's admonition to keep his mouth shut, as he pushed the door open and entered the darkness. A man moved from the shadows to greet him. Not the usual thick bouncer with a bull neck, but a stringy well-dressed Filipino with a thin face in a purple pastel suit.

"Are you lost?"

"I'm looking for a poker game." Jack heard his own voice, and it sounded shaky. This guy would kick him out on his ass if he didn't take charge.

The Filipino man gave him a soft smile. "I'm looking for a virgin with a million bucks."

"Have you tried up in Fresno?" Jack strode past him through the dark and smoky room to the bar. He took a stool and ordered a beer. The place didn't look half-bad. The tables were full and busy.

The Filipino slipped onto a stool next to him. "Do you have a note from your mother?"

"Do you have balls?" Jack sipped his drink. "If you do, they're going to get kicked to Fresno if you keep pestering me." Jack watched the man, thinking he had gotten under his skin. Maybe he had gone too far.

The man sniffed and savored a grin. "What's your preference besides gin rummy? Go Fish?"

They probably played this game to sort out the easy marks. Jack gave him a hard stare. Maybe this was why Herm had warned him against coming here. "Where are your five dollar tables?"

"Poker for five dollars?" He glanced around as if searching the room then faced Jack "We don't have five-dollar tables here. Have you tried those sleaze halls down the road? You'll love the mariachi music and the zesty chilies."

Jack wanted to clock the guy. Irritation was his game, so he turned to the smoke-choked room. The tables lit up by overhead lamps were full. He strolled among them, stopping to watch. These were all five-card draw tables. The Filipino came up beside him, close.

"You have to be eighteen to play on the main floor. We don't like to get busted for contributing to the delinquency of minors." The man picked at a nail. "It would ruin our reputation."

Herm and his friends had already warned him this place had a reputation. Yet, it looked much tamer than the other seedy cardrooms he had visited. Why didn't this place have muscle-bound bouncers and cute gals serving drinks?

"If you don't like draw poker, there's a Hold'em game in the back, but I wonder if you could afford the stakes?"

Jack patted the bulge in his pocket, and the second he did, he remembered that he should not have brought his entire roll in here. Herm had warned him to hide a bankroll in the car. To take only what he would risk losing. He studied the distance to the door halfway across the room from where he stood.

"So who's the one who doesn't have balls?" The Filipino laughed under his breath, snorting.

Jack put his hands in his pockets. This guy wanted to get into his pores. "What's the buy-in?"

"Fifty dollars." He folded his arms across his chest and gave Jack an arrogant glare. "And a two-drink minimum. We don't sell sodas, and you must have school tomorrow. What—second grade or third?"

"Kindergarten. Let's go see your game."

The man shook his head in warning, "A fool is soon parted with his money."

He turned on his heels, leading Jack through the maze of tables, down a hall, through another door, until he came to one that was closed. He knocked. It opened into a tightly packed room with two eight-player tables and a small bar at the far end. Smoke settled into rings around the hanging lamps. A husky doorman ushered him in, closed it, and took his seat by the door.

From the table in the back, a black man's hand full of diamond rings shot up. "Over here."

A cocktail waitress pointed to an empty seat.

"Welcome, my friend. Your first time here?" The man, the color of dark chocolate, smiled, and diamonds sparkled from their settings in both of his front teeth. Jack had dropped into this stranger's world. Black Diamond was a card player. Had Herm been warning him about a man? Jack's cheeks felt suddenly hot. He forced a smile as he shook the man's hand. It was sweaty and soft, pillow soft.

"I'm Ephraim Diamond. My friends call me Epha." His smile had an irresistible magnetism.

Jack wiped his upper lip. Herm's warning to stay alert, watch everyone, made him fidgety. One game here, then he'd take off.

Then he took a breath. Here he was sitting with a professional gambler, a notorious cardsharp he had been warned to avoid. But he had to know. If he was ripped up here, then he'd know to stick to bucking hay.

The dealer called for the buy-in. Jack worked the bills off his roll under the table. The others were from the ethnic strata that cut across this valley of immigrants—several Mexicans, an Arab, a slight Filipino man, and two Indian men who spoke with the thick accent of the Punjab community up near Visalia. And Mr. Diamond. Jack smiled. How would Sugar handle playing with this group?

The first two hole cards were dealt. The blinds started the betting. He had two unsuited cards, an eight and three. A folding hand, for sure. The betting went around. He forced himself not to smile: he'd played the same game with Herm's friends. Only his tablemates' skills and quirks were unknown to him. He stayed in the first hand as long as he could despite a lousy flop. He checked when he could, called when he had to, and studied the players' ticks and tells. He folded on the turn when the dealer flopped a five of diamonds, and the Arab pushed him out with an aggressive raise on Mr. Diamond's wager.

Jack sipped his beer and studied the players. It was all pretty much the usual movements—flicking of ears, resting hands flat on the table, scratching an ear, rubbing an eyebrow, and on and on. It would take Jack a few hands, but he could figure these guys out except for one. Mr. Diamond astonished him with his concentration—his head, his hands, his lips were perfectly still and his eyes soaked up everything. He touched his down cards once, and he never lifted a corner to recheck. He bet aggressively as the game wore on, pushing everyone out except the Arab.

Diamond won a game on the river with a straight, king high. Jack had seen the straight coming and wondered why the Arab stayed in, betting so heavy with only a pair of tens.

By the middle of the third hand, Jack could hold his own. Most of the players were average from what Jack saw, and already one of them was down to a stack of five chips. Conserving his chips, Jack went out early on the next hand. *Play few hands.* Herm's voice rang in his head.

One of the Indians took the third pot with three fives. Still, through winning and folding, Mr. Diamond didn't show any sign of concern or favor any habit that Jack could tie to a particular draw of cards. He understood better Herm's concern for his own expressions of euphoria and smart-aleck faces. Any of that nonsense here and Mr. Diamond would clean him out.

When Mr. Diamond raked in a large pot on the sixth hand, wiping out two of the Mexicans and the Arab, Jack understood the pattern of his play. His was a bluffer's game. He won early. And with the advantage of chips, he could push the weaker players out late in the hand. He played on their fears more than their cards. The last couple of hands, he hadn't needed to show his cards when players folded early. That only mystified the players—was he bluffing or not?

The man's impassiveness continued to impress Jack. He played so many hands he had to be bluffing unless someone was feeding him cards. Jack studied the dealer's every movement and couldn't detect any bottom or false dealing. When Jack was dealt two eights for hole cards, he sensed the game turning. He let Diamond lead. Jack held perfectly still, not nervously checking and rechecking his down cards like the Indian player across the table. On the turn, the dealer placed an eight of diamonds on the table. Trip eights. He let it sit. He called Diamond's bet and raised it double.

Diamond reraised aggressively.

The man's game was clear to Jack. He counted on pushing players out with big bets late in the game.

Jack called him all in, pushing the remainder of his chips into the middle. For the first time, Diamond rubbed his chin with a forefinger. Jack held his eyes steady on his cards.

"I will call you, young man." The dealer slid Diamond's chips over to match Jack's. "Maybe your luck has not entirely turned."

The last card, the river, a deuce. With no more chips, Jack turned over his pair of eights, and all eyes went to his opponent, who frowned for the first time that evening and refused to turn over his cards.

Jack ignored his pettiness and just raked in his chips, doubling his stake in one hand.

These men didn't play a game he couldn't handle. He played the rest of the night as if he belonged. They didn't have anything on him but experience.

Close to midnight, he drained what was left of his only beer and was up to $425. Not bad for a beginner. He'd have Adrian out in no time. Mr. Diamond was gracious when Jack settled his tab and rose to leave, shaking his hand and inviting him back anytime. The bouncer at the door let him out the back exit, straight into the parking lot.

The thick wad of bills in his pocket lifted him, and a smile burst on his lips until it threatened to split his face open. He loved

Mr. Diamond's exasperated look, one of unexpected defeat when Jack flopped over his pair of eights. He wanted to drive right out to Herm's, but it was late.

The lot was much darker than when he arrived. He craned his neck, searching for his car. Hadn't there been a couple of lot lights on when he drove up? Even the dual pink band of neon tubes that wrapped around the top of the building were off. He stumbled between rows of cars in the pitch-blackness looking for his Olds.

He stood on his toes scanning the roofs of cars. By the time he heard the footsteps and turned, a club was in the air above his head. He jerked up his arms to block the truncheon, but a foot smashed into his crotch, knocking the breath from him, bending him over. A hard smash on the back of his head fired a shock of pain down to his feet. His legs buckled, darkness rushed in, and he crumpled, throwing his head against the rough blacktop, and sending him to a place of futile dreams.

Chapter 27
Bread of Suffering

THE CAGED BULB IN the center of the ceiling glared day and night. Adrian told time by the lurching of his stomach. No one had a watch, and no clocks were visible to him from the small cage he occupied with fifty other campesinos. He had counted when they came, when they left, when they fainted, when they took a dump in the corner pot, the odor so rank it leached any good feeling about his life right out of him.

Minute merged into minute. The hours slithered along in dark days until weariness became an afterthought. At first, his anger exhausted him. Dragged away in cuffs in front of Darcy, his teammates, the whole damn school, and shoved into this rat-hole. He imagined the rumors that flew around: He killed someone. He raped a girl. He punched a teacher.

He doubted he'd ever be invited to Darcy's again. Had his scholarship vanished too? He vacillated between wanting to kill Kauffman for treating him like a criminal to a sinking shame—his arrest would mark him forever.

He'd helped a friend and look at him now. Where was Jack? Where was his father? His mother was useless. The day she came, she had stood by his cage and wept.

Packed in here, shifting his weight from foot to foot to ease the pain, his loneliness cast a pall that turned into a lump of red-hot coal—*these bastards want us to hate them. To take out our anger out on them.*

He calculated the days by how many meals they slipped through an opening in the bars. Meals fit for pigs. He drank the porridge it was so runny. The coffee stank of something medicinal. Birds would choke on the bread.

On the sixth day, Ella visited. They only allowed her a brief time. He worked his way to the edge of the cell. She stood in the dank light of the hall. Her tortured face striped by the iron bars between them. Darcy's father wouldn't allow her to come. Jack was busy working on bailing him out. She told him about his father.

His father in jail too! He didn't hear anything more Ella said before a crisply uniformed deputy ushered her out. He stared at the empty hall. Cells on both sides of him were packed with campesinos. His father was the one person he depended on to figure things out. If his father couldn't help him. He closed his eyes to calm himself.

Jack…Jack was trying. The boy was flat broke. What could he do?

The jailer called another name, and a visitor entered the hall. Adrian shuffled back through the crowd to his place in the middle. He stood under the naked light. Jammed into this square cell, he only possessed enough room to breathe; room to shift his weight from left to right; room to turn to stare at the back someone's greasy head, instead of some fellow's nose or whiskered face. And just enough room to simmer. Everything he had worked for was circling down the drain.

With so many men, unwashed, unshaven, and underfed, odors flooded in until they were all living in a cesspool. The jailers wanted them to breathe deeply of it, to take it in until it corroded something human inside them. Adrian stood next to Pedro, who stood next to someone else, men with names that he would have remembered if fatigue hadn't stunted his memory. When he closed his eyes, he imagined frigid air from the earth's depths shot through his shoes, ramming its way up his shins, through his thighs and groin, right up into his guts. After so many days, it became too cold to think of much else besides marshaling the strength to stay on his feet.

When a man dropped to the floor exhausted, they would gather around and try to revive him, lift him, cajoling him to endure this gringo justice until some angel bailed him out. *He was not forgotten. This will not go on forever. There will be an end to it soon.* Sometimes the men rose and took their place among those who set their jaws to endure. Other times resolve washed from their spirits, and they began to whimper until it became an agonizing cry. The jailers in their pressed uniforms shoved their way in and dragged those men away. At times Adrian could hear their wails from down long halls as they traveled deeper into the bowels of justice.

Whimpering would not save him. How did one get enough steel inside to keep from breaking down?

What they called dinner arrived—a tepid gruel, a cup of coffee, the steam more nutritious than any food, and a piece of hard bread. Hard bread for hard people. He chewed it slowly. He must stay hard and unbreakable to resist the fragility of defeat. He ate the crust with a wry smile, relishing the sharpness on his gums. Was this his bread of suffering? *This will not go on forever. Endure. Stay calm.*

He closed his eyes as he sipped his coffee. In the dark of his imagination, the entire world was on fire, flames licked buildings, incinerating it all. He carried a torch, setting fire to the world.

The iron door clanked open, and another campesino was shoved in. It clanked shut with metallic certainty. No one was taken out. Now there were fifty-one. Everyone gave an inch here and there for the new man. Whispering came from the edges. Eyes turned to the new man, who spoke in quiet tones to those around him. Chewing stopped. The news passed from ear to ear.

"Cesar has fasted now for ten days." Pedro cupped his hand around Adrian's ear. "No food or drink. He is with our suffering. No one is to strike back or to let the gringo pain enter his soul. We are not to hate them."

Adrian stared back at Pedro, while a piece of crust bit into his gum. He did not grimace. *We are not to hate them.*

"Pass it on, brother," Pedro said, smiling as if all the meanness of the moment had lifted. Adrian could not say that. Those words would not form on his lips. When Adrian hesitated, his neighbor nudged him with an elbow. An eon passed before Adrian turned to the man nearest him, cupped his hand to the man's ear. He repeated the sentences to those around him, giving to others words he was not convinced would help. But he said them anyway, hoping they would extinguish the inferno inside: *We are not to hate.*

Chapter 28
Planter's Hat

As soon as Jack showed up at school Monday, Coach drove him over to the doctor's office. Doc Barton sewed six stitches into his scalp in a conspiratorial silence; neither did Jack offer any story. Explaining the stupidity of walking into a pitch-dark lot with a pocketful of cash eluded his loquaciousness. This morning he had woken a bit after one, chilled and damp, lying next to his Olds. He had to squint to keep the parking lot lights from stabbing his brain. He felt the sticky blood on his scalp and staunched the bleeding with a T-shirt. At home, he bandaged it with masking tape and another T-shirt. In the morning, he slipped out before his mother could fuss over him, and drove to school with Herm's admonition to stay away from the Black Diamond whispering in his ears.

After returning from Doc's, he had only made one morning class; his head throbbed, and he felt weak. At lunchtime, Jack didn't eat at his usual place in the cafeteria, but under the oak in the quad. Now with his back to the tree, he rehearsed the different ways he could avoid the subject of money with Ella. She found him propped up against the bole of the tree.

"Aren't you eating?" She sat in the grass and set her tray beside her.

He shook his head. "Have you heard anything from Adrian?"

"The union bailed out Mr. Sanchez." She pushed the French fries around on her plate.

"Did you see Adrian this weekend?"

She nodded. "He's pretty low. The jail's a pigsty. He's packed in with a whole bunch of others."

Jack stared off into the quad, kids lounging in the sunshine, laughing, talking. He deeply regretted his friend wasn't here to enjoy it. He hung his head. Thinking of Adrian in that ratty jail made him wish he had never seen the combine, never met Herm, and hadn't cracked the door open to his father's past.

"So are you going to tell me what happened?" Ella pushed her hair over her ear.

"Happened what?"

"Marcy saw you in third period. Said you have a horrible cut on your scalp like your head has been split open or something."

He was about to tell her a lie, and say it was nothing really, that he just fell during practice. But news traveled fast along the girl grapevine. Marcy hadn't wasted any time sending in her report. He'd have to tell Ella soon enough about losing the money she gave him the other day.

"Can I see it?" She leaned close, and he bent his head around. She gasped.

"Jack, it's so ugly. How did that happen?"

Doc had shaved a patch of his scalp, and the stitches couldn't look too pretty. He told her about playing at the Black Diamond, winning big, and then getting rolled in the parking lot.

She kissed his cheek then leaned her head on his shoulder, snuggling close. "Please, Jack, no more gambling. I don't care about the money you lost. I'll help you raise more."

"I need the whole thing in the next week or two."

"I've been talking to people. Darcy has some money, but her folks are forcing her not to get involved. They think Adrian deserves getting arrested. But there're others who want to help. I've been talking to Kathy."

"Your sister?"

Ella nodded. "She thinks it's stupid what happened to Adrian. She wants to help."

"She's always had a thing for quarterbacks."

"And cops!" A mischievous grin came over Ella's face. "You won't believe what's been going on the last couple of weeks with her and a certain cop."

"What? She get a ticket for wearing a skirt that's too short?"

"She's getting back with Earl."

Jack shook his head slowly. "No. No. How can she do that?"

"He's been coming around a lot like he used to."

Jack groaned and rubbed his forehead, trying to sort out all this news. Earl Kauffman was the epitome of every evil that festered in this valley. Now he would know everything Jack was up to, gambling to bail out his friend.

"You told Kathy everything I'm doing, and now she'll tell Kauffman. He'll use her to get to me, I know he will."

"It's not like that, Jack. I'm sure."

"You've never had a gun shoved in your face. If you had, you'd never trust that guy."

"She'll help us, Jack. I don't think you'll have to worry much about Earl anymore."

"I appreciate whatever she can do, but I'm not going to let Adrian rot waiting around for people to help. Sheriff Grant makes his jail a stink hole on purpose." Jack touched her hair. He didn't think Ella was naïve, but he didn't see how Kathy dating Kauffman again could help him or Adrian.

"If she wants to help us, she can slip some arsenic in his coffee."

"Oh, Jack, you don't understand much about women."

"I know enough."

What he didn't like was the enormous weight that hung over his head. The full force of it would crush him if he didn't find a way to spring his friend. He had urged Adrian to help rescue that blasted combine. Adrian's presence of mind had saved him from getting a worse beating. He kept Jack from nearly killing the old man. And Adrian paid the full price of Jack's confused thinking. He had misjudged how easy it would be to take back what was rightfully his. He had underestimated the Black Diamond. His whole life seemed boiled down to one wrongheaded decision after another.

"You okay?" Ella asked.

"I gotta go." He pushed himself up from the ground. He had to keep moving, keep pushing, or this anvil of recriminations would drop for sure.

➤

"I TOLD YOU NOT to play the Black Diamond," Herm said, leaning against the counter still littered with tequila bottles and beer cans. The three Mexicans stared at him across the table. The sun had just set on Monday, and the cramped kitchen stank in the Central Valley oven.

"Yeah, well, I didn't know Black Diamond was a gambler. There wasn't much I could do about it once I was at his table." Jack held a dishtowel packed with ice Herm had applied to his throbbing head.

"You beat the Black Diamond." Pancho Villa shook his head slowly while flashing Jack an admiring smile.

"*Cojones grandes*," Silver Tooth said.

They all laughed, even Jack, though he grimaced in pain.

"Yeah, but he also had me rolled." Jack winced. "Almost five hundred dollars gone like that."

The three Mexicans moaned, sighed, and shook their heads.

"It most likely wasn't the Diamond's doing." Herm handed Jack a shot glass of tequila. "This will help."

Jack sipped the drink; it burned down to his shoes.

"It's not the Black Diamond's style to roll players," Herm said. "He usually takes it at the table. He's the best around."

"You beat him, yes?" Silver Tooth said, "That is a *milagro*."

"No miracle. Skill," Herm said. "But you pissed someone off. Who'd you smart mouth?"

Jack held the ice bag to his skull, his eyes skirting over the green and white pattern of the Formica table.

"Ah." Three of the Mexicans sighed at once, raising their chins knowingly, chatting with each other in rapid-fire Spanish.

"You met the Filipino, sí?" Silver Tooth asked with a wry smile.

Jack pressed his lips together.

He slapped the table. "Sí,"

"Did you smart-mouth the Filipino?" Herm gave him a scrutinizing glare.

"He's a jerk."

"That's his job," Herm said. "To sift people out, make sure they're not cops or crooks. He spots the easy marks and keeps Black Diamond's table full. I told you not to go in there."

"Muchacho, what did you say to him?" Silver Tooth asked.

Jack laid out his conversation with the Filipino.

"Muchacho, he kicked your cojones to LA." They all laughed uproariously. Jack felt a dagger of guilt twisting into him. His scalp tingled. The slight, effeminate, unlikable man had deserved to get kicked around a bit.

"Amigo, listen here." The Mexican's bushy Pancho Villa mustache pulsed up and down as he spoke. He pointed a finger at Jack. "Do not say one word of threat you do not intend to do at that very moment."

"You have to cut that crap out." Herm reprimanded him. "You have to keep to yourself."

"You cannot go back there." Silver Tooth wagged a finger.

"I'm not going back." Jack set down the ice pack.

"None of the card rooms in Delano are safe now." Mustache man said slicing the air with his hand. They all shook their heads in agreement. "If the Filipino is after you, it's *muy malo*."

"Why is that?" Jack asked.

"You see, Filipinos are lower than Mexicans in the minds of the Anglo," Mustache man said.

"True," Herm said. "But that's not the reason the Filipino is so dangerous. He harbors a special vendetta. His uncle is Larry Itliong."

"The union guy who started the strike?" Jack asked.

"Exactly." Herm tapped his cigarette ash into an ashtray. "He grew up with some tough fellows, the Itliong brothers. He resents the fact he had to be either a picker or a gambler, so he takes his frustrations out on unsuspecting marks. You had grower's son written all over you. A rich kid who comes in with a pocket full of cash and pushes his way around. He's not going to take that from some punk kid. Not in his house."

Jack rubbed the back of his neck. "I really pissed him off."

Herm nodded. "It would have been better to spend more time in the Delano card rooms, but the Filipino will have you rolled anywhere you play, to make his point. He knows you won't go to the cops. If you can beat the Black Diamond, then you're ready for Bakersfield."

The Mexicans nodded, eagerly agreeing. "But keep your mouth shut, sí."

"Cicero's on Fourteenth Street's a safe place. They have twenty-five- and fifty-dollar tables on the main floor." Herm leaned an elbow on the table. "The big money's in the backrooms. That's where the growers play. I'd tell you to stay away from them, but that's just wasting my breath. You go shooting your mouth off with them, worse will happen to you than a knock on the head."

Jack hitched in a breath and pictured himself playing those big guys. Jack could taste the satisfaction of taking Kolcinivitch down.

"And wear a hat," Herm added in an offhand way. "You don't want to give anyone ideas on how to handle your fancy talk."

The room fell quiet; all eyes were fixed on Jack.

"You know how your father got his nickname, Sugar?" Herm asked.

Jack gave a slight shake of his head.

"He was always sweet about taking folks' money. The more he soaked them for, the more they wanted to play him again."

"Sí, *dulce*," Silver Tooth said.

They all swigged their drinks, snorting their laughter, wiping their mouths on their sleeves. They poured more rounds until the joviality over his gaffe with the Filipino and the marvel over his exploits with the Black Diamond lay thick and warm in the air. Jack rested his forehead on the table and adjusted the ice pack, disgusted he had let six-hundred dollars so easily slip away. He had to find a way not to let his mouth undo the magic of his game.

➤

TUESDAY AFTERNOON COACH LET him out of practice to rest. Instead of heading home, Jack hauled his father's ball card collection down to Bakersfield to a sports memorabilia shop on Truxton Avenue. Earlier he had talked to the owner on the phone. The owner was willing to appraise the cards.

Jack laid them on the counter, and the man shook his head as he casually flipped through the cards, sneering at the lesser names. He mildly raised a brow when he pulled out the pristine DiMaggio, the Mays rookie card, a Mickey Mantle card, and a few others. Examining them carefully, he frowned, hemmed, and jotted notes. Pulling out a thick catalog, he flipped through the pages searching for values. Jack followed the man's finger as he found the price listed in the catalog, reading it upside down. He offered to buy only thirteen of them, including the Willie Mays rookie card and autographed pristine DiMaggio for $325 cash.

"But that's a signed DiMaggio." Jack pointed to the card in a plastic sleeve laid out on the counter. "The book says it's worth five hundred dollars in excellent condition."

"That's what a collector might pay for it. I don't make money collecting cards, I sell them."

Jack gathered his cards slowly, settled them into the Tupperware, and patted them down into neat rows.

"If you want to leave them here on consignment, I can probably sell them for a lot more. But it's going to take a couple of months. You gotta put them in the catalogs and place ads in hobby magazines. It takes time and costs money."

Jack snapped on the Tupperware cover. "I don't have time."

"Most folks don't." He closed his catalog and crumpled up his notes. "There's no guarantee I'll find a buyer either. That's a risk I take shelling out even a dollar for your whole lot."

Outside on the sidewalk, standing in the bright sunshine, traffic on Truxton flicked back and forth. San Francisco was a five-hour drive north. LA was four hours south. He could spend a week negotiating with shop owners before he got a decent price.

Sitting in his car, he knew he'd regret parting with them. He didn't need more than a couple of hundred dollars and some gas money to get started. One card in the whole lot was worth $500. He fired up the Olds, swung a U-turn, and took off toward downtown. He found the outfit he wanted squeezed between a used furniture emporium and a liquor store. It took nearly an hour to bargain the scruffy pawnshop owner up to $225 by continually putting a finger on DiMaggio's face, reminding the pawnbroker of its value.

"Well, I don't know that for certain." The man handed him a receipt with his final offer of $235.

Jack took the money. The shop owner slid a red ticket stub across the counter. He had sixty days to redeem his collection. Sixty days, that's it, the fellow repeated. Jack watched as he slipped the plastic container of cards into a glass case next to a tray of diamond rings and locked it, clipping the keys on a hoop ring at his belt.

At home in his bedroom, Jack taped the pawn ticket inside his top desk drawer and covered it with a pile of schoolbooks. Later, after his mother went to bed, he stood before the mirror over his dresser adjusting his baseball cap. He had worn it every minute since Herm mentioned it yesterday. It covered his wound. Not even his mother suspected anything. He would need to wear one when he played cards. But his Delano cap made him look every bit a high school kid. He tossed it on his bed, scrounged around, and came up with an old Giant's cap he had bought at Candlestick a few years before. It made him look even younger. He remembered the photo on the farm office wall of Herm and Sugar. The two were young but had the gaze of men who knew the score. And they wore hats.

He snuck down the stairs in his socks, not letting the tired boards betray him. In the farm office on the second floor, he flicked on the light and closed the door with a gentle click of the knob. Sugar and Herm smiled at him as they stood in the furrows of a freshly plowed field, hats on their heads, and a gleam of satisfaction in their eyes. Jack loved that photo. Herm's was a planter's hat, with its round crown, wide brim and a flat top. Sugar's was more of a fedora style with an oblong crown pointed in front, and a shaped rim turned slightly down over the eyes. He looked self-assured and determined in his khaki pants and a chambray shirt.

Jack's eyes floated upward where he hadn't looked in years and spied his father's gray felt hat hanging on a hook near the ceiling. What harm could there be in trying it on? He moved a few items on the credenza, hoisted himself up, and reached for the hat. He lowered himself to the floor quietly. He replaced everything on the credenza, not one item out of place. He would have it back up there before morning. He just wanted a look-see in the mirror.

Standing in front of the mirror, he adjusted it. It fit a little snugger than the last time he tried it on since his hair had grown out. First, he slid it down low over his right eye. Too jaunty. He wouldn't be taken seriously. Then he set it straight on but with the brim low over his eyes. A man with something to hide. He flattened the rim and fixed it straight on his head. He looked older, more settled. He smiled the way his father had in the photo, and lightly touched the brim with a finger. He tingled inside, content and self-assured, ready for an adventure.

He set the hat on his dresser. His mother had been very busy since Jack had come home with the combine, fixing things, running errands, unpacking her boxed up belongings. He doubted she would miss an old hat hanging up high on a peg.

Chapter 29
Necessity

WHEN JACK'S TURN CAME up to pitch on Wednesday, Coach insisted he sit it out, fearing his stitches would open up. Jack convinced him otherwise and took the mound on the hottest day of the year so far. He shut out a weak Trasco High squad through five innings with curves, fastballs, and sweat. In the top of the sixth, a Trasco player hit a sharp double over Barton's head at third. Coach trotted to the mound and took the ball.

Jack didn't argue. He was soaked down to the yarn in his socks. After the game, he spent a long while under a cold shower. Outside, Ella leaned against his car waiting. She took his hand and looked into his eyes.

"I'm talking to everyone. I think I can get the money."

"I'm not going to play in West Delano anymore. It's too dangerous."

"I don't want you to play anywhere." She held his hand tight.

"I'm going to play in Bakersfield. It's safer there."

"What about school? Graduationis less than six weeks away. You can't let your GPA slip."

"I'm all caught up in my classes."

"Except algebra."

"I'm going to pass."

She frowned and bit a fingernail. "Are you going to do this in LA?"

Jack watched the line of cars leaving the lot, boys honking and making noise. "I owe Adrian."

"We all do, Jack." She left him standing in the white afternoon light. He watched as she stomped off, unhappiness in the hitch of her shoulders, in the tight determined swing of her hips. He turned to his car and settled behind the wheel. He closed his eyes. Losing a few hundred dollars was one thing. But his friendship with Adrian was impossible to measure. He fired up the motor. It lolled with a tired-sounding lope. It had to carry him places tonight. Bakersfield lay due south, straddling Highway 99, thirty minutes on the fly.

➤

CICERO'S WAS THE ELEGANT daughter of a dusty and dried out Bakersfield, its plush purple carpet splashed with diamonds, spades, hearts, and clubs. Jack arrived after seven, as Herm had suggested. A husky fella in the lobby nodded his way as Jack strode through the lobby, touching the brim of his hat in return. He sauntered into the main hall. In a crisp white shirt and pressed khakis, he fit right in here.

He only brought in fifty dollars. The rest of his money was stuffed under his spare in the trunk of the Olds parked close to the door. At a cashier's window, the woman gave him a hard once-over but took his bills and slid him fifty dollars in chips. He touched the tip of his hat and smiled. She tittered and smiled from the side of her mouth. Jack strolled by several tables of five-card draw. He wasn't interested in that game. He was beginning to think Hold'em was only played in the back room when he spotted a livelier table in the far corner, one he recognized. The hand concluded, and a seat opened up. He climbed in, stroked his greenbacks onto the felt, and pulled his chips in front of him. He felt a little lightheaded, fearing a tap on this shoulder, and a rough escort outside, but no one gave him even a second glance. The dealer spun out the first two down cards. The small and big blinds began the betting.

He chatted and complimented the others on their play while carefully observing the dealer's habits. The players were good, solid men of the area—plumbers, carpenters, a roustabout from Oildale, and even a lawyer. Jack could tell that because the slim man had clean fingernails and spoke so precisely. With his amiableness, Jack found that the men dropped their guard a bit, and the signs and tells of their play began to appear. A few of them were veterans of the table and bet with strategy and care; they lived the game.

By eleven, Jack was up $175 and ready to call it a night. He shook hands all around, and cashed out with the same woman, tipping his hat when she finished counting out the bills. She blushed. In the lobby, he stopped to ask the bouncer a question about area restaurants. When a group of men, laughing and carrying-on strolled by, he followed them out. Slipping behind the wheel, he locked the doors. A good first night, but he needed to pick up the pace, or it would take a month to spring Adrian.

On Thursday night, he returned at seven sharp. He purchased chips from his favorite cashier and strolled the floor until he saw a familiar face. The lawyer sat at a fifty-dollar table between two players who appeared dicey. He took a seat, nodding at his fellow players. From the very first hand the lawyer had a rough go of it; the two men who flanked him kept the bets high on worthless hands, bluffing him right out of his chips. Jack folded nearly every deal until that game ended, with the player to the lawyer's right taking in most of the chips. Jack had lost almost half his chips, but others had been cleaned out.

Jack stood. "We need to draw for seats."

"I think we're okay," the winner said, a man in a purple shirt and lying eyes. "Let's just keep sitting where we are."

"We're not fine."

"I agree." The lawyer pushed back his chair and rose.

"We'll redraw after the next game." The dealer gathered the cards and began shuffling. "You can go to another table if you don't like it."

"I'm not moving," Jack insisted. "I just want you to play by the rules."

"What're you saying?" The dealer stiffened his back.

"Is there a problem over here?" A man in a gray suit rested his hand on the back of a player's chair and glanced around.

"He lacks clarity of the rules," the lawyer said, nodding toward the dealer. "We're starting a new game, and we want to redraw for seats, but…"

The pit boss stared down at the dealer, who then sorted through the deck and placed seven cards, numbered two through eight, face down on the table.

"Dealer holds the ace," the pit boss said.

Jack leaned over and shuffled the cards around on the felt, then picked a five of spades. Players took their seats in order of their numbers. Jack held his position. The lawyer now moved to his right, away from the two men who had been suckering him all night.

From the first deal, Jack's cards turned to him. The two squeeze boys were now on opposite sides of the table and weren't able to force players out. An hour later Jack closed out the game, cleaning everyone out but the lawyer, with a magnificent straight flush that apparently no one saw coming. Taking away what he lost in the first hand, he was now up to $195 on the night with more time to play.

Before the next game, the lawyer leaned over to Jack. "Let me buy you a drink."

A few minutes later, seated at the far end of the card room at a cocktail table, Jack sipped a Coors while Todd Hennley worked on a Bloody Mary.

"Thanks for saving me from those two charlatans." Todd stirred his drink.

"They must have been paying the dealer and he didn't want to mess with a good thing."

"You play really well for such a young Turk. Where'd you learn to manage a game like that?"

"Necessity."

Todd leaned an elbow on the table and rested his chin in his hand. "I love hearing stories about necessity."

Jack told him about his mother's tax problem, the stolen combine, how he stole it back, and of Adrian's illegal arrest, his incarceration, and the necessity he had to raise $2,500.

Todd shook his head, slowly taking it all in. "Was your father a grower?"

He nodded. "Is it the hat?"

"At first I thought it was a tad pretentious, but now I realize it's really you."

Jack raised the hat and turned his wound to him.

"Man, that's nasty."

Jack told him about his unfortunate run at Black Diamond's in Delano.

"So, you're more than a man of fashion?"

"You could say that. But now I like it."

"It looks good," Todd said. "How much do you have so far?"

"I'm at four hundred and fifty dollars. I have a ways to go."

"Let's get back to the game. Every minute your friend's in that filthy place is a minute too long. We can talk later."

They played together until 11:30 when Jack had enough for the evening and cashed in, now up $325 on the night. He winked at the cashier after she counted out the money, and she flashed him a sly smile. Todd walked with him to his car.

"I admire you for what you're doing." They shook hands. He agreed to meet Jack again that weekend.

➤

AROUND MIDNIGHT JACK PULLED into the brightly lit gas station off Route 99, in Delano. He cut the engine by the pump, clambered out, and pushed the nozzle into the throat of the gas tank and set it to fill. While leaning against the pump exhilaration and fatigue coursed through him. He had almost $500 in his pocket. If he could juggle school, baseball, and gambling, he could spring Adrian in no time. His friend would be back on the team and life would return to normal.

The *ding, ding* of a car pulling up to the pumps behind him interrupted his reverie. He heard the door slam, and a customer filling his tank. Jack felt too weary and uninterested to turn around. When the nozzle clicked off, Jack racked it on the pump. He froze at the sight in the next bay over. Deputy Kauffman had one foot up on the bumper of his cruiser. They both stared at each other in the cold morning.

"Hey," Kauffman said, an unfamiliar nonchalance in his tone.

"Hey," Jack said, stunned at the sight of Kauffman. Jack gathered himself, strode to the cashier, paid for his gas, and walked calmly to his car.

"You're out awful late, aren't you?"

"A friend was helping me with my algebra."

"I heard you're working on numbers, but not for school."

Jack felt suddenly flushed. "Who's telling those lies?"

"You calling Kathy a liar?"

Jack felt a ball of iron in his stomach. He knew this would happen.

"You haven't heard?"

"Heard what?"

"Kathy and I are back together."

Oh, yeah. Ella's beauty queen sister. Kathy must have told him everything about his plans.

"That's great." Jack still could not imagine Ella's beautiful, sophisticated sister with this oaf. Not since the friendly Earl Kauffman had become irascible Deputy Kauffman. "Congratulations."

Kaufman stepped up on the island, and Jack moved to his door.

"I would never have shot you, you know that, don't you?"

"It didn't look that way to me." Jack slowly opened the car door, not wanting to appear nervous. The cold steel barrel of the deputy's .45 pointed at his face still haunted Jack's dreams.

Kauffman stood over Jack, so he eased his door open and slipped inside. He didn't have the energy to argue with him tonight. Neither did he want to get hassled. Not with all this cash in his pocket. Jack snapped the door shut. Kauffman stepped down beside the Olds, resting his hand on the window frame. Jack turned the motor over.

The deputy leaned down so Jack could see him. "I wouldn't have shot you, Jack."

His voice was pleading as if he were asking for forgiveness. Jack had no room in his heart to reconcile this new Kauffman with the old Kauffman.

"But you still wanted me to fink on my best friend."

"Yeah, but you didn't, and things worked out for you, didn't they?"

"Not for Adrian."

Kauffman rolled something around in his mouth, thinking it over.

"That came from the top. I was just doing my job."

Jack had much more to say, but he didn't want to start a fight. It appeared Kauffman didn't either. Was this another game or an apology?

"Cops are supposed to do good, aren't they?"

Kauffman raised up, hitched his belt, and tapped the roof of the car. "Drive careful."

Jack rolled out of the station onto Cecil. In his rearview, he spotted Kauffman climbing into his squad car. Jack passed under the 99 and lost sight of the station. And no one followed him as he headed down the dark county road toward home.

That night in bed, he lay awake trying to figure out Kauffman's game. Was this a new side of him, the human being Kauffman? Only time would tell.

Chapter 30
Playing With Sharks

AFTER PRACTICE ON FRIDAY, Ella and Darcy waited by his car, both of them leaned against the fender, heads down, arms crossed. They had been crying.

"What happened? Adrian okay?" His friend's face flashed before him: his lifeless body on the concrete floor, the breath beaten out of him by some bastard cop. He hugged Ella, and she clung to him as she recounted a conversation with Mr. Sanchez at his home.

Adrian's public defender wanted him to cop a plea. If he agreed to plead guilty to assault and battery, they would drop the grand theft charges. A generous deal according to the DA, which would reduce Adrian's jail time to less than a year. Jack stopped hearing her words, submerged in the loathing of what he had brought on his friend. Yet certain words slipped through: *a felony, jail time, not graduate, lose scholarship...*

Darcy couldn't stop shaking, so Jack drove them to a coffee shop. He assured her this travesty would never stand. If Adrian was convicted for something he didn't do, Jack wouldn't be able to live with himself. He had to find someone interested in the truth.

It took a while to calm the girls. Later he dropped them in the school parking lot and watched them drive away in Darcy's teal VW bug.

He headed out of the lot toward Highway 99, but he kept making wrong turns—left here, right there—not recognizing the streets of the very town he called home, unexplainably confused at the signs that read south and north. Landmarks had disappeared, the Sierra Mountains to the east shrouded in the afternoon haze. He peered through the windshield, into the brightness. Blinded by the afternoon sun, he clamped on the brakes.

A horn blew, startling him. Then it turned into a deafening chorus. He had braked halfway into an intersection, blocking cars behind him. The light glowed green ahead of him.

"Get moving, fella," someone yelled.

Off to his right, a sign finally made sense: Bakersfield 22 Miles. He remembered why he needed to make that road. He swung onto the on-ramp, jammed the gas pedal to the floor, and the Olds thumped up the ramp onto the 99.

➤

A MAN CANNOT WIN at cards with a sour face. Herm had tutored Jack well in that truth. He greeted the cashier with a smile and a tip of his hat, and bought $400 worth of chips, nearly all of his cash.

"Good luck to you." She winked and flashed him a demure smile. The fun of the chase settled in. He needed to play big tonight at the highest stakes tables he could find. Last night Todd had said that the county jail was a filthy hole. He should know. He did criminal defense. Todd wasn't at any of the tables. The maximum bet on the floor was fifty dollars. There were tables with higher limits, the pit boss told him. But one had to be invited. The man said this with a condescending smile that made Jack want to wipe it clean with his play.

He settled at a table in the middle of the room facing the long, blacked-out windows running the width of the card room. Must be where the high rollers played and hooted at the lesser folk. He went on a losing streak for the first few hands, missing many hints the players were giving off. He played tight, holding back, not going beyond the flop, refusing to wager on the weak combinations in his hole cards. The blinds began to eat away at his chips. He considered changing tables when a slick-looking fellow with a sharp nose and a neatly pressed maroon dress shirt took a seat, making it seven players.

Jack now sat fifth from the dealer, and his cards took a sudden turn for the better. A pocket pair of queens were dealt him face down. Three clubs in a row appeared on the flop, seven, eight, and nine. A possible straight flush in the making. On the turn, the queen of clubs showed up, giving him trips. A strong hand, but Maroon shirt had a hungry look in his eyes. He pushed in fifty dollars.

The player next to Jack folded. Jack had too good a hand not to work it, so he called. So did another player. The pot now had more than $200. On the river, another lady, the queen of hearts, showed her beautiful face. A rare hand indeed. He contained his glee. Odds were against any of the other players drawing four face cards in the same hand, even the straight flush. Maroon shirt guy couldn't have anything better than four ladies. He could have three kings. But Jack had him beat. Maroon shirt guy jiggled his hands with determined movements as if he believed he had a winning hand. He pushed in another fifty dollars.

Now it was fifty dollars to Jack, and, without hesitation, he pushed it in, not containing his smile. Jack flipped his queens over and leisurely reached for the pot.

"Not so fast," said Maroon shirt. A miserable sinking knot mushroomed in Jack's stomach at the sight of Maroon shirt's flop: a five and nine of clubs, giving him a straight flush.

It was against all probable odds, but there it was in front of him on the green felt. The men around the table mumbled and cursed as Maroon shirt raked in a pot of almost $400.

Down $150, Jack had been warned that marginal players often withered away if they didn't mount a comeback. Jack refused to let his disappointment get the best of him. He should have figured he had the flush, but four queens, my God, how often did that come along. He kept alert, studying the men and their moves, and he noticed a curious thing. The players were distracted while the dealer chatted them up. He shuffled, sorting through the deck lightning fast. Then he flipped a small section of cards, turned it, and slipped it into the deck. His long slender fingers, dexterous and quick. The dealer had planted a set of cards on the bottom. The player to the dealer's right cut it, leaving two stacks side-by-side. When the dealer set the bottom half on the former top half, the secretly stacked cards were now at the top of the deck. Then just before spinning them out to the players, with his pianist's fingers, the dealer reversed the cut, sliding the top half underneath into its original position. A false shuffle done with magical deception.

Jack scratched his bottom lip in admiration and disgust, and not one player said a word.

Jack sipped his beer and wiped his hands on his jeans. That deal explained the last hand. He had been set up, thinking he couldn't lose with four queens. If it had been a no-limit table, he would have pushed everything in, letting his greed outrun his wits.

"You playing?" The dealer nodded to him. "It's five bucks to stay."

Jack stroked his cheek. He tossed in his chips. After two clubs in his hole cards, and two more on the flop, he knew this had to been another setup. A flush was solid, but Maroon shirt would have a better hand. He tamped down his urge to blow their scam wide open. But he decided to play it cool and see if he could turn their game to his favor.

The dealer spun out an eight of hearts on the turn, the third heart on the table. Maroon shirt could have two hearts in his down cards. At Maroon shirt's turn, he slid in thirty dollars. The simplest remedy would be for Jack to move tables, but if they were targeting him, they wouldn't stop until he was broke.

Out of the corner of his eye, he noticed the pit boss leaning against a wall not too far away, staring him down. Maybe they had figured out his age and decided to clean him out before they kicked him to the street. Maroon shirt had one large stack of five-dollar chips and such a disgustingly satisfied grin. Jack stroked his chin and kept his mouth shut.

"Too rich for my taste." Jack pushed his cards into the center.

When an ace of hearts came on the river, everyone called, and Maroon shirt turned over a two hearts, king high. Someone guffawed from the other side of the table. Jack leaned back and sipped his beer while the winner stacked his chips and ordered a round for everyone. Watching the dealer go through his routine again, Jack glimpsed a reflection in the glass wall behind the dealer's head. A parade of men headed in from the lobby, five at Jack's count, weaving their way across the gaming floor.

As they passed, he recognized Kolcinivitch, his left arm in a sling. The bastard should have both arms in a sling. Jack lowered his brim over his eyes. The stocky, black-haired man behind him was DiGorda in a crisp madras shirt and pressed slacks. The others he didn't recognize but they seemed comfortable with each other. They all disappeared into a door at the back of the room. The high-stakes game Herm had mentioned.

The sight of Kolcinivitch made Jack's heart race. He wanted to take the large grape grower's last penny. Strip him clean. The beer in his mouth turned sour. He wiped his lips with the back of his hand. If he couldn't win out here with these small-time grifters, the big boys would surely eat him up. When the dealer finished his liar's shuffle, Jack leaned forward.

"We need a new deck."

The dealer hesitated, cards in hand, ready to play and eyed Jack with a black look.

"The bottom card." Jack pointed. "The ace of clubs, the one you keep touching, is bent."

The man turned the deck up to show the ace of clubs. "It's not."

"You touched it at least three times. We need a new deck."

With a grudging roll of his eyes, he retrieved a new one and ripped off the plastic cover. Shuffling it up, he passed it to his right. The man slid it back, and the dealer did his false shuffle again.

"We need another deck."

"What's the problem now?" The dealer stared, his irritation mounting. The Maroon shirt fellow leaned in, touching his chin with a knuckle.

"I'm sure you didn't mean to, but you miss-shuffled."

"Not likely, pal." He looked irate.

Jack pointed to the dealer's neighbor. "After you cut it." He pointed to the dealer. "You cut it again."

A fat guy across the table shoved back his chair and scooped up his chips. "I'm leaving."

"That's a false deal," Jack said again.

Todd Hennley promptly took the empty seat. Jack nodded at his lawyer friend, but everyone at the table seemed dazed.

The dealer pegged Jack with a sullen glare and didn't move.

"What's going on?" Todd asked.

A man nodded toward Jack. "This fellow over here thinks the dealer's fake shuffling."

Without any more argument, the dealer unwrapped another deck. He carefully shuffled it and cut it with extra care. Then dealt them out. "Is that okay for you, buster?"

"Please don't wrap your index finger around the front of the deck like that. If you'd like, I'll show you how to hold the cards."

A couple of players laughed. Another player collected his chips and left hastily. The dealer was tight-lipped. He laid the deck on the felt then rubbed the back of his neck.

"Just want a fair shuffle and a fair deal," Jack said. "That's all I'm asking, mister."

The man took up the cards and reshuffled methodically. He held the cards correctly and dealt the down cards all around. The combinations came easier to Jack now, and after a hand, the men loosened up. Jack could read their apprehension, their caution, their greed, and the rank fear in Maroon shirt's eyes. He didn't draw more than a measly pair of twos for the rest of the night. Yet, he kept betting as if it wasn't his money, gambling away his chips in lousy moves against poor odds. Jack made sure those one-dollar and five-dollar chips steadily piled up in front of him as he called and bluffed and pushed men out.

Around midnight the table emptied, and Jack had taken nearly all of Maroon shirt's money. When the man gathered up his few chips to leave, Jack nodded with a wide grin.

"Nice game, mister. Let's do this again real soon."

He grunted as he slouched away. Jack was up nearly $500 on the night.

A bit before one, Jack and Todd sat at the bar going over Adrian's plea bargain offer from the DA.

"From what you tell me, I don't think he needs to make that plea."

The more they talked, the more Todd became intrigued by how the two boys ended up on the grower's property that night.

"So you were stealing back your own property?" Todd shook his head.

"Exactly."

"This is a case I'd like to get involved in. I'll be glad to do what I can for Adrian."

"Can you see him tomorrow?"

Todd agreed to see him immediately. If Adrian decided to let Todd represent him, it seemed likely he could get the charges dropped. But it would take time.

"I figured that. But I've got to spring him quick."

Just as they were finishing, a player from their last game approached them.

"I like the way you play, young man." A farmer, in worn dungarees, offered his hand. "You took all my money tonight, but I'd play you anytime."

Jack thanked him and pressed his palm into the man's earth-hardened hand. As Jack watched the farmer amble away, he wondered if what the guy liked most was, that even with the sting of losing his money, he left knowing winning and losing was driven by chance tamed by good play alone. That was about all a man of the land could ask for. A fair deal, something even gamblers deserved.

Jack had almost $900 now. Adrian wouldn't be in Sheriff Grant's torture chamber much longer if he managed the odds. The way things had worked out tonight put him at ease. He didn't have to sit by and let these experts at lies steal from him. There were always people who'd take all your money if you let them.

Chapter 31
The Lion's Den

J ACK DUNCAN."

The confident voice called to him across Cicero's purple art-deco lobby. Jack stopped on his way to the main room. A stocky man with bushy black hair in a madras shirt stood in a corner, hands in the pocket of his khaki slacks, sizing Jack up and down with a dark pair of searching eyes. It was the powerful Thomas DiGorda. Jack recognized him from the baseball game at Arvin.

"How'd you know my name?" Jack asked.

"Where'd you get that hat?"

Just feet away the Saturday night action picked up. The tables filled while the room buzzed with clanking chips and the voices of men and women winning and losing.

"It's my father's. I borrowed it for a while."

DiGorda nodded again as if he were letting it all soak in, trying to fit things together. "Heard you got a bump on the head the other night."

"You hear a lot."

"At first, I heard Sugar Duncan was in this joint last night, but I knew that couldn't be true. So I asked around."

"Asked who?"

"Take off the hat."

Jack looked into the main room, eager to get to the tables. Was this guy going to squawk about his playing in here? "Why?"

"I want to see for myself."

There was intensity in the man's ways, but Jack also saw a curiosity that bordered on fear. Did he just brush by and get on with his game? But this was the great Mr. DiGorda.

"I'd like to get into your game."

"Depends."

Jack doffed his hat and turned slowly.

"Damn," the grower said under his breath.

"Damn right." Jack turned back around.

"You beat the Black Diamond?" DiGorda wiped his bottom lip with a knuckle.

Jack resettled his hat. "Yeah, I beat him clean. Then he rolled me."

"Not what I heard. You have the Duncan disease in spades is what I hear. Can't stop pissing people off." The man rested his hands in his pants pockets. "That true?"

Jack shrugged and faced the card room, searching for a place to sit. "Do I get in your game or not?"

"You're a good player, like Sugar. But you better control yourself. Is that a problem for you?"

Jack sucked in a breath and let it out slowly. He turned back to the squat grower. "If a man tries to cheat me, I'm going to say something. You gotta problem with that?"

For a full second, DiGorda appeared stunned, screwing his mouth up tight. Then he broke into a laugh, one that bubbled up from somewhere deep in his stocky frame. The gravity of the moment drained away. He slapped Jack on the shoulder as if they were old grape-growing buddies raised together in the dirt.

"You'd stare down a lion to win a game, just like Sugar." He stuck out his hand and introduced himself even though Jack knew who he was. He nodded for Jack to come along. Jack followed poker-faced, lean and ready.

A green felt-covered table for eight centered the dark room DiGorda introduced Jack around, letting him shake hands with the three other men. Clasping Kolcinivitch's gritty palm felt like meeting Judas. Everything in him wanted to finish what he started in that dark grape field. Instead, he gave the land thief a brave smile. DiGorda had warned him about keeping his mouth shut and so had Herm. Right now, he needed their money more than he needed revenge.

Manny, the dealer, had everyone draw for seats, and Jack picked up a five. He seated himself directly across from Kolcinivitch, who looked older in the light. His face looked sun-weathered, with sharp creases, and his left arm in a sling. He stared Jack down as if he were trying to place his name and face. Jack figured all of these men knew he was the son of Sugar Duncan. That's why they sent DiGorda out to confirm the rumors. But did he recognize Jack from the night in the grape fields?

Jack swallowed his fear and studied Kolcinivitch's chips, tall stacks of green $50s and blue $100s. There was enough to solve Adrian's problem. Jack forced himself not to stare. Manny, the house dealer, took Jack's cash and counted out $700. He slid stacks of green, blue, and red chips across the felt.

"What's going on? We have a thousand-dollar buy-in." Kolcinivitch clutched a glass. "What's this penny-ante stuff?"

Jack cringed inside but refused to bat an eye. He had another $150 in the car for emergencies and gas. He didn't want to appear eager, but he'd go get it if he had to.

Everett Champs, a skinny cotton grower from Tulare, waved Kolcinivitch off.

"Let it pass. This man took down the Black Diamond and nearly cleaned out Carter last night. His money's good here." Champs still had the telltale lilt of an Okie transplant.

"Take off that stupid hat." Kolcinivitch glared at him.

DiGorda puffed on his stogie. "The hat's fine. Leave him be."

Jack watched Manny with keen interest as he shuffled, cut, and dealt the first round.

"There's no false shuffling or second dealing here, young man." Les Gilinsky spoke in a thick Eastern European accent. He was a grower Jack had heard of, one with a reputation for running a good outfit. He laughed, and they all joined in. Except for Kolcinivitch. It sounded to him like they had setup that little scam to see if they could wipe him out. He hoped these guys were as easy to rattle as that Carter fellow in the maroon shirt had been.

No easy marks at this table. They played fast and fierce, betting, calling, and chatting just enough to get under each other's skin. No one wasted his money on weak hands. Jack folded early on the first few hands. They were full of weird quirks, gave off few obvious tells, and played the odds deftly. Black Diamond had played like this. It took a while to figure him out. Picking up a new hand, he leaned back. His mouth had dried out. He absentmindedly rubbed his lips.

"This too much for you?" Kolcinivitch locked eyes with Jack, his lips turned down in a permanent scowl.

"I'd like something to drink."

"Good idea." Everett Champ signaled the dealer, who buzzed the bar.

A cocktail waitress appeared and took everyone's orders. Jack asked for a beer, and when it came, he savored a long pull, letting it roll around in his dry mouth. Kolcinivitch ordered a double Scotch, straight up. The man slurped it noisily. Jack needed all of his wits and let his beer sit. It bothered Jack that Kolcinivitch had read him so easily. He could have stayed on the floor with the farmers and truck drivers, more dreamers than gamblers, and eventually made his money instead of risking everything here. But it would set some things right if he sprung Adrian with Kolcinivitch's own dough. That made him smile.

"This weather sure makes a man thirsty," Les Gilinsky said.

Kolcinivitch grunted and slugged down more of his Scotch. Jack rechecked his down cards and kept his smiling. After a while, the game started to clarify. DiGorda had a pugnacious way about him; he bullied as much as he bluffed, and it generally never got him anywhere. He possessed a natural caution that never allowed him to put too much at risk. Everett had a good old boy way about him, friendly, chatty, wanting to have a conversation about the weather or the harvest while trying to push players out with big bets.

Kolcinivitch was by far the most fascinating and most difficult man to plumb. For all of his bluster and rude manner, he grew calm and pensive when his money was at stake. But behind those black eyes, Jack saw anger. In the way he flicked his hands, the way he tossed his cards, and flung his chips into the pot instead of sliding in stacks that could be easily counted. He was a brittle stick of dynamite, cracked and unstable, ready to explode at the slightest jarring. But that told Jack little about the cards the man held.

So far, it was the sweet-talking Les Gilinsky, with his thick accent, raking in the chips, winning two pots in a row. Then Kolcinivitch played hard on a hand, winning on the river card when he drew an ace of spades to complete a flush. The pots were larger than any stakes Jack had played before.

DiGorda chomped on the stub of a cigar in the corner of his mouth.

He called and raised it another $100.

Jack took a breath. With a pair of nines without seeing the flop, the betting was getting way too wild, but this was no time to flinch. He called.

Manny wheeled out the three-card flop—a king of spades, a deuce of clubs, and a one-eyed Jack of hearts. Kolcinivitch picked up his betting, juicing the pot. Jack felt good hoping it grew but could beat him with a Jack or a king. The waitress came by with another round of drinks, and Kolcinivitch now worked his third Scotch, straight up. Another double.

"Heard someone died over at your place, Ethan." Gilinsky rearranged cards in his hand.

DiGorda unwrapped a cigar, bit off the tip, spit it out, and lit it up.

Kolcinivitch turned to the thin-faced grape grower and sneered. "Yeah, already shipped her home to Mexico. Her bawling daughter with her. Cost me seven hundred and fifty dollars out of my own pocket."

"A true hero." Everett Champ chipped in.

Kolcinivitch had a big smile on his face as if he was proud of his good deed. Was he referring to Sabrina and her mother? A throb began right behind Jack's eyes. The old woman had looked weaker the last time Ella saw her. He stared at the cards spread out on the table. He was all alone in here with men who would break him in two if they knew what he was up to. He checked his down cards because he suddenly forgot his hand.

"What'd she die from?" Jack asked, wanting to intensify the distraction.

Kolcinivitch moved his right hand up and down from his ear to the table, a definite nervous reflex. Jack knew he couldn't have more than a pair of kings.

"The doc said it was her asthma. She had to be at least ninety."

"I heard it was poisoning," Gilinsky said.

On the turn, Manny dealt a seven of clubs. The betting grew intense, and Jack decided to stay in, hoping he could steal the pot. Kolcinivitch tugged on his wattle under his chin, his eyes aglow with the thought of winning. DiGorda sent up puffs of smoke. He blinked and let out an enormous cloud of smoke. A real sign of unease. But no one folded.

Gilinsky pushed in another $100. Kolcinivitch and DiGorda called.

"What kind of poison?"

When no one answered, Jack concluded they were all buried in their own thoughts. He felt good about the odds, so he pushed in every one of his chips. "A hundred and I'll raise a hundred."

Manny counted the stack. "Two hundred to stay in."

Everett folded.

Instead of betting, DiGorda leaned toward Jack. "Listen." He pointed across the table. "You have to spray. If you don't catch that fungus and strangle it before it spreads, we'll all be out picking someone else's fruit just to eat."

"It was her asthma. But the pesticides didn't help her. Besides, I had no choice." Kolcinivitch had a sheepish look. "I found a canker fungus on my eastern division. There were already signs of measles down a couple of rows. If I didn't get it quick, I could have lost the whole section. We cleared people out of that section. But when we sprayed the wind rose and it carried over to the central division and over sprayed a group of pruners. I didn't know that would happen."

"Blast it!" Gilinsky shot back. "If Chavez gets a hold of it, he'll bring the State Ag people down on us. We need to clean up our own mess. That's why I think it's better to give him what he wants."

"The state people will do what we tell them to do." DiGorda exhaled pale smoke as he spoke. "We could never agree to stay out of the fields for thirty-six to forty-eight hours after a spray. Besides, that pesticide usually doesn't hurt anybody."

Kolcinivitch wiped his mouth with his sleeve. "My guys check that eastern division every day. I drive it myself every Sunday morning just to make sure we got it all. If we didn't, a lot of jobs will disappear. We'll have to yank up the entire section and replant it. I can't get all sentimental about losing one scab. I got another five hundred coming soon for the early harvest. We have to spray, and we have to pick if we're going to eat."

"It's to you, when you're ready, Mr. DiGorda," Manny said, trying to push the game along.

"You know my place wasn't the only place that old lady worked," Kolcinivitch said. "She spent the whole winter in the Coachella Valley. Probably worked on Ed Nolan's place. She could have gotten sprayed anywhere."

"She was poisoned. And she died at your place, right?" Jack questioned Kolcinivitch with his eyes.

"It's two hundred to you, Mr. DiGorda," Manny said, surveying the table.

Distractedly, DiGorda threw in his chips.

"It was her asthma," Kolcinivitch said.

"You could have waited. Thirty-six hours is reasonable." Gilinsky tossed his cards onto the pile, folding. "What do we miss? A little trimming and bundling?"

"So her death could have been avoided?" Jack glanced at each of them. But none of them responded.

Kolcinivitch tossed in his chip. "Not when you're ninety."

They all looked to Manny who flipped his river card—a nine.

"To you, Mr. Duncan." Jack felt good about trips and their distant thoughts. He pushed his remaining chips into the pot.

Manny counted and stacked them. "Two hundred and fifty dollars to stay in."

"Red Monks, Red Monks, Red Monks." DiGorda slapped his cards on the table. Gilinsky and Champ laughed heartily. Kolcinivitch glared at Jack, profound and hateful, and folded his hand. Jack raked toward him a pot of almost $2,000 and change.

Kolcinivitch still had chips in front of him. The rest of the night, the men argued back and forth over a quarter an hour raise for the pickers. About what it would do to their profits; about how many hours a worker should stay out of the fields after pesticide spraying. About lunch breaks and the productive operation of a farm, and about grape rust and mite infestations, soil acidity, and bankruptcy if any of this were to happen at once.

They debated over Chavez. What did the little bastard really want? Did he intend to drive them into bankruptcy, or did he hanker to control their operations? They argued, drank, smoked, and played until the room became rancid with stale air. A closeness moved in on them all with DiGorda's cigars, the cigarette smoke, the constant swearing at the weather, and the pests that plagued their vines.

These men were so overcome with concerns for their business, none of them seemed to notice that the pile of chips on the table grew in front of Jack.

Jack eased his way in between the chatter, until around midnight when he had nearly cleaned out Kolcinivitch, who threw down his last losing hand in disgust, he decided it was time to go. He joined Champ and Gilinsky, who cashed out and stood to leave.

Jack rose, and a wide smirk washed across his face. "Thank you, gentlemen. It's been a pleasure."

Kolcinivitch eyed him. "You're gloating because you think you took me down tonight, punk."

"I don't think anything." Jack tapped the large stack of $100 bills in front of him. He divided it into two stacks, more than enough to bail out Adrian. He would like to give some to Sabrina. Make her way easier, if he could find a way to get her some cash.

"Enough of this." Everett Champ rose. "Come on, Jack. I'll buy you a coffee for the road."

Jack stood and stuffed the rolls of bills into his jeans pockets.

"We'll settle up someday." Kolcinivitch stretched as he rose.

"Anytime," Jack said. "Any place."

Chapter 32
Water Rights

IT WAS AFTER MIDNIGHT when Jack strolled out Cicero's front door and met DiGorda on his way to his car. The grower turned to Jack.

"You're a good card player."

"Thanks."

"It's a bit of good luck your mom was able to pay off her taxes like that."

"Yeah, our combine just showed up one morning." Jack wondered if he knew it had been stored in his friend's shed. "Everything's going to be fine."

"You must know that Kolcinivitch needs those water rights."

"Enough that he would try to force my mother out with nothing but a few clothes."

"I don't know about any of that, Jack. That sale was about her back taxes, nothing more. But listen, you're a smart kid. Talk to her. You got a small stake now, maybe you can help her. And Kolcinivitch will pay nicely for those water rights. That would set her up fine." He patted Jack on the back. "Talk to her, Jack. Tell her Ethan Kolcinivitch is not some monster, and he wants to make things right, financially, as far as he's able to."

"Sure."

"Listen, come play again sometime. We like to have new blood every now and then."

He took a drag off a stub of a cigar and puffed out a cloud into the night air.

Jack plunged his hands into his pockets. "Appreciate it, but I don't have much time."

"Just come when you can. Let us know what Shirley is thinking. There's always a way to work out a deal, so everyone's happy."

"Yeah, sounds good." Jack glanced at his car.

"You know where to reach me." DiGorda strode to his Caddy.

Jack slipped into the driver's seat and let the motor warm up. He began to think these people had invited him into their game as a way to get to his mom. He patted the wad of cash in his pocket. Walking away with their money could have been nothing more than a goodwill gesture, a way of ingratiating him into thinking good of their motives. The thought that they might have gone easy on him, letting him rake in big winnings, bothered him. He gunned the motor. That consideration would have to wait. What mattered now was springing Adrian, and the county lockup wasn't far.

Chapter 33
Road to Delano

I'M HUNGRY," ADRIAN SAID as soon as he slammed the car door shut. Sunday morning when the sun had just cleared the Diablo peaks the two of them pulled out of the parking lot of the county jail in downtown Bakersfield. The last time Jack had seen his friend, he was lean and wiry. Now he was pale and thin as if muscle had been stripped from him. His smile had faded too, but Jack didn't think the frown would stay long. Who would be cheery after two weeks in jail?

Jack pulled into a diner near Highway 99, and the two found a booth.

As soon as the waitress set two cups of steaming coffee on the table, Adrian took a large gulp of his. "Man, that's good." He wiped his mouth with his sleeve. "You wouldn't believe the crap they serve in there." His face brightened. Adrian ordered a short stack, scrambled eggs, bacon, sausage, orange juice, and coffee. Jack asked for eggs and bacon.

"Sorry I didn't get a chance to visit while you were in the hoosegow."

"Hey, I heard from the girls you were busy raising cash to spring me." He gulped the rest of his coffee and held up his empty cup for the waitress to see. She hustled over and refilled it.

"Busted some dollars loose from the growers themselves. That's how I paid your ransom to the county."

Adrian cracked a wider smile. "I'd like to hear about that." Their food came, and he dug in so fast, the eggs, the toast, the pancakes, the bacon, all disappeared in a ravenous feed. While he ate, Jack told him about playing at the Black Diamond, getting mugged, and coming down to Bakersfield to play.

"That's where I met Todd Hennley."

Adrian nodded as he shoveled more food into his mouth.

Jack went on to tell him about playing at Cicero's. About meeting the growers and getting in on their game.

"That's where I won most of the money for your bond."

"Who'd you play?"

Jack ticked off the names. When he got to Kolcinivitch, Adrian gave him a hard look. "No kidding?"

"He plays like a turkey before Thanksgiving." Jack stuck his neck out and sliced at it with his hand.

Adrian put his fork down. "How do you know they weren't setting you up for something? These guys are disciples of Machiavelli."

"You know, I had that feeling last night. Maybe it was all too easy, but, hey, here you are, buddy." Jack spread his hands.

Adrian cracked another smile and went back to eating.

He set down his coffee cup. "You surprise me."

"Yeah, in what way?"

"You never used to play cards. Said it was pure evil. Now, you've turned into a real shark, taking money from fat cats."

"Hey, I got rolled at the Black Diamond." Jack turned and lifted his hair to show him the scar.

Adrian grimaced. "You've really changed."

"The times change us all, don't they?"

Adrian looked up from this feast. "They do."

"Was it tough in there?"

"Have you ever stood six inches from another person for twenty-four hours every day? They pack the cells so tight you have to stand. At night, there's no room for all of us to lie down, so we let the old guys lean against the walls. Maybe they'd get two hours here, an hour there. It's tough. Some of them didn't make it. It's like standing on an iceberg. Then your mouth is so dry because of the crap they feed you."

Jack shook his head. No wonder his friend was so thin. "That would have pissed me off to no end." Jack imagined how he would react. "I would have killed someone."

"I know you would have." Adrian drained the last of his coffee and set the cup down. "For the first week, that was all I thought about. Then one day I watched one of the other guys go berserk. The guards had to come in and haul him away. We heard them dragging him down the hall and yelling at him to shut up."

They ate quietly for a few minutes. Jack studied his friend, who seemed to be considering his words carefully.

"I had a lot of time to think things through."

"Guess there wasn't much else to do."

"Have you ever wondered if what we've worked so hard to get aren't the things that really matter?"

Jack rubbed his bottom lip. "I'm doing what I want. Playing baseball, that's what we always dreamed about."

"Yeah…" Adrian's voice trailed off, and he turned to the window. "Everybody's busy going someplace, aren't they?"

"You're exhausted. I'll get you home. Good food and sleep, and you'll feel better."

He turned his hard eyes on Jack. "I see things more clearly now."

Jack flipped some bills on the table and slid out the booth. "You need to sleep in your own bed."

The two rode in silence. His mother's simple wish for some peace and security; his full ride to college. Those were dreams worth cherishing, worth all the effort he put into making them come true. His mother needed help opening a store, and that was worth working hard to help her. He'd given a lot of thought to what he wanted. But now Adrian, talking as if he questioned everything that was possible to him. That was just him talking through his fatigue. There was nothing here in the valley for either one of them.

"Do you know what road we're on?" Adrian asked.

"Yeah, Highway 99."

"You know where it goes?"

"Sure. It's the road to Delano. You haven't forgotten where you live, have you?"

"This is the same road the Joads traveled."

In the morning light, Adrian's face appeared intent, serious. His eyes were fixed straight ahead, peering into the sketchy morning mist as if searching for something.

"That was fiction by that Steinbeck dude. You know that. We all had to read it last year."

"It's all the same, Jack. It's a road people take to find something they want. Thousands and thousands of them every year. They have a dream of something better. All they get is the all-American shaft by people who are good at concocting stories to keep particular groups of people down."

Jack clutched the steering wheel and stared ahead. This is a road he had driven a thousand times before. It was just a concrete highway. What was Adrian talking about?

"The growers say they're fighting communists and anarchists. Everyone knows there are communists here. But those guys are so whacked out, no one wants to listen to them. No one wants to give up their freedoms and their property. Communism would strip us all of our dignity more than anything the growers want to do. So who are we fighting?"

"Not sure."

"We're fighting ourselves. But we don't know that because we're so caught up in lies like Vietnam. If that country goes, then the whole world will fall like a set of dominoes to communists, and farms around here will become communist collectives. The growers are just baiting us with this stupid red scare to hide the real war. The real war is the war of who we want to believe we are."

Jack shrugged. "Believe what?"

Adrian leaned toward Jack. "That we're all Americans."

"That's not hard to believe."

"It's hard to take for those who want a docile immigrant to hoe their fields."

"Yeah, but why is that so difficult for some people to take?"

"Because to dream of a better life is dangerous. If we can dream like any other human being, like any other American, then we have hope for something better than getting treated like we're pieces of dirt."

"But you can't change them. The growers are going to think what they want."

Adrian wagged his index finger. "No, my friend. We have to fight for the right to control our own lives."

Adrian slumped in the seat, drained by fatigue. Jack floored the Olds, and the big eight-cylinder coughed to clear its throat and then shot forward into the foggy morning. They sped up the two-lane highway that split the belly of the valley of plenty and drove as men into the heart of the most fertile land in the world. As it had been in times before, their road home had become a path of decision, a road they all traveled—the road to Delano.

Chapter 34
The Year of Fruit

S HIRLEY MET JACK AT the back door. He had expected this. Out all night, he had called her from the lobby of county jail around 5:00 a.m. Awake and worried, she seemed to understand. But when he stepped inside the back door, she gave him an exasperated glare. She led him to the kitchen table. She sat in front of an empty mug of coffee, wrung out by worry.

"We need to talk."

Jack slumped into a chair. She served him a plate of eggs and bacon and potatoes. On top of the waffles and eggs he had eaten with Adrian earlier, he was stuffed. Fatigue must have bored a hole right through his stomach, he ate so much.

"Sugar's hat's gone. Do you have it?"

Jack looked up from his plate of food. "I borrowed it."

"You've been down in Bakersfield?"

"I told you, bailing out Adrian."

"I got a call."

"Yeah."

"An old friend said she heard Sugar was back playing again at Cicero's. I knew that wasn't true. When I saw his hat gone, I called over at Ella's, and she told me you were on a mission to bail out Adrian."

"That's what I did."

Shirley folded her hands in front of him and appraised him.

"Without getting myself killed, either."

"Did you play Ethan Kolcinivitch?"

Jack stuffed his hands into his pocket and pulled out two wads of bills. He neatly stacked the $100s on the table.

Shirley pursed her lips. "That all Kolcinivitch's money?"

"Most of it. Some's DiGorda's, Champ's, and this Gilinsky fellow."

"Les Gilinsky was there?"

"You know him?"

"He's the only one who ever called after Sugar died."

"How much do you need to open that dress shop you're always talking about?"

"For three thousand dollars, I can have a very nice place."

Jack counted off ten one hundred dollar bills and slid the stack across the table. "When I get my two grand back after Adrian shows up in court, you can have that too."

"I'm very proud of you, what you've done for Adrian."

She stood and stared down at him, both happy and angry at the same moment. After a long pause, she took up the bills, counted them and took them to the counter. She took a brown manila envelope, which she held to her chest. She laid the envelope flat on the table, the blue UCLA logo in the corner clear and bright. She gripped it so he couldn't take it.

"You opened it."

"I had to know so I could decide something."

"Decide what?"

"To tell you everything." Shirley folded her arms on the table. "You have a right to know what happened to your father. But you need to promise you'll take this scholarship and never look back."

"I intend to take it."

"I just want your word on what you'll do."

"I'm going to play baseball, you know that."

"No matter what I tell you." Shirley eyed him hard.

"I already know most of it."

"Herm knows *some* of the story. He doesn't know the parts you want to know." Shirley tapped the table with her index finger. "I just want to hear you say you're going to play baseball."

He didn't like her shoving his own life down his throat, but after these past weeks of having to outwit lawmen, fight a grower, and then shake down even more growers to get his friend out of jail, leaving to attend college would be a deliverance. "I don't see anything changing my mind on UCLA."

His mother slid the manila envelope across to him. He tore into it and read the letter. "A full ride, room, board, and tuition."

"We have to sign and return it." She handed him a pen. He signed the offer letter then handed it to her. He watched her sign it, fold it, and slip it into the return envelope.

"It says you can move into the dorms on August first." She read over the school schedule from the packet. "School starts the last week of August. You have a lot to do to get ready."

He leaned back, hands laced behind his head. He'd be living in the dorms in LA, playing ball, going to school with Ella and Adrian.

"Why did you think I wouldn't take this scholarship?"

"I've done everything I could to get the land back. I've always been afraid you'd get involved, and it wouldn't turn out well."

As much as he wanted to know the truth, he could understand why she kept things from him.

"I'm fine with what you've done, Mom. I'm ready to go."

She reached across the table and laid her hands on his. "Sugar was a good man. He loved this place as much as anyone could love a piece of land. We had a great life together. We worked right beside each other, every day. A few years before you were born, he planted about a hundred acres of Thompsons to see how they would sell. We had a good crop in a couple of years. He understood the changes around Delano, the weather, the soil, the water, a perfect climate for table grapes. He knew we needed to switch over to table grapes. So he made plans to remake the land.

"We were making good money growing durum, but the real cash was in table grapes. We had to convert the land, buy the vines and plant them, build housing, and the like. Vines take three years to mature before their first harvest. So, we took out a mortgage."

"Your father visited a few of the ranches to see how they ran migrant farm housing, so he knew what others were doing. He'd come home disturbed about how it stank; the leaky roofs; the cold, damp conditions; workers sleeping in gullies and on the ground. He began talking to the growers in the area, trying to organize improvements. The largest growers didn't want to change. They believed migrant labor was beholden to them, that they owed the growers what little they possessed."

"Sugar decided to make changes himself, so he hired a man to design housing we planned to build on a southern section. He wanted to show others how it should be done. He was very proud of his ideas."

"The trouble began when he showed the plans for migrant housing to the banker. The man said Sugar had budgeted way too much money, beyond what growers in the area were allocating to labor housing. We learned later the bank was afraid it would raise the bar for the other growers and cause cash-flow problems."

"What does all this have to do with Kolcinivitch?" Jack asked.

"Everything. The bank gave us the mortgage." Shirley paused to catch her breath. "It was secured by the value of the property at the time. We started building and tearing up the land and planting vines. We wouldn't have a cash harvest for three years, so we needed all of that mortgage money plus all of our savings.

"The first year of the fruit harvest, we had a modest crop. We were going to be okay. That year your father sent a letter around to the growers about how they mistreated the migrants, and his recommendations to improve their lot. Then he gave that speech in San Francisco."

"The night he died?"

She nodded. "Even though I was devastated by his death, we were going to be okay. We just needed a couple of big harvests, and we'd be back on our feet. But shortly after your father died, Kolcinivitch put his property in Arvin on the market. Barely a thousand acres. But he had to put it on the market because he used State Water Project water, and the law required after ten years of taking public water, the farmer must sell his land. So he was forced to sell."

"A few days later the largest tract to ever come on the market came for sale: the Sierra Vista Ranch owned by DiGorda. Those two parcels stayed on the market for some time. They suppressed the value of farmland in the entire area. So the bank called our loan."

"How can it do that?"

"It's the way farm mortgages work. When the land you use for collateral for a farm loan falls below the value of you of what you owe, the bank has the right to call the loan. Even if you're current on your payments, they can throw you into default. They had every legal right to foreclose, and they didn't waste any time. They seized our property and sold it at auction."

"Kolcinivitch bought our land at auction from the bank?"

"For a pittance of its worth. Turns out, he was the only bidder. I sued the bank for fraud but lost in court, twice. I spent everything we had trying to get the land back. Kolcinivitch and the banker knew each other. But we couldn't prove the banker had rejected other bidders. He just said he didn't have any."

"Was the banker friends with the owner of the Sierra Vista property too?"

"We believed so, but we couldn't prove it in court. But everyone knew Kolcinivitch and DiGorda were best buddies." She pushed her coffee cup away from her.

Jack rose and paced the kitchen. "So they worked together to depress the value of our land. Kolcinivitch's friend calls the loan. Then he buys it cheap at auction. Leaving you with what?"

"Very little. This land and a little cash. Most of the proceeds from the sale went to pay the note. The judge gave me most of the profit from our last harvest. What we had left went to legal bills trying to unwind the auction."

His mother covered her face with her hands. "It was an awful time after Sugar died. Part of me doesn't even want to think about it again."

"Do you think Kolcinivitch had anything to do with Dad crashing on that road?"

She grew quiet.

"The night before he gave his speech, Kolcinivitch showed up at our front door."

"Here!"

"I talked to him." His mother sat straight and stiff. "He threatened us, said if we didn't stop our efforts to change the way things were run, we'd be sorry. I pleaded with Sugar not to go to the meeting. But he went anyway, and, well, you know what happened. We told the sheriff. Nothing came of it. Kolcinivitch said he never stepped foot on our land. Said we were just imagining things. It was his word against ours."

His mother drew circles on the table with her finger, her eyes cast down as if trying to conjure pleasant memories.

The air suddenly grew thick and muggy, overbearing in its weight. The shacks on Kolcinivitch's land—the stinking, rotting shacks people lived in—flashed through his mind's eye. The mark on the plat map still hanging on the wall in the upstairs office. Kolcinivitch's shacks were in the same spot his father had wanted to build his farm housing.

"What about the water rights? They're worth something."

"In Spring Gulch? That water is going to stay in the ground as long as I live. When I'm dead and gone that ape next door can dig up whatever he wants—if he's still around."

"Thanks for telling me." He put his hand on her shoulder. "I've got to get some rest. I've got a game tomorrow." He pushed his weary body up the stairs and fell into bed. He dreamed of a slim man in a planter's hat trudging across a harrowed field, reaching out his hand—but they never touched.

➤

MONDAY MORNING. THE EARLY light filtering through Jack's bedroom window brought him no solace. He sat up, bare-chested and impervious to the chill, his arms at his side in lank repose, his mind stuck in a loop of ruminations. *Dad was run off the road and died alone in the dark. Because he cared about people.* Black and white snippets, clips of his father's easy ways, his bright smile while dancing with Shirley in the living room, then watching her play while leaning on the piano—lean, hardy, and tall. If he stayed in bed, he would drown.

He dragged himself up, pulled his legs and arms through clothes in a mindless rhythm. Hope in a better future for his mother slipped away.

He stood by the window, opening it to take in the fresh morning air. Trellised rows of vines, heavy with a budding crop. *Dad planted those.*

"Jack," his mother called from downstairs.

Everything around him had his father's hard work stamped on it. Numbness swamped him. He couldn't move away from the window. That thief Kolcinivitch owned it all now, and there wasn't one damn thing he could do about it except stare at what used to be.

"Jack, you're late."

He grabbed his jacket off the bed. He scooped his backpack and gear and trudged downstairs. In the kitchen, he sipped some coffee, ate something his mother gave him, and nodded as she rumbled through her warnings about getting distracted. But the land next door kept vigil in his mind. How much had it been worth when the bank seized it?

"Jack, are you listening?"

Not really, he wanted to say. "Yeah, I heard every word."

"I have my doubts." She handed him the car keys. She'd find a way to the game today. He told her not to bother since he wasn't pitching anyway. He'd be home after the game.

"Not too late," she called after him as headed toward the door. He stopped at the screen.

"How much would the land have been worth if they hadn't manipulated the property values?"

"Jack, that's done now."

"Kolcinivitch wants to buy your water. How much would you sell it to him for?"

"That man will have to kill me to get a drop of my water."

"What if he paid you full value? What he should have paid you ten years ago for the land."

"He never will."

"Humor me. What should it have been?"

"In fifty-eight farmland was going for about a thousand dollars an acre. He paid less than two hundred dollars from the bank."

"No wonder you're pissed off."

"It's not just the money, Jack."

"I know. But he should have paid four million."

"I'd give him this acre, too, with its water if he paid me that."

Jack nodded. "I'll tell him that." He pushed the screen door open, and it slammed behind him. All the way to the car he could hear his mother laughing, something he hadn't heard from her in a long time. On the drive to school, his mother's laughter danced in his ears. The money would never bring back his father. But maybe he could get Kolcinivitch to pay for his misdeeds, one way or the other.

Chapter 35
Ella's Detention

A T MORNING BREAK, JACK waited in the quad until a minute before third period, but Ella didn't show. She hadn't been home last night when he'd called either. Her father grumped at him over the phone, saying he didn't know where she had disappeared to. She didn't have a debate scheduled. She could have been at one of her girlfriends, studying.

His eye twitched thinking of that smug Kolcinivitch smirking the other day about the woman dying on his ranch as though he'd lost a cow or a chicken. That had to have been Sabrina's mother. He hoped Ella was too busy with school to find out.

At lunch, he sat in their usual spot in the cafeteria. Darcy told him Adrian had to report to the library for make-up work. He ate his tacos with a few of his friends and their girlfriends and Darcy. But no Ella.

"Adrian will probably have to do that right up till we graduate," Darcy said. He had a mountain of homework to make up before graduation.

"Have you seen Ella?" From the day he met her, Ella had an internal sense of duty, one that didn't allow her to flake out on friends. Or at least call him. He glanced around at the bustle in the cafeteria. She wouldn't sit somewhere else even if she were mad at him. She had other friends, but it would be beyond her not to say something. He stood and studied the food line in case she had come in late.

"Maybe she's sick today," Darcy added. "She didn't sound too well over the weekend."

Her father hadn't said anything about her being sick last night. Jack surveyed the dining hall one more time.

"The attendance office has a phone you can use in emergencies. You just have to tell them a reason, like there's been a death in the family or something."

A death. Jack stared at Darcy, but all he saw was Sabrina's mother. Her cold body in a wooden box shipped away like so much produce.

He strode the empty halls to the attendance office and explained that some distant relative had died and he needed to call home. She gave him a sly grin, reached under the counter, and set out a black phone. Just as he picked up the receiver, Ella came out of the vice principal's office on the far side of the counter. Her jeans streaked with dust; her sneakers caked with mud. Tear tracks streaked down her dirty face. She took a seat by the door, not even noticing him. She wiped her nose with a tissue and rubbed an eye with the back of her hand.

"Ella, what's going on?" Jack sat beside her.

"They killed her."

He took her hand. "You did the best you could."

"I tried to talk her into going to the hospital. But no one would leave the property, not even if it meant dying."

Jack reached his arm around her. He felt her trembling.

"Miss Carter." The vice-principal in his white shirt and tie, with his chest puffed up, held out a slip of paper over the counter. "Here's your readmittance slip. And your detention notice."

"Detention?"

"You aren't a party to this nonsense, too, are you, Mr. Duncan?"

"To what?"

The vice-principal gave him a searing look.

"Only a couple of more weeks to graduation, Miss Carter. This is not the time for shenanigans, particularly for issues that don't concern you."

She rose slowly and took them from his hand.

"And don't be late for detention, Miss Carter."

She brooded over the paper. She looked ready to explode. Jack took her arm and led her into the hall.

"You tick him off and he'll give you detention in your sleep."

"The heck with him. He has no business telling me what concerns me."

Outside in the quad, Jack guided her to a bench. "So, what's going on?"

She caught her breath. "I was there Saturday when Sabrina's mom died. They came in and just wrapped her up and slapped her in a box. They threw her box in the bed of a pickup and took off. They took Sabrina, too. They're gone."

"I heard Saturday night."

"Sunday you weren't around, so I went down to the Forty Acres."

"What'd you do there?"

"What do you think I did?" She looked up at him. "I volunteered."

He shrugged and looked away. The sun blazed across the courtyard, and they sat in the only shade. He glanced down at her dirty jeans. "Were you in the fields this morning?"

She shook her head. "The migrant housing over at Kolcinivitch's." She wrung her hands. "I filed a complaint with the Rural Legal Assistance. I took two attorneys to where Sabrina's mother died so they could document my claim."

"What can they do?"

"They're going to put it to him hard. What a pigsty."

"And those shacks shouldn't even exist."

She looked at him quizzically.

Now wasn't the time to tell her his father's housing plans, so he stood. "You eaten?"

"No." They went into the cafeteria where kids were beginning to clear out. She filled a tray, and Jack followed her to a table. She picked up her fork, and while scooping up some beans she said, "I've accepted an internship for the summer."

"You're not going to LA?"

"Probably not till the last day of August.

"Who's the internship with? The UFW?"

"No, the Rural Legal Assistance office. They're right here in McFarland. I'm going to help them inspect the farmworker housing on the ranches so they can sue the growers."

"You tell your father about this?"

"Does my father have to know everything I do?"

He vaguely remembered throwing that line out at her not too long ago. "That's why he's so angry at you, isn't it?"

"Kolcinivitch called and cussed him out for letting me run around on his ranch." She wiped the corner of her mouth with a finger. "Like I'm a child or something."

"I'm surprised...I mean, you were all set to get out of here the day after graduation."

She set her fork down and took Jack's hand. "Seeing someone die like that changes things. I can help change this, Jack."

"You're going to change a hundred years of habit in one summer."

"What I'm trying to say, Jack, is that I'm changed."

He nodded slowly, not full understanding what she meant. It wasn't like Ella to take a position on something she hadn't clearly thought through."

"Does this change anything between us?"

She flashed a reassuring smile. "Only if you're a shallow-minded bore...which you're not."

"But what can you accomplish in a few months?"

"I don't know, Jack, I don't know if it'll be two months or two years. The attorneys I followed this morning...I liked how they handled things. This work intrigues me."

While he admired her determination to make her life count, she had thrown him a curveball. They had planned to attend college together for so long. But when he stepped back and thought about Ella, she had been preparing for a decision like this since the day he met her. There was no use pressing her any further; she would tell him what she planned when she was ready. He glanced up at her—her mud-smeared jeans, makeup-less face, and not-so-perfect hair, she even had bits of dirt under her fingernails, were all part of her ability to throw herself into something meaningful. He leaned close and kissed her.

She brushed him away. "Oh, Jack. I'm all dirty."

He gazed into her eyes. "You're the most beautiful girl in Delano."

A smile broke through her glumness. "You're the only one who thinks that."

"I'm the only one who matters."

She touched his chin with a finger. "I have to eat and get to class. I can't get any more detention."

"If you do, I'll go with you. I'll get caught up on my algebra."

"I bet." She laughed and didn't stop smiling the entire day.

Chapter 36
Riding the Bench

THAT AFTERNOON, ADRIAN AND Jack strolled into the locker room. Coach came over and stared at Adrian as if he were an apparition. He grinned wider than it seemed possible. He asked Adrian to his office, and after a while, someone shouted for Jack. Coach wanted him. In his jersey and jeans, he made his way to the man's office. The three of them sat in the cramped confines of an athletic office smelling of old socks and stale coffee. Coach asked right off how he got all that bail money.

"Legally. I didn't rob a bank. No one lent it to me either."

"Someone give it to you?"

"You could say that."

"Legal, you say?" Coach rubbed his chin with an appraising gaze.

"Most definitely."

"Okay, we'll leave it at that. Excellent job." Coach called Principal McGrew to make sure Adrian could play. Jack and Adrian left his office before the conversation ended. Later, when they ran sprints in the outfield warming up, Coach called Adrian over by the dugout. When he returned to running, Jack knew from his frown he wasn't going to play.

"McGrew said I'd been out nearly three weeks and had to get checked back into school. I tried to do that today, but there's a paperwork problem. I don't know what it's about. And Coach didn't want to risk a forfeit if I was ineligible."

During the Turlock game that afternoon, Adrian rode the bench while Jack played center field. It didn't seem fair to him that Adrian couldn't play. But their season had come too far to risk a forfeit. In center field, Jack punched his glove and settled his hands on his knees, watching Stoddard pitch. Turlock didn't have a bad team, but today they were swinging at everything as if they'd completely lost hope in their season and just wanted to get this over with. Stoddard was obliging, striking out the side in the first inning, and inducing ground ball outs in the second and third. It wasn't until the fourth inning a ball was lofted Jack's way. He tracked it easily and caged it safely in his mitt. There was no fire in the Turlock boys. And Delano had just enough enthusiasm to squeeze out a couple of runs by the fifth inning. The Delano bench was quiet, with Adrian at the far end, with his elbows propped on his knees, cap pulled down low, a fatigued slump to his shoulders.

Jack sat next to his friend, but there were no words between them. Jack would be up soon, so he strode the length of the dugout, took a bat off the rack, and ran his hand up and down the length of the smooth ash. The smell of wood and sweat, the yammer of the home crowd, calling out to kids they knew, the faint breeze that tickled the flags—this is what he loved, a trouble-free place where the rest of the world passed by unnoticed.

He pushed away the thoughts of the old woman dying in a shack, of Ella's red eyes over her grief at the woman's death, of the big world that lay outside the chalk lines of his make-believe world. If they lost this game, there would be another tomorrow. But Ella's world played for keeps. He glanced back at his friend, slumped at the end of the bench, with a distant glare in his eyes as if his thoughts were still in that Bakersfield jail. He'd be much better off if he could play again, get his old fire back—pretend the tragedy of others wasn't his affair. He made his way down the bench and touched Adrian's shoulder.

"You'll get out there soon."

He looked up at Jack, a mystified glow on his face. "If you hate them, they win."

"Hate who? What're you talking about?"

"Just something I heard, that's all." He nodded and went back to his contemplating.

At the sharp snap of wood against leather, Marty yelled from the on-deck circle as he waved runners around the bases. His teammates scored, the home crowd cheered, parents yelled out accolades to their kids, and the Delano bench broke into a crescendo of shouts. Jack turned to the field, cheered on his friends, and in the length of a breath, his world regained its balance.

Chapter 37
Over Pumped

ON HIS WAY THROUGH town, Jack drove past Robert's Guns. He made a U-turn and parked. The door chime jangled as he entered.

"Hello there." A gray-haired Sol Roberts greeted him. "I thought you'd forgotten." The man set a leather rifle case on the glass counter. He unzipped it, opened the flap, and lifted the shiny Browning Auto-5 shotgun out. He held it in both hands, presenting it to Jack as if it were a trophy. The barrel, its mechanisms and trigger, was a shiny black. Not one spot of rust. The wood had been meticulously restored. His father's initials looked freshly carved in the dark wooden stock.

Jack rested it in his palms. "This looks brand new."

"Just like the day I laid it in your Pa's hands." Sol grinned broadly.

Jack set it on the leather carefully and pulled out a wad of cash.

"I was going to give it to you as a gift. But you look flush, young man."

Jack peeled off enough twenties to pay the bill. "I'm planning on doing some target practice. I'll need some more shells."

"Skeet shooting is best with this gun. Try Miller's Range out on the 83 and Garces Highway." Sol set three boxes of shells on the counter. Jack zipped up the gun, took up the shells, rested the shotgun on his shoulder and made his way to his car. He placed them all in the trunk and then set out for Bakersfield. He wanted his father's baseball cards back.

It didn't take him long at the pawnshop to conduct his business and leave with his cards under his arm. There was a relief having them stowed away in his trunk. It was shortly after six when Jack rode by Cicero's. He hadn't planned on going in.

He only had a couple of hundred dollars with him. The rest of his bankroll was with the baseball cards and the Browning. The fifty-dollar table was almost full, and he played a few hands, not really too excited about his efforts. He lost then won, and by eight o'clock his interest waned so much, he rose to leave when he heard a familiar voice.

"Jack." Les Gilinsky hailed him from the other side of the room. "You and I should talk." Jack followed him to a dark corner of the bar, away from the gambling floor. Seated at a cocktail table, Les hunched forward.

"Ethan's madder than a bitch cheated of her whelps. Wants to play you again."

"I figured he would."

"Is it true your mother paid off her back taxes?"

Jack told him about finding the combine on Kolcinivitch's land, fighting the man in the dark, and the arrest of his friend.

"Is that how he got his face all banged up like that and the sprained arm?"

Jack nodded, smiling sheepishly.

"And with your dough, you've bailed out your friend?" He slapped Jack on the shoulder. "There's honor somewhere in this valley." Les rubbed his whiskery chin. "That slimy conniver probably had that tractor salesman beaten too."

"It looks that way."

Les looked him over with watery eyes. "Shirley has every reason to believe Kolcinivitch would do such a thing."

Jack appreciated his words and couldn't help but notice the farmer's furtive glances as if making certain no one lurked close by, listening. The farmer leaned across the table. "You know about Kolcinivitch's aquifer?"

Jack shook his head. "What about it?"

"He's pumped it nearly dry. The water table has dropped so bad his land's sinking in places. Your father built a water bank in the lowland to recharge the aquifer, but Kolcinivitch filled it in and planted over it, the fool. He's been irrigating with state water for a couple of years now. That's what forced him off his other place before he purchased yours."

"Stole it, rather."

"That, too." Les continued. "The water rights attached to the little parcel of yours, you know about that?"

"Yeah. They've been mentioned."

"Your father used that water to recharge his aquifer. Kolcinivitch needs that water. He's madder than a sow gone rabid at Shirley redeeming her land."

"DiGorda asked me if my mom would sell him her water."

"If she would do that, it would keep him off her back."

Jack didn't want to say what dollar figure he had in mind. "What do you think would be a fair price for her water?"

"Without water, the only thing he has left is a few more years of cash flow before he is forced to sell the land. The federal government set up the State Water Project during the Depression. A drought had threatened the agricultural bounty of the entire San Joaquin Valley. The feds financed an extensive system of aqueducts, canals, and pumping stations that carried water from the Sacramento River Delta down to the dry lowlands. Any farmer can draw from it through his local water district. But if a farmer used subsidized water, after ten years he had to sell his land. Kolcinivitch had already been forced to sell his land near Arvin for the same reason. Now he was on the verge of it happening again. That's why Shirley's spring water has become so valuable to him."

"He should be willing to pay big money for it."

"He should. But he won't."

"He doesn't have any choice if he wants it."

"Oh, he does. He can sue. He's known for getting what he wants through the courts. He's beaten Shirley in court before. There's no reason to think he won't try it again. I can picture him running up your lawyer bills to force her out. If it ever does go to trial, there's always the chance a judge will grant him access to water that should be flowing through Spring Gulch. It's happened before in the valley."

Jack now understood his mother's fears.

"If you can't come to an agreement on price, then you've got to be prepared to fight."

That would be a losing proposition for his mother. That wasn't the way Jack wanted this to go. Yet, Kolcinivitch needed the water. But how far would he go to get it?

"My mother will never sell it to him."

"Why don't you play him for it?"

"In a card game?"

Les nodded. "If you don't do something, there will be a nasty standoff."

"What're you proposing?"

"His land for yours—straight up."

"He'd find a way to cheat me or worse. If I win, he'll kill me."

Les considered that, pinching his bottom lip between his finger and thumb. "There are ways to make this happen without you getting killed. If you decide to do this, I can help." Jack could see a glimmer of a plan in the man's eye. His mother had said nice things about the fellow sitting across from him with big brown sympathetic eyes. He had even differed with the other growers about the labor struggles.

"I don't know if I'll ever talk my mother into letting me wager her land."

"Just wanted to run it by you. You never know."

➤

THAT NIGHT BEFORE TURNING in, he opened his bedroom window and looked out over the nearby grape fields. The rows of Thompson vines stretched out into the darkness under a moonless sky. The big dipper slung low in the inkiness. Owning the land his father had broken and planted was an impossibility. Just a few weeks ago, it hadn't mattered much to him if they owned this place again. Yet, now, overlooking the vines, he felt something that drew him. Rightfully, it should be his mother's. Someday his to work if that's what he wanted to do.

But gambling their one acre in a winner-take-all game of chance didn't seem rational. If he read the cards wrong, if he made a bad bet, if he allowed himself to be cheated, his mother would be out in hours. Kolcinivitch would see to that. If she became homeless, he could never leave here without making it right.

Then pleasant thoughts flooded him. If he did win, he could walk away proud that his father's life hadn't been for nothing. That the bankers and their friends couldn't trample on folks and simply walk away with all the chips.

➤

FRIDAY AFTERNOON AT PRACTICE, Jack announced to the team that Adrian had been reinstated. Just in time for the big game. Arvin was up next, and every man had to be ready to do battle. The afternoon's workout went well with Adrian participating for the first time in several weeks. Everyone was intense and focused, their spirits lifted to see their best hitter and fielder back in uniform. Adrian hustled through his work but still had a brooding glare. He hardly spoke or shouted and never joshed with anyone even when Marty egged him on. His timing looked off during batting practice. He pulled up, holding his side, during wind sprints.

While everyone trotted in for a shower, Coach asked Jack to stay and throw some batting practice for Adrian, sharpen up his swing. Adrian would have none of it. He insisted he had to get home to help his folks.

"Lot's going on there," he told Coach. Jack had witnessed the sheriff deputies tearing their place apart as if they were a demolition crew. He imagined as the oldest boy, Adrian's help was needed putting their home back together. But Adrian hadn't confided in him, so he didn't know exactly what was going on. Besides, it was a Friday night, and Jack had promised Ella a special night out. But first, he had some important business to handle.

Chapter 38
The Price of Water

FRIDAY NIGHT, JACK BLASTED down the 99 toward Bakersfield as darkness swept across the valley. He and Ella hadn't seen much of each other lately because of her involvement with the migrant legal issues and his baseball, and his gambling, according to her. She didn't care for his card playing, but she understood why he was doing it.

Despite their busyness, Jack had something planned tonight. Something they hadn't done for a while. They used to dance regularly at the Rainbow Gardens, a dance hall in Bakersfield that was a lot of fun. It had been one of her favorite places.

Before he could have any fun, he had to take care of some business. His conversation with the growers wouldn't take long. Once they heard what he had to say, they'd want him gone. So, he wore his dancing clothes: Levi's, cowboy boots, and a new shirt.

In Cicero's parking lot, he donned Sugar's hat. Inside, the cashier winked at him as usual and told him the big boys were in the back room if that was the game he was after. That, indeed, was the game he was after. He gave her a warm smile, gathered his chips, and made his way through the tables bursting with action.

He barged into the dark room, and the four men around the smoky table stopped their chatter, glancing him over. The single lamp slung low over the green felt table held the players in a circle of light. DiGorda exhaled a swish of blue smoke that drifted upward, swirling in the amber glow. Eerie tendrils of bluish stink wound around the four growers. It appeared the men had vines growing out of their ears and mouths. The odor was that of an old barn, one that hadn't been mucked out, the acrid fragrance tempestuous in Jack's nostrils.

He took a breath and hoped it wasn't his last.

He strode to the table, taking his seat among the men. Only the slap of shuffled cards echoed in the silence. A waitress entered from a side door and set drinks all around. Kolcinivitch bit quickly into his double Scotch. She placed a full bottle next to him. DiGorda puffed away and appraised Jack. Gilinsky stacked chips then counted them. Everett Champ stared into his drink.

"Did I disturb something?" Jack glanced around again.

"Nah!" DiGorda's words came out clothed in blue. "We're just getting warmed up for the real cussing."

The men laughed. Kolcinivitch spit out his Scotch, nearly choking on the liquid.

Jack spread his hands in a question.

"You the only one around here who doesn't know what's going on?" Kolcinivitch's voice spewed acid.

"Depends on what it is."

"Chavez and his damn fast," Everett Champ said. "It's killing us."

"What I read, it's killing him." Jack signaled the waitress and ordered a beer. She took his order, never asking for his ID. No one in this place had ever asked him to prove his age. Hanging around the growers, no one would.

"I hope it kills him," DiGorda said.

"I hope it kills him right now." Kolcinivitch slammed his glass to the felt. "Or we're going to be in real trouble come harvest."

Just then the dealer showed up, took over shuffling, and the game got underway. The cards flew, betting got heavy, and the tension eased. At the end of the first game, Jack had to know.

"I don't understand how a man fasting can hurt you guys."

Kolcinivitch growled and took another slug of Scotch. Just the mention of Chavez, not even by name, brought a grimace to his face.

"Look, it's simple." DiGorda pointed his stogie scissored between two fingers at Jack. "Say you have economic assets that need to bring a certain return. Some costs are fixed. See. There's little you can do about them. Then you got the variables. You got the weather, which is a demon to you every other year. Treats you like a jilted woman—blows too hot or too cold just to mess with you. Don't give you no rain just to remind you who's really on top. Then you got the Feds and their stranglehold on water. They tell you how much and how little you can use, and what time of year you can use it. How much runoff you can put back into it. Like they know the first thing about what we do every day, breaking our backs, risking it all to bring in a crop. We can't do much about either of them, but they aren't fixed. They change with the wind. Then you got labor. See, that's something we have to manage, or we're going to come up short. Real short. If we can't say how and when and where labor is used, then where are we? You hear me."

Jack lifted his cards to view his hand. "Sounds like farming's a tough deal."

Kolcinivitch swore and jammed his drink down on the felt. "You don't control labor, you don't have an operation."

"Labor is the only variable, Jack. Our only variable." DiGorda leaned in as though he was holding a debate. "Look, you can't give up control of everything or you can't run your business. Chavez wants to organize all our workers under his control. We can't let that happen."

"When he fasts, that threatens your variables?"

"It's not just the fast, Jack. It's the boycott. Since his fast started, the boycott has become a nationwide holy crusade. Mothers in Maryland won't buy our grapes now. If this keeps up, we're screwed."

Jack felt a surge of enjoyment, watching these men turned inside out because of the actions of one small Mexican-American man refusing to eat. They shivered at his very name, and still, Jack had a difficult time putting his finger on the point of tension that drove these men to think the way they did.

"Then you got that Kennedy fool." DiGorda almost choked on that name. "What's he thinking coming back here?"

"What about him?" Jack asked.

Kolcinivitch glared at him. "You don't know squat, do you?"

"I don't know what you know."

"Lay off him, Ethan." Gilinsky took up the bottle of Scotch and refilled Kolcinivitch's glass. "Chavez is breaking his fast next week and Kennedy's flying in to sit with him as he eats."

DiGorda puffed. Kolcinivitch rubbed his face. Champ shook his head slowly.

"It didn't do go well last time RFK came out here, did it?" Jack asked.

"He stirred a pot that needs no stirring, that's for sure." Champ had an exasperated look. "And he's going to do it again if he has his way."

"Someone needs to take care of him before he does any more damage," Kolcinivitch said.

The room froze.

DiGorda wasn't smiling. "He's just joking."

"Heard he told Sheriff Grant to read the Constitution last time he was here," Jack said. "Do you know if he ever got around to it?"

All four of them laughed. Champ pushed back his chair and slapped his thighs he was laughing so hard.

"We don't pay Sheriff Grant to read anything." DiGorda laughed. "I'm not even sure he can read."

"I heard he tore up his copy of the Constitution."

"I doubt it," Champ said. "He never owned one."

"He wouldn't know where to find one." Kolcinivitch poured himself another drink.

After everyone calmed down, DiGorda leaned forward. "Jack, look. We're not making fun of the Constitution. It's a fine document if you ask me. But we have certain ways of handling difficult labor situations out here that have worked for us for a long time now. You can't just hand over power to a bunch of Mexican and Filipinos who think they can run things better than we can. That's the issue here."

Jack held his cards close to his chest. He took in all the men, staring hard at him, searching him. They wanted to know, did he see things their way? Had they had this same conversation with his father in this same room? Maybe Sugar had sat in this same chair, these same men judging whether he could be part of their cabal. He threw down his cards.

"So, Ethan, you want to buy my mother's land. You can purchase it outright with the water rights if we can come to a fair price."

"Fair price sounds good to me." The big man set his Scotch down and for the first time sounded congenial. "What price did you have in mind?"

He calculated his father's hard work planting the fields and his mother's years of anguish. It all added up. There was Herm's voice in his head, to play it cool, not to go off half-cocked with the growers.

"I'm thinking about 3.4 million dollars."

Kolcinivitch's face turned nasty red; his mouth tightened in an angry pucker.

"Now, Jack." DiGorda leaned over the table, ever so amiable.

"You know what your problem is?" Kolcinivitch rose. "You think all this," he said spread his arms, "just grew out of the ground on its own. When I came here as a kid, my father had a hundred dollars and couldn't speak English. We broke this land ourselves, planted every vine, and made this place what it is today."

Jack leaned back, possessed of a real calmness. "My father did the same thing from what everyone tells me."

DiGorda put a hand on Kolcinivitch's arm, and the big man slowly lowered into his chair. "How did you come up with that figure, Jack?"

"That's the balance of the price he should have paid for my father's land. You know, when the bank called his loan because of the manipulation of the value of our land."

Kolcinivitch fidgeted in his seat as if trying to hold back something. He finally blurted out: "Your mother had her day in court, twice. Twice the courts said it was a fair value considering the current market conditions."

"Look, Jack. No one was cheated." DiGorda stretched out his hand practically pleading. "You gotta be reasonable about this."

"Did you own the Sierra Vista Ranch at the time?" Jack pointed at DiGorda.

"Sure." DiGorda shrugged. "I had to put it on the market when I did. Since I used state water, I had to sell it after ten years. This is all well-traveled territory, Jack. I didn't know how it would affect the value of your father's property. Besides, I didn't have a choice. I had to put it on the market."

"Who owns it now?"

DiGorda took a deep draw on his cigar.

"Who owns it now?" Jack repeated.

"My cousins."

"Despite the fact selling it to your family is illegal, you still farm it. But my mother lost her land, and now you want the last bit of it for nothing."

"I'm willing to pay a fair price," Kolcinivitch said.

"What's fair?" Jack leaned forward.

"Anderson just sold his five hundred acres for one thousand and three hundred dollars per. Your place has a house on it that I understand needs considerable repairs. So I'll probably tear it down." Kolcinivitch rubbed his stubbled chin. "I'm thinking about ten grand. That'll give Shirley some cash to move and set herself up. She can buy a place in town for that."

Jack gave a sigh and leaned back, shaking his head. "Won't do at all, Ethan. I'm still thinking around 3.4 million dollars."

"You're not looking at this as a business transaction," DiGorda said. "You're letting your emotions carry you." He leaned on the table. "Look, Jack, every price is determined by the market. Not how you feel about it."

Jack spoke low and steady. "My father did an extensive study of water usage for his entire acreage. He charted the monthly water usage by the gallon to irrigate the vines. He built the settling ponds on the north side of the ranch to recharge his aquifer. He calculated that Spring Gulch water would replenish the aquifer through those ponds to fifty percent of its annual usage after peak season irrigation. With the annual precipitation and runoff, even during lean years, his aquifers would never be depleted below seventy-five percent capacity at the beginning of peak irrigation months." Jack pointed at Kolcinivitch. "But you graded over the settling ponds and planted them so you could increase your yields. You don't let the land recharge naturally."

The men stared at him open-mouthed.

"Unlike Sheriff Grant, I can read." Jack took a breath. "I've read all of my father's surveys and plans for the ranch. And I know this—you'll over pump your aquifers, and then you'll need to buy federal water if you're not doing so already. So, eventually, your land will come on the market, and at current market prices, land without water isn't worth much." Jack leaned back. "So, I'll just wait to sell the property. Someone will pay peanuts for your property, probably just cover the mortgage. But they'll pay full value for mine, and together they will have a self-sustaining property. So, that's how I came up with 3.4 million dollars. Considering everything, I think it's a fair price."

DiGorda rubbed his bottom lip. Kolcinivitch poured a tall drink and kicked it back. Gilinsky pursed his lips and gently nodded his head. Champ Everett gave him a blank stare.

In the silence of the moment, it became apparent to Jack that his father, besides being a good man, was a good farmer, one who truly understood the land and its ways. He felt a shining inside, one that warmed him to this moment. He sat tall and met their shocked gazes.

Kolcinivitch composed himself and folded his arms over his chest. "So what you're saying is that your one acre with water is as valuable as my four thousand without water if they were all one operation."

"That's it in a nutshell."

"Listen, big balls." Kolcinivitch puffed out his chest. "The water is all from the same aquifer. But you don't seem to think that's true, so I'll make you a proposition. One that even your father would see as fair."

"Yeah." Jack wanted to hear this.

"Play me for the land. I'll put up my deed, and you get Shirley to put up hers. I'll put up a five thousand dollar buy-in; you can come in with what you have there. The winner takes the deeds. The loser takes the cash on the table. Even if you lose, you'll get something. But if you win…" He spread his hands, palms up.

All the eyes in the room were on him. He could hear himself breathing. He glanced at Les Gilinsky. Had the grower said something to Kolcinivitch about their conversation or did he just come up with this idea on his own? Jack pushed back his chair and gathered his chips. "I'll let you know."

"What's the problem? Your big balls suddenly go cold?" The grower stood. "You think you can run with the big boys and not put everything at risk like the rest of us."

Jack wanted to take everything the man owned, including his pants. But he kept his mouth shut, for once, and played the bluff the way it needed to be played.

"I said I'll think about it."

"Don't wait too long, buster. Because I got options."

"We've all got options." Jack rose with his chips and turned to the door. He made his way to the cashier and cashed them in, then rolled the bills into his pocket. Making his way to the car, his footsteps were barely tethered to the earth.

He could beat Kolcinivitch ten ways to Sunday if the man didn't cheat. If Jack could find a way to arrange a fair game, he could have his land back. Sitting behind the wheel, he imagined himself owning the ranch. The first thing he'd do would be to tear down those ratty shacks Kolcinivitch called housing. After that, he wasn't so sure what he'd do. Would he stay and work it with his mother? He had never considered that before.

He'd consider that when the time came. First, he'd have to talk his mother into trusting his game with her deed. He drove out of the lot with his brain on fire with possibilities, and the night was still young. Once he reached Delano, he'd find a pay phone and call Ella. He felt like dancing.

At the bottom of the on-ramp to Highway 99, he pushed the pedal to the floor, and the lazy straight-eight guttered and guffawed, then grabbed hold of the gears beneath him and shot forward into the stelliferous night.

Chapter 39
Blackboard Café

WHEN HE PULLED INTO the circular drive of Ella's house, the front porch light blinked on, and she stepped out into the warm starry night. Unusual that she would meet him on the porch. Her father insisted he come inside so he could give him a once over, then they could leave. But there she was—outside waiting for him. He wasn't going to keep her waiting, so he hustled out. She stood in the dim glow in tan cowboy boots, clutching a small leather purse hung over her shoulder. She wore a jean skirt and a tight emerald blouse that matched her sparkling eyes. Her lips were red with anticipation. Teased up in a messy beehive, her auburn hair lingered in stringy bangs around her eyes, with long strands falling over her shoulders and around her breasts, a style he saw in photos of Bridget Bardot. Stunning. He couldn't stop smiling, taking her in. He opened the door, and she slid in.

Once he was behind the wheel, she snuggled up to him, the fragrance of her White Shoulders a freshness that bore away the putrid air he had been breathing lately. This was an Ella he hadn't seen before. An Ella he liked very much.

"You look ready to dance. How about Rainbow Gardens?"

Ella wrinkled her nose. Rainbow Gardens was an all-ages dance club. Some of the best bands of the Bakersfield sounds play there— Tommy Collins, Jelly Sanders, Jean Shepherd, and many other

Bakersfield guitar pickers. But it was cavernous, with poor acoustics, only creaky wooden chairs around the walls, and food only a hardened cowboy would eat. If you were dance crazy and didn't care about mingling with a few hundred other couples, it would do just fine.

"Buck Owens is playing at The Blackboard Café."

"We can't get in that place." The Blackboard was honky-tonk in a rough section of Bakersfield. They had the best bands and the biggest bouncers; toughs who kept a tight lid on who got in to keep the brawling down. Buck Owens and Merle Haggard showed up there regularly when they were just starting out, but now it would be a special event. The club would be packed and rowdy. On the other hand, it would also be smoky and dark; the perfect place to hide out if the cops ever showed up, which they only did when a fight broke out.

She spoke softly, nearly under her breath. "You go into gambling halls all the time. You buy beer and hang out with growers—who knows what else. Now you're afraid to take me with you?"

The warm charm of her challenge set Jack straight. He wasn't afraid of taking her anywhere. "Blackboard it is."

He couldn't keep his eyes off her. As beautiful as she looked, she wore a pensive frown.

"What gives? You don't look in a dancing mood."

"Oh, I am." Her lips were tight as if she were controlling herself. Something was digging at her.

"You still upset about Sabrina's mother?"

"I've moved on to other controversies."

"Those controversies have anything to do with you standing outside when I drove up?"

"My father's furious. He wants me to stop working with the Migrant Legal Aid office. His friends are calling, cussing him out that he lets me run all over their properties. He's pissed off that he can't control me anymore."

Jack pursed his lips at that thought. They must have had a monumental argument.

"That why you were outside when I drove up?"

"I'm lucky my clothes weren't outside with me. The day after graduation, I'm moving into town with Emily." She explained her plan to work right up to the day she had to drive down to LA.

She had planned to go to LA after graduation, but now she would be here all summer. "That's a change."

"A good one. Besides, you're not going right away either. You'll be in the state championships, and that will keep you around until late July."

"We still have to beat Arvin. That's not a given."

She lit him up with her confident smile. "You're going to win. I know it."

"Oh, baby, you're right about that."

She leaned her head back on Jack's arm and closed her eyes. "Let's just forget all this crap and have a good time tonight."

Jack felt a surge of ascent run through him. He hit the gas pedal, and the Old's pummeled forward down the macadam toward Bakersfield.

The Blackboard Café took up a corner lot on Thirty-Eighth and Chester Avenue near downtown, a squat stucco building that had been painted white a couple of decades ago and forgotten about. A large painted sign in red letters took up half the side of the building facing the parking lot. "Dancing 7 days a week."

There were no motorcycles parked in front, always a good sign. Hells Angels had taken to making the place a stopover on its big rides up north. From the signs of the crowd hanging out in the lot, smoking and shooting the breeze, it should be hopping inside.

At the door, a big old boy a couple of heads taller than Jack with tatted up arms and biceps as wide as the Kern River stood in the doorway. His roughed-up cowboy hat inched down close to his brows. He held out his oversized palm as Jack tried to pass.

"Hey, Pardoner, how old are you?"

"Old enough to shoot gooks between the eyes, and vote for Buck Owens for president."

A twangy steel guitar riff and a mellow baritone in a bluesy lament blared through the open door.

The bouncer gave him a leering grin. "I'll tell him that. Right now, you need to take your baby ass out of here."

Jack had a good story ready for such events. "We're friends of the band. They told us to meet them here."

The bouncer gave him a narrowed glare, full of doubt.

"Don Rich is not going to be happy if you don't let us in." Rich played lead guitar on the Buckaroos.

"Say I call Don over here?" The bouncer nodded toward the dark inside, "He's gonna vouch for you?"

"You call Don over here during a set, he's going to break his Fender over your fat head."

The big man gave out an intimidating growl Jack didn't like. He raised both of his beefy hands to grab Jack, just as Ella stepped between the two. Her beehive stood taller than Jack's head, making her look older, a lean, beautiful, and self-assured woman.

"Mister, we've come a long way to hear Buck. You can throw this guy out if you want to, but I'm going in."

His eyes grew large, and he pulled his chin in. He slowly lifted his hands out of her way. Then he swept his right palm forward in an arc, ushering her inside with his best cowboy manners. She strutted past the two into the darkness. The bouncer grabbed Jack with his meat hook hand and pulled him close.

"You better keep that woman real close. And keep your big mouth shut. I hear one squeak out of you, I'll throw you so far even that cute gal of yours will never find you." He released Jack's arm.

Jack straightened his shirt. "Hey, everything's cool."

In the darkened room, Jack took Ella's arm and steered her toward a cocktail table against the wall a few rows from the dance floor. Ella sat facing the band. Jack pulled his chair around beside her. The music reverberated through his body. He couldn't help moving.

Ella jigged her shoulders swaying to the beat. She leaned into him. "Let's dance."

Jack led her by the hand to the packed dance floor. Couples were swing dancing, western style. She moved her hips, catching the beat. Jack swooped her under his arm, leading her through a turn. She danced her styling, hand curling in the air, on the tether of his fingers.

The Buckaroos banged out their twangy guitar rhythms, and Buck's lyrics caught Jack's feelings.

We were made for each other.
I'll be yours eternally...

Eternally with a girl, with Ella, hadn't crossed his mind before. He always focused on the next game, the next semester, the next thing to do. But tonight her satisfied smile, the concentration in her green eyes, her toes tapping, and her slender body gliding past him as he led her in a twirling turn, made him feel alive. There was so much more than playing baseball. He pulled her close, for a promenade, the tempo of their bodies swayed with the beat.

I'll give you love that's above,
And beyond the call of love...

With Ella's soft hand in his, she swirled a turn, her skirt flared, her long hair swished in a twirl. The beat brought her again into his arms. Inches from her face, he saw a different Ella, one he hadn't seen before tonight. A grown-up woman. So much had happened since that first bus ride to Berkeley. On that ride home, he knew she was a special girl. But now their life was about to change. They were both about to fall off a cliff together into a different world. This woman in his arms was the most real and vital part of him. He loved everything about her. Right about then, Buck went into another song.

I don't care if the world don't turn,
Just as long as you love me...

His hand rested firmly on her shoulder blade, not wanting to let her go. Did he have her love? If he did, it would be enough. Whatever came his way, he could take.

Their bodies together, he whispered in her ear, Buck's words, "I don't care if the world don't turn, just as long as you love me."

She pulled back, looked him straight in the eyes, and he knew. And when the twanging stopped, and the band took a breath, he wrapped his arms around her, and they stood together in the middle of the floor. With his mouth to her ear. "I love you. I want us to be together forever."

She pushed away a bit with a ravishing smile so real he didn't need her words. She searched his eyes as if trying to look into him. Her green eyes misted up in a sheen, a radiant glow all around her. She leaned into his ear as the Buckaroos struck up a new song, her warm body molded to his, and Buck's voice mingled with hers. Jack could not tell her words from the singer's. Maybe they were the same...

I got the hunger for your love...

Chapter 40
Workout

TUESDAY AFTERNOON'S WORKOUT ON the ballfield dragged on in the wilting heat. Jack kept sharp, tossing batting practice to the team. He ran wind sprints, Adrian beside him, sweating and subdued, his friend moving better than the day before but still, his stride was stiff, understandable after two weeks crammed in a cell. Adrian had a troubled look as he worked to regain his form. He missed two fly balls, letting them drop in when he misjudged their trajectory. His teammates shouted encouragement, while Coach ground his teeth, his jaw flexing.

At the plate, Adrian laced pitches all over the field when he made contact, then stroked wildly at easy balls. When he finished, Marty came out of his crouch and patted him on the back.

"Keep at it. We need you to come up big for us Thursday."

Adrian slung the bat over his shoulder, a laborer with his shovel, and nodded in his wordless way. Jack hustled to catch up with him in the locker room, to try to ease his friend's mind. By the time Jack had showered and dressed, Adrian had already left. Jack ran to the lot with his hair still wet. His friend's beat-up Chevy accelerated up the street, rumbling as it headed east toward home.

Jack wanted to follow him, but he remembered his last visit to the Sanchez home. His father's arrest and the destruction of their house could account for his listless play. His family must still be under pressure from the sheriff. It was part of Adrian's make up to stand behind them. Then there was all the make-up schoolwork he had to complete before graduation. He had to graduate. All of his plans hinged on that.

Then there was his time in jail. It had cut into Adrian in unspoken ways.

Climbing into his car, Jack let the Old idle. Images of the swaggering Arvin boys coming to town filled his mind. Only a few more days of practice left. They would be desperate for vengeance, and they'll bring every grudge and baseball trick. Delano had to be ready to go.

Chapter 41
The Lawsuit

THE NEXT MORNING JACK strolled into the kitchen before seven. Shirley sat at the table, a half-filled coffee cup in front of her. From the redness of her eyes, she must have been up all night crying. He set his books on the table and fetched a cup, poured some coffee, and swung into a chair. His mother pushed a stapled set of papers toward him. He had never seen these kinds of papers. He scanned them.

"You're getting sued?"

"By that idiot next door."

Jack flipped the page, and the word "water" bled off the paper. Page after page, "water" was everywhere.

"It says we defrauded him of his divisible rights to Spring Gulch by blocking up the spring on our land." Shirley pointed at the section. "Our land." She pushed her index finger into her chest. "That water is on our land."

"Does he have a divisible right?"

"That's what he has to prove. But now I've got to pay to defend this." She pushed her chair back, letting out an exasperated breath. "Can't let him do this. But we don't have the money. He knows that."

"Are you going to at least talk to an attorney?"

"I'll go see Hank Edwards. But the only money I have is what I've put away for the shop. We can't just keep throwing money down this rat hole."

That jackass next door hadn't even waited for an answer from Jack. He just plunged ahead. He wanted to force a reply—either sell for a pittance or play him straight up.

"They're all friends." Shirley folded her arms and leaned against the sink. "Lawyers and growers. Then they have the judges in their pockets if they want them. I thought opening a shop in town would be my way out of this mess, but now this."

"This is a ploy, Mom."

Jack told her about his conversation with Kolcinivitch. How he offered to pay ten grand for the place. But once he showed the grower how he came up with the value at $3.4 million, Kolcinivitch challenged him to play him straight up—his land for hers, winner-take-all.

"Oh, Jack, you're in way over your head. I could never put you in that position. He'd kill you before he'd let you out of that room with a deed to his property."

"Les Gilinsky said he'd help me to set it up so it would be safe. I know I can beat him. The lawyer who helped Adrian can set it up, so it's legal."

Shirley gave him a hard look. "I trust Les, but not with your life."

"You can't take him on in court, Mom. Les said he has a fair chance of winning rights to some of the water. Then what are you left with?"

The disdain in her eyes made Jack turn from her. "I'm not done here, and I don't need you to tell me what I can't do."

"He's just trying to force us to make a decision—play him or sell out to him."

She eyed him warily as if she wondered whose side he was on.

"It's our only and best chance of getting everything back. Worst case, you'll have the cash to move with. Best case, you won't have any reason to move at all."

An argument began to brew in her eyes. Grabbing his books, he turned to the back door. She called him. He let the door slam behind him. Time to get to school.

JACK DIDN'T SEE ADRIAN around campus that day, hearing he was holed up in the library trying to save his semester. Later at Wednesday's practice just as everyone finished stretching, Adrian sprinted onto the field. He stood in front of the team spread out on the grass stretching. He opened the pocket of his glove and struck it several times.

"Let's get to work."

His tone was so bright everyone jumped to and sprinted through their drills. He ripped through his workout, his raw intensity a harbinger. During batting practice, he played third base to practice handling hot liners. Hustle and command oozed from his smooth slide to his left to spear drives. He leaped and stretched to glove balls above his head, then ones slicing off to his right, a dynamo of excellence. Marty gave him a holler. Boys hooted and clapped.

He sprinted full out to center, smoothness in his steps, hunger in his stride. He chased down fly balls with ease, catching them over his head, over his shoulder, a running basket catch here, and a diving save there.

Adrian's enthusiasm for the game had been reborn.

Jack jumped on the mound and slapped his glove. Practice picked up. Boys shouted encouragement, ran the bases with abandon, dove for balls that dirtied their jerseys and came up clutching the ball.

Their captain was here to lead, and with tomorrow's game looming large in their minds, order had been restored. Today they were world-beaters.

Practice over, Coach called everyone to the mound. Mercifully, his pep talk was short. He dismissed them, and Adrian raced all of them to the locker rooms.

Jack sat at his locker, elbows resting on his knees, drenched in sweat, but feeling ready. A few lockers away, Adrian slumped on the bench, hanging his head.

"You looked good today, buddy. Great to see the old Adrian."

"It's been a while since I worked that hard." He pulled off a sweat-soaked T-shirt and flung it into his open locker.

"You sure brought it today."

Adrian beamed. "I got a lot going on. But I can't let the team down. We've come this far."

"How's your dad?"

"Man, he's right back at it. Out organizing."

"It sucked, man, what they did to him. It still seems like a bad dream."

"I'm not living a dream. Neither is my family."

"Neither is mine."

Adrian unwound his taut body, standing bare-chested and tall. "We're going to win this game. Then I got to move on."

"You out helping your dad? Haven't seen much of you lately."

"I got called into McGrew's office the other day."

"What'd he want?"

"Said the board was considering not letting me graduate."

Jack shot up. "What? That's bull."

Adrian shook his head. "He'd heard I was helping my father on the picket line. Said if I kept it up, they would flunk me."

"No way."

Adrian gave him a shrug.

"But you have to graduate."

"You know, Ella's always talking about putting her body on the gears of the machine. That's what I've been up to lately. It's not a bad feeling, knowing something might change."

Adrian turned and left, and Jack detected a slump in his friend's shoulders as if he carried an unwelcome weight. It shouldn't be that way, Jack thought, kids saddled with the ills of their parents. But that wasn't the way things were—Adrian trying to measure the importance of everything he'd worked for, and now his graduation in jeopardy; Ella at odds with her father, and making new enemies every day. And what about Jack's mother facing a lawsuit she couldn't afford, and probably couldn't win? Jack didn't know what to do if his mother became homeless.

He had promised her nothing would interfere with his moving to UCLA come August, but everyone he cared for, their lives were in flux. Ella's determination to work in the legal aid office this summer had taken over her life. Jack had no idea what would happen to Adrian if he didn't graduate. And his mother's dilemma had become a dark cloud over their lives, a raging storm ready to break over both their heads.

Tomorrow's game was supposed to be the biggest game of their high school career, but instead, it had shrunk in consequence. If he allowed himself to think that way, he feared failure. He couldn't allow it to happen. Tomorrow's game represented everything he had worked for since little league. He had to clear his mind of the politics of grapes and pitch the best game of his life. But he couldn't erase the images that flashed through him—Kolcinivitch showing up on his mother's doorstep after his father was killed, Adrian hauled off to jail by Kauffman, him getting slugged by the same deputy. It all boiled inside him as he dressed, fusing into a ball of heat in his stomach, pulsing in his brain in a tumor of hate. Striding to his car in the twilight, he feared the tension would split him wide open.

➤

HE SHOULD HAVE HEADED home to study, but instead, he turned east toward Miller's Shooting Range. Dusk wasn't too far off when he reached it on Highway 83. He parked and bought fifty clay pigeons.

"Don't know if you'll get them all off before dark." Miller counted out Jack's change.

"Just keep pulling. I'll take care of the shooting."

At the shooter's stand, Jack unzipped the Browning from its leather case and slotted in five rounds—one in the chamber, four in the magazine. The gun felt smooth and tight in his hands, the steel cool and uncaring. He took his stance, laid his cheek on the stock to line up the sight. The wood platform overlooked the range, a deep depression of bare land lined on both sides by eucalyptus trees. The pigeon launcher sat beside a shack to his right.

"Pull," he yelled. The clay disk slingshot in an arc right across his sight. He squeezed the trigger, the gun bucked into his shoulder, and the disk shattered into bits.

"Pull." He tracked and squeezed, and the disk disintegrated over the range. His shoulder buzzed; he seated the wooden stock solidly in the crook of his arm.

"Pull." Track and squeeze.

"Pull." He shot in a rapid fury of bursting shells and exploding clay, shattering and falling. He reloaded in quick, sure movements with never a hesitation. Just as the sun dipped below the trees, he blasted the last pigeon out of the air.

He rested the barrel on his shoulder. A pall of gunpowder gathered over the shooting stand. He felt spent, the buzzing in his head diminished, but not the misery festering in his heart. As the gray cloud drifted over him, the grit of burned gunpowder stung his nostrils, for a moment he felt shiftless, his future seemed obscured and rootless, enveloped in a haze.

Chapter 42
Arvin Redux

THURSDAY AFTERNOON THE ARVIN boys strolled onto the Delano field, bats over their shoulders, gloves in their hands, and arrogance in their eyes.

Jack ignored them and continued his warm-up as his teammates jogged in the outfield. Boys brushed by one another without a nod, everyone focused on running, swinging, catching, and throwing. In the afternoon's heated stillness, the echo of bats on balls, of boy's sliding in the dirt, of balls thudding into mitts, filled the air.

City cops posted at the corners of the stands eyed fans as they filed into the bleachers. Folks milled about, and long lines formed for cold drinks and hot dogs under the wilting sun. Cheerleaders danced behind each dugout, their pom-pom enthusiasm sounding less sporty, more like incantations of war. A thickness carried in the air that went beyond the heat.

The umps called the two coaches and starting pitchers to the mound. Jack trotted over. Their words were stern—no brushbacks, no hitting batters. Jack eyed the string-bean Arvin pitcher, but the guy wouldn't look his way. The boy just kicked at the dirt like a nervous stallion. Accidents were the same as provocations, the ump said. Watch the hard slides, make them clean. Swearing and name-calling would earn an ejection.

The meeting broke up, and Jack took the mound. The home plate ump asked for the ball. He looked it over then tossed the catcher a new one from a pouch at his belt.

"Play ball," the ump shouted.

An Arvin player stepped into the batter's box.

The top of the first inning, Jack held his mitt at his belt and stood tall. He leaned in to take a sign when a squad of riot-helmeted cops jogged into his line of sight behind home plate. The crowd grew quiet. Sunshine glinted off their badges. Jack stepped back. A phalanx of them guarded the Arvin bleachers, and he didn't like it all.

"Time to play," Coach shouted from the dugout. Perched one foot on the top of the dugout steps, Coach eyed him. Jack gripped the ball and leaned in, studying the batter as he took his practice swings. He'd faced this boy before, a wiry wisp of a kid who liked to slap the ball in play and sprint to first. He could only hit fat mistakes over the plate. Jack leaned in, focused on the dark circle of the catcher's mitt, wound up, and threw a fastball that floated inside, twisting the boy like a corkscrew. Jack worked as if in a dream, kept his grip firm, nodded at the signs and tumbled through his pitches, punching out batters for three quick outs.

The bottom of the first inning, in the dugout, Jack wiped his face with a towel. A cheer went up from the visitors' bleachers. Delano's first two batters had struck out. Marty stepped to the plate, swinging his arms in a fusillade of practice strokes. The Arvin pitcher delivered a ball that dove at the plate; Marty twisted around almost full circle. Two more bottom dropping fastballs, and Marty slugged at the dirt with his bat and stomped back to the dugout.

"That guy's got some sinker working today," Marty yammered as he strapped on his gear and snapped his chest protector on. "We've got to find a way to beat their butts, Jack. This guy's going to be hard to hit."

Top of the second inning, Jack took the mound. The heavy-footed DiGorda stepped into the batter's box, and Jack looked him down. The hefty player wagged his stick back and forth. Jack sniffed at the hot air. DiGorda's demeanor hadn't changed from a couple of months ago, and Jack wanted to wipe the smugness off his lips with a fastball to the gut. The boy kept winding his bat in tight circles, crouching.

Jack tossed an off-speed pitch, slow and low for strike one. A lot of shouting came from the Arvin bleachers. They had brought half the town.

He took the toss back from Marty and a whole flood of people piled in behind the line of cops. Signs and placards were raised above the sea of heads and the chanting began. Hand on his hip, Jack stared over Marty's head.

I'm not going to let them wreck my game.

Flashes of the first game with Arvin ran through his mind. Jack turned to the outfield. The championship was here for him.

Stay focused on the batter.

Jack wanted inside this boy's head. He threw a heater right down the middle. DiGorda swung from his back foot. Marty called time and jogged out. Jack held his mitt close to his mouth.

"What're you doing giving him a pitch like that? So what if he walks. The guy's a loaf of bread on the bases. Keep it low. He can only hit the low pitch if his mother tosses it to him."

The ump signaled to hurry along. Jack nodded and sent his catcher away. He kicked at the dirt. Low and away, my foot. Jack moved his pitches in and out, until the big guy imploded in frustration, swinging wildly for an out.

Bottom of the second inning, the Delano boys at bat, the twisting sinking fastballs continued. They darted to one side then the other, making the pitches unhittable. The Delano players slumped on the bench. Expectation slowly drained away by those wily pitches.

The bottom of the third inning, a moan went up from the bench when Adrian struck out. Coach strolled over to Marty.

"Seen anything unusual on those balls?"

"Nothing to see. The ump changes them so fast. He must have a couple of dozen already rubbed up."

Coach propped a foot on a concrete step, chewed and spit seeds. He didn't flinch when Barton struck out for the second out. Jack glanced down the bench. A blackness had taken over, belief and hope had evaporated in the heat.

Jack stood and clapped when Retuda stepped into the box.

"Let's go, hit one to LA," he yelled.

With the boy's twisting unhittable sinkers, he notched three quick outs. Delano took the field for the top of the fourth inning. Jack answered with two strikeouts and a third out on a fly ball.

In the bottom of the fourth inning with Jack on deck, Coach told him to keep an eye on the ball in the catcher's glove. See if he could spot anything. Jack stood in the on-deck circle. He winced when his teammate swung wildly at a dropping curveball. The catcher held the ball still long enough for the ump to call a strike. Jack caught a glimpse of it. He turned to the dugout and nodded.

There's something on those balls, he mouthed.

Coach nearly ran to home plate, signaling timeout. He pointed to the ump.

"I want to see that ball."

"What for?"

Coach held out his hand. Jack leaned on his bat, edging close.

"We need to move the game along," the ump said. "It'll be dark soon."

"I can stand right here till next season if you like." Coach kept his hand out. The catcher tossed the ball to him. Coach looked it over. "I want to see the ball he just threw."

"I got a whole pouch of 'em here." The ump patted his bag full of balls.

"Let me see them all."

He handed Coach a ball.

"Is this the one he just threw?"

"Can't say." He handed over another one.

"None of these are used." Coach motioned for another one. The ump reluctantly tossed him one.

Coach turned it along the seams and touched a flat scratch roughed along the leather stitching.

"We got a problem here."

The ump took it. The first and third base umps moved in. Each of them looked it over.

"It's odd to me, but it's your call." The first base ump nodded to the home plate ump.

He shook his head. "Could be a scuff from the dirt, anything hard will put a bruise like that."

Jack leaned over Coach's shoulder. That was no dirt scuff. Jack took in the pitcher, tall and unashamed up high on the mound, blinking at them with squinty eyes, an innocent glare on his face. Looked like the work of sandpaper. No way were they going to hit pitches from this guy with him chopping the ball like that.

Coach pointed to the mound.

"You gotta check the pitcher's equipment and warn him."

The ump motioned the pitcher to home plate. The stringy player strolled up. Jack edged closer. The ump examined his mitt and frisked around his waist.

"What about that?" Coach pointed at his cap.

"What's wrong with my cap?" the player asked.

"Let's see it." The umpire held it by its bill and searched inside the sweaty crown. "I don't see nothing."

Coach grabbed it and shook it hard. A tiny square of sandpaper fluttered out of the hatband, glued in by the boy's sweat. Coach picked it up and turned it over. Something of what Jack loved about the game slipped away. Today was for the championship. The best against the best. And this guy was cutting the ball. All those strikeouts were fake.

The ump tossed him from the game, and the lanky kid stormed away into the dugout.

"You gotta call a forfeit." Coach's arms akimbo, he spoke in a determined tone.

"The rules say it's at the umpire's discretion." The man crossed his arms over his chest and gave Coach a blank stare.

"But—" Jack began, but Coach cut him off with a raised hand.

Coach bit into the ump, citing chapter and verse from the book of rules. Boos sifted in from the stands.

"This whole game's going to get out of hand if we don't get back to playing." The ump backed away. The cops held back the demonstrating farmworkers, water behind a dam ready to break. They had kept strikers out of the stands by containing them behind home plate. Their shouting filled the air.

"You going to play ball or not?"

Coach nodded with a disgusted glare.

The ump called for another pitcher, who trotted to the mound. Coach stood by and watched as he went through his warmups. The ump warned the new Arvin player not to use anything on the ball, or the game would be forfeited. Coach trotted back to the dugout.

The game was stuck in a scoreless tie and three innings to go.

"Let's play ball," ump yelled. The catcher crouched, and Jack stepped into the batter's box. He hacked at the pitches that floated by. His muscles felt empty of force as he twisted all the way around in a futile effort.

"Strike three."

On the bench, Jack slumped between Marty and Retuda. Coach strutted up and down, spitting shells as he went, then he took up his perch on the dugout steps.

Adrian slid down beside Jack. The tightness around Adrian's mouth and eyes had settled in.

Jack prodded him with an elbow. "What?"

"They should have called the game." Adrian slammed his mitt to the dirt.

Coach had argued that line and lost. They couldn't lose their concentration right now.

"He should shake down the new Arvin pitcher. Make him stay honest, the way the game's supposed to be played."

Jack understood his friend's anger. But it wouldn't help anything.

With Barton up to bat, Jack rose and shouted encouragement with such force and volume others chipped in, cupping their mouths, screaming for Barton to whack it hard, hit it home, make the ball fly out of here. Babe Ruth it. Make it go to Hollywood. Take it yard. Do your mother proud.

The crowd erupted in a cheer when Barton slapped a hot grounder between second and third, and it bounced into left field.

Marty slapped Jack's shoulder. "Keep it up."

The next hitter, Retuda, lined a bouncer to short, which the player scooped and threw to first for the third out.

The top of the sixth inning, Delano took the field with slow, uneasy strides. Jack set three Arvin batters down.

In the bottom of the sixth, a Delano player walked, then quickly wiped out in a double play, ending the inning.

"Come on, let's go." Coach clapped as he waved the team onto the field for the top of the sixth inning. "Game's not over."

The top of the seventh, the last inning, Jack took the mound steeped in sweat with the sun sagging off toward a distant line of eucalyptus trees, casting afternoon shadows across home plate. Jack fed the first Arvin player a curve. It crossed the part of the plate covered in shadow, brushing the player back. The boy squiggled away, his upper body bending back in a rubbery twist.

The Arvin coach yelled at the ump. The ump motioned at Jack, warning him. Jack took the toss from Marty and stood astride the mound, staring back. Trying to get too fine, hitting those dark corners could work against him. He went back to work, and the batter fouled off five straight pitches. Finally, Jack lost him, serving up ball four on the outside.

Jack watched the Arvin player trot to first base. Now he had to watch the runner, keep him close to first base. Two batters later, the player slapped a hard bouncer past Smithy over third into left field. With runners on first and second, Jack bore down, striking out a boy for the second out. Down to their last out of the game, the next Arvin batter fouled off four straight pitches. Sweaty and flagging, Jack unwound with a big overhanded curve that he intended would move away but instead it floated up, and the big boy swung, squishing the ball into a high chopper between first and second.

Barton dove and came up with it, twisted and threw a bullet to second, but it flew over the outstretched mitt of the second baseman, squirting into right field. The runner advanced to third. By the time Smithy retrieved the ball, the runner had turned home. The throw from second came in wide, pulling Marty to the left, and despite his heroic effort, the runner scored the first run of the game.

The Arvin celebration angered Jack. Their fans made too much noise. Jack stomped to the mound. Coach came out and reminded him to compose himself, find his strength. He forced himself to focus on the batter, on his lazy swing. Jack settled and threw three straight strikes. The team trotted into the dugout for their last chance to win the league.

"Come on." Coach clapped and slapped players on the back, "Let's win this right here." He stomped up and down and gave each boy up to bat some last-minute instructions.

The bottom of the seventh, the first two batters went down swinging. When Adrian strolled to the plate and took a few practice swings, the home crowd went wild, chanting his name. Everyone on the bench rose, clapping and yelling encouragement.

Adrian had struck out twice, but his fielding had saved several runs, tracking down long fly balls. Now Adrian, crouching at the plate, looping practice swings, was taut and intent. He lashed the first pitch hard into right center, a low drive that dropped to the grass, and he slid into second under a late throw from the center fielder. The team broke out in hoots and hollers. The cheerleaders woke from their sleepy routines and danced about.

Marty slugged the next pitch to the hole between first and second, and Adrian took off, all arms and legs in flagrant motion. The big Arvin catcher stood astride home plate, waiting with mitt out. Both teams rose to the edges of the dugouts, shouting for their man. The stands heaved forward, arms raised in a cacophony of shouts. Cheerleaders screamed and bounced their pom-poms, and Adrian rounded third in a tight turn, churning up chalk, steaming toward home as the ball arced on a bead over his head. It thumped in the catcher's glove. Adrian slid in the dirt as the catcher on a knee, swung his mitt smoothly down for a clean tag. The ump shouted in his emphatic way, "O-u-t."

The Arvin squad erupted in cheers, backslapping, handshakes, and hugs.

Jack slumped hard on the wooden bench and pulled his cap over his eyes to hide from the world. It truly ached to hear that last out called, to have their season-long dream dashed in a single play, and to know he had just thrown his final pitch of high school.

He heard his teammates milling around him. A big hand rattled his shoulder. It was Marty.

"We better go get Adrian before he gets killed."

Jack found Adrian on his knees in the dirt staring at home plate, his hands resting on his thighs like he was praying, rocking back and forth. Jack elbowed a couple of the celebrating Arvin players away. He grabbed his friend under his arm, Marty took the other, and they lifted him, carrying him to the locker room where they set him on a bench. They all dressed in silence for everything that needed to be said between them had already been said.

Chapter 43
The Party

JACK TOOK A LONG shower and an even longer time in front of his locker, dressing slowly. He packed his gear for the last time. When he left the building, the janitor followed him to the gym door and locked it behind him. The upper windows of the locker room went dark as he trudged to his car, plunging the lot deeper into shadows. He lugged his bag, slumped shouldered, to his car where Ella waited for him, leaning against the door.

She wrapped her arms around him as he stood in the yellow-shadowed light. She didn't talk. They both knew their time here had passed. In the soft glow of the early evening, with the sounds of a city awake behind them, he held her tight. It never helped to talk about defeat, to salve the emptiness with platitudes of good effort or the empty promise of winning another day. The only way to bear the bitterness of this defeat was to allow the sting to hurt.

Barton had invited everyone to his spacious house for a team barbecue. Jack drove with Ella beside him, quiet and pensive. The party had its good moments. He and Ella sat on a sofa in the living room, talking in the low moodiness of pain no one wanted to mention openly.

When the beer was passed around a few of the boys became loud. Some found a way to laugh, even though it sounded stiff. Jack drank a beer. In time, Marty loosened everyone up with some outrageous jokes. Retuda and Stoddard started a card game in one of the bedrooms. They wanted Jack to play, but he would have none of it. He ate a hamburger, said polite things, and picked at a bowl of grapes. Ella shoved them away from her, refusing to look at them.

She chatted with friends, brushed her hair off her face, smiled through her bright teeth, and nodded every time she was asked if she was moving to LA. She didn't say anything about her summer internship. Neither did she explain her intentions beyond the summer.

Around eight o'clock Adrian strolled in, and Darcy, who had been sitting across from Ella and Jack, rose and slid away to the other side of the house. Ella asked Jack what had happened between the two, but he only shrugged. He knew Adrian was coming, but he didn't know Adrian wasn't with Darcy anymore. Apparently, Ella didn't either, and that surprised Jack.

In winning and losing, Adrian had always been the same fellow. But Jack had never seen his friend so disconsolate after a loss. Jack didn't question his friend's judgment for not holding up at third as the coach had told him to. That was the way he had always played—all out. They won so many games because of his full-throttle play that Jack had no qualms with the way his friend rolled the dice. Sometimes you get your number, sometimes you don't.

Toward midnight, Jack stood next to Ella as she spoke with some of her girlfriends; he realized she was not talking about college. That had been their main topic of conversation the last few months, leaving home to attend university somewhere. Kids were making plans, preparing to make the next biggest transition in their lives, their voices saturated with excitement. Ella only stood by and listened.

On their way home, she rested her head on his shoulder, staring out the windshield with a dreamy look. He knew she was thinking about not going to LA, but it was unlike her not to tell him.

"Everyone's pretty excited about graduating," he said.

"Two weeks to go. It's so close I can taste it."

Jack could taste it too. At one time, graduation meant freedom for both of them, but Jack was beginning to doubt Ella's resolve to move away. It was not like her to drag out a decision. If she was going to stay, she had already decided.

"How long will your internship last this summer?"

"Not that long."

"Then you're heading to LA?"

"Maybe not. A fulltime position may open up; I've been encouraged to apply for it."

"That mean you're not coming to LA?"

"It means I'm not decided yet. Lots of people take a year off before college."

"Yeah, to backpack through Europe and see the world, that sort of thing."

"Well, I'm not going on some grand tour." She snuggled close and looked up at him. "Have you ever thought about the fact that this is your home?"

"I may not have a home here soon if Kolcinivitch has his way."

"It's not the house you live in, Jack, it's where your heart is. If I can make a difference here, that's what I want to do."

He glanced away from the road to take her in. Her green eyes glistened in the moonlight. She watched him quizzically. She was always trying to divine his thoughts, and now his thoughts could not be more transparent. He was thinking about losing that game, about losing her, and about taking her in his arms and kissing her.

Chapter 44
Dropout

THE NEXT AFTERNOON, AFTER school, Jack strode to the door at 617 Hadley Street. A thin wooden veneer covered the marks of local justice. Jack knocked, and it took a moment before the door opened slowly. A worried looking Mr. Sanchez peeked through a small opening before swinging it wide. His dark eyes scanned the road before he waved Jack inside. The room had been pieced back together. A jagged white scar wrapped around the upright Virgin's slender neck. She had been brought back to life with Elmer's glue and hopeful hands.

Mr. Sanchez asked Jack to sit, but he stood on the very spot where they had both been laid out cuffed and afraid for their lives. Neither spoke of it.

"Adrian wasn't at school today," Jack said.

"Yes, he worked."

"Instead of going to school?"

Mr. Sanchez shrugged. "I told him to go."

"Doesn't he plan on graduating?"

The older man looked away as if he wanted to answer but couldn't. "He will be home soon. Ask for yourself." He motioned again for Jack to sit and left the room.

When Adrian showed up later that evening, he tramped in with dirty jeans and a sweaty shirt.

"I thought that was your car outside." He had a tired slump to his shoulders as he settled down hard into the worn rocker. His mother brought him a plate of food.

"I didn't see you in class today. I was just wondering what's going on."

Adrian ate with the ravenousness of a workingman.

"Two weeks left of school, you know."

Adrian looked up as he swallowed the last of a tortilla. He wiped his mouth on his sleeve and set the plate on the coffee table. "If things are going to change, someone's got to do something."

"You're upset about losing yesterday."

Adrian shrugged. "Not really."

"Oh?" Jack leaned forward, elbows resting on his knees.

"I'm not angry because I know how things work."

"What're you talking about?"

"Baseball," Adrian said, scooting forward. "We used to think the game was safe, where we could all play on one field by the same rules. For most of us, that's how it works. But some people do what they want."

"You dropped out of school because they cheated?"

"I didn't drop out of anything. I was told yesterday after the game that I wouldn't be graduating."

"Is that why you broke up with Darcy?"

"Darcy's father made her dump me. I was seen on a picket line."

"Two weeks to go. How can you let this slip away?"

Adrian had a dark look in his eyes. "The patrones won't let us have an education unless we see things their way. That's the way it is, Jack. Unless someone changes it."

"You've been working a picket line, that's what you missed school for? What about college?"

"I may take a year off. Cesar wants me to join a boycott team on the East Coast."

"I can't believe you'd let college just pass by."

He picked at a tortilla on his plate beside him then eyed his friend. "When you take dignity away from people, you take more than education can restore."

"I can't believe you'd throw away everything you've worked so hard for."

"There are many good things to work for, Jack."

"I know it's important to you, to help out with the strike and boycott," Jack said, trying not to sound preachy. "You knew that would happen with Darcy if you got involved with the UFW. Didn't you two have plans?"

"I think about her all the time. But I also want to live in a world where everyone is treated like humans." He leaned back in his chair and smiled at his friend in a disarming way. "I think, Jack, that's the only difference between us."

Chapter 45
Memories of Home

Saturday morning Jack's mother dragged a large suitcase down the attic stairs, one that looked right out of the Depression. She set it by his bedroom door. She wanted him to get ready to move on with his life. He shoved it under the bed. He had time to pack.

He moped around the house, sulking over his friend's decision. He still could not fathom what he had done. He had to keep busy, or he felt that something would come loose inside, and he'd do something…something unpredictable.

Before lunch, he hammered some new boards on the old barn where they had peeled off. He finished and stowed the ladder. Jack went around to the backyard where his mother worked on her knees weeding her garden. He hoped she would be here long enough to harvest her crops.

"Kind of late for spring planting, isn't it, Mom?"

Her garden took up a large section running the length of the back fence. She shielded her eyes with her hand. "Plenty of things to plant if I can get the ground in shape. You done with that barn?"

"Good as new. Need a hand?"

She pulled up a clump of weeds. "There're enough here for both of us."

Beside her on his knees, he worked in the opposite direction, down an oblong stretch, pulling clumps of dried earth out with the webbed roots of weeds, exposing the dark soil. When he reached his end, he grabbed a spade and methodically turned over the earth—kneading it, breaking up clumps, letting it breathe, until the musty aroma of the rich loam filled him with possibilities. Anything would grow in this land as long as it had water. He worked in the hot sun all morning. Leaning on the wooden handle, he wiped the sweat from his forehead with the sleeve of his shirt and surveyed the patch of dark earth.

"We used to grow everything we needed right here." Still, on her knees, she brushed a wisp of gray hair off her face with her wrist. She peeled off her work gloves. With her fingers splayed, she dug both hands into the loose dirt.

"Look at this, Jack," she said, with a lilt to her voice he had not heard for some time.

He knelt beside her. She pushed her fingers deep and moved them around as if searching for something.

"You lose something?"

Her face flushed in the sun, but a glare of pleasure rose high on her cheeks. She seemed lost in the memories of the home she once had.

"Feel this?"

He humored her and slipped his fingers into the earth's coolness.

"I used to watch it all grow from nothing."

"I know." He didn't remember those days the way she did, but he didn't doubt her. They must have been pleasant, and full of everything she had ever wanted. Now they were gone. She had spent the last week talking to attorneys, which only added to her dismal outlook. She couldn't afford the retainer to defend herself. Even if she could, she had little chance of prevailing. Without any likelihood of her ever needing the water for any agricultural purposes, in all probability, her neighbor had some rights to it. Now she had to choose. She could try to keep the water rights and the value it brought to the land. If she lost her full rights to the water, the property would be worth very little with a dilapidated house on it. Or she could sell it outright and take the money for a new life. Ten thousand dollars was enough for her to get settled in town and start a shop.

Memories of every Duncan happiness passed over him like palpable breath on his skin, alive and full as if it resided here in the dark loam. He pulled his hands out of the wet earth and rocked back on his knees. He held his dirt-covered fingers in front of his face.

"I'll put in some squash and some melons. We'll have ourselves a summer harvest."

He feared she was only dreaming, a last pleasurable exercise before reality set in. So he imagined with her, the lush leaves of the melon plants filling the garden, of food growing from seeds. He rested on his knees, taking in a full breath of the unearthed loam. Whatever he said about this place—the dilapidated house, the twisted barn, the weed-infested yard, the riot of troubles clustered with the land—it was home. It would never stop being home.

The two worked in silence, kneading the earth with their fingers, yanking out weeds, spading shovelfuls of moist loam, preparing the land to produce. He felt an attachment, the way she must feel, and he didn't think he would be the same person without this feeling.

➤

SHE DIDN'T CONFIDE IN him what she decided. But later in the day, she drove into Bakersfield to peruse second-hand shops. She returned late that afternoon with a well-used heavy-duty metal sewing machine, a headless wire mannequin, and other supplies. Jack helped her unload them into the living room. She arranged the dressmaking equipment like a proud new shop owner. Jack set down the headless mannequin in a corner and leaned against the wall.

Watching his mother hunched over her new machine, adjusting the settings as she plied the foot peddle until the threaded needle hammered up and down, Jack was confident she could survive financially once she had her shop underway. He didn't know if she would survive emotionally if she didn't have this place to come back to. But it appeared as if she was trying.

He leaned against the doorjamb of the dining room where she set up her equipment. "Are you just going to let him take the water?"

"The only decent advice I've gotten is to settle with him. Let him have it. The courts will give him most of the water since I'm not using it. If I give him some water, I can stay on the property."

"Once you settle, it will never be enough."

She cut a thread with her teeth. "Don't you think I know that?"

"Did you talk to my friend, Todd Hennley?"

"He's the only one who gave me the time of day. The others made sure I knew the growers have deep pockets and get what they want from the courts."

"There is another way."

"I'll never let you gamble away the whole shebang. Even if you win, you won't win."

"Once he has the water he needs, his offer to pay you anything will pass."

She fed a piece of cloth under the presser plate as the needle chattered, laying down a stitch. She flipped up the presser plate to inspect the seam.

"So I should let you get yourself killed?"

"I've talked to Todd and Les. They both agreed to sit with me throughout the game, to witness who wins."

She put aside her sewing. "You think they'll protect you?"

"I don't think it's right to give in to him."

"Jack, if I go to court, I'll end up with nothing. I won't have enough money to start the business. Eventually, we won't have a house to live in."

"Eventually, you won't have a house to live in anyway."

She went back to sewing. Upstairs at his desk, he tried to concentrate on his US history. He slapped the text closed. He couldn't focus, he was so disturbed by his mother's dilemma.

Later that day, Jack drove over to Miller's Skeet Range on the outskirts of town. He purchased a hundred clay pigeons and took his place in the firing stand. Working fast, he got through the hundred targets quickly. He only missed five. The gun felt lighter in his hands, his shooting more accurate. He loaded the Browning into the leather sleeve and zipped it up. He'd clean it later. Right now Ella expected him to pick her up for another night of dancing. At least there was one bright spot in his life.

➤

THE NEXT NIGHT AT the kitchen table Jack watched his mother scan the classified section of the paper. She motioned toward the stove where several pots sat warming. He scooped out some meatloaf and spinach and took a seat across from her

"Les called today." She set her paper down. "Said Kolcinivitch wanted to settle this in a game of cards." She eyed him across the table. "Said he'd see to it there was no cheating."

"One more game and that's it."

His mother stared at him.

"What's wrong?" he asked.

"I just hadn't heard someone say anything like that in a long time. Your father said those same words—just before we were married—and he meant them."

Both of them were quiet.

"What did you tell Les?" Jack studied her.

"Graduation's a week from this Friday. You're leaving next Tuesday with Ella, right?"

"Ella's staying for the summer." He leaned forward on the table. "She has an internship in town. She'll be coming down in August."

"What about Adrian? Are you two still planning on driving down together?"

Jack shook his head. He told her about Adrian not graduating because of his involvement in the strike. And how he was planning to take a year off to work with the UFW before finding a way to get his diploma.

Shirley studied her food as though she was trying to parse the recipe. She was visibly upset that everything, all the plans they had of escape, were dissolving into nothing.

"I know if I play him, Kolcinivitch has a plan to get your deed, one way or the other. It's up to me to have a better plan once I win the game." Jack studied her silence.

"He's not going to let you walk away from the table with all the marbles."

"That doesn't mean we can't do something to make sure I can walk away with all the marbles."

"I'm not interested in hearing about anything except you leaving here to go play college baseball." She pointed her fork at him and raised her eyebrows. "Eat your spinach."

➤

AFTER SCHOOL, JACK SPENT time with Ella studying and preparing for finals. She had a big debate coming up the last week before graduation, which seemed odd to Jack. And with final exams and graduation parties, both their lives took on a whirlwind pace. Jack had an algebra final on Friday. He found himself thinking in terms of probabilities and odds. He had better odds of winning a card game against Kolcinivitch than he did of passing his algebra final.

During the last week, Ella disappeared between classes. Starting her internship early, she inspected several migrant housing camps and returned to school possessing a new level of indignation.

Late one night at home, after a full day of working and studying to catch up with his algebra, Jack emptied his pockets onto the dresser, setting out his car keys, wallet, and a few coins. Lastly, he pulled out the deck of cards, and set them on his desk by the window, next to the planter's hat. The collection of baseball cards was perched on the corner of his desk. He flung open the window over his desk and flicked off the lights.

Under the starlight, the rows of vines appeared as faint humps in the shadows, vanishing into the darkness. They had been there every day of his life. His father's life work. He picked up Sugar's hat and settled it on his head. With his hair long enough to part on the side, the hat fit snugger than it had before. He tipped the brim over his eyes, and he wondered at the fit—he had grown into it. Would he ever grow into what it took to run an operation of this size?

He doffed the hat and tossed it on his bed. If he took the property back, his mother would run it. She could do it better than anyone. He didn't see himself as the patrón as they liked to call the growers around here. A man like DiGorda or Kolcinivitch or the others. The word just didn't seem to fit him. But if he won the property back, he could make that choice, if that's what he wanted.

Or did he only want to prove a point? If he didn't play this one last game, he would always wonder if he had it in him to pull it off. But most of all, he wanted his mother's situation settled. Losing was a possibility. Losing was always a possibility. He hefted his father's cards. Cards could make him rich, but they could also strip him of everything. He had to think clearly, weigh every possibility, and have a plan.

Chapter 46
The Confession

O N SATURDAY WHEN JACK drove up to Herm's, the '59 Caddy was parked against the side of the house. This was the first time he'd seen it since the old man had stopped him on the road.

The two sat in the cluttered kitchen. Herm knew all about Jack's escapades in Bakersfield, but they reminisced over the highlights—Jack sniffing out a cheating dealer, meeting Todd, the attorney, and DiGorda questioning him about beating the Black Diamond, then inviting him to play with the growers. And how he took down Kolcinivitch and used the money to bail out Adrian.

Herm's smile grew brighter as the story progressed, until he slapped the kitchen table with glee, wanting to know more. When Jack told him about Les Gilinsky saying that Kolcinivitch planned to strip them clean of their water rights, his look grew pensive.

"Les said he'd probably file a lawsuit," Jack said. "Drive us off the land by bankrupting us in court—if we didn't sell to him."

Herm rubbed his bottom lip thoughtfully.

"The last time I played the growers, I gave him a fair price." Jack told him how he figured the worth of the land.

Herm shook his head. "That's a lot of cash. He'll never pay it."

"I know. That's why he finally filed a lawsuit against my mom, claiming he has a right to the water in Spring Gulch."

Herm sucked in a breath. "I feared he'd pull that someday."

"He doesn't want to go to court. The night before he served my mom, he said if I thought my land with water was worth as much as his was without it, I should play him straight up—deed for deed. Winner takes both properties; loser takes the cash on the table."

Herm ran his hand over his stubbly chin. "Sounds dangerous, far more dangerous than any court battle."

"You don't think I'm good enough?"

Herm scratched his head, thinking through the question. "What if you just let his craziness pass and go on down to school? If I were you, I'd convince Shirley to take the ten grand and move into town."

"Things have gone too far for that. I either play him for it or see him in court."

Herm shook his head slowly.

Jack leaned his chair way back, balancing it on two back legs. "I don't get it. You're the one who put me up to all of this, giving me my dad's playing cards, telling me stories about him."

He rose, poured himself more coffee, and leaned against the sink. "It was mighty unfair for you not to know the truth. Guess I didn't think things through, but I was hoping that with a fresh pair of eyes on it, you might prevail in court."

"That's malarkey, and you know it. She's already lost two cases. That's why you gave me those cards, wasn't it?"

"You have a future away from here. You need to take it."

"You know what?" Jack stood and glared at the old man. "Sometimes I wonder why you opened this whole can of worms in the first place."

"I gave you those cards because you deserved to know the truth about your father. That's all." Herm looked suddenly haggard; fatigue filled his eyes. "You can put yourself through college playing baseball. If you have to, you can play cards. But playing head-to-head with Kolcinivitch, I never intended that...that's suicide."

"I'm not saying I want to." Jack buried his hands in his jean's pockets. Herm slouched over to a chair and took up a deck of cards.

He shuffled it once then set it on the table. He looked away at a wall, leaving Jack to stare at the side of his gray-haired head.

"Jack, I'm warning you, get out while you can."

"I see your Cadillac's finally made it back. Was it in police impound all this time?"

"It was. Cost me a pretty penny to get it back."

"Feels good to have your property back, doesn't it?"

Herm shook his head slowly. "You just don't give up, do you?"

Jack leaned against the sink and shoved his hands in his pockets. "So when are you going to tell me the rest of the story?"

Herm glanced up at him, a guilty look in his eyes.

"You stopped me on the road to give me that police report, I remember distinctly you giving me that deck of old cards and saying they were all I needed to get my land back."

Herm fixed his gaze on Jack.

"Now you want me to just up and leave."

"If Kolcinivitch played by the rules, you'd have a chance." Herm tapped the top of the deck of cards on the counter.

Jack put his hand on the cards. "Did you give the same warning to my father?"

Herm spoke to the table. "I told him not to push them too far. I said it a hundred times, but he never listened. He would never back down."

"Did Kolcinivitch and DiGorda have him run off the road?"

"Who else would do it? He was a burr in their saddle that rubbed them way too hard."

"Are you positive they were involved in the death of my father?"

He hesitated, looked away, then back to Jack, as if he were considering a lie.

"Tell me the truth."

"I heard Kolcinivitch boasting about 'getting rid of the local problem' at an Association meeting. I knew he was speaking about Sugar. That's when I stopped going."

Jack remembered the ominous threat Kolcinivitch had made in the card game the other day, the one DiGorda said was just a joke. "Was it their thugs who beat you that day they stole the combine?"

"Thugs don't wear uniforms. It's hard to know what team they were playing for. But look where the combine ended up. Who else could have sent them?"

Jack pushed back his chair and stomped to the front door. He heard Herm call after him, but he pushed on. He fired up the Olds and jammed it in reverse. From the front porch, Herm waved him to come back. Jack punched it, and the car stormed backward down the dirt drive. He skidded in a tight turn onto the road. He shifted into drive and sped off, leaving a plume of dust on the county road.

He drove crazy fast along the dirt roads, kicking up a cloud of debris, thumping through potholes, shaking every loose part. The undercarriage rattled, threatening to fly apart. He headed east toward Miller's Range. Soon he steered into the lot at Miller's Range and slammed to a stop. The engine ticked off the heat as he stared out the windshield. It didn't matter what plans he laid for his future, his past would always haunt him.

Herm had wanted him to know about his father, what kind of man he had been. But he had opened an old wound, one that refused to heal. He couldn't prove Kolcinivitch had killed his father. His mother couldn't prove it either. That's why she had lied to him all these years, but all the signs pointed to that man. Suspicions hardened into convictions—his father's death wasn't an accident. But getting justice for Sugar wasn't in the cards. Not around here. He felt on fire within, and all the restraints built into his life slowly burned away.

He grabbed his gun and ammo, swung his door open, and barged to the range's shed to purchase a hundred clay pigeons.

On the stand, he loaded, took his stance, and called for his target.

He aimed, squeezed the cold trigger, and clay disks exploded. He worked in a feverish rhythm, smoothly loading, steady aim, easy pressure on the trigger, and the clay disks exploded into a cloud of dust that drifted away on the stifling valley breeze. If only his hatred could be blown away so easily.

Chapter 47
Revenge

IN THE DAWNING HOURS of Sunday morning, Jack lay in bed, mulling over a plan, one that felt unnatural when considered in isolation—a moral choice forbidden by both men and God. One that could change his life forever, if he went through with it. But if he measured the pain caused by valley hooligans, cutting his father's life short, and the injustice poured out on his mother, defrauding her of the land, and the wrong that had accrued too much weight for him to carry, it would be a just action, one he could live with.

His friends already had their dreams pissed on by these men of the land, so why not do something to redress the wrongs? He dressed in boots and jeans. He shouldered his way into a thick plaid shirt too warm for the day, but suitable for his purpose.

During a game last week, Kolcinivitch had mentioned that he drove the western division of his property Sunday mornings, checking his vines for a spreading fungus. Like every grower he knew, the man would be up early inspecting during the cool of the morning. Jack had checked the old farm map in the office. An isolated road bordered the western division. A road the grower had to use to examine the entire length of his vines.

The early mist, curling off the grapes in strings of steam, was barely visible by the time Jack neared the backside of Kolcinivitch Ranch. He pulled off the county road, onto a narrow path between some trellised vines, and snugged the car out of sight. He slung the Browning over his shoulder in the haphazard confidence of a man convinced of the necessity of his deed. His boots clicked in determined steps on the rough dirt road.

He flicked past the green rows of trellised vines stretching across the quiet land, the morning calm a lie against the truth that raged up at him from the earth. This had been his father's ranch, vines planted by his father's hands, taken by a man in a swindle, and no one cared.

Jack leaned into his stride, all six feet of him, limber and ready. The grower would drive right along here. Once he spotted Jack, he'd stop to talk, most likely threaten him as he usually did. The grower would not miss the opportunity to say something insulting. Once the man had his window down, he'd raise the Browning and even things out between their families. He wouldn't touch the man's car or body. He'd collect his empty shells and trot back to the car.

He'd leave no car tracks. No spent shells in the dirt. The anonymous wind would wash away the scent of gunpowder. Nothing would be left to see but the man's blood seeping into the fertile earth. When they found him, the community would be shocked. Then suspicion would blossom into blaming their favorite target. The sheriff would run around accusing but never figure things out. Sheriff Gates couldn't even remember to put cream in his coffee anymore. Growers liked that about him. They'd soon forget the same way they had forgotten his father. That's the way justice worked around here.

He'd go back to shooting every few days out at Miller's. So many in the valley owned a Browning auto-5 so it wouldn't raise any lawman's hackles that Jack had one. As soon as he graduated, he'd get out of here.

A car appeared out of the haze. A rooster tail of dust spewed up in the distance. A wind kicked up, and a tingle of grit irritated his eyes and parched his mouth. His stomach felt light. His step became heavier.

Time to bring truth to bear with some enlightening buckshot.

The car drew close enough for him to spot a red pennant on the antenna, flapping in a jagged craziness. In the undulating action of the flag, Jack couldn't see the black eagle in a white circle. But he knew it was there, splitting the air with unmistakable vigor. While way off, the old beater slowed as if wary of the blue steel across his shoulder. Jack stepped to the side a couple of feet. Just campesinos looking for work. It didn't matter that they saw him with the gun. No sheriff would ever talk to them. No farm worker flying a UFW eagle would ever trust a sheriff enough to ask directions.

He hitched the gun up and searched a point up the road, expecting another plume of dust to appear. Under the bleaching glare, the old station wagon crept toward him. Jack closed the gap with purposed strides. Closer now, he saw that the paint was actually a faded yellow. It looked familiar. Through the windshield, he saw the driver talking to someone in the back.

A man with a gun.

They had good reasons to be afraid. Jack stretched out his steps, and the wagon rolled forward until the driver became visible, a blond-haired fellow. The man stuck his head out the window as Jack passed.

"Hey, buddy where you going?"

Jack didn't stop—but that car, that voice. He stopped and pivoted, the barrel of the Browning swung toward the vines. The man's arm rested on the car door. His shaggy hair flopped over his forehead. He stared at Jack through a pair of bookworm wire glasses.

"What's it to you?" As soon as he spoke, he remembered. He was the guy at the gas station who took him to meet Chavez.

The back door opened, and a man's unsteady foot tested the ground. Then the other foot slipped down, and the man feebly pulled himself forward.

"Cesar, no." A woman's emphatic voice spilled from inside. The driver jumped out and propped him up. A diminutive Mexican with a wan complexion in a crisp white guayabera shirt leaned against the station wagon. He could hardly stand by himself. His face was drawn as if all the energy had been drained from him. Yet a familiar smile crinkled the edges of his black eyes.

Cesar Chavez, the same man he'd met a month ago, but the glow of a healthy roundness in his face had disappeared. Now his cheeks were sunken. His jaw appeared chiseled down to the bone.

"Where you going with that gun?" His voice was weak and trembled. He leaned on the blond-haired man. A stiff wind probably could blow the strike leader over.

Jack could hardly believe the man's appearance. He didn't need to explain himself to him, did he?

"Something I need to do."

"Killing is no answer."

"Who said anything about killing?"

"Your eyes. They say everything." Cesar took a labored breath. "Violence will not bring back the dead."

"What do you know? What've you had taken from you?"

Cesar attempted to smile. Someone laughed from inside the wagon.

"You ignorant—" the blond man began.

Cesar raised his hand, and the man left off.

"Come with me. See for yourself."

"Where you going?"

"To a celebration, twenty-five days of nonviolence. Come."

Jack had heard of some meeting at the park in Delano. "That the one Senator Kennedy's going to?"

"He's waiting for Cesar now," a woman said from inside. "We're going to be late." Impatience saturated her voice.

Cesar didn't appear in a hurry. Neither did he take his eyes off Jack. The man held out a shaky hand. "Give it to me."

If he gave his gun, nothing would change. Today it was in his power to right one wrong. One that would never be avenged otherwise. He glanced up the empty road ahead.

"You got someplace to go. I do too." Jack turned on his heels and strode away.

"You know," came the weak voice from behind, "only men find justice through nonviolence."

Jack stopped.

"Justice will come. But it's a struggle one must be willing to sacrifice for."

Jack half turned.

"The poor have nothing but time. We will get justice someday. I'm sure of it. But there is no time for revenge. Come." Cesar held out a hand. "I will help you find what you seek."

Jack stared at the simple man under the blazing sun for a long while. His dark eyes appeared clouded with memories, as if every hour of stoop-labor pain, every unpaid cent of workers' sweat since the first planting of the valley played across his thoughts. Not one of them had been wasted. He was alive to them all. They had starved him thin.

Jack couldn't hold the man's piercing glare any longer. He turned to the empty road. A tiny speck arose in the distance. He shielded his brow with his hand. A rooster tail far down the road grew in the morning light.

The high whine of a car reversing and tires biting into the dirt followed him as the old wagon chased him down. The yellow Buick swerved in front of him and jerked to a stop. The window rolled down, and a man leaned out.

"Cesar wants to talk to you."

Jack leaned down close to the back window. A determined but thin face stared back. He reached a gaunt brown hand through the opening and gripped the barrel. "This is a day to celebrate nonviolence." Chavez fixed his black eyes on him.

The sound of a motor echoed in the distance. He glanced up. A pickup cruised along the edge of the fields toward him. A man's head and arm hung out the window, inspecting the vines. Jack struggled with the Browning, but the annoying little man wouldn't let it go.

"Not today, Jack." His voice was firm as he pulled the shotgun into the window. Another hand grabbed the gun. The safety clicked on. "This man you seek to kill is not worth your life."

The pickup glided closer. Kolcinivitch's head searched the edges of the vines as it rolled closer. The Browning slowly disappeared into the darkness of the car. He tried once more to yank it by the stock, but there must be ten hands on it now. The car devoured his anger, inch by inch, as the last of the black barrel slipped through the window. Someone ejected the shells.

Just then Kolcinivitch's truck pulled up behind the wagon. The grower stared as he leaned out the window.

"What're you doin' here, Duncan?"

The blond man opened the door and stepped into the road.

"We're on our way to celebratory Mass in Memorial Park. Twenty-five days of nonviolence—would you like to join us?"

"Fat chance of that."

He gunned the motor and sped around the wagon, laying down an enveloping cloud of dust. As he passed, Jack glimpsed the man's profile—sad, deluded, a slave to his avariciousness. A man to pity, not murder.

The back door opened, and hands pulled him in. He barely had a few inches of seat, and the back door slammed him in against Chavez. Squeezed tightly against the door, the rattling of the old car, the warmth of bodies exhaling, the meditative quiet as if they were on a mission for God, pushed him into a haze of unreality—where were they headed?

Ten minutes later, they pulled into a crowded Memorial Park in central Delano. People were everywhere, and the driver rolled slowly through the crowd. Reporters surrounded the car, snapping photos, tapping on the window, trying to get Cesar's attention, sticking microphones against the glass.

The wagon stopped, the door yanked open, and Jack piled out. Strong arms supported a frail Cesar, who with great difficulty made his way to the seats in front of an altar. Helen Chavez with her pious lips, black hair covered in a black lace mantilla, took her place beside a lanky, thin man in a dark suit, skinny tie, and wavy brown hair.

People crushed in behind the single row of plastic seats for dignitaries in front by the altar. Hands pushed Jack behind the row of plastic chairs. He stood behind Cesar. Someone pressed through the crowd and jostled Jack as he filled the spot beside him—it was a smiling Adrian. He wrapped his arm around Jack's shoulder and pulled him tight.

The priests in their gold and green vestments performed their ritual—praying, chanting, pouring, and lifting the golden chalice. Nuns passed a plate of bread and a cup of wine, first, to Senator Kennedy, who took a piece of bread and passed it to Cesar, who then tasted food for the first time in twenty-five days.

Several men helped Cesar to stand and hobble to the microphone. In a weak voice, one laden with the pathos of the moment, he spoke. The words washed over Jack until the final sentences—

When we are really honest with ourselves...only our lives... belong to us. So it is how we use our lives that determine what kind of men we are...so I am convinced that the truest act of courage, the strongest act of manliness, is to sacrifice ourselves for others in a totally nonviolent struggle for justice. To be a man is to suffer for others. God help us to be men!

The crowd broke into a rhythmic clapping, rising to a crescendo as Cesar shambled to his seat.

¡Viva la causa!
¡Si, se puede!
¡Cesar! ¡Cesar!

The cheering, chanting, and clapping became deafening. Jack smiled for the first time that day, carried along by the gladness of the crowd. He had witnessed something truer than any truth he had ever learned. It floated in the air along with the aroma of carne asada grilling on hundreds of barbecues, mariachi and tejano and banda music all mixed into one cacophony of joy.

People were celebrating their freedom. Freedom to suffer for their hope in something better. None of them wanted to live without justice. And justice wasn't a fruit to be picked or kowtow for at the whims of the powerful, but a right worthy of fighting for.

The diminutive brown man, who sat slumped-shouldered in front of him, had said to him weeks ago at Forty Acres, at the beginning of his fast that he had come here to Delano of his own accord. He had come with a purpose—this was his road to Delano—to suffer for others so they could learn to fight for justice. Jack must find his own way, his own path, his own fight for justice.

Chapter 48
Ground Rules

HOURS LATER JACK SAT behind the wheel of his car parked among the vines. Witnessing Chavez break his fast for nonviolence with Senator Kennedy and the farm workers celebrating as if they had achieved something significant, something life changing had stirred him. That they could celebrate, yet not one major grower had agreed to sit and speak to the union about better wages and working conditions. Not one thing had changed except the peoples' attitudes toward using guns and sticks to get their way, about paying back the growers with the same violence they paid out with vicious generosity. Thousands at the rally were prepared to take the risk of nonviolent action.

Jack felt foolish he ever thought of shooting the likes of Kolcinivitch. His death would only solidify the growers' convictions that they were right, that farm workers could not be trusted, and their violent intentions had to be put down by force.

The grower's death would have stopped the lawsuit, but his mother wouldn't be safe. The next property owner could easily revive it.

If Jack wanted to see any justice done for his father, he would have to come up with a better idea—a winner-take-all game: her one acre for Kolcinivitch's four thousand. A fair bet if Jack ever saw one.

His mother was stubborn. He had to find a way to convince her it was the brightest and best path out of her predicament.

His plan clarified. It was risky to walk into the lion's own lair. But a winner-take-all game was too big to pass up. He didn't see any other way. He smiled as he keyed the ignition and the motor fired.

➢

A FEW DAYS LATER, a beef stew simmered on the stove in Shirley's kitchen. She stirred it slowly.

"Mom, will you come back over here so we can finish talking?"

Jack, Shirley, and Todd Hennley had been sitting at the kitchen table for most of the afternoon, and now it was evening.

A sheaf of papers was stacked in front of Todd. Next to the attorney sat a young woman with her notary book and stamp. Shirley wiped her hands on a towel and slid into a chair across from the two men, reluctance written all over her face.

"Here's the check from the County for the return of Adrian's bail." Jack slid it across to her. The DA had dropped Adrian's case after Todd took it on.

"That's a lot of money."

"You can use it for your shop, Mom."

"Is this some kind of blood money to convince me to let you get killed?"

"Shirley." Todd folded his hands on the table. "This game's going to be tightly controlled."

She sighed under her breath.

"I'm pretty sure we can use the backroom at Cicero's. I've had several conversations with the owner."

"And if that doesn't work out?" She eyed the attorney.

"We have other neutral venues."

She wiped her mouth and stared at Jack. "Why are you so set on this?"

"We've been over this." Jack tapped the table with his fingers. "If he goes to court and wins the rights to your water, which he will, you're left with a property of little value."

Even as he laid out the logical reasons for playing this game, deeper passions drove him. He hoped she couldn't see those on his face. Jack didn't lie to himself: he wanted to take the bully down. Even if his chances of walking away with both deeds never reached above one percent, a margin that allowed no room for error, he would take it. Winning would require him to play the game of his life. With Todd and Les Gilinsky there, he had every reason to believe he would get away with winning.

For the last week lying awake in bed, he had replayed all the games the two had played, dwelling on the man's obvious tells, his distracted drinking, his penchant for overbetting his weak hands. He analyzed everything he remembered to ferret out every nuance of the man's play. He was confident he could control the tempo of the game and not let Kolcinivitch's bluffing and bluster distract him.

"I know how the courts work around here," Shirley said. "I'm concerned about Jack. When are you going to give this up and go on with your life?"

Jack wanted to say never.

Todd leaned forward. "I spoke to Kolcinivitch's attorney at length. He's agreed to increase his buy-in to ten thousand dollars. Jack's would stay the same at two thousand dollars. If Jack loses the game, he will leave with the cash winnings but without the deed."

"And if Jack gets killed doing this?"

Todd opened his mouth to trot out more arguments when Jack butted in.

"We're just going around in circles here, Mom. We've covered everything in detail."

They had spent the last hour going over how Todd and Jack had worked out the ground rules for the game. It would be played at a neutral site. Les Gilinsky and Champ Everett promised to stay for the entire game. Les was someone Shirley trusted. Todd would pick up Kolcinivitch's signed and notarized deed from his attorney in town, and transport them both to the game. Todd agreed to hand over both of them to the winner.

"I'm telling you, we've thought of everything." Jack settled back in his chair. "I'm not leaving here until you sign this so we can get on with it."

She bit her bottom lip. She fiddled with her spoon, letting it clatter into her plate. She savored something in her mouth, moving her lips. After what seemed like an hour, she reached for the deed and signed it. The notary did her work to make it official. The date was set. The game was on.

Chapter 49
The Last Game

THE GAME WAS SET for Sunday morning.

Friday evening their graduation ceremony took place on the athletic field. That night Jack and Ella joined their friends at an all-night party at Barton's house. Sometime early Saturday morning on the patio with a beer in his hand, Jack told Ella what he planned on doing. She had hugged him so tight he thought he was going to burst. Then she sauntered away and spent the next hour talking to Darcy, only shooting him furtive glances every now and then. In that hour she stared at him across the room, it felt as if they had spent a whole life together. She looked older, wiser than she had on that bus ride to Berkeley what seemed like a lifetime ago.

When she came back, he asked her what that was about. She said she wished him the best, but she wanted to see what it would be like not having him around. She feared if he played Kolcinivitch, he would get hurt. It bothered him that she didn't believe he could take care of himself, but it was like Ella to make her point without nagging. Despite her fears, he had every intention of coming away alive from the card game.

The party broke up around four, and Jack drove Ella home. They held hands as they rode along in silence until Ella said, "He's not going to let you win."

"We've got it figured out, Ella."

"What if he cheats you?"

"I have a plan."

His plan was not to lose. It wasn't a case of over-confidence as Herm used to accuse him of. If he weren't confident in his skills, he would never take on such a pugnacious idiot, a guy who slewed from cheerfully pleasant to hatefully aggressive in consecutive breaths. But the man had serious flaws in his game. Ones Jack had seen the grower practice with regularity. He could take him down, but it would be tough.

At the heart of Jack's game lay his powers of observation; his ability to recognize a man's tells and a penchant for bold action and a grasp of the odds. That's what had always saved his skin and his cash.

"Even if you win fair," Ella said, "you're naïve to think he's going to let you walk away with the deed to his property."

"That's what he's agreed on."

The whole ride home, she stewed until Jack explained how the game was going to go down. Kolcinivitch had also agreed that if one of them got caught cheating, that person would forfeit the game. Todd Henley would sit as a witness, and several other growers were to attend. It was safe as playing at Cicero's.

"This is my last game. Promise."

His words seemed to mollify her, but it was hard to tell. She gave him a long hug, then a quick kiss, a brush of her lips across his. Then she slid out the door and disappeared inside her house.

Later up in his bedroom, he lay awake listening to the groaning of the old house. His thoughts went to his friend Adrian, out on the roads every day trying to find equality and justice using nonviolence. He hoped his friend achieved everything he worked for. He also hoped his friend survived. The roads were dangerous around here.

Cesar and his people hadn't returned his Browning. They wanted him to come out to Forty Acres in a few days to retrieve it. Jack wouldn't need it anyway. Without a gun, that left him with his skills, his wits, his abilities. Maybe he could pray. The last time he'd seen Adrian, his friend had said he would say a rosary for Jack, that he would be as wise as a serpent. Maybe God would help him gamble better. Didn't seem like a prayer God would answer. He closed his eyes in the darkness and spoke to someone he didn't really know too well. He asked only for the wits to not get blown away by this devil.

He slept until noon on Saturday and spent the day packing. It seemed odd, packing to leave this place. Once he had the deed in hand, his mother could knock down the fence separating the properties, and get back to work. Part of him wanted to see it while it happened. She would need help managing the land, but she would make a good grower and a good *patrona*.

Opening the window, he stuck his head outside, surveying the fields. They were turning green and leafy, growing with warming weather. Leaving here would be harder than he thought it would be.

➤

EARLY SUNDAY MORNING JUST as Jack prepared to leave the house, the phone rang. It was Todd. The venue had to be changed at the last minute if Jack wanted to play today. The UFW had set up an illegal picket at Kolcinivitch's ranch. The grower didn't want to leave the area while the strikers and the cops were in front of his place. They could play in the grower's house if he wanted to get the game in today. Otherwise, they'd need to put it off for a couple of weeks.

Jack thought it over.

"I have both of the notarized deeds," Todd assured him the other witnesses and the dealer would be there. "I've already contacted all the parties, and everyone's okay with the change. So it's up to you."

"Let's play." He didn't like the changes one bit. But he knew Kolcinivitch was trying to get an early harvest of one section. The UFW must have caught wind of it.

"I'll meet you there." Todd's line clicked.

Jack drove the county roads slowly, steeped in thought. Todd would be there. Les and Champ Everett had both agreed to come.

They still had a neutral dealer, someone from Cicero's. He needed to relax and just play his game.

When he turned into the county road leading to Kolcinivitch Ranch, two sheriff's deputies greeted him. One was Kauffman.

"What'ya doing here? This place is going to blow up." Kauffman had his hard-shell riot helmet strapped tightly under his chin.

"I got business with Kolcinivitch this morning."

"You going to that meeting too? I've already let a few other folks through." He leaned in. "Drive careful. We're having a devil of a time keeping these two sides apart." He waved Jack through.

Jack tapped the accelerator and rolled through the protest. Along the edge of Kolcinivitch land, a line of thugs swung bats and sticks, ready for a melee. Across the road, a row of farm workers carried signs. They marched in single file on the edge of a lemon grove. On a flatbed truck, a familiar figure raised a bullhorn. He spoke vehemently about why the pickers needed to come out of the fields; why they needed to hear what the union had to say for their own welfare. Jack wasn't surprised at the man's passion.

As he slowly motored past the flatbed, he caught the eye of the speaker. Adrian paused and nodded from the platform at his friend, giving him a warm smile.

This is where I need to be, he seemed to say.

Jack cruised through the protest and spotted the entrance to the ranch a couple of hundred feet down the road.

➤

Todd Hennley turned off Highway 99. He had carefully written down the directions, and the paper lay beside him on the seat. Right next to him were the two brown envelopes containing the deeds. He turned down County Road 43, which he knew led directly to the front entrance of Kolcinivitch Ranch. About a half mile down, he stopped at a roadblock set up by two Kern County deputies.

Todd rolled down his window. "What's up, Deputy?"

The deputy touched the brim of his cowboy hat and leaned toward the window. "Good morning. We have an illegal labor action going on down the road. It'll be clear in a couple of hours."

"I have an appointment with Mr. Kolcinivitch. He assured me I could get through this morning."

He glanced down the road, then back to Todd. "You say he's expecting you?"

"Yeah. I need to be there for a meeting in thirty minutes."

The deputy sauntered over to confer with his partner. He came back to the window. "Let me see your ID. I'll make some calls."

Todd knew this was the only road into the ranch. And if it was closed on this end, it would more than likely be closed on the other side too. Besides, if he tried to go around, it would take him a couple of hours. He reluctantly pulled out his wallet and handed over his driver's license. The deputy went to his cruiser that straddled the road. He pulled the cord of his microphone through the window and stood by his cruiser eyeing Todd, talking on his radio. Talk and wait. Talk and wait. Then a flurry of back and forth on the radio. The two deputies conferred again as if they weighed a decision. This time, they both strode to the car. Concern filtered through him. What was this all about?

"Mr. Hennley, can you step out of the car, please?"

"What for?"

"Just routine."

As soon as he stepped out, a deputy grabbed his arm and swung him around. Then pushed him against the car.

"Hey, what is this?"

"Put your hands behind your back."

"Tell me what's going on."

"Are we going to have to add resisting arrest to your charge sheet, counselor?"

Todd slowly moved his hands behind his back. "The least you can do is tell me what's going on."

"Outstanding warrants. Lots of them."

"That's ridiculous."

"If it's ridiculous, then we'll get it straightened out, and you'll be on your way."

They marched him to a cruiser and folded him in the back seat. The deputy slipped in behind the wheel and slammed the door.

Todd stared at the back of the deputy's head through the wire mesh. "What are the warrants for?"

"Failure to appear. Serious outstanding fines."

"Traffic tickets? I don't have any outstanding tickets or fines. This is some mistake."

"Like I said," the deputy said as he fired up the cruiser, "if it's a mistake we'll get it ironed out and get you on your way."

Todd ground his teeth. "I have to be at a meeting in thirty minutes…"

The deputy turned his profile to the mesh. "That's just going to have to wait. Right now you got some business with the county."

➢

JACK TURNED INTO THE entrance of Kolcinivitch Ranch. The ranch house lay at the end of a dusty farm road about a quarter of a mile deep into the lush grape fields. The vines were thick with purple and green clusters. There would be an excellent early harvest this year. By an outbuilding, he backed into a space between two pickup trucks.

A man let him in the house and showed him into a dining area where a round table was covered with a felt tablecloth with four chairs. On a sideboard along the wall, a couple of bottles of beer in a bucket of ice sat next to two-fifths of Scotch. The window facing the road remained shut. A limp overhead fan stirred the stuffy air.

"Jack." Les Gilinsky strolled into the room. "Did you have trouble on the road?"

Jack nodded and wiped his forehead with his sleeve. "Cops are everywhere out there. Didn't think they'd let me through."

Kolcinivitch entered, tall and beefy, in jeans and a sports shirt, surliness on the curl of his lips. He quickly opened one of the bottles of Scotch.

"Where's Everett?" Jack glanced around.

"Ah." Les had a rueful grin. "He had trouble getting away."

Jack nodded, biting back his disappointment. That should be okay as long as Les and Todd were here.

"Where's the dealer?" Jack wanted Manny from Cicero's to handle the cards, and the dealer had agreed to be here early. Without Everett, he would be okay as long as he had his dealer, Les, and Todd. Jack glanced at his watch. Todd should be here by now.

"He's coming." Kolcinivitch swirled his drink, clinking ice cubes against the glass.

Les frisked both men. "So you're both clear about how this works."

"Yeah." Kolcinivitch slid into a chair across from Jack. "I win and send this punk packing." He laughed and then slugged down his drink.

Jack did not mind the man's cockiness. Bravado was often a cover for a bad case of nerves. However, he refused to begin without his friend. "We can't start till Todd shows up with the deeds."

Gilinsky checked his watch. "Let's give him five more minutes."

"Five minutes?" Jack stirred in his chair. "If he doesn't show, we don't have a game."

Kolcinivitch eyed him across the table, dark and calculating, both calloused hands splayed on the table. Jack hitched in a breath and soaked in the surrealism of the moment. He was sitting on his father's land, and the genuine possibility of owning it again began to grip him. He eyed the gruff bruiser sitting across from him. What if Herm was right—there was no card game in the world that would pry this land loose from Kolcinivitch.

A door slammed, and Jack heard voices in the hall, then footsteps.

Les stood and turned to the hall. "Ah, the dealer."

Jack heard the dealer greeting someone. At the sound of the man's voice, Jack's stomach knotted up. The dealer strolled in. Kolcinivitch rose and shook his hand, and Jack tapped the table with his index finger. At the sight of the Filipino from Black Diamonds Jack flicked his chair back and stood.

"Well, well. Are these today's combatants?" The well-dressed dealer glared at Jack. "Fancy seeing you again." The slightly built Filipino sized Jack up and down with his dark eyes as if he were buying a sofa. "Last time I saw you, you were sleeping in the parking lot. Are you aware you snore?"

"What're you doing here?"

The sharp-faced man wore a tailored gray suit, black shirt, and gray tie with his black hair slicked back. He gave Jack a sly grin.

"Manny had a death in the family," Kolcinivitch said. "So I called my friend here. You gotta problem with him? He's one of the best dealers around."

The Filipino took a seat, broke the seal on a new deck of cards, and shuffled them. An innocent smile crept across his face.

"Yeah, I got a problem with this."

"I don't see that it matters much," Kolcinivitch said. "He can deal cards just fine."

The dealer gave Jack the most simpering grin. He wanted to spit in the Filipino's eye. Jack slowly lowered himself into his chair. He felt the room closing in, and a hammering went off in his head saying it was best to get up and run. He couldn't leave with the notarized deed to his mother's property floating around. If that ended up in Kolcinivitch's hands, his mother's land would be gone without even a fight. They'd be forced out with nothing to show for it. He would wait for Todd to arrive, and then they could leave together—with his mother's deed.

Jack wiped his mouth with the back of his hand.

Les rose. "Need to frisk you."

The dealer stood, opened the flap of his jacket, and winked at Jack. Les had the man empty his pockets and patted around his waist. Kolcinivitch watched with a sneering grin.

Jack tried to hide his confusion. A death in the family just wasn't likely. He appreciated Les's thoroughness, but the Filipino didn't need much to throw a game in Kolcinivitch's favor—if that's what he wanted to do.

The Filipino set to work. "So as I understand, this is a blood feud, right? Play to the death."

"Well, we don't want to put it in those terms," Les said.

"What's wrong with those terms?" Kolcinivitch barked, pouring two fingers of Scotch.

Jack thought this odd. Kolcinivitch had to know he wasn't a good card player once he swallowed too much of that stuff. That must have been a ruse, too. He watched the man sip it as the dealer shuffled. No water. No ice.

"By the way," the Filipino said, glancing over at Jack. "My name's Joe."

Jack nodded. "And you know Ethan."

"Indeed, we do go back. He first started playing at my club years ago." He pushed the deck Jack's way.

Jack figured. That unsettled him even more, leaving him with a weightless feeling in his stomach.

"I don't want to start till Todd gets here."

Kolcinivitch raised the glass to his mouth and eyed Jack. "He better get his ass here soon."

Someone banged on the front door. A man came in and tapped Les on the shoulder and motioned him to follow. A few minutes later Les returned with the two brown envelopes. He laid them in the middle of the table.

Jack stared at them in unbelief. The two deeds. Where was Todd?

The big grower leaned forward and inspected them. "Yeah, these are them. How'd they get here?"

"A deputy delivered them." Les wouldn't look Jack's way as he spoke. "Said they arrested the fellow bringing them over here for outstanding warrants. But he insisted those envelopes get here. So the deputy dropped them off."

The dealer snorted. "Imagine that. A lawyer going to jail for breaking the law."

Kolcinivitch slouched in his chair, a cool look on his face.

Jack stared at the two deeds on the table. He sat right in the middle of Kolcinivitch territory, surrounded by his thugs and sympathetic cops. No dealer from Cicero's, no Everett Champ, and now no Todd. The pulse in his temples beat out a warning. Someone had cooked up a way to get Todd out of the picture. Todd would never have unpaid traffic tickets. Jack's whole plan had evaporated. He had to get his deed and run for his life.

Jack took a deep breath to stay calm.

The Filipino pointed toward the center of the table. "I take it these envelopes are the prize you two boys are scuffling over?"

"You could say that." Kolcinivitch flashed a smile for the first time and patted them with his palm.

"Wonderful. We only need the buy-in, and we are ready to commence with the fracas of the grapes."

Everything inside Jack screamed to run. He rose. "We can do this another day when Todd can be here." He reached for his deed on the table, but the big grower slapped the envelopes first.

"You ain't going nowhere, punk. Now sit." The man pushed Jack's hands away.

Jack lunged forward to grab them. But Kolcinivitch pushed Jack's hands away and slid the deeds closer to him. He turned to the sideboard behind him, grabbed an envelope. He dropped it on the table and pulled out a thick stack of hundred dollar bills. He piled the cash on the table.

"Ten thousand dollars. Like I said. We're going to settle this once and for all." He twisted around again and opened a drawer in the cabinet. When he faced Jack, he held a large shiny revolver with a foot-long barrel. He laid it on the two envelopes in the middle of the table. "Like I said, they ain't going nowhere."

"Whoa!" The Filipino pushed his chair away from the table.

Jack froze his hand in mid-air.

"We said no guns!" Les Gilinsky's face turned a shade of crimson.

"Yeah, well, you didn't tell me he would chicken out. We've gone to a lot of trouble to put this together. We're settling our problem one way or the other."

Every muscle of Jack tensed. It was either the game or nothing. Running out of here with his deed wasn't in the cards. The shiny chrome gun gleamed under the dull light; the long barrel reminded him of a cannon. He stared at it in stunned silence.

The Filipino came back to life, flippant as ever. "Ah. What a marvelous weapon." He leaned forward and picked it up by the barrel as if it were a toy.

"Hey, put that down." Kolcinivitch flinched.

"Not on your life." He lifted it higher, out of the grower's reach, holding the chrome barrel with two fingers as he inspected it. "You said no weapons, but if you must have one, this is marvelous. A man-sized weapon for sure. Big, big, big." He flipped it in the air and caught it by the handle grip.

Kolcinivitch flinched. "You idiot! Be careful."

He ejected the cylinder and spun it with his finger. "A long-barreled .44 Magnum is a beautiful weapon. Fully loaded, ready to kill. I love it." He clicked the cylinder closed and slipped it into his outside coat pocket, handle down. Jack could see the chrome barrel sticking out. "I'll keep this for the one who's caught cheating."

"You're going to give it to the one who cheats?" Jack bent forward, incredulous at what he just heard.

"Hardly, young one." The steely dealer picked up the deck of cards. He spoke as if he were discussing the weather, calmly, smoothly. "I will give it to the honest one. He can do with it as he pleases." He shuffled with lightning moves. "Like he said," nodding to Kolcinivitch, "it's a fight to the death."

"Give me the gun," Kolcinivitch said in a threatening tone as he held out his beefy hand.

The Filipino didn't even look his way, but continued shuffling, letting the clapping sound of the stiff cards speak for him.

"I said—give it to me or I'll—"

In one swift motion, the Filipino pulled the Magnum out of his pocket and pointed it at the blustering grower. "Or you'll what?"

Kolcinivitch half raised his hands and surged backward, screeching his chair across the wood floor. "What the—?"

"I hate threats." He held the revolver steady with two hands. One finger rested close to the trigger. "Just ask Young Warrior here." He nodded toward Jack.

Jack grimaced. Electricity ran through him thinking of that night playing the Black Diamond himself and then getting cold-cocked in the parking lot. All because Jack had pissed the Filipino off, disrespecting him with big-talking threats. And now Kolcinivitch had hit the same raw nerve, and the Filipino didn't waste one second letting them know who was in charge. He remembered Herm telling him the Filipino had an inferiority complex; he had to show up anyone who tried to bully him, particularly rich white guys.

"Now, are we going to play cards or are we going to have a gunfight? You decide." He clicked the hammer back, plunging the room into a dazed silence.

After a tense moment, Les spoke. "Let's all cool down."

"I am cool." The dealer kept the gun steady pointed at the grower's face. "I want to know—do we have a game here or do we have a sham? If the game's a sham, then I elect to end it right here. Myself." His eyebrows were furrowed; his eyes narrowed into slits of concentration.

Kolcinivitch had a calculating look about him. Was he going to call off the game if he couldn't get away with intimidating everyone?

From the way the grower scowled, Jack wondered what kind of friendship the men had. With the Filipino here, maybe this would be Jack's best chance at a fair game. Better than he had imagined.

The grower leaned forward. "Come on, Joe. Put it down. I just didn't like the way you were handling it, that's all. I didn't mean to threaten anyone. I think you're a great guy. You know what you're doing. You holding onto it is just fine. Let's get this game going. I don't have time to mess around with that rat's nest of idiots outside who want to skin me alive."

The dealer's arm relaxed. He slowly lowered the hammer and pulled his finger away from the trigger. Jack exhaled. Kolcinivitch slumped in his chair, his shoulders relaxing. The Filipino returned the gun to his pocket, brushed his black hair back with a swipe of his hand. Then took up the deck of cards.

"Are you in?" He nodded to Jack.

Jack rubbed his chin. Kolcinivitch looked sheepish with his eyes on the money, and the smugness seemingly wiped off his face. He had seen this turning in the man when they played in Bakersfield. After the grower stopped his antics, Jack could always get a decent game out of him. Yeah, he was ready.

Jack pulled out a wad of cash wrapped with a rubber band. He counted out $2,000 in hundred dollar bills. He slid the stack into the center.

"*Here we go,*" the Filipino said with auctioneer's emphasis. He raked the bills to him. He counted the money with quick, practiced motions. He then slid the two brown envelopes with the deeds away from Kolcinivitch and set them on his right, on Jack's side. He stacked the money on his left.

"We have twelve thousand dollars and two deeds. I understand the one who becomes homeless walks with the pot." Joe snorted. "A bon voyage present." Joe counted out ten thousand dollars in stacks of chips, tens, fifties, and hundreds to each player. He then unwrapped a new deck of cards and shuffled it deftly.

"Can we cut with the jokes?" Les said. "Just have ourselves a quiet game?"

Kolcinivitch pointed with a glass in his hand. "You know his real name isn't Joe. It's Joker."

"Thanks to American TV, my given name is Joker Guzmán." He shuffled the cards dramatically, then glanced up at Jack in a moment of sincerity. "My father was a great Red Skelton fan."

"I hate Red Skelton." Kolcinivitch arranged his chips.

"Shameful," Joe said. "Shameful." He set the deck in front of Jack to cut. Then Joe took it up and dealt out the first two whole cards to each man.

Jack watched Joe with curiosity as he dealt. Something didn't ring true about what he'd just said. *Joker Guzmán*. Herm said he had a different last name, but he couldn't remember it. Joe worked efficiently—no false shuffling, no sleight of hand, and no bottom dealing that he could see. Jack rubbed his chin. Time to calm himself, focus on the game, and stop worrying about his disappointment that Todd wasn't here.

Jack studied the room. The window behind the dealer was closed, and the entryway behind Jack led to the front door. Almost directly behind Kolcinivitch, a swinging door led into the kitchen. It would be his last choice if he had to make a quick getaway. The window facing the yard appeared to be the most direct exit out of here if things got crazy. He would have to get it open first. He fidgeted in his seat, working for a comfortable spot.

"It's to you." Joe nodded toward Kolcinivitch.

The grower edged up the corners of his two down cards. He slugged down some Scotch and rolled his mouth around, still mulling his hand. Jack had only a king-seven combo. Jack wanted to see the flop before he decided to fold, so he called Kolcinivitch's bet.

Joe dealt the flop: an ace of clubs, a Jack of spade, and a deuce of hearts.

Kolcinivitch studied the cards. The way he kept rolling his mouth, twitching his fingers on his glass, Jack wondered. Finally, he pushed in $500.

"I'll call." Jack pushed in his chips.

The dealer dealt the turn: an eight of clubs.

Kolcinivitch put in $200 more.

Jack tossed his cards. "I fold." He wiped his mouth and fidgeted in his chair.

"Good move, Young Warrior."

Joe scooped the cards into a new stack.

"Get yourself a beer." Kolcinivitch motioned toward the sideboard.

Jack rose and grabbed a bottle. The doorway leading into the kitchen lay between the sideboard and the wall. He popped the cap on the beer and lingered by the door, glancing through the small window. The kitchen was long, narrow, and full of shiny appliances and a polished floor. At the far end, there was a backdoor, probably twenty feet away. He had no idea what lay behind the door. The window to his right was still his safest bet. As he returned to his seat, he glimpsed through it and spotted his Olds squeezed in along a line of pickups.

After an hour of playing, he was down a thousand dollars. He didn't like the sight of Joe pushing chips into Kolcinivitch's growing pile. He knew he had to keep his cool and let the cards come to him. They would in time. They always had.

They played on. Jack wiped the sweat off his brow after every deal, watched his pile gradually diminish. It wasn't the big pots that broke a man, but the little ones that threatened to whittle down his nerves and his chips. If he lost too much, he would begin to think defensively, and that would limit his boldness.

The room grew tighter after each hand. When he drew a queen, the grower drew an ace. If he had two aces, Kolcinivitch flopped three queens. And if he made a straight, his opponent produced a flush.

He began to wonder if Joe was feeding the grower cards. Jack watched Joe deal each card. His hands were fast, smooth, practiced. Not one thing seemed out of the ordinary. He wished he had another pair of eyes here. Beads of sweat accumulated under his arms and soaked through his shirt as if he had slaved all day under an unforgiving sun. He wondered what Sugar would do in a game this taut. He then thought of his mother pushed from the house she loved because he lost. His collar turned cold with sweat.

"Can we open the window?" Jack wiped his forehead with his sleeve.

Kolcinivitch nodded. Les rose and flung it up, letting in a hot breeze that carried with it the ruckus from the road.

"Shouldn't you be out there?" Les asked.

Kolcinivitch grimaced. "If I go out there, I'm going to kick some ass. It's probably better I'm in here, away from those idiots." He made a noise under his breath while he studied his cards then threw them face down. "Some loudmouth must have ratted that we were picking this morning. No way could those UFW fools had figured that out. They're too stupid."

Jack felt Kolcinivitch's accusatory eyes burning his skin. Blood rushed to his cheeks as he pushed his cards into the center and scooped in the pot of around $400. He had thought the same thing himself when he saw Adrian and the strikers this morning. Jack didn't know there was any picking this morning, so he didn't know why Kolcinivitch had given him that evil eye.

When Kolcinivitch heard the distant turmoil, the faint shouting, honking horns, and an echoing voice on a bullhorn, he seemed rattled. It was a pleasure seeing his friend get under this arrogant man's skin.

If Kolcinivitch focused, he played a solid game with an understanding of the odds. Jack had never seen this side of the man. He observed every movement of Joe's hands as he shuffled, cut the cards, and dealt. He worked faster than any dealer Jack had ever played with. Jack remembered Herm saying the best dealer's sleight of hand was so undetectable they could bottom deal and false shuffle right in front of you and would never see it. Then there was this guy's last name. What had Herm said it was?

And why didn't Herm trust the Filipino? Then there was the whole episode of his pointing that cannon of a revolver right at Kolcinivitch's face. It sure looked convincing. But it could have been a charade.

Jack patted his upper lip with his index finger, pondering if he should fold with a pair of sixes when he noticed Kolcinivitch slipping his right hand under the table for a second then bringing it up. It was something he had seen earlier, but it was so momentary, so liquid, it hardly warranted paying attention to. If it was a nervous tick, he hadn't seen it in the man's play before. It was too apparent for a polished cheater. Jack decided to stay in, pretending to focus on Joe but eyed Kolcinivitch's movements carefully. Jack had two pairs, kings high, and the top card showing in the flop was an eight of spades. Nothing suited, he could have a pair, but Jack didn't think he had much more. On the turn, a six of clubs showed. Two clubs, a diamond, and a heart. He could have a flush, which would beat two pair. But the grower's betting was listless. The pot didn't have more than a couple hundred in it.

Joe dealt the river card: an ace of hearts.

"To you." Joe nodded to Jack.

"Three hundred dollars." Jack slid his chips in.

Kolcinivitch snorted and called. Jack flopped his two down cards, two pairs, kings and sixes. Kolcinivitch turned over his two down cards, an ace and eight. He had gotten his card on the river. Jack's heart sagged right into his shoes.

"Another lucky draw for the grape man."

Kolcinivitch scraped in the pot in with a twisted grin while Jack studied the two pair on the table. He had seen Kolcinivitch put his left hand down four times. Doing that with his hands was so obvious and stupid. Was he just trying to throw Jack off? He settled back. Sweat beads formed on his forehead, and heat rose on his neck under his collar. He forced himself to smile.

"You're looking flushed there, Young Master," Joe said as he dealt, the cards flying, two down to each of them. "My mother used to say it's a lack of *betute* in your diet."

"What's that crap?" Kolcinivitch asked.

"Stuffed frog. It's a delicacy in my country." Joe held the deck in front of him and nodded at Jack. "To you."

Jack didn't need any frog. He needed to figure this game out. Jack's mouth tightened. Were these men colluding? He had a pair of kings and a wave of slow-cooking anger rising inside. Kolcinivitch had a glint in his eyes that Jack had never seen before. Was he gloating?

He wracked his brain trying to remember what Herm said about Joe's last name. It wasn't Guzmán, he knew that much.

He wondered if he had stumbled onto their scheme. If they were working together, there was no way Joe would hand him the .44 Magnum. Even if he did, what would he do with it? He had already been through that in his mind. It would solve very little unless it came down to self-defense. And Jack was on a grower's land, playing a game of cards in his house. Local justice would grind him into fertilizer.

When Jack's pair of kings held up taking in only $100, and Kolcinivitch hadn't moved either hand suspiciously, Jack wondered if they were giving him just enough hope to think he could win. If that were the case, bluffing wouldn't get him anywhere since Kolcinivitch must know Jack's cards too.

If he didn't know them, he had a way of getting the winning hand. Jack won the next three hands, gaining back nearly $500. Kolcinivitch had been all over the place, touching his head, his ears, his left eyelid, and hadn't moved his left hand once under the table. Jack could not discern a pattern, a strategy, any secret signals between them. He couldn't help but think they were giving him just enough hope to keep him from turning suspicious.

The Filipino spun out another hand, the blue-backed cards flying to them. Jack studied his two down cards, the edges bent slightly up. He saw the signal again, three quick up and downs with his left index finger. He wracked his brain to figure out their game. If he called the grower out for cheating, and it was only a nervous twitch, there would be no going back. Kolcinivitch would overreact, and who knows what would happen. The wooden handle of the chrome weapon stuck out the dealer's pocket. He settled himself. He had to be sure before he was worn down to nothing.

If Kolcinivitch continued mashing down the Scotch, already he had poured three-quarters of a bottle down his throat, he would start making mistakes soon. His tells should become more exaggerated, slower, easier to spot.

Jack studied his cards. He didn't want to think about coming home without the deeds. But the possibility was becoming all too real. It would kill his mother to lose her home. He imagined her laid out on her bed in a new dress, hands folded on her stomach, and her skin pasty and pale with death.

Kolcinivitch pushed in a large bet. Jack folded right off, throwing his cards to the table.

"Need some better cards, Joe." Jack wiped his mouth.

The grower tossed his too, a disgusted look on his face.

"The cards speak for themselves."

It rattled Jack that the Filipino, with his expert shuffle, could possibly be false dealing at will. He could even be feeding Jack those winning cards for the last four hands. Could he control everything: the good cards, the best cards, and the ones that could sink his hand? If that were true, why were they signaling each other, if that was what they were doing? None of this made sense.

Les fidgeted beside him.

Joe dealt another hand. "To you, Young Warrior."

The echoes of a chant drifted in on a warm breeze: *Huelga. Huelga. Huelga.* Followed by sharp and angry shouting. Kolcinivitch's mouth tightened—his face drew taut with concern. Then he turned to the game.

Jack decided to fold whenever he thought Kolcinivitch had bogus cards. It might keep the surly man guessing, wear down his patience, and force him into rash play.

A winning hand came to Jack, and he threw in $300.

"Brave wager, Young Master."

Kolcinivitch lifted the index finger of his right hand then slowly pushed in a stack of chips. Now Jack saw everything Kolcinivitch did as a possible menace—a touching of the right nostril, a scratching of the forehead above the left eyebrow, a tug on his left ear, a clearing of his throat, a lifting of a finger. They must have a system worked out that was too difficult for Jack to decipher. Kolcinivitch didn't once have the look of concern or frustration Jack had seen when the man played at Cicero's. Jack took a deep breath and tried to ignore what was becoming impossible not to notice.

Kolcinivitch won the next hand with a full house, aces high. And there hadn't been one distinguishable tell. Just those strange movements of his hands, a jumble of signals with no pattern. If Jack lost, he didn't doubt they'd be evicted tomorrow. For a second, he saw all of his mother's belongings stacked on the road, hauled out by sheriff's deputies evicting her. He rubbed his chin and stared at his cards. He had to find the man's pattern.

Kolcinivitch gave him a hard look. "It's not as easy as you thought, huh?"

Jack shrugged. The man must have been playing him in Bakersfield, letting him believe he wasn't good. Especially when he drank. This whole game must have been a setup.

"Well, now, fellow gladiators. We are *mano a mano*—Goliath and David, a young rock thrower from way back."

Kolcinivitch smirked. "David's getting down to his last few rocks from the looks of it."

Jack had let the fear of these two cheating distract him from his game. His nerves must be so visible, even his opponent sensed it.

The Filipino shuffled the deck and dealt out another hand. Over the next few games, Jack lost another $600. His energy ebbed trying to decipher how they were cheating. Kolcinivitch continued to move his hands all over. With an unsmiling mouth, he touched his nose, his hair, his ears. So much movement destroyed his concentration.

Jack decided to give up watching for patterns when he noticed his opponent's right hand resting on the table next to his two down cards. When he lifted his index finger twice, Jack thought he saw the dealer run his fingers along the bottom of the deck. The Filipino's fingers moved so fast, Jack couldn't tell if the next card came from the top or bottom of the deck.

Jack held his index finger to his lips. If Kolcinivitch had just signaled for a card, Joe would have dealt from the bottom. Then the grower would have a winning hand.

"To you, Young Warrior."

Jack rubbed his lips. He felt certain Kolcinivitch had nothing but junk, ten high. Jack had a pair of queens. The intentness in Kolcinivitch's eyes betrayed him. He was waiting for Jack to break. He had never seen the rancher so focused, so tuned to every nuance of the game.

Jack felt his finger on his bottom lip, something he had been doing on and off for a while now. The Filipino stared at him. Jack lowered his hand slowly. Had he been signaling his own tells? Maybe the grower wasn't cheating after all, but just watching him unravel on his own. If that were true, he was beating Jack at his own game.

He rolled his shoulders to loosen up. He had let the stakes of the game erode his confidence. He had allowed his fear to dictate his body language. All the other games, he had little to lose, but now with so much on the line, the pressure had pushed him into playing a different game. Jack felt his hope drop through the floor into the basement. With less than $4,000 in chips in front of him, sweat clung to his T-shirt, soaking through.

Kolcinivitch flashed a smirk that edged up one corner of his mouth. The man actually looked happy. Why not? He had figured out Jack's game.

Jack had to flush the two of them out. Now was the time with his two queens and Kolcinivitch's tens. If he didn't take a risk here, he could lose any hope of a comeback.

"All in." Jack pushed every chip into the middle.

The Filipino blinked languidly, not showing any emotion.

Kolcinivitch jerked his head up. His eyes grew large, then he wiped his mouth, tipped the edges of his cards up, flashing an appraising glance at Jack. His eyes smoldering, he threw down his cards. Jack raked in the pot.

Winning that hand convinced Jack the man hadn't been cheating at all but using his own tells against him. All that moving with his hands and signaling was an elaborate bluff to get under Jack's skin. Everyone knew how Sugar played, always able to read a man's tells. That had been the strength of Jack's game too. The grower had planned carefully to confuse him, use his strength against him. Psyching out an opposing player was a game Jack could play too.

"Lucky hand." Kolcinivitch slugged down more Scotch.

"I beat you once. I'll beat you again."

Kolcinivitch smirked. "Winning one game or two don't mean squat."

"I'm talking about that time in the fields. I could have beaten you to death. You go and blame a Mexican because you're a sorry, chicken-assed excuse for a man." Jack leaned over the table. "That guy you had arrested stopped me from killing you, but he ain't here now. He's out there trying to put a stop to your harvest."

The big rancher leaned back and smiled wryly. "I don't know what you're talking about. He was trespassing, trying to steal my property."

"You always keep stolen property on your ranch?" Jack met his eyes straight on.

The rancher chewed on something. "That old windbag owed me a lot of money. How was I supposed to know it was yours?"

"Did you have to nearly kill him?" Jack couldn't believe Kolcinivitch was admitting to having Herm beaten.

"He must have fallen and hit his head. My guys just pushed him off. That wasn't anyone's fault but his own."

Jack doubted the man had what it took to tell the truth. He shook his head slowly and stared at his cards.

"Young Warrior, let's play cards." He flashed Jack a warning glare and dealt the next hand slowly. Jack relaxed, laying his hands right next to his cards on the table, not moving except to breathe. Kolcinivitch swallowed the rest of his drink in one gulp and wiped his mouth with the edge of his hand. Jack's effort to unnerve Kolcinivitch seemed futile. The man played smarter than ever with a keen understanding of the combinations. Jack's chips edged slowly away—fifty dollars here, a hundred dollars there, two hundred in one hand he felt confident he would win.

By late morning, he was down to less than $3,000. Sweat soaked his armpits and chest. He tried to use every angle to regain some momentum, but every ace, king, or pair came to him at the wrong time.

The truth seeped over him—Kolcinivitch played a strong game. He had duped Jack into thinking he could win. Jack flushed inside. Herm had warned him. He leaned forward to study all the up cards on the table, trying to convince himself the game wasn't over.

"Young Warrior. You battle like a hero. There is still time for a valiant charge." The Filipino dealt another hand. He gave Jack a confident nod.

"Another couple of hands here," Kolcinivitch gloated, "even Sugar's old truck will belong to me."

"You've wanted to steal that, too, haven't you?"

Kolcinivitch looked up at him. "You don't know nothin', that's your problem."

"You're right. I don't understand why you'd kill my father."

Kolcinivitch leaned back in his chair and gave Jack a long glare.

Joe held up a deal, holding the deck in midair. He glanced from Jack to Kolcinivitch and back. "Your father was Sugar Duncan?"

Jack nodded.

"A tragic death. A great loss. But to accuse a man of such a deed while locked in mortal combat takes either great courage or monumental indiscretion."

"I'll agree with that." The grower slouched and eyed Jack. "Like I said, you don't know nothin'."

Jack heard Herm's voice in his thoughts. *Keep your mouth shut, and you'll have a better chance of winning.*

Jack tossed his miserable cards into the center of the table. He counted less than $2,000 in front of him.

Les leaned on the table and turned to Jack. "Your father killed himself."

"What?" Jack couldn't believe what he heard. "How did you come up with that?"

"We told him for years to stop siding with the Mexicans and the Filipinos." Kolcinivitch held his cards close to his chest. "He never listened."

A hot ring settled around Jack's neck right under his shirt. He rubbed the back of his neck. He felt the room closing in, thinking about his father killing himself.

"My dad didn't kill himself."

Kolcinivitch snorted, stifling a laugh.

"I'm not saying suicide, Jack." Les folded his arms and rested them on the table. "We warned him something would happen if he insisted on changing the way things worked in the valley. No one here knows who did what. But you can't just go around saying that how we're running our ranches is wrong. And that we're immoral for how we treat our workers. We've been doing things this way for a hundred years. You don't just start handing the help control of the ranch."

"He just wanted you guys to treat them better."

Kolcinivitch laughed. "You ever been to Mexico?"

"Not really. Why?"

"Because if you looked at the farm housing on this ranch then compare it to the shacks with dirt floors they lived in every day down south, then you'd say we treat them pretty damn well."

"That's like letting the slaves free but not too free. So it's okay if blacks live in ghettos and work at low-wage jobs. It's better than where they came from."

"You're starting to sound like that King fellow."

"That King fellow was an American hero."

"Yeah, some hero. That's why he got a bullet in his brain." Kolcinivitch pushed in a pile of chips. "He deserved what he got from the way I see it. The same's going to happen to Chavez if he doesn't back off real soon."

"You guys, we must finish this game," Les said. "I can't be here all day."

Jack laid his cards face down on the table. "When you set this up, Les, you knew all along how it would go."

"We had to resolve the water issue with your mother," he said. "She is a very stubborn woman. What will happen here will be best for everyone. Shirley will have the money she needs to move on, and we can get back to the business of grapes."

"You guys rigged this game against me?" He looked from Les to the grower across from him. Heat rose in his face.

"We ain't rigged nothin', you idiot. That's what's making this so much fun."

"Ethan," Les pointed across the table, "has been the top Hold'em player in Kern County for some time. We were surprised you didn't know that."

His chance meeting with DiGorda at Cicero's, getting invited to play with the growers, it hadn't been chance at all, instead a calculated plan to strip him clean. Jack glanced over at the dealer, asking with his eyes if it was true.

"Yes, Young Warrior. He is a champion of cards and Scotch, as much in his mind as in actuality. You seemed so sure, so self-possessed, I didn't feel obliged to throw a ripple of doubt into your confidence. To top it all, you are the son of Sugar Duncan, are you not? If anyone could tame the beast, it would be a Duncan. But as for the game being rigged." He shook his head. "Why rig a game you couldn't win anyway?"

The Filipino's smug look dissolved, and he fixed Jack in the glare of his coal-black eyes.

Kolcinivitch threw down his cards. "None of that matters now. Let's just finish the game."

Joe nodded. "It's to you, Young Warrior, be certain the odds are fair."

"What do you want?" Jack said to the frowning grower.

"To see you crawl out of here with only the shirt you're wearing. If you go out of here naked, that'd be even better. Before I kick you off my property," Kolcinivitch pointed a thick finger at Jack, "I'm going to break you in half."

"Ah, such bravado…impressive. It is to you, Young Warrior, bloodied, but not out. You are still breathing. Play your cards." He spun out another round of cards.

Jack collected himself. He pushed his cards to the center. "Tell you what. You guys seem so sure of yourselves. Why don't we make this game really interesting? Put in the deeds. Put in all the money. Let's make it high card wins—winner takes all."

Kolcinivitch threw up his hands. "No way. I have you by the throat."

"What are you afraid of—a true game of chance?" Jack gave him his bravest face.

The big grower mulled it over for a moment. "Okay. Put in your car keys. I want to see you walk out of here."

"You want my boots, too?"

The Filipino gave Jack a warning glare—*better mind your mouth.*

Jack threw his car keys on the table.

"Deal them down." Kolcinivitch tapped the felt.

The Filipino spun one card off the top to Kolcinivitch, and in the mystery of card sharking, in the smooth, natural flow of the deal, out of the corner of his eyes saw the Filipino's long index finger glance across the bottom of the deck and plucked Jack a card.

Jack laid his hand on his card. "Whoever gets the high card walks out of here with the whole shebang, right?"

"Cut the crap." Kolcinivitch turned over—an ace of spades. "Hot damn." He slapped the table.

Jack flopped over an ace of hearts. Both men shot to their feet and grabbed at the deeds, but Jack snapped them up first.

As the big grower leaned over the table, pointing a threatening finger at Jack, a blue-backed Bicycle card fell out of the grower's open shirt by his belt buckle. It lay face down on the table. The dealer reached over and flopped it—an ace of clubs.

"Ah, we have a cheater." Joe wrapped his hand around the handle of the revolver.

"No!" Kolcinivitch growled.

"Oh, we shall have blood tonight." The dealer, erect and serious-mouthed, backed up and slowly raised the revolver from his pocket. When the barrel cleared his jacket, Kolcinivitch lunged.

Jack fell back against the wall. Blood rushed to his face. The two grappled, swinging the weapon this way and that. A shot rang out, an explosion of smoke and sound, striking Les in the arm. He screamed and fell to the floor, the wound gushing blood.

"Go, Young Warrior," the Filipino said, still struggling to control the weapon.

Jack, with the deeds, squirmed past the two grappling bodies. Just as he dove through the window, Kolcinivitch wrestled the gun away and fired a shot at Jack, grazing a pant leg as he disappeared through the window. Clutching the envelopes, Jack hit the dirt on his shoulder and rolled. He vaulted to his feet and sprinted toward his car, sliding to a stop when he spotted two muscular men leaning against the trunk lid. A shot rang out behind him. It splintered the trellis of grapes in front of him.

Kolcinivitch, leaning out the window, shouted, "Get him!"

Jack took off. The two men pursued.

He sprinted up the farm road, clutching the envelopes. He willed his legs to pump as he stretched to reach the county road. About halfway up, he heard a motor coming on fast, the gravel crunching under speeding tires.

The noise in the road ahead grew steadily louder. Almost there, Jack veered off to his right down a row of vines running at an angle. A truck tore up the road after him, the engine whining. Jack raced past stooping pickers, jumped over trays of grapes. His side aching, he stumbled up onto the paved road, right in front of a line of strikers hoisting pickets and banners.

Frantic to get away, he looked up and down searching for a way out. The beefy toughs closed in behind him. Deputy Kauffman, a few paces away, gawked at him.

"Whatsa matter? You look like you saw a ghost, Duncan."

A pickup turned onto the road. Kolcinivitch rolled out of the cab. If Jack ran into the strikers, Kolcinivitch wouldn't hesitate to fire.

"What's going on?" Deputy Kauffman yelled.

Jack turned to the vines. The burly men stood on the shoulders, panting, holding their bats aloft.

"Return my property, Duncan." Jack turned toward the voice. Kolcinivitch stood in the middle of the road and leveled the long barrel of the revolver at him.

"Kauffman!" Jack pointed toward the man with the gun.

Kauffman peered down the road and shouted, "Put that gun down, now!"

A shot boomed across the vines. Jack swiveled to run, but someone hit him hard from behind, wrapped strong arms around him, and dragged him down. Before they reached the ground, the strong arms around him suddenly went limp, and they both slammed into the pavement hard. A deadweight pinned Jack down.

Men shouted. "He's got a gun. He's shooting again."

"Kauffman!" Jack yelled. "Do something."

Kolcinivitch cocked the Magnum and aimed.

"Put it down, Ethan," Kauffman commanded.

"Get out of my way. He's a thief."

"Do something," Jack shouted again.

The deputy drew his service revolver and peeled off a shot, then another. Kolcinivitch froze, dropped the revolver, and then crumpled to the ground. Cops ran to him.

Jack twisted around to see who lay on top of him. It was Adrian. Jack worked his way out from under his friend's limp body. A red blot on Adrian's back grew larger in ragged pulses.

Jack eased his friend over. He cradled his neck in his arm. Adrian wheezed shallow breaths.

"Adrian, man, what did you do that for?"

His friend tried to say something, but no sound came out.

Jack yelled for someone to get an ambulance. Kauffman stood over them, his pistol in his hand.

"Ambulance is coming." The deputy knelt beside Jack.

Adrian coughed and tried to talk.

"Quiet now. Help's coming." Jack stroked his friend's forehead.

"Did you win?"

The blood-splattered envelopes were on the ground beside him. "Yeah. I got everything back."

Adrian smiled, the dry edges of his mouth barely moved. "Good."

"No, man, it's not good. I can't believe what you've done."

Adrian reached up, grabbed Jack's shirt, and pulled him close. The pain etched on his face. "You're the patrón now?"

He stared into his friend's brown anguished eyes. "Hold on, hold on." He held his friend's head that lolled to the side in a growing weakness.

Jack watched his friend's shallow breathing until he wasn't breathing any longer, and his eyes closed on the sunlit day. He held his friend's face close to his chest.

"Adrian, Adrian…"

Adrian's face grew pale, his eyes closed in peace. Every one of his friend's hopes and dreams had vanished. Jack scanned the crowd, the fields, the workers lined up to mourn their friend. Down the road, men had gathered around the stricken rancher. A rising bitterness clotted in his chest, as he cradled his friend.

"I am the patrón now," he said to his friend limp in his arms. "And this is my home."

The End

Acknowledgment

As a lifelong Californian, I am often amazed at the events that have unfolded in my home state while I only possess a vague understanding of their causes and effects. When I ran across a book of essays on the history of nonviolence beginning with the life of Socrates, I had no idea where my reading journey would lead me. The penultimate essay surprised me. Just before the excerpts from Martin Luther King's speeches, which I anticipated reading, was a brief bio of Cesar Chavez. Followed by a series of excerpts from a biography by Jacques Levy. The subject of nonviolent action took hold of my imagination. The life of one man who used nonviolent action in a most innovative way stood out to me.

After I finished reading Levy's book, I found many more to read on Cesar Chavez and his movement. I began searching used bookstores and library stacks. The characters and plot of a novel began to take shape. In the Delano City library, a librarian offered me a cardboard box of newspaper clippings stretching from the late 1950s through the 1970s. This was the only collection of clippings I could find, as the local newspaper did not maintain an archive. From the clippings of front-page articles and op-ed pieces, I heard the voices of the growers in their own words. My story began to grow and take on different dimensions. My inspiration for Sugar, I found in an essay on a shelf in a used bookstore. His gambling and death are my imagination, but not his desire to seek change in the valley. I am so thankful for librarians and the local bookstore owners, new and used, who keep the repositories of our history available to the public.

When I began writing, my group of many years, Tom Allbaugh, Lyle Smith, and Mary Mullin read each section and helped me improve the book. My Newport Beach group, John Glass and Scott Barnes, gave me valuable feedback. I workshopped portions of the book at Squaw Valley and spent two different times on Cape Cod thanks to the Norman Mailer Colony. There I worked with Marita Golden and Jeff Allen. At the Napa Writers, I worked with Ron Carlson, a real treat.

To the Historical Society of Southern California for their grant to assist with the book, I thank you.

Special love and appreciation to my wife, Barbara, a constant believer.

Special props go out to my publisher, Tyson Cornell, whose equanimity in the face of near calamities, I found reassuring. To the entire Rare Bird staff who made this happen—thank you. I would be remiss if I did not mention Marc Grossman, spokesperson for the Cesar Chavez Foundation, and former speechwriter for Cesar Chavez, a special note of gratitude for his zeal for historical accuracy. Any errors in how these events actually played out are entirely mine.

If I could thank one additional person, dear reader bear with me, I would say a word of thanks to a man who lived a life worth remembering, a life worth reading about, and certainly one worth writing about—Cesar Chavez.

We should never forget the true heroes of our culture.